Unwell

Unwell

a novel

LESLIE LIPTON

iUniverse, Inc.
New York Lincoln Shanghai

Unwell
a novel

Copyright © 2006 by Leslie Lipton

iUniverse books may be ordered through booksellers or by contacting:

iUniverse
2021 Pine Lake Road, Suite 100
Lincoln, NE 68512
www.iuniverse.com
1-800-Authors (1-800-288-4677)

This is a work of fiction. All of the characters, names, incidents, organizations and dialogue in this novel are either the products of the author's imagination or are used fictitiously.

ISBN-13: 978-0-595-41412-3 (pbk)
ISBN-13: 978-0-595-85926-9 (cloth)
ISBN-13: 978-0-595-85762-3 (ebk)
ISBN-10: 0-595-41412-5 (pbk)
ISBN-10: 0-595-85926-7 (cloth)
ISBN-10: 0-595-85762-0 (ebk)

Printed in the United States of America

To my parents:
Who couldn't get all the thank-yous they deserve.

To Andrea Nolon and Courtney Weaver:
Without whom I never would have
gotten where I am today.

Acknowledgments

Writing acknowledgments feels similar to how I imagine writing an Oscar speech would feel: I'll never remember to thank everyone who deserves it, and, if I did, I'd have to write a whole separate novel.

In the meantime, I'd like to thank everyone who had a hand in the creation of this book, including the people who read various drafts (even when the manuscript just kept getting longer and longer) and selflessly provided their insight and wisdom, namely those friends who squeezed it into their busy high-school schedules: Nora Nussbaum and Laura Gunderson. I'd also like to thank the teachers who witnessed the creation of this book firsthand—Ann V. Klotz, Julia Heaton, and Sarah Rutledge—as well as those teachers who discussed eating disorders with me ad nauseum, namely Gene Gardino and Suzanne Fehrenbaker. You were mentors more than teachers, and thinking it over with you day after day made the details of this story richer and clearer.

I'd also like to thank Lohk Min Lee, who stuck acupuncture needles in my head to cure writer's block and never stopped telling me I was a writer. At my tender age of two, he was my first audience. Thank you to Nancy Nelson, who selflessly provided suggestions about the publishing world and who was always as excited about my work as I was. And thank you to Amanda Urban, who originally suggested I expand this story into a novel—without your encouragement this would still be a seven-page short story, sitting in a file on my old Gateway computer. Thanks, too, to Michael Heyward, for his time and energy in printing off as many drafts of the manuscript as I needed (which were many). Without him, this truly could never have happened.

And thank you to all the people who have had a hand in the editing, creating, and revising of this book at one time or another:

Christina Capote, Susan Leon, Nicole Caputo, Peter Holm, Joyce Ravid, and Kelly Evans. Also deserving of thanks are Cynthia R. Pegler, MD, Jane Karp, MD, and Lynn Grefe, CEO of the National Eating Disorders Association.

A friend by the name of Rachel Posner also deserves mentioning, though I haven't spoken with her recently. Rachel, your hugs sustained me, and we'll always be soul sisters; I miss you. And thank you to Gail Furman, PhD, for putting up with my craziness and really starting to help me.

Of course, I must also include my family—extended and otherwise. In addition to reading drafts, they provided encouragement, advice, and unending support. My parents read the basis for this novel when it was only a short story for a high school English class, and my aunts read revisions as new manuscripts came along. I hope the final product has made them proud.

Thank you to Andrea Nolon for reading my stories even when she didn't have to, for treating me like a friend when I so desperately needed one, and for being the person I could turn to when I needed the most help of all.

And finally, thank you to Courtney Weaver—the best friend a girl could have—for her walks to school, her talks, and her love. She took me seriously when it seemed that no one else could understand, and for that I'll always be grateful.

~ 1 ~

The phone rang, and Stefanie reached for the portable that she always kept near the bathtub, a Friday night tradition. The house invariably would be empty. Her parents would be at a cocktail party somewhere along Park Avenue in some friends' grand apartment, probably overlooking the New York City skyline. They would be talking with the parents of other girls her age, joking about their children's teenage years and what a pain they were, and women with high-pitched, squeaky voices would be exclaiming, "So nice to see you" ... "We should do lunch" ... "Have you lost weight? You look fantastic!" Stefanie would run the water until steam rose against the tiles, dropping in bath beads and bubble bath. Then, as she sank below the hot water, she would turn on the radio and daydream.

Beneath her, the city would be busy. There was something nice about the city on Friday nights. It was fun. Relaxed. Happy. Cars moved hurriedly along Park Avenue, their passengers eager to begin the weekend after a long, tense week. Lights shone from apartment windows, neon signs erupted on restaurant windows, and people spilled over the doorsteps of local bars, drinking beer and shouting at the television that showed the New York Knicks attempting, yet again, to end a losing streak.

Cell phone static erupted on the other end of the telephone connection, breaking Stefanie's reverie. Holding the phone away from her ear, she waited. Sometimes it was Annabel Cohen, who called on Friday nights from the bathroom stalls of restaurants or from inside her closet—the large, white walk-in where she spent her time after a fight with her mother or where she tore through her clothing looking for something "party appropriate." Or sometimes she called from a street downtown that she was unfamiliar with, when it had suddenly dawned on her that if she didn't find a taxi in the next few minutes she would be more than a half-hour late (her grace period) for her curfew. Soon Annabel's voice rose from the receiver. Stefanie bit down on her lip, wondering what the crisis was tonight.

On these nights Stefanie was expected to smile casually and listen to the raging, or alternately excited, monologue that crossed over the phone lines. She wasn't supposed to talk; just to listen. Listen to the details of the new life that Annabel had so effortlessly plunged into, a life that Stefanie hadn't felt ready—or invited?—to enter. Listen and occasionally contribute an *ah-huh* or a *hmm* or *cool*, just to let Annabel know that she was still listening. Usually she imagined in these phone calls that she was a famous columnist paid to give advice. A Dear Abby.

But she wasn't paid.

The phone rang again. What was it this time? Annabel calling back to say she had found the invitation to the party she was meant to attend? Who cared? But this time it was Laura and the voice on the other end of the phone sounded hysterical, something like: "Skirt ... doesn't fit ... don't have anything ... in five minutes."

"What? Slow down ... I can't understand what you're saying."

Laura was another friend. She called frequently, though not as often as Annabel, and was more emotional. Laura overreacted about little things—the color of lipstick, a pair of jeans she wanted to wear that was in the laundry, a boyfriend who had forgotten to call her the moment he got home. At least these things seemed little to Stefanie. But still, she could pacify Laura. That was what friends were for; that was her duty. Even if it was unwanted sometimes.

Tonight, Laura's voice shook from her sobs, and Stefanie could imagine her slumped against her bed with puffy eyes and tears rolling down her cheeks. If tonight was like any of the others, her new boyfriend, the latest in a long string of boys Laura loved and then lost—all long before Stefanie had had even one boyfriend—was picking her up in minutes, and she had just realized that her black leather pants had gotten tighter. Oh, the tragedy.

When Stefanie had managed to convince Laura that the Ralph Lauren denim miniskirt with the cute back pockets and blue stitching around the waistband would work just fine, she sighed, hung up the phone, and flopped back into the water. As the water stirred, the scent of vanilla reached Stefanie's nose, but it wasn't pleasant anymore. The rippling surface of the water distorted Stefanie's legs. Her thighs wiggled like Jell-O, and her stomach formed an island above the layer of bubbles. Laura had always been the skinny one. She could eat anything—ice cream at Serendipity III, frozen hot chocolate, deep-dish chicken fajita pizza at Pizzeria Uno on 86th, as many Starbuck's Frappacino's as she wanted (one at every store they passed), and all the chips and guacamole they could manage at Zocolo's on a Saturday night—and never gain a pound. Yet Laura couldn't see that and had recently been experimenting with fad diets. Sometimes, when Laura's meal consisted of only lettuce leaves and her own consisted of a cheeseburger with french fries, Stefanie wanted to punch her. She was so goddamn skinny. And there Laura sat like a saint, all virtuous and pure, eating a grapefruit before every meal or testing the theories of Dr. Robert Atkins. It was sickening. If she thought that *she* needed to diet, then what did she think of Stefanie—who didn't scan AOL's headlines for the latest diet secrets? Annabel was thin too. She played sports every afternoon at the Asphalt Green and was on three varsity teams—one for each season. Annabel's mom was also a health-food nut. She had the food pyramid pasted to the refrigerator and worked out with a personal trainer three times a week. "Thin" was encoded in Annabel's DNA.

The bathwater was cold now. On the radio a song about hipbones and thighbones was playing as part of a Friday night "Recapture Youth" special. In nursery school, Stefanie remembered how they had sung that song to learn about the parts of the body. What went where? It had all been a big mystery. Fourteen years later, she and her classmates, grown, scattered among the city's elite single-sex private schools, knew what connected to which bone. Now, as she listened, her eyes scanned her own figure. In fourteen years, the song's meaning and purpose had changed. Laura could see those bones; Annabel could see those bones; but, in her mirror, Stefanie could not. Maybe it was not a coincidence that they were out on dates, and she was alone in an empty house. People only liked those whose bones were visible. Damn them. Suddenly Stefanie felt very tired. She stood and reached for a towel, watching the water slide down her abdomen and legs.

She shuffled down the hallway in her furry, leopard-print slippers and sank into the couch, her wet hair dampening the down pillows. Her parents wouldn't be home for at least another two hours. Fridays had always been her parents' time alone, but ever since Stephanie had outgrown the need for babysitters (who were usually girls from the junior and senior classes at school), and ever since she had begun to sleep over at her friends' houses on the weekends, her parents had been much more willing to take their Friday nights for adult time.

The apartment now was empty but not quiet; noise from the street filled the rooms of Apartment 8B, bouncing off the wood floors and the black marble table in the otherwise white kitchen. There was the noise of a party somewhere nearby—a welcome sign of life— and from down on the street came the whooping sounds of roaming teenage boys.

When Stefanie was little, she had been afraid of walking past the pink living room, the least-used room in the house, that connected the bedroom side to the kitchen side. She had thought that someone would be in there, waiting to kill her. Stab her, shoot her, kidnap her, rob her. She had spent evenings alone hidden in her bedroom, often under her canopied bed, convinced that she had heard a strange noise. Thankfully, she had outgrown those days. In the dark, she still sprinted past the living room and into the kitchen, but it was OK. She was braver now. She bit her lip. Gnawing at the areas that were chapped. Waiting to taste the sharp metallic flavor of blood.

Stefanie had signed on to the Internet earlier, but her buddy list had been empty. No mechanical voice had greeted her with, "You've got mail," so she had signed off. There had been no point in waiting to be harassed by the pedophiles who stayed online even when nobody was around. They probably wouldn't bother to send her an instant invitation to view their live sex cams. They probably wouldn't waste their energy to solicit Stefanie's attention. She wouldn't be worth it even to them. Besides, she imagined that tonight not even they were sitting in front of the computer. Judging from the sounds on the street, everyone was out—except her.

Her parents were out at a party. Laura was out on a date. Annabel was with the popular kids from school—that was happening more and more. Even Julia, one of Stefanie's earliest childhood friends, was busy. She had known Julia since the days of nursery school when Julia had taught Steffie to cartwheel and Steffie had taught Julia to tie her shoelaces, but they had been spending less time together recently. And tonight was Friday; Julia's family always went to their country house on Fridays. They took Julia's grandparents and disappeared for the weekend. They were like that. Stefanie could remember the times when they had invited her along for weekends in the Berkshires, but it had been almost a year now since she had been to the wonderful little place with the tree house in the back yard. The invitations had fallen off. Occasionally, she wondered who might have been invited in her stead.

In a vain attempt to block out the noise from the street and from her own thoughts, Stefanie flipped on the TV. News ... boring. Horror movie ... too scary. Western ... outdated. No ... no ... no ... infomercial. She stopped.

A tanned, blonde model lounging on the beach next to a box of chocolate chip cookies smiled out at Stefanie and held up a bottle of pills. "With these I lost thirty pounds in twenty days," the Barbie doll chirped. "I lost all this weight, and I've kept it off. I feel great, and I can even eat these." A plastic smile stretched across the expanse of glaring white teeth before they bit into a chocolate chip cookie.

Stefanie felt her face flush in anger; she couldn't watch a moment longer. With a click of the remote, Stefanie sent Barbie back to her dream house, thinking that after filming that infomercial, she probably spit the cookie in the trash and promptly scrubbed away any stray remnants from between her porcelain veneers.

Stupid advertisers. Stupid marketers. They fed girls the notion that dieting was necessary, good, normal. Those products were as fake as the digitally enhanced models used to sell them. Stefanie felt betrayed, and yet ...

The slippers made a dull padding sound on the wooden floor as Stefanie headed to her room. She would just read her magazine and go to bed—she wasn't going to waste herself on mindless television, and anyway she was tired.

A magazine lay on the floor. On the cover was that actress from *Girl, Interrupted*—Winona Ryder. Writing scrolled along the side of her pretty face: *Top Ten Ways to Lose Weight FAST!*

"Screw ... the ... world!" Stefanie screamed as she sent the latest issue of *Seventeen* flying across her bedroom, nearly toppling a lamp and sweeping a flurry of papers from her desktop. She hated the fucking magazines too.

Leaving the magazine where its flight had ended, Stefanie took out her journal. The green leather was still shiny and smooth. She'd always wanted a journal—something to show her children someday, some way to look back on her life. She'd always written but had never kept a journal. Not formally. Three weeks ago, on the morning of her sixteenth birthday, she had emerged from her bedroom to find the beautiful book resting by her seat at the breakfast table. The inscription—written in her mother's scrawling, perfect script—read: *To our lovely sixteen-year-old. Happy Birthday! We couldn't love you more.*

The book fell open to a blank page, and Stefanie began to write, wondering if her mother's inscription was still true. If they loved her so much, why were they out for dinner tonight? Why had they left her?

On the previous pages, her black pen had made calm, winding brooks, but tonight the waters were rough and capped in white, as if a harsh wind was blowing, battering the jagged shore with angry waves.

Before Stefanie marked her place with the white satin ribbon, she reread what she had just written.

Why are people so stupid? Why do they care about what they weigh? Why does our society care? Why am I the only one who knows a number on the scale shouldn't matter?

She closed her eyes against the dark of the room. Thoughts of Julia, Annabel, and Laura raced through her mind. She imagined what they were doing at that very moment. Stefanie's mind flashed again to the blonde Barbie-doll model that had held up the bottle of pills and taken a bite of the chocolate chip cookie—her perfect abs ... her toned thighs ... her thin face. And then, there were those words again: *Lose Weight Fast!* Stefanie's eyes opened, and she looked around at the darkness.

She couldn't sleep.

1:34 … trip to the bathroom, 2:30 … phone rings—prank call, 3:58 … can't sleep, 4:42 … room is too warm—turn down heat, 5:15 … can't sleep, 6:01 … an ambulance drives by, 6:12 … room is too cold—turn up heat, 6:28 … can't sleep …

Stefanie leaned over and retrieved Mr. Whiskers from the floor. The poor stuffed bear hadn't had a good night's sleep either, and she apologized for knocking him off the bed. Outside it was still dim, but Stefanie pulled back her curtains anyway and flipped on her desk light. Eight floors down, she could see one of her neighbors walking his dog. On the corner, two children held their father's hands and jumped up and down, reveling in the clouds of white that their warm breath made in the frozen air. She remembered when she had done the same thing with her father and imagined the trio sitting at the Amity coffee shop, sipping hot chocolate over Belgian waffles or pancakes.

They didn't do that anymore, not since her parents had begun to stay out late on Friday nights. Now they all slept until nine—catching up on sleep lost during the busy week. And when they did go out on Saturday mornings—having fought through impatient crowds off to the gym or out walking dogs or shopping, or with those other younger children who hadn't yet outgrown the Saturday morning breakfast ritual—the cold never seemed quite as pleasant.

Shivering, Stefanie pulled on her bathrobe and slippers. For a moment, she contemplated working on her English essay, "The Stigma of a Scarlet A," about *The Scarlet Letter* and Hester Prynne, but hesitated. What was the rush? It seemed pointless to begin when she would have the rest of the day to work on it.

Julia, Annabel, and Laura were busy again today, independently of each other of course, but still busy. Julia was away in the Berkshires, probably playing in the leftover snow from the week before; Laura was no doubt still sleeping, recuperating from a late night out and preparing for another one tonight; and Annabel would be going downtown, possibly to SoHo, with those new popular friends, where they would spend the day shopping at tiny unknown stores, having lunch, and then shopping again.

Sometimes Stefanie wished that she had somewhere to go and someplace to be, but then she also considered herself lucky—she wasn't involved in any of these plans, so her only distraction would be the television or the Internet. As she was still disgusted with the television and could confidently predict that no one would be online, she was safe. There would be no distractions; she could definitely write the essay later. She'd start with her psychology homework, much less demanding than her English; she would knock that off quickly. Stefanie climbed back into bed with her psychology textbook.

It was a strange phenomenon. Annabel got new friends, Laura got a boyfriend, and Julia got to spend less time with the friends that she'd had since childhood. And Stefanie? She got more time to study and get better grades. Teachers had always said that Stefanie was a bright student but undisciplined. Now they said she was finally reaching her potential. So it was worth it to read a textbook on Saturday morning, especially when there was nothing else to do. Besides, she sort of liked the new attention. Loved it, in fact. And more of it would have suited her just fine. Her teachers noticed her now. They asked her to help other students. They looked in her direction when they asked a difficult question. She was the authority on what they had actually been assigned for homework and whether it had been difficult. Her teachers' praise and respect made Stefanie comfortable in their rooms. She liked knowing that she had something to offer—intelligence—and that other people recognized it. There was something magical about being asked to explain something to the class. When everyone's eyes were trained on her, she felt powerful and special. She'd never been special before, but all of a sudden she was. She used to fade into the background. She had been one of those "OK" students, neither worth the attention afforded to the smart ones nor the attention afforded to the troublemakers. Now, as her grades got better and she volunteered more in class, everyone had begun to notice her.

The hastily written notes in her blue teacher's plan-book instructed her to read pages 97–145 for next week. The assigned section was about eating disorders. As Stephanie flipped through, she looked at the pictures. She stuck a Post-it on the first page and made a note to show Laura. Laura, the dieting one. Just looking at those girls was enough to make anyone stop dieting.

Yet, while looking at them, it dawned on Stefanie that these cases were the extreme. Just because these girls chose to starve themselves to lose weight didn't mean that that's how it always had to be. They had carried dieting too far. But wouldn't it be okay just to go on a normal diet? A diet that was healthy? It wouldn't even be considered a diet, really just eating sensibly. That's all; that would be it. She could stand to lose a few pounds, but she wasn't crazy. She could never be on of those girls.

The knock at the door startled her. Her father's head appeared in the doorway, and then he approached the bed, forgetting to wait for her to invite him in. He walked uneasily in her room, traveling into uncharted domain. It struck her as he walked slowly, still under the influence of sleep, that he was slower than he used to be. His eyes were the same as they had always been—one looking slightly away toward the left, not quite focusing—but the hair around his temples was graying. He wasn't a young surfer from California; he was her father. Looking into his eyes, Stefanie did not see the macho, self-described fitness guru that he thought he was, but the father that he had always been. He was the hero from her childhood, back when he had done everything right, when she had stood up for him in any situation because she couldn't bear to see him hurt. There was softness in his eyes, and by looking into them Stefanie could tell he still loved her. She couldn't help but think that she and her dad were still close, even if they didn't go out every Saturday as they did when she was younger.

He sat at her feet, and the edge of the bed sank under his weight. "What about breakfast, Stef? Why don't we go out?"

Stefanie grinned. Just like old times. She imagined them as the perfect duo, the father-daughter pair from every sappy TV show from the eighties—*Full House, Growing Pains, Charles in Charge, Family Ties*. They would pass maple syrup across the table and laugh and joke and talk. And she would leave feeling full. In fact, most of the time, she'd spend so much time having fun that she wouldn't pay attention to her eating, and she'd stuff herself to overflowing before she even realized it.

Her father picked up the magazine from the night before and placed it on her lap. "It was on the floor," he said as he touched her foot gingerly, but she pulled her foot back and buried it in the covers, recoiling from the weight of his hand. Winona Ryder's perfect features, defined stomach muscles, and the words *Lose Weight Fast!* leapt off the page and sailed toward her. Her father was still waiting for his answer. "So how about it?" he asked.

Stefanie shook her head. "Can't. Too much work ..." Her voice trailed off. She felt like she was being strangled. She thought of her self-inspection the night before. Bones ... bones ... bones. She remembered the models that pranced across the pages of her magazines. She wanted to eat breakfast, but she knew that if they went out, she'd overeat, as she usually did. She'd just grab a low-fat yogurt on the way out the door. That would be better. But she knew he was disappointed, and so was she. Why was she such a rotten daughter? Why couldn't she just have said yes? Her father walked back out into the hallway with his head down.

A picture of a girl at 5'5" and seventy-three pounds stared out at Stefanie from her open psych book. In the space below the image, the girl's personal essay recounted how she had done that to herself. Stefanie continued reading. That was only one of the images. The others were just as—if not more—disturbing.

She could never be one of those girls. Why would anybody want to look so pathetically emaciated? How had they managed to be blind to the blatantly obvious truth? They were killing themselves, and their eyes showed determination. There was no pain, only numbness. Surely they must have known what they were doing. Couldn't they see the thinning hair that was so obviously thin and wispy, even in the pictures, and understand that something had gone terribly wrong? Were they crazy? There could be no other explanation.

Her head was resting against the spine of her textbook, and Stefanie realized that she had drifted off. In her dream, Barbie, the blonde model from the night before, had locked herself in a single-stalled bathroom. Barbie was staring at the mirror, watching her lips mouth the words of the "Bones" song while the radio played in the background. As she hummed, Barbie swung her hips back and forth and stared into the mirror, watching those same bones that Stefanie had searched for when she had heard the song. In the reflection, Barbie's thighs were getting bigger and bigger. They were going to explode; tendons and ligaments would be all over the bathroom. Stefanie cringed at the prospect. Then Barbie's stomach extended, beginning to look pregnant but only in the mirror. Ignoring the reflection, Stefanie stared at Barbie. As the image in the mirror grew larger, Barbie got smaller. Her ribs became clearly visible under a thin layer of skin. And her thighs, which had looked like inflated balloons in the reflection, were in reality no wider than the straight pin that clowns use to pop balloons at the circus. Barbie was obviously delusional. And all the while she sang that awful song. She was one of them—one of the girls from her textbook with sallow faces and empty stares.

Despite her disgust, Stefanie found herself pitying Barbie.

Caught somewhere between alertness and sleep, Stefanie remembered that the textbook had said that eating disorders had created lots of issues for those girls. It made them lose their hair. It made them sickly. It killed their immune systems. It was not a healthy way to live. An eating disorder could result in death. But yet, it had also made them feel more in control; these girls had more friends; they could relate to other people. Losing weight had given them a purpose and a sense of accomplishment. In truth, it didn't sound like an entirely negative proposition. The girls wouldn't really *die*, after all. No one was that stupid. They'd just be thinner, and thinner was prettier. Stefanie was beginning to understand. Thinner … prettier … more confidence … more friends … more attention …

The door to the bedroom vibrated as someone knocked. It was her mother's special patter. Stefanie called out, "Yeah?" as she rubbed the sleep from her eyes and straightened the pages of her book. "Lunch time," her mother called from the hall. "There are sandwich fixings on the table and an unopened box of Oreos in the breadbox."

Stefanie slid off the bed, quickly splashed some water on her face, brushed her teeth, and pulled on the same pair of jeans she had worn the day before. When she reached for the zipper, she sucked in her stomach and became acutely aware of a tightness that hadn't been there before. "Damn zippers!" As she jumped up and down in an attempt to stretch the jeans, Stefanie bent over and looked at the two rolls of fat on her stomach. *Okay*, she thought, *I've really got to do this. I'll just lose a little weight … just until my jeans fit and my thighs don't jiggle … and maybe until my stomach's flat.*

She could have had Oreos at lunch, but she restrained herself and settled for graham crackers instead. *I'm going to get healthy,* she told herself. Today she would begin a new lifestyle. It wouldn't be a giant change, just an improvement.

* * *

As dusk fell over the city, coaxing it out of its afternoon stupor, Stefanie walked briskly from the neighborhood Blockbuster, the evening's entertainment tucked snugly under her arms. She'd be by herself again tonight, but it was OK. She felt a sense of peace and almost a sense of satisfaction.

- 3 -

On Monday mornings Stefanie walked to school alone. For the fifteen minutes before the redbrick building and its inherent stresses became her focal point, her companion was her Discman. After staggering out the front door and mumbling a hasty good morning to the doorman through that last bite of powdered doughnut, she would raise the volume and turn right, away from the stolid solitude of tree-lined Park Avenue and toward the more boisterous Lexington. On cold mornings she would usually stop at the little coffee shop on the corner and buy a hot apple cider. Spinning the black leather aluminum stool by the take-out counter, she would ask the guy behind the counter for an extra cinnamon stick, which she would suck on when the cider was gone. It was a particularly good Monday if she arrived at school with cider remaining. Her homeroom met in the cafeteria on Mondays for a class meeting, and it was always nice to have warm cider to sip while eating the muffins and bagels, her second breakfast.

That morning, the column of mercury in the glass thermometer ended just below the thirty-degree mark, and Stefanie had to keep her head down to protect her face from the whipping wind. It was a hot cider morning.

"The shinbone's connected to the knee bone, the knee bone's connected to the thighbone, the thighbone's connected to the hip bone ..."

Once Stefanie was inside, the song began to play in her head just as she stepped around a table and up to the counter. The impatient server stared at her while drumming his knuckles on the side of the cash register.

"One hot apple cider, please." The room was revolving; the walls were falling inward, and the chairs were going to topple. She needed an escape. *Am I going crazy?* The pulse of the music echoed through her head. A harmless nursery school song—long forgotten until the other night. Now she hated its beat and the way she was reminded of her friends who called and complained, even though they should have been happy. Those bones—they could see those bones. They should look in the mirror and be proud.

Outside, Stefanie wrapped her hands around the warm cardboard cup and breathed in the smell of the apples mingled with cinnamon and spices. The cars were moving in a straight line, the walls of the store hadn't collapsed, and she had made it back outside. Her sanity was returning.

But her mind was still singing about bones. The repetition of the song was getting obsessive, but she couldn't stop it. As the chorus played again, Stefanie felt for each bone. Holding the apple cider in one hand, the other reached inside her down jacket and traveled the length of her body. Hoping none of the people she passed would notice, she began at her shoulders and carefully assessed each indentation, curve, and protrusion. Tracing the pointy edge of her shoulder in toward her body, she grabbed at her collarbone and tried to shake it, her fingers pulling at either side. She pressed at the sides of her rib cage and in the center of her chest, where her sternum ended. Her hand reached her hip bone, and she tried to wiggle her fingers behind the bone, pressing down as hard as she could. She couldn't do it. There was so much work to be done—so many spots where she knew bones were meant to be but where her fingers felt only flesh—the top of her chest, her stomach, her thighs, her butt. But there were ways, she assured herself. It was only a matter of choosing the best one. She needed a plan.

When the music finally stopped, Stefanie stuffed her Discman back into her backpack. The desire to listen to music was gone. The wind was still cold, the cider was gone, and she had forgotten to ask for the extra cinnamon stick.

When she entered the cafeteria, there was already a group seated around a table. They weren't all her closest friends, and ordinarily the unwritten but accepted laws of lunchroom decorum would dictate that she should find her own table. But Julia was there, so this morning she could join them. That was acceptable.

It didn't really matter where she sat. While the other girls discussed the trivial events of the weekend, she usually studied. Even if she had something to share, no one would really listen anyway. They only listened if you were cool. If you went to all the parties—or just to the one where no other classmates happened to be—then you were cool. Talking about these parties was the only way to get everyone's undivided attention. Otherwise, the girls didn't stay on any one topic long enough to allow anyone to interject. One moment they were talking about guys, the next it was homework, the next it was teachers, then grades, then parents, then friends, then back to guys, at which point the cycle would begin all over. It was typical teenage ADD. Their conversation blew wherever the wind carried it, and even minutes afterward it was hard to recall what had even been said. She'd come to accept it as a function of an all-girls school, and she dropped her backpack on the floor next to the one remaining seat.

Today they were serving the chocolate muffins with melted chocolate chips that were always warm in the center. A fourth grader walked by carrying a plate of five, and Stefanie felt powerless, seduced by their fresh-out-of-the-oven aroma. Stefanie wandered up toward the counter, wishing that she were in middle school again. No one would care; no one would look at her strangely. She wouldn't be the only one at the table eating a muffin.

Standing head bent over the steaming muffin tins, she could see that some were still too hot to touch. She tried to imagine the pleasant burn against her tongue. Certainly, one couldn't hurt her; surely it wouldn't do any damage. But what about her new lifestyle? What about the new, healthy Stefanie Webber?

That thought seemed to somehow shake her out of her daze.

The muffins would be there again. She could have one next time, once she had lost a few pounds. She always ate as though there would be no next time, but there would be. She would need to remind herself of that.

Julia's laugh carried across the cafeteria, and Stefanie wondered why they didn't hang out anymore. There had been no fight, no falling out, no harsh words as there had been with other former best friends. No name-calling or gossiping, no spreading rumors or rolling eyes. They never gave each other the silent treatment. They had just stopped talking. There was no body language or annoyance or anything that would have signaled the end of a relationship. She had seen it happen before, had done it to other people, and had had it done to her, but this time there was no definitive moment between them that Stefanie could remember. The invitations to the Berkshires had just stopped coming. They stopped going out for dinner on the weekends. Julia didn't call to ask what movie Stefanie wanted to see on Friday afternoon. They both quit tap dancing lessons—not enough time—so that shared time of the week ceased to exist. The separation would have been mutual, but Stefanie hadn't wanted to lose her friend. Out of sight, Julia laughed again. A knot formed in Stefanie's stomach—she hated to admit to herself that she missed Julia; she hated to be that needy. But whatever had been just wasn't there. Not anymore.

Next to the counter were the cereal dispensers. That was it; she could have cornflakes. They were healthy, and everyone else was eating cereal. She'd fit right in. A triumphant grin spread across her face as she escaped from the tempting pull of the muffins with only a bowl of cornflakes. But she had taken a while standing there next to the food, longer than she had thought, and her seat at the round table was gone. There was no room to pull up another chair, and Stefanie was forced to collect her bag and her cereal—that second breakfast— and move to one of the long tables. She tried to smile as she left, to make it look like she had someplace else to be, but she knew that she didn't. How she hated those girls, and yet she wanted to be with them. It didn't really make sense. She took out the psychology book and flipped it open to the anorexia pictures. She needed to talk to Laura, needed to tell Laura her plan. They could help each other.

Laura never ate in the cafeteria on Monday. She had breakfast at home, where she avoided saturated fats as if they were the plague and where she could eat "healthy" foods, like granola bars or fruit. When she finished choral practice and joined the class downstairs, she never felt the impulse to have a second breakfast. Stefanie could use Laura's strong will, her determination. If she could channel them into herself, then she knew she could succeed.

When Laura arrived—thin and lanky with spandex leggings under her skirt and her golden brown hair pulled up into a sloppy half-ponytail that only Laura could manage to pull off—they talked momentarily about their weekends. Laura mentioned that the date had gone well, and she thought she was in love—again—with Robert, the boyfriend du jour, despite the leather-pants-versus-mini-skirt fiasco. Laura would look good in anything. Stefanie could see the truth about Laura—she was thinner than average and didn't even work at it. She was just built that way. Where Laura's kneecaps were bony, Stefanie's were covered in a layer of flesh. The bathing suits that Stefanie had outgrown in the sixth grade would still fit Laura. Stefanie couldn't even pull them up to her hips.

Laura was talking about how Robert could be much cuter if he would only cut his hair and let her pick out his clothing, when Stefanie cut her off. "I've decided to lose some weight." You had to be that direct with Laura, or else she wouldn't understand—or maybe she just wouldn't care. Stephanie continued, "I think that we can help each other. You know, form a routine and follow it together—like a support group. What do you think?"

She knew Laura would protest. Laura would insist that Stefanie didn't need to lose weight. Laura would say that appearance wasn't important. And yet the song sang about hip bones, Barbie talked about diet pills, the smiling brunette promoted her lose-weight-fast tips. If Laura needed to worry about weight, Stefanie did as well.

She was fifteen pounds heavier than Laura and an inch and a half shorter; she was the heavy one.

Stefanie also knew that Laura would lie. All friends do—harmless little white lies to make a friend feel better. Laura had to protest. She had to, but having fulfilled that obligation she would then be allowed to accept the offer. Stefanie only had to wait. Laura would agree, and they would create a plan. Their common goal would draw them closer together than they'd ever been. They would jog together in Central Park or along Fifth Avenue. They would go to the gym together and spot each other while they lifted weights. They would mix protein shakes in their kitchens and drink them together—experimenting with different recipes and flavors until they found one that was palatable. She would finally have a friend— she wouldn't be alone any longer. Stefanie's heart beat a little faster than it had a moment before. That feeling of anticipation made her pulse flutter.

Then, just as homeroom began and the teachers called for the girls to assemble with their advisors, Laura nodded. She was in. Stefanie had been right. She knew Laura; she knew that she would concede in the end.

The last bite of cereal in Stefanie's bowl went uneaten as the girls rushed for the tables where their advisors were waiting. Stefanie was flushed and excited. Laura would help her. A new lifestyle—and then a new life—was underway.

When she got to the table that Ms. Olson, the psychology teacher and Stefanie's advisor, chose for every meeting—the one at the far end of the cafeteria—everyone was passing around pictures from someone's sweet sixteen party. Stefanie took this opportunity to retrieve her journal from the bottom of her bag. She opened to a new page, marked the top right corner with January 8, 2001, and wrote, "Let the games begin."

It was an appropriate line. She would look back at that page until the words melted together, until she had memorized the color of the ink and the way that the writing slanted on the page. It galvanized her today and would from that day forward.

Stefanie's psychology class met in the smallest classroom on the second floor because there were only nine of them. This class was purposely kept small so that conversations could be personal. Stefanie was the only one from her group in that section. Although it felt disloyal, sometimes she was thankful for having this one period alone—where she could be away from her friends, away from their critical stares and their complaining. And Ms. Olson's tiny classroom, with the candy bowl on the desk and the oversized pillows that they occasionally lounged on during discussions, was a wonderful place to escape.

Stefanie took her usual seat next to the window and waited. They always sat in the same seats, not because they were assigned but because they were familiar. The rest of the class would file in within the next few minutes. Ms. Olson would follow a couple of seconds later, and class would begin. Today's topic, following the reading, would be anorexia and bulimia. Stefanie had already opened her textbook and turned to the correct page when her teacher entered the room.

Ms. Olsen began with a handout on intervention and what people should do if they suspected that a friend has an eating disorder. In one of the real-life stories, one girl recounted how she regretted supporting a friend's diet by saying they would do it together. The friend had stopped eating altogether soon after.

Stefanie had heard it all before: the guilt of the friend over inciting the eating disorder; the trauma of the parents when they found out that their daughter was starving herself; the loss of many precious years for the girl who was starving, years spent kowtowing to a vicious disease; the regret when lasting consequences began to appear, and the ability to have children, to develop a woman's body, or to prevent osteoporosis were all gone. Stefanie's thoughts roamed to Laura. Laura was already thin; she didn't need to diet. She shouldn't be dieting, in fact, and she didn't need encouragement from any vague meal plans. But Stefanie intended to make a healthy plan for both of them. She would draw on Laura's strength to adhere to the rules, and meanwhile Laura would be eating healthily. It would be mutually beneficial.

"Ms. Webber, I asked you if you care to share your reactions to this weekend's reading assignment. You've been unusually quiet today."

Ms. Olson perched on the corner of her desk. She sat there with her legs crossed, her thin knees showing in the folds of her skirt, her curly brown hair just resting on her shoulders. She was at once both intimidating and friendly. She always said that from the corner of her desk she could see everyone, everyone could see her, and she could tell if they were paying attention. She was good at that. At twenty-seven, having only been at the school for three years, she could already tell when somebody hadn't done her reading, was bored with a lesson, or was tired from having been up late the night before, probably watching reruns of *Friends* or lingering online with friends. Ms. Olson wanted all her students involved in the discussions and was nothing if not persistent.

"Stefanie?" She just wouldn't give up.

"It's considered a disease, like leukemia, so we can't fault them; but why does anyone consciously do that to themselves?" That was what she said, but what she said belied an admiration for these girls' war on weight. What strength they had, she thought, to diet so successfully and lose weight. She felt the tiniest bit jealous. Why couldn't she do it, too? The answer was that they were sick and she was healthy. No, she considered, rejecting her thoughts. She didn't really want to be them, did she? It was stupid. Still, it would be so nice if she could lose a few pounds—just a few pounds.

"It's a good question, Stefanie. We don't know why a person does that to herself. I suppose there are many reasons ..."

It had been a rhetorical question. She hadn't expected an answer, but it appeared that her teacher was going to try and give one. Ms. Olson was sitting next to the candy bowl. It was filled with miniature Snickers and Hershey's Nuggets, Stefanie's favorite: the cookies 'n' cream variety. Their whole class knew those were her favorites, and they always saved her some whenever they raided Ms. Olson's bowl. But recently, the bowl had stayed full longer. The other girls claimed they were giving up sweets. Stefanie was sure that she was the only one craving that creamy taste of white chocolate melting against her tongue, and she hated herself for wanting it.

Her teacher was pacing the front of the room, enumerating the reasons why anorexia nervosa and bulimia nervosa strike teenagers at such an astounding rate. There were new societal pressures that pushed teenagers harder than ever to be perfect. There was a generation of parents trying to live vicariously through their children, pushing too hard and being overbearing. There was new technology—DVDs, the Internet—that spread waif-like images of beauty, convincing people that their self-worth was tied up in their bodies. In a time when most parents were absent either physically or emotionally, there was the need for children to get the attention that they craved. And it wasn't surprising that this need for attention was often met by abusing a body they had been conditioned to hate.

Suddenly, Stefanie flashed back to that morning's muffin tray, and then her eyes began to burn. What right did Ms. Olson have to speak about eating in moderation? She hadn't had a dessert in ten years; she probably lived off lettuce and low-calorie, non-fat dressing. It was all a lie—the biggest lie. All the skinny people lied about the secret of moderation. And as for the girls in the book Ms. Olson was holding, they almost certainly never ate chocolate, and they were the really skinny ones. The walls of the classroom seemed to have grown less solid and began to melt into the floor. Stefanie knew she was chewing on her lip. She could feel it begin to split and knew that she would need to get to the bathroom for a tissue. The air in the hallway would be good anyway, and she excused herself to the safety of the ladies' room.

As she dabbed at her lip with toilet paper, Stefanie leaned back against the locked door of the stall. Was she going crazy? The question knocked the wind out of her, but she tried to ignore it. Of course she wasn't crazy. She was correct—and sensible. The anorexic girls didn't eat chocolate, and the bulimics threw it back up. But they went to even greater extremes than just depriving themselves of candy. Stefanie thought of her own breakfast. Those girls wouldn't have even eaten the bowl of cereal, much less a powdered doughnut too. Why had she eaten an extra breakfast? What purpose had that served? She hadn't even been hungry.

She stood in the bathroom, locked in a stall by herself. Everyone else was in class. Bulimics throw the food back up. She felt for her hip bones again, but they still seemed nonexistent.

The toilet came closer as Stefanie bent down to kneel on the cold tile floor. She wasn't sure what she planned to do until she got there, and then it seemed like the most natural thing in the world. The index finger of her right hand reached for the back of her throat, and Stefanie felt each stomach muscle contract upward. She was pushing the finger down farther and hoping that nobody would come into the bathroom, when she suddenly pulled her finger out of her mouth, wincing in pain. Her nails. She should have been more careful; she didn't want her throat to bleed.

She sat on the bathroom floor and cried. The tile was cold against her bare legs—exposed beneath the plaid uniform kilt—and Stefanie wondered what had happened. Her right index finger had two indentations where her teeth had left their mark, and her throat felt raw where her nails had caught. She was shaking. Why was she doing this? Those girls were stupid. She didn't want to be one of them. But she had tried it; she'd only tried it. It wasn't as if anything had happened. Everything was the same. She hadn't thrown up. She wasn't bulimic. She wasn't anorexic.

The door opened, and Stefanie heard someone enter the stall next to her.

A second girl's feet appeared under the stall on her other side, and Stefanie listened to the two girls' conversation. Girl Number One had been to a party Saturday night. She's eaten chips and dip and even some guacamole ... so fattening, she proclaimed. Girl Number

Two could empathize. She'd eaten leftover cake from her younger brother's birthday party yesterday afternoon. But it was OK. Neither one had had breakfast that morning.

She needed to get back to class; Ms. Olson would think she was trying to slack off. Leaning on the sink for support, Stefanie wiped the tearstains off her cheeks and fled from the bathroom before the girls in the other stalls could come out.

She slid back into her seat and tried to look like she was absorbed in the lesson. When Ms. Olson looked her way, Stefanie forced herself to smile, but under the desk, her hands were still shaking.

- 4 -

*A*llowances: one juice a day, one soda a week, two desserts weekly. That was the end of her daily journal entry. Above it, Stefanie had detailed "the plan." Squats, sit-ups, leg lifts, a regimen behind a daily workout was listed carefully beside bullet points. They had collaborated, Stefanie and Laura, to come up with it, and before lunch had ended they had drafted a pledge and signed their names to a back page of Stefanie's notebook. Those signatures were an agreement, a promise to follow the restrictions until each had reached her goals. Stefanie had signed without hesitating. Why should it matter when she didn't even know what her goal was yet? That could be defined later. All she needed to know now was that soon she would be happy. Like Laura and Annabel, she would be able to see those bones.

Outside it was dark, and the streetlamps cast circles of light on the sidewalks. One day had passed, one day of her new lifestyle. Stefanie thought back on dinner and was pleased with her success. She had managed to avoid apple pie and garlic rolls, and she had eaten relatively little—only a lamb chop, after carefully cutting off the fatty portions, and a small bit of ratatouille. All was going according to plan.

"Stefanie, it's getting late. Don't you think you should be getting to bed now?" Her mom's voice echoed down the hallway.

"I'm getting ready for bed, Mom. Goodnight. I love you."

Stefanie reached over and turned off her lamp so that her mother couldn't see any light from under the bedroom door. She still had her exercises to do.

She was aiming for thirty sit-ups, but after twenty-three, her muscles refused to do more. She was forced to give up. After a semester and a half of school with only one measly PE class a week, which involved no cardio fitness anyway—she just wasn't in shape. She wished she'd joined a sports team. At least then she would have to work out. The leg lifts were even harder, and she only managed to do eighteen of thirty. But it was only the first day. There was time to improve, and Stefanie promised herself that she would. Tomorrow was a new day.

She lay on the wooden floor of her bedroom, staring up at the ceiling. Her stomach muscles tightened from the unaccustomed workout, and, as she felt for her hip bones in the hopes that they might have appeared, Stefanie wondered how Laura had done. Laura, who was thin and perfect—why was she on a diet at all? A rush of competitiveness surprised Stefanie. It wasn't a contest. She was just aiming at being healthy; why did Laura's success matter? Still, she would prove to Laura that she was just as good. She would beat Laura. Tomorrow was a new day.

Before she set her alarm clock and slipped between the covers, Stefanie took out her journal. Under her journal entry she wrote the date again: *January 8, 2001*. Below that: *Day One*. She wrote two numbers: *twenty-three, eighteen*—the amount of sit-ups and leg lifts that she had done. Finally, she wrote two more numbers—*thirty-five, thirty*—and circled them, her goals for the next day. Then she fell into a dreamless sleep.

When Stefanie woke in the morning, she hurt. It hurt to move. Her stomach muscles seemed to be protesting, still angry from the night before. But Stefanie smiled; pain was good. Pain meant progress. The sun was shining outside, and the wind was calm, eliminating the hated January windchills. It was going to be a good day. She was ready for Day Two of her new lifestyle.

She'd never really noticed it before—her face was round. While Stefanie brushed her teeth, she stared into the mirror. Her face was unequivocally round. Her cheeks looked like a baby's—puffed out—and her cheekbones were invisible. There was certainly a lot of work to be done.

She hated the mirror for what it showed her. She didn't want to look at herself, didn't want to see all the changes that she needed to make, but she couldn't seem to pull her eyes away. She was entranced. Slowly, she lifted up her shirt. Her stomach looked the same as it had the day before. Why was she doing sit-ups and leg lifts if they didn't change anything? Of course, it was too soon to see a difference. Intellectually, Stefanie understood, but she still wished that her stomach could have flattened and her ribs could have come closer to the surface overnight. Just a little.

A knock at the door broke Stefanie's concentration, and she pulled her eyes away from the mirror. Just as her mother entered the room, Stefanie let her shirt fall. Her mom might think it strange that she was standing there, brushing her teeth, in only a bra, but her mother was holding the *New York Times* in front of her and wasn't really paying attention. She liked to read all the headlines before she did anything else in the morning. "Come have some breakfast, Stef. It's getting late."

It *was* getting late. Stefanie grabbed her backpack and swung the strap over her shoulder. She needed to hurry if she wanted to walk to school with Annabel.

In front of Stefanie's place at the table were powdered doughnuts. Her glass was filled with orange juice, and there were some strawberries sweetened with sugar in a bowl. She paused for a second. Her mother was at the sink buttering an English muffin. An English muffin—it was healthier than a doughnut. No wonder everyone always said that her mother was so health conscious. That was what Stefanie wanted. She wanted the praise that her mother got; she wanted to be known for her being healthy—and thin.

She passed over the doughnuts and went to the pantry. More doughnuts ... mini muffins ... cinnamon buns ... banana cake ... her mother wouldn't eat any of these items; neither would Laura or the anorexic, skinny girls. Finally, in the back, behind the boxes of pancake mix, cereal. That was an acceptable breakfast. Stefanie returned to the table gripping the bran flakes and poured in some milk. She felt suffocated; the doughnuts were still in front of her. The powdered sugar would taste so good. The doughnuts would be soft inside her mouth. Her teeth would sink in the soft ring of fried dough, and the sweetness would fill her mouth. Stefanie closed her eyes, trying to erase her thoughts. She wanted a doughnut, a mini muffin, a cinnamon bun, or banana cake; but she couldn't. She couldn't allow herself to eat any of that. She couldn't sabotage the entire day just because she wanted something sweet and caloric.

When she opened her eyes, her mother was watching her intently over the rim of the coffee cup. The gold band along the rim, falling right below her eyes, looked like morning war paint. "Are you feeling okay this morning?"

Stefanie, reaching for a spoon, tried to sound nonchalant, "Sure, why do you ask?"

"You're eating my bran flakes, and you used to say that they tasted like cardboard." Her mother was obviously perplexed.

"I'm trying to be healthier. I'm going to eat more reasonably and do some exercises. I want my stomach to be flat and strong—muscular."

Stefanie held her breath and waited for her mother's answer. She didn't know what type of reaction she would get. Madeline Webber had only been on a diet once in her life—probably to see what she could do rather than because she needed to lose weight—and was generally a proponent of the eat-everything-in-moderation philosophy.

But her response was surprising. Her mother was pleased. "Good for you. And breakfast is the perfect place to start. You know, it sets the pace for the rest of the day."

Ten minutes later Stefanie met Annabel on the corner of Park Avenue. There had been a time when their walk-to-school conversations had been sweet schoolgirl banter about what happened last night on the WB. Not anymore. Fictional boyfriends—Jesse or Dean from the *Gilmore Girls,* or Simon from *Seventh Heaven*—had been shelved and replaced by reality, by Annabel's monologue about her real-life boyfriends. She could talk forever on that subject—their IMs, their cell phone conversations, their plans to steal a few hours from their busy schedules to hang out at whoever's house might be empty or unsupervised later in the week. Usually, Stefanie tried to listen. She didn't want Annabel to think that she didn't care, although she really didn't. But without her, the diminishing circle of Stefanie's friends would close even further.

But that morning Stefanie couldn't concentrate. She was thinking about her mother's words, trying to process their meaning and the unexpected discomfort they had provoked.

What had she wanted? What was her mother supposed to say? Stefanie wasn't sure. She only knew that what had been said was not what she had wanted to hear.

"Good for you ... good for you ... good for you ..." The words played back in Stefanie's mind with each step she took. Her mom supported her diet. Her mom condoned the plan; and with those few words she also affirmed what Stefanie believed: She was fat. If it wasn't true, then her mother would not have congratulated her.

Annabel was still chattering away, oblivious, but to Stefanie her voice seemed to be humming the song about bones. And the infomercial blonde was tap-dancing through her thoughts. *What was the secret? Why was everyone else so thin? Why couldn't she be like everyone else?*

They had reached the school. Annabel stopped talking and disappeared in search of her new friends. Stefanie went to her first-period classroom, her psychology book open on her lap.

As the clock ticked away the minutes until the class began, Stefanie wondered about the girls that stared up at her from the worn pages of her book. Did they spend their weekends alone the way she'd been doing lately? When they arrived at school, did they sit by themselves in empty classrooms to pass the time until the first class? She didn't think so. She peered at the girls' pictures. Skin and bones and not much else. Most were scantily clad in only underwear to get the maximum effect of their boniness. A few were runway models dressed in haute couture fashions, with spindly legs showing from underneath short skirts. In every picture Stefanie saw bones protruding from unusual places, places normally covered with flesh—the collarbone, the shoulders, the rib cage. All these girls were the same, and they had each other. They were part of an exclusive club—no normal people allowed—and it almost seemed fun.

The door to the still-empty classroom opened, and Stefanie looked up. Laura entered, closing the door securely behind her. "I was so good!" Laura said, beaming. "I worked out yesterday, and I only had a salad for dinner. And I didn't even have my juice this morning ..."

Stefanie didn't want to hear anymore. Laura was beating her. Stefanie was losing at her own game. This hadn't been the plan; she wanted to be the successful one. She wanted people to admire how skinny she had become, and she didn't want to share that attention with Laura. She hated her friend for her accomplishments, but then she felt herself being pushed along; strength and determination were building. She could do this. She would do this. Day Two had begun, and it could be better than Day One. Stefanie felt calm. Knowing that she would work harder, she could feel happy for Laura. Why shouldn't they both be healthy? There was no reason to be competitive.

And yet, as Stefanie sat down to lunch that day, she couldn't refrain from looking at Laura's tray. A small portion of rice, two packets of saltines, and a cup of potato leek soup ... Laura grinned, and Stefanie easily returned the smile. She was willing to bet that Laura thought she was having a healthy lunch. But all those carbohydrates? How healthy could that be? As she placed her tray on the long table and took a seat, she felt a certain satisfaction. It held a salad with beans and tuna fish and only a tiny bit of pasta salad. Laura took a bite of rice, and Stefanie's smile widened. Pride stretched its edges. She was finally succeeding.

~ 5 ~

"CD complete," a mechanical voice announced. Stefanie watched the clock as she waited for the music to end. It was late afternoon, and her mother had suggested that she help make dinner. Instead, she was sitting at her computer, downloading a child's song and then copying it onto the CD that spun rapidly inside the CDR/W drive.

"The shinbone's connected to the knee bone, the knee bone's connected to the thighbone, the thighbone's connected to the hip bone ..."

The song made her angry. It brought out her hostility. She hated the infomercial models; she hated diet pills; she hated the bones that the song sang about—the ones that she couldn't see. She hated herself. And she hated Laura for her dieting success, Annabel for her perfect body, and Julia ... just because. She hated them all for drifting away, for being able to squeeze magically through some keyhole passage into a self-possessed teenhood, a kingdom for the light and lithe, somewhere beyond her grasp. Well, if they could sail into it, she would find her own way in. She would mount an assault.

She restarted her CD and pressed "Play."

No one else would have understood. She would use her CD, on continuous loop, as encouragement. Every time she heard the lyrics, she would find the strength to deny herself. She would skip dessert every night; she would do another set of sit-ups; she would run for five more minutes around the reservoir in Central Park despite the frigid weather. She felt powerful. Unbreakable. Indestructible.

With a black permanent marker, Stefanie titled the CD *Motivation*. She set her alarm for the next day and programmed it to wake her up with the new CD. It would be a good way to start the new day.

So ended Day Two, with Day Three close behind.

Stefanie fingered her lip as she walked down the empty hallway toward the basement. The basement was dark. Apartment-building basements were always that way; she could remember being afraid to go down there as a little girl, afraid of the people who hid in those exposed pipes, afraid that the gray floor would turn into quick-sand and swallow her. She'd always had a colorful imagination. But the gym was down there. The co-op had put it in a few years back, making the building a more desirable place to live, and it had quickly become the hot spot for all the fitness-conscious—or possibly obsessed—people. The equipment was new. There was a basketball court, a television, and stereo equipment. Her parents preferred to go to their gym downtown, where they took workout classes from the toughest trainer in the TriState area, so they didn't use the apartment gym frequently. Stefanie had only been in there a couple of times and had been perfectly happy to keep it that way, but now it was different. Now she had to go. She didn't want to, but she had to—or Laura would win again.

There was a treadmill, weightlifting equipment, a stationary bike, and an elliptical trainer. She'd heard horror stories about treadmills; people had fallen and nearly been killed by the moving belt. There was weightlifting equipment, but she didn't know how to use it. She did know how to work the stationary bike, but she also knew that it didn't burn enough calories. Her only option was the elliptical.

After programming in her weight and choosing the Fat Burn option, Stefanie began to pedal. Moving her legs felt good. She was doing something healthy. This was what The Plan had been all about. Her muscles were beginning to feel the workout—the oxygen deficit was accumulating. To push herself along, she hummed to herself, "The shinbone's connected ..."

She pushed herself slightly harder, faster. Her heart rate steadily rose, and it became more difficult to breathe. But what did that matter? Somewhere across town, Laura was doing the same. With each lift of her leg, Stefanie heard, "Beat Laura. Beat Laura. Beat

Laura." Her programmed session ended, but she kept pedaling. Laura would have kept going; Laura would have barely been out of breath, so she had to keep going. Ten minutes, twenty minutes, thirty. When had this dieting game become a contest?

Other people began filing into the gym now, and Stefanie listened to their conversations. They all knew each other, had obviously grown accustomed to these evening workouts. One man complained about his youngest daughter—she'd been going through the terrible twos and had just graduated to the more-terrible threes. Another had just closed an important deal at work. A woman asked advice about an upcoming vacation: Where should she go, Nevis or St. Barts? Of course, she'd heard great things about Anguilla, too. Other conversations swirled around the room: work, bosses, guys, girlfriends, children, workouts …

It was after six fifteen, and the working crowd had begun their routines when Stefanie, exhausted and panting, finally allowed herself to step down from the elliptical. Another woman climbed on, and Stefanie ruefully noticed the woman's model-type figure. Was everyone else in the world gorgeous and thin?

There was a scale in a corner of the gym. It would be tempting to measure her results so far. The Webber household had always been without a scale. Her parents had instilled in her the importance of not being dependent on a number. She was only weighed once a year at the doctor's office, that was all, but now she was curious.

Stephanie stepped on the scale. The weights clanked against the metal beam as she moved to balance them. One hundred twenty-eight—she had been eight pounds lighter the year before. Eight pounds in a year, without growing taller. How could that be? One twenty was acceptable if you were five feet, four inches. One twenty-eight was not.

She turned from the scale, and a room of mirrors confronted her. In every direction, she found herself looking into her own eyes. She imagined she was looking into those funny amusement park mirrors where the body becomes distorted, stretched out of shape—

33

unrecognizable. Your head became larger. Your chins doubled. Suddenly a waist became way too small and hips way too big. It was a life-size, moving caricature. You could stare into those mirrors for hours and not even recognize yourself. The reflections of the others in the gym were perfectly proportioned. What was their secret? How did people do it? How could she stop her thighs from wiggling? How could she flatten her stomach?

How had she not noticed that she had gained so much weight? And was it too late now to change it? Though she surreptitiously tested for her bones multiple times a day, perhaps even hourly, she couldn't see any difference. Nothing had changed. Not yet.

Stefanie was too tired to oppose the tears of frustration that now trickled down her cheeks. The room had gotten blurry. She blinked, but the mirrors melted into each other. She saw her thighs and stomach bulge. Her upper arms widened, and, when she turned to look back at the scale, the number seemed magnified. Everyone was looking at her. They were judging her. They could see what she had eaten for breakfast. They knew that she'd overeaten for years, that she was addicted to Ms. Olson's chocolate candies. They were disgusted and with good reason. Stefanie was disgusted with herself.

What could she do?

Try harder.

This time she would prove to them, all of them—the models, Laura, Annabel, her classmates, her parents, the people in the gym. She would not give in. She was unbreakable, indestructible. She would win.

The tears came faster now, and Stefanie turned away from the equipment. She didn't know these people, but she didn't want them to see her cry. They might know her parents, or she might see them riding the elevator or passing through the vestibule. She didn't want to give them anything more to talk about. She fled from the fun house to the newfound safety of the gray hallway with the quicksand floor.

Dinner was on the table when Stefanie reached the apartment. Her parents were already seated, waiting for her. She approached the food slowly, reminding herself that she would only eat a small portion of each item. A small bit of chicken, some vegetables, and a little salad: that was a decent, healthy dinner.

She could feel her parents' watchful stares as she ladled out her portions. Without looking at them, she assumed they were smiling. She was making them proud. They never would have told her to diet; they wouldn't have hurt her feelings for the world. She, in all her imperfection, was all they had. She was their only child—the child they had always wanted, the daughter who had come late in life, but whom they loved nonetheless. But Stefanie knew they had always wanted a thinner daughter. Who wouldn't? She could finally fulfill their hopes and expectations.

The plate in front of her was empty. She had finished her meal in a meager seven minutes. It wasn't enough. She could have eaten for twenty-one minutes more and still been hungry; but no, she couldn't allow that. Her body just had to acclimate. She had learned about it in science class—animals could adjust to their surroundings. And humans were essentially animals, so why shouldn't she be able to adjust as well? She would just have to be patient. She didn't want to disappoint her parents.

The dark of the room felt familiar as Stefanie stared at her ceiling. This was becoming her nightly routine; she hadn't slept through the night for days, but tonight was the worst. She watched the numbers on her clock change from 1:15 to 1:16 to 1:17 to 1:45 …

She was hungry. Too hungry. Breakfast wasn't for another six hours. Would she make it that long? Stefanie closed her eyes and tried to fall asleep. If she could only drift into a dream so that she could stop thinking about food. If she could sleep, she wouldn't have to eat. But sleep refused to rescue her.

In psychology class, they had been taught that hunger kept the body awake and that the way to make oneself sleep was to eat. But Stefanie didn't believe that. She could sleep without eating—she was different. Besides, they had been talking about girls with eating disorders. Just that fact made her different. *She* didn't have an eating disorder.

It would be so easy to walk down the hallway and into the kitchen. They had cookies in the pantry and leftover chicken in the refrigerator. There was ice cream in the freezer and fruit on the counter. She could make a whole meal, maybe even two, and then she wouldn't be famished anymore. But that wasn't part of her plan. She and Laura hadn't made any allowances for midnight raids in the kitchen. Laura—she was probably at home in bed, fast asleep. Laura wasn't craving food. Laura was strong. And she had to be also.

The clock read 2:00. She couldn't just lie there. There were magazines on the night table, and the CD she had made.

"The shin bone's connected to the knee bone, the knee bone's connected to the thighbone, the thighbone's connected to the hip bone ..."

She sat cross-legged on the floor next to the stereo, the volume turned low so as not to wake her parents. They couldn't know that she wasn't sleeping. As her ears strained to hear the lyrics, her eyes strained to see the pages of her magazine under the dim glow of her flashlight. She was looking at models. They were strong too, just like Laura. They were strong and beautiful. Their hair was perfect, pulled away from their faces, or left to hang purposefully, never sloppy. Their features were flawless. Eye shadow brought out the blue, brown, or green of their eyes, their cheeks brushed in soft rosy pinks. Stefanie traced the outlines of the bodies with her finger. They were all active: one was playing beach volleyball, perfectly accessorized with the Gucci sunglasses and the string bikini, and another was water skiing, water glistening on her smooth legs. There was no cellulite or fat to conceal. Their bodies were perfect. Nothing of hers was perfect. Stefanie chewed on her lip and reached for a tissue.

The title of an article caught her eye as she flipped page after page, looking at the next beautiful, flawless model. *How to Love Your Body*. There were girls doing yoga, girls getting their nails done, girls sunning themselves, and girls snacking on the deck of a beach house. Every one of them was smiling, filled with what the article called *joie de vivre*. Stefanie hated them. Of course they were happy—why shouldn't they be? They were all thin and pretty. Not one of them wore jeans larger than a size one; she was willing to bet more than a few even wore zeros. She thought of her own jeans hanging in the closet—fours and sixes; no wonder she didn't love her body. How could she? When she had a body like those girls, she would be happy. Then she would claim some of that *joie de vivre* for herself.

Stefanie was suddenly tired. The music had stopped, and, as she removed the CD, Stefanie saw the word *Motivation* written across its silver front. She'd get there eventually; one day she'd be happy too.

As she lay in bed, she could feel her eyes finally closing ... slowly, painfully ... as if it were an unusual movement. And then, too soon, a familiar alarm was going off. She reached over to turn it off. Beams of light spilled into the room from both sides of the drawn curtains. It was almost time to leave for school.

It took a lot of energy to pull off the covers and even more to stand. The room spun, but Stefanie dismissed it and struggled toward the bathroom. She couldn't fall now, not onto the hard tile floor. She fought off the fatigue and made it to the sink. Standing in front of the bathroom mirror, she tried to wipe the sleep from her eyes. She lifted her nightgown and looked down to examine her stomach. Where were those damned ribs? Why couldn't she see them? All her work hadn't made a difference. The hunger from the night before—the whole sleepless sacrifice—hadn't changed a thing. Now, from behind her belly button, she heard a rumbling, a distant thunder that seemed to be spreading. There was an emptiness inside her. But damn the emptiness, what did it matter? She was strong, just as strong as anybody else. All she had to do was to try harder, sacrifice more. They would see.

But it seemed easier to get back into bed, much easier than completing another day. Another day, and tomorrow would be the same, as would the next day, and the day after that. Stefanie could see a whole future of next days stretched out in a line, waiting for her, and the prospect was daunting.

"Stefanie, are you awake?" Her mother's voice disrupted her deliberations.

She couldn't get back into bed. It wasn't an option. It wouldn't make her happier. No one could sleep forever.

The "bones" song was beginning to play, and Stefanie stretched out on her floor. She could do whatever she wanted. Her parents didn't know what went on behind her closed door early in the morning and late at night. It wasn't that she was doing anything wrong, but she didn't think they would understand. They wanted it both ways. They wanted her to be thinner but not weight obsessed. She couldn't explain that being thinner would bring happiness. She knew she had lost some weight, even if she couldn't see her ribs yet. Her jeans slipped a little farther down on her hips, and the sleeves of her shirts were less tight around her upper arms. She was losing weight, which she was certain her parents condoned, but they might not like the way she was doing it. They might argue, they might tell her to stop, and they might hate her if she didn't. When they had watched the occasional eating disorder special on TV, her parents had never understood what desire drove those girls. Stefanie could see what drove them, why they did what they did. She didn't have an eating disorder, but Stefanie could understand. At least she was beginning to understand. She might starve herself too if she had their willpower.

To the beat of the music, Stefanie began her sit-ups and leg lifts.

Day Four: I added more exercises to the routine before school. It's all part of The Plan. I'm trying even harder now. I'm going to lose this weight. I'm going to succeed. I'm going to be happier.

There. She had committed her goals to her journal in ink. She couldn't erase, couldn't take it back. Those additional sit-ups and leg lifts were part of The Plan now. Under the entry Stefanie wrote how many exercises she had completed; then she wrote a second number and circled it, her goal for the next day.

"I have to go, Mom. I'm late. I'll eat at school." Stefanie was standing at the door wearing only one shoe. "I promise; I'll eat as soon as I get there." She stepped onto the elevator, uncrossed her fingers, and pulled on her second sneaker.

6

Skipping breakfast hadn't hurt her, so skipping lunch wouldn't either. And it would only be for a few days. Only until she had lost those unwanted pounds.

The hallway was empty. Stefanie had never seen it that way, at least not during the noon hour. Then again, she'd never skipped lunch before. There were girls who did, certainly, but not her. She had never been on a diet or understood the reasons for doing work during lunchtime.

She, Annabel, Julia, and Laura used to have their own designated area in the cafeteria. Since fourth grade, when they had first been allowed to choose their own tables, the four of them had sat together in the left-hand corner, at the table closest to the ice cream freezer. Sometimes other girls joined them and sometimes they sat alone, but they were always together. Until ninth grade, this had been the ritual. Now, in tenth grade, the routine had changed. Laura ate little and finished quickly, rushing to get to yet another choral practice. Annabel's new crowd sat at a different table. They spent lunchtime creating inside jokes, always keeping Stefanie on the outside. And Julia … maybe she went out for lunch, maybe she had a different lunch period, or maybe she just didn't want to eat at their table anymore. It was possible that she had simply grown to dislike her old friends. Or maybe Madeline Webber was right: Julia was swayed easily by the opinions of others, and she simply got tired of people after a while. As Stefanie's mother had pointed out occasionally, Julia had acted this way before, but Stefanie only vaguely remembered it. Her mother's words were meant to help her put the situation into perspective, but Stefanie couldn't see what remembering would do for her. It didn't make the hurt go away.

There was no reason to be at lunch. Finishing the meal alone. Being ignored. Sitting at an empty table. Why bother? Nobody would even notice that she hadn't shown up.

Noise from inside classrooms drifted out to the hallway where Stefanie sat. Lunch periods varied. These girls would have their lunch later, after the lower and middle schools had had time to vacate, and there would be more places to sit. Bored, Stefanie tried to listen to the different lessons. English was to her left, European history to the right, math farther down the hall, beyond history. She thought she heard French *ouis* and *nons* moving toward her; straight across the hallway, Stefanie heard the distinct tones of Ms. Olson teaching another psychology class.

Ms. Olson's voice was soft and friendly. She was giving the same lesson that she had given Stefanie's class earlier that morning. Stefanie wished she were in the classroom now, listening in a back-row seat. It wasn't that she needed to learn today's lesson again; she just felt less exposed in there. The staring walls of the hallway wouldn't see her, and her only company would be the soft pillows in the corner of the classroom, the bowl of chocolates on the desk, and Ms. Olson.

Noise moved toward her. The hallway filled with girls.

Julia walked by with a girl named Taylor, and Stefanie waved. Taylor saw and gave a raucous laugh, pushing Julia playfully. When she regained her balance, they continued down the hallway, and Julia forgot to wave back. That was just the way things were now.

It was time for class, but she couldn't get up. She didn't want to go to class, and she felt too weak to move. She wondered if her science teacher would believe that the gravitational force had suddenly increased in the second floor hallway. Could she say she was talking with a teacher? Whose name would she give? Not Ms. Olson's—she didn't want to be a burden. Could she claim she was sick? No, not now, she had been fine that morning. She would just have to get moving.

Stefanie stood up and dragged her feet toward the stairs, staring at the floor. Someone was standing there, blocking the way, and if she didn't hurry she was going to be late. The person didn't move as Stefanie tried to get past.

"Stefanie, is everything all right? Do you need anything?" It was Ms. Olson.

What could Stephanie say? That she was scaring herself? That every time she stood the floor shook and she thought she would fall? That she knew she had become obsessed with becoming thin and was doing some very unhealthy things? That she wanted to talk to someone but just didn't know who she could trust? That she didn't know where to begin? That as the days progressed she felt more and more miserable? That the old but suppressed feeling of wanting to die had resurfaced?

She was afraid to open her mouth, afraid that no matter what she said, Ms. Olson wouldn't understand. And there was nothing wrong, really. "I'm fine, honest. Just a little tired, I guess."

Ms. Olson was moving aside now. "OK. But if you need anything, feel free to come talk to me."

Stefanie nodded and walked by. Her legs not only looked like gelatin; they felt like it. Silently, she prayed that her teacher couldn't see them shaking. Why hadn't she told the truth? She had gotten her opportunity … but what was the truth?

The door to the science room was closed when Stefanie got there. Damn it, they had already started; now she would have to explain.

"Sorry, I was answering a teacher's question," Stefanie slid into her small metal desk, grateful for the fake smile that she had managed to force onto her face.

She could have said more to Ms. Olson. She should have said more. She wanted to explain everything but she didn't know how; her vocabulary was failing her. How could she explain the emptiness that had begun in her stomach and had now spread outward? Or the tears that she longed to cry? And more important, why would Ms. Olson want to listen? Why should anyone care?

She wanted to turn back the clock—turn it back to the safe, warm, happy, innocent moments when all little girls basically came in identical party-dress packages of sherbet-colored smocking, matching hair ribbons, and shiny Mary Janes. She wanted a clock that never ticked its way into the future—a future where girls sorted out into extravagantly different shapes and sizes that neither growth spurts nor wishful thinking could correct. She wanted to feel safe.

7

Over and over, Stefanie replayed the bone lyrics so that the shin, the knee, the thigh, and the hip melded together like a run-on sentence. Her resentment toward those lyrics increased as the week passed. They taunted her. She imagined the singers with their spiteful smirks jeering at her, glad that she was failing. They were pleased each time Stefanie yielded to the persistence of her stomach. They laughed when she ate fruit after school and exchanged high-fives when she struggled to break her own records for sit-ups and leg lifts alone in the dark of her room, her parents oblivious. Still, the word *Motivation* spun around and around in her stereo, and Stefanie listened carefully to every word. The jeering voices of the singers pushed her along. With each chorus, she became more determined to feel those bones.

Friday night. The house was empty again. Her parents had left early and would be home late: theater, and dinner after. Laura was on a date tonight, and Annabel and Julia were at the movies—sneaking into whatever R-rated movie happened to be showing—with Annabel's new friends. Julia had tagged along, not busy for once, and Stefanie had been invited too, but she had declined. Why miss out on a night of sit-ups and leg lifts? She could stay home and work out. She could stay home and finish her homework. Besides, the movies were the breeding ground of junk food. Popcorn, nachos, sour gummy worms, chocolate-covered gummy bears, chocolate-covered raisins, Hershey bars ... those were six very good reasons not to go.

Skipping her customary bath, Stefanie stood in the shower while hot water poured down on her head. She breathed in the steam that filled the bathroom and touched a hand to the wall of the shower, trying to steady herself. The glass walls were wobbling. Would they fall? Would she? She was so dizzy. Her head was floating far above her neck, detached from her body, and her torso seemed too heavy for her legs to support. She had heard a story once about a girl whose ankles had collapsed—could hers? Maybe she should have eaten, maybe then she wouldn't be afraid of falling. She wished she weren't in the oppressive heat of the bathroom anymore. She could have been with her friends. Why hadn't she accepted their invitation?

She closed her eyes and stood still; it was too late to go now. The movie was well underway, and then they would be moving on for a snack at whatever house was having a party tonight. It would be chaos—people from different schools congregated in someone's living room, possibly drinking, probably hooking up, most likely unchaperoned. She would have been ignored anyway. She wouldn't have had fun. Julia and Annabel would have gotten snacks later—and dessert—and then she would have been jealous. Or they might not have, and then she would have been angry that they were dieting also. And who needed to see a stupid movie anyway?

Twenty seconds passed, and the glass stopped quivering under the touch of her hand. Her head was back where it belonged on her neck, and her ankles were as strong as ever. She stepped out of the shower and heard the phone ringing.

Laura would be the only one calling; the other two wouldn't need her that night—they had each other. Was Laura feeling ignored by Robert? Was he not paying enough attention to her? Had her denim miniskirt stopped fitting? Was she threatening to run away from home again? It didn't matter. The phone continued to ring, but Stefanie's mind wandered elsewhere. When had she stopped caring?

A fifth indignant ring and then the answering machine picked up. Good. Laura never left a message. The caller ID would tell her who had called, but as far as Laura knew, she had never checked the caller ID. Stefanie wouldn't have to call her back.

She looked into the mirror. Her eyes scanned her figure—ever searching, ever watchful. Today had marked one week, well, Day Five officially, since she started and nothing changed. She had been down in the gym every day. She'd done her exercises. She'd faithfully followed her allowances, cutting back wherever possible. Maybe she'd done a better job at it than Laura. But she still looked the same. At least sometimes she looked the same. A Jekyll-and-Hyde experience: sometimes she could see the change, sometimes not. But the times when she did see the difference, she dismissed it as wishful thinking. She stared harder at the mirror. A roll of fat from her stomach still bulged over the elastic of her underwear. Her upper arms still hung flabby and limp. The waist and legs of her jeans were still tight. And her face was still unmistakably chipmunk round.

Stefanie closed her eyes and pictured a beautiful girl on the beach in a string bikini. She had auburn hair and chestnut eyes, and she was thin. She raced into the waves, laughing and beckoning to her friends. They joined her to splash in the water. The girl was smiling and happy. A light wind gently eased puffy cumulus clouds to the east. The clouds were soft marshmallows. Stefanie opened her eyes. The girl had vanished. All that was left was her reflection staring back at her blankly—and a craving for the marshmallow sundae she imagined her friends sharing. Stefanie sighed. The hair and eyes of the girl she saw now were the same as the girl she had envisioned, but the girl she saw in the mirror would never wear a bikini and wasn't smiling. They were two very different people.

The hallway seemed cold after the warmth of the bathroom, and Stefanie pulled on her pajamas. On the back of Stefanie's bedroom door there was another mirror. A mysterious magnetic force pulled her gaze to it, and she examined her body again as she dressed.

It was getting silly. How much could she have changed in the time it took her to walk down the hallway from the bathroom? Still, she had to look. What if something had changed and she missed it?

Were her calves smaller? She prodded them, testing to see if they still jiggled. She'd read somewhere that that was normal, that it was just relaxed muscle. But she didn't believe it. You couldn't trust everything you read in books anyway. What about her pajama pants? Were they slightly looser? Hadn't she had to pull the drawstring tighter? No, she was lying to herself. They fit just the way they always had. Stefanie turned sideways to examine her profile. If only she hadn't had that salad with the two slices of turkey, her pants might be looser. Why was she so intent on undoing any progress that she had made?

She'd never looked this bad before.

Ms. Olson had explained how girls with eating disorders have distorted body images. The skinnier they became, the more fat they saw when they looked in the mirror. It was called *body dismorphic disorder.* Their eyes played tricks on them.

Could she have that? Was the body she saw distorted? She leaned in to get a better look. It couldn't be. Those girls were seriously ill; they had real diseases. She was healthy. As much as she wished she could tell herself that she wasn't seeing clearly, she couldn't. Her mirror showed the truth—she needed to lose more weight, and she would. She would skip dinner. That would cancel out her lack of restraint at lunchtime, and everything would be all right—she could fix things. A little more effort, and she would free herself from those pounds. She'd be thinner and happier. Everything would be okay again. Next time, she might even go to a movie with the girls too.

Her parents always left dinner in the microwave with the timer already set—a throwback to a time when they thought they had to do everything for her when they went out for the evening. All Stefanie had to do was push the start button, and in three minutes she would have a meal. Voilá. But she didn't want dinner.

She stared at the microwave. For the moment, its walls held back her enemy. If she opened the door, the assembled army would advance. The foot soldiers would lead the march down her throat, the cavalry of calories would follow. They would take her stomach prisoner. The sugars would break through and capture her veins, using them as rivers—a wartime travel system. Fats would invade her body, racing through her circulatory system to the places where they would set up camp: her stomach, her thighs, her face, her arms. How could she contain the army?

She couldn't leave the food in the microwave; her parents would see it and ask questions. She couldn't throw it in the garbage; her parents would find it and be even more suspicious. What to do? She looked at the kitchen clock: 7:33. She had to get rid of it but not in a place where her parents would notice, where they would realize what she had done.

She was still staring at the microwave. If she removed the food without tasting it, she would be safe. Her mind was a strong enough defense against the invaders. Slowly, she opened the microwave door and set the food on the counter. She wanted it. It smelled so good. Couldn't she take just one bite? One taste: wouldn't that be OK? Her only defense was wavering; she wasn't safe. Before she surrendered, she needed to get rid of the food.

Stefanie walked out of the apartment. The back hallway smelled of garlic and lamb. Her neighbors in 8A were obviously eating in tonight. There was a trashcan out here that only the building's workmen emptied. Her parents dumped their garbage into that can outside their kitchen door, and the doorman took it away and left it on the street for garbage pickup. They would never think to look at its contents. They wouldn't find the uneaten meal; they wouldn't be suspicious; they wouldn't question. They'd never know. Behind her, the back door of her apartment was still open, and she could see the white walls of the kitchen—so different from the gray, cold, unfriendly hallway. Stefanie shivered and poured the food into the garbage. It hit the bottom with a plunk; Stefanie was already inside her apartment, double-locking the door.

Before she'd left the apartment, she had put some sauce, a bite of chicken, and some remnants of the rice on a plate. Now she stirred them together with a knife and a fork. She dunked her fingers in the sauce and wiped her hands off on a napkin. She would leave the plate, knife and fork, and napkin on the counter by the sink. Her parents would see it and the now-empty container and think that she had finished it. She smiled at her cunning, but it felt wrong somehow. Deceptive. Sneaky. Her stomach tightened thinking about the lies she would tell to her parents, who trusted and loved her. But what choice had they left her?

In her room, Stefanie lay down on the floor and let the *Motivation* song play. She was tired—too tired and weak, though she hated to admit it, to do the obligatory sit-ups and leg lifts. She just wanted to lie there. Maybe she would never get up. Maybe she could just stay there until the day when the sun blew up and enveloped the world. It would be so easy—and not such a bad way to die.

From where she was lying, Stefanie could see the pictures and papers taped to her mirror. They chronicled her childhood, from birthday parties to tennis tournaments; everything important was displayed there. She saw a third-grade participation certificate from PE class and her ninth-grade science award. She had loved biology. There were pictures of Annabel, Laura, and Julia when the four of them had gone to the beach together. They were wearing bikinis and splashing in the waves, unashamed of their girlish, stick-figure bodies. *To be that carefree* ... Another picture had been taken by Stefanie's father at an apple orchard on Long Island. Her hair was still highlighted from the summer sun and the juice from a Jonagold apple was dribbling down her chin as she flashed a wide seven-year-old smile at the camera. It had been a glorious late September afternoon. Cool enough to keep away the honeybees, but warm enough not to wear a jacket.

Stefanie remembered that day vividly. She had been punished right after that picture had been taken. They had gone home early. The excursion had been abruptly terminated after they'd run into the mother of Stefanie's classmate, Diane Delafield. Stefanie had gotten in trouble at school that week for pulling Diane's hair, but it hadn't been her fault. Diane had started it. And Diane's mother had blabbed it. Mortified, Stefanie's mother had packed her into the car while her father had paid for the apples and proceeded, for the next three hours, to lecture her. She remembered her mother telling her, "Stefanie Webber, you should be ashamed of yourself," and her father asking if she felt guilty. Guilty? Guilty was a word that Stefanie didn't know. Did it mean sorry? Did it mean angry? Or was it about that free-fall feeling in the pit of her stomach, the kind that made her feel like they should pull the car over?

From her position on the floor, Stefanie stared up at that picture. The quick-pull-over-the-car feeling in the pit of her stomach, the kind that came when she knew she'd disappointed her parents, was what Stefanie had learned that guilty meant. Yet at the same time, she felt a strange swell of pride at her extraordinary self-control. But there were people starving in the world. She knew that she should care about them, and, more than that, her parents had spent money on her dinner. They wouldn't like what she had done, and it was even worse that she planned to lie and allow them to think that she'd eaten it.

Ms. Olson said that the girls in the textbooks were wasting their lives: the ultimate crime. In class, they had talked about how those girls were wasting their skills and their intelligence. How could that be justified?

She had only thrown away her dinner. She hadn't thrown it up. And it wasn't as if she was wasting her life. Their situations were different. Those girls were *emaciated*; she was *fat*. They refused to eat even when their lives were in danger. Her life wasn't in danger, not even close. But Stefanie's stomach still felt like she was on a roller coaster, heading over the first big drop.

Stefanie knew that she had to do something. She had to scare off her weak self, the one who felt guilty for doing something that would benefit her. Weakness was simply unacceptable. She hated *that* Stefanie, the lazy one with no self-control or will power. She had to become the new Stefanie. At least *she* wasn't quite as lazy; at least *she* tried to fix things.

Sit-ups. They would be her panacea. They would make everything better. They would chase off the weak Stefanie. Her stomach muscles screamed for mercy, but she wouldn't surrender. She refused to waste all her efforts. She was fighting for her life against that deadly army of fat cells and calories. She squeezed her eyes shut and tightened her muscles. One last one—OK, no, one more—you completed it, but come on, do another one. Stefanie's chest touched her knees again, pushing to complete one last sit-up, and her back crashed to the floor. She hadn't been breathing. Her cheeks had grown scarlet red and warm, and her eyes had filled with tears. But she had to keep going. She was ten sit-ups away from her goal for the day—fifty. She had to continue. She had to make it. She couldn't give up.

God would give her strength. Her mother had always said that when she needed help she should turn to God, and he would help her. Stefanie didn't pray. She went to church on holidays, like Christmas Mass and Easter Sunday, more to please her mother than because she believed. She wasn't an avid Catholic. To her, religion was a set of morals—there to guide. She didn't have to follow rules and talk to the sky to be a good person. Who could say that God was in the sky anyway? She believed that there was a God, but could he do all that her mother claimed? She'd never really tested her mother's theories. Maybe now was the time.

Please, please, please, please …

Dear God (it seemed as good a way to start as any), *please help me. Please let me lose a lot of weight. Please let me beat Laura. Please give me the mental strength to deny myself cookies. And please give me the physical strength to get through the exercises that I have to do daily. Please show me the way to do this. Please give me a reason to believe. Please let me lose a lot of weight and soon.*

Her mother told her that faith could accomplish anything—faith in oneself, in people, or in God. That was what she needed—faith. She would have to believe.

Amen. Had the talk with God worked? Did he really listen? Would he answer? Stefanie pushed on her stomach again. It still protruded more than she would have liked, and her ribs didn't seem any closer to the surface. How could that be? She had asked nicely;

she had been polite. Maybe it would take more time. Maybe God was backed up tonight, and she would have to wait until tomorrow or the next day. Or maybe a lazy girl like herself wasn't worth his attention.

Please God, help me. I need help. This is important. Please let me lose a lot of weight. She repeated the prayer and wondered if she had done it wrong the first time around. Maybe that was why God didn't appear to be listening. Then again, what was she waiting for? A sign?

"The shinbone's connected to the knee bone ..."

Stefanie's breath had returned, and the CD was still spinning inside the stereo. It was time to finish the sit-ups.

"Forty-eight, forty-nine, fifty." She wouldn't have been able to do one more, but she had reached her goal. At least when she spoke to Laura the next day, she could discuss the evening candidly, without exaggerating.

It had become routine for Stefanie to write in her journal before bed, recording the day's successes and failures and setting goals for the following day. Now she picked up her pen and began writing. She wrote about faith and God. She wrote about Ms. Olson, psychology, and wastefulness. And she wrote about the apple orchard and the free-falling feeling—her mother would have called it guilt—that was in her stomach even now, as she went to bed.

Day Seven: 50 sit-ups, 50 leg lifts.

She wrote another two numbers and circled them: sixty and sixty. She'd get there tomorrow.

~ 8 ~

*E*veryone seemed to be impressed. Her parents may not have known that she was trying to lose weight; but nonetheless, they complemented her on her appearance more frequently. Her mom encouraged her saying how great it was that Stefanie was trying to make herself more "fit." Her dad complimented her on how gorgeous she looked. Her friends were jealous—even Laura.

Laura had failed. After only two weeks, she had given up. She said it wasn't worth it, that there was nothing she could do to change the way she looked, so why should she fight it? She wanted to eat saturated fats and carbohydrates. She wanted to have candy and ice cream and eat breakfast in the cafeteria on Mondays. She liked sharing salted French fries—almost as much as she liked French kissing. She was tired of dieting.

But Stefanie held out, more determined than her friend. The results of her late-night efforts were finally becoming visible. Her jeans were looser, and the number on the scale had begun to shift. She was even beginning to see the lines of her ribs when she lifted up her arms in front of the mirror.

When the people in the gym had begun to recognize her and talk casually to her before or after a workout, she knew she was making progress. When the girls at school started making pointed comments about eating disorders whenever she was around, she smiled at the new mark of her success. Girls who complained about their excess weight looked at her enviously on their way to lunch. One girl asked her how she did it, but Stefanie just shrugged, a false air of confidence enveloping her. She was competing with the world now, and she was winning; she wasn't going to share her success. People noticed her. Happiness was on its way.

And yet, she wasn't satisfied. There was something burdensome about this new attention. Everyone expected her to be Little Miss Healthy now, and sometimes she feared that she might one day disappoint them all. Besides, as much as people were noticing her, it never seemed to be enough. She lived to hear others' compliments, but she was still lonely, and every day the emptiness inched its way further through her body. It wasn't good enough yet: the attention, the weight loss, her new life. She wasn't quite there. She'd have to do more, lose more weight, eat less.

* * *

Her mom was putting food out on the table: swordfish, mashed potatoes, eggplant. Dinnertime again. How could she avoid it? Stefanie did not want to sit down and eat. She'd been so good all day—no breakfast and no lunch. She couldn't give up her weeks of hard work. For strength, she thought about her new life. Now people expected something of her; they *wanted* her to diet. They liked the "New, Healthy Stefanie," and she liked their praise. How could she give up that recognition?

She was already at her seat; there would be no skipping this meal. Her parents would not support the idea of skipping dinner. Every night her mind played tug of war as she waited for the food to be placed on the table. Should she eat? Should she make an excuse? Should she refuse? It was so much easier when her parents went out; then she could slip into the hallway and throw her food away and be free from the internal conflict. She used to resent it, but recently she had found herself wishing that they would go out more often.

Her parents took their seats. The smell of buttery mashed potatoes made Stefanie weaken. She reached for the spoon and dished out a generous helping. The smell of sautéed eggplant annihilated her remaining self-restraint. She gave up. She would eat. How much damage could one meal do? It wouldn't hurt anything. Some mashed potatoes, eggplant, and swordfish—that was a healthy meal.

She filled her plate and laughed as her father told a story about the traders at his office, but inside she was angry with herself for capitulating. Wasn't she supposed to be dieting? Each forkful rose almost involuntarily to her mouth. She was going against The Plan; she was betraying herself.

Howard Webber now began to talk about the stock market. It had been a good day; they were up for the month. But Stefanie was only half listening. She was thinking about the calories and wishing that she could just put the fork down. She couldn't. It was impossible. She was powerless before a higher force. Her firewall had fallen; her defenses were in ashes. She was smoldering; she didn't want to stop. The food just tasted too good.

Madeline Webber talked about her tennis match of that morning. She had a weekly game at a fancy indoor court. Tennis was like her second religion. Stefanie scowled and twisted her tongue around inside her mouth. Her mother had always been considered healthy, thin, athletic—that was what everyone said. Her mother had played tennis, maybe even gone to the gym, and what had she done? Stefanie had sat in a classroom and spent only forty-five minutes in the gym that afternoon. Madeline Webber wasn't even on a diet, and still there was the gym and tennis and God only knew what else. No wonder no one ever called Stefanie healthy. Compared to her mother, she had work to do.

How could she be enjoying this food? This wasn't the way things were meant to happen. She was supposed to be strong, determined. It should have been so easy; so why wasn't it? She shouldn't relish the garlicky taste of the eggplant or the creamy flavor of the mashed potatoes. Shake your head stoically. Now, Stefanie. Push the food away. Say "no thank you" and force a smile. That's a good girl. That was the point of a diet.

Empty bowls and dishes sat in the sink. Her parents watched the evening news. Stefanie stood beside the running shower. The noise of the water rushing against the white tiles drowned out Stefanie's thoughts. She stood undressed, before the mirror. The radio was on, as it always was when she was alone and bored. But, lost in thought, she couldn't have named the song that was playing. Where were the new bones that she had seen the night before? Where were her ribs? Was her stomach more extended? Had she gained weight? Had her dinner already settled into her waist and hips?

She had to do something. People would stop caring about her again. The girls would stop `commenting about how thin she had gotten. They would stop giving her admiring glances. Her teachers would no longer watch her carefully, and people would stop asking, as they often did now, whether everything was all right. All the attention lately made her feel worthwhile and loved. Finally, she was cared about. Without the diet, she'd return to being unimportant. No one would care. She wanted to stand out. She wanted to be special.

Stefanie could feel tension building inside her. She slid to the floor and laid her head against the outside of the shower door. The cold tile against her legs made her shiver, but she didn't want to get up. Then she cried.

Could she disappear? Could she stay in the bathroom forever, where people would never see what she looked like? Could God just change the world's opinion of what is beautiful? Or could he just give her a new, prettier, thinner, better body? And why, she wondered crossly, did she have to do all the work anyway?

She sat on her knees over the toilet. Ripples chased each other across the glasslike water, emanating from the points where her salty tears were now falling. Its perfect surface was broken into a million tiny fragments, as tear followed tear—a steady stream of deadly bullets.

But there was another way, she knew. Foolproof and easy. All she had to do was push her finger to the back of her throat and induce vomit. Other people did it, and it worked for them. Even Princess Diana had. So why couldn't she?

She used the toilet bowl's smooth sides to calm her shaking hands and rested her head against the wall. Too much food … too much food … She had to. It was the only way. She was brave. She was strong.

Her finger groped for the back of her throat. She reached her smooth palette but nothing happened. Her finger kept going. She was blocking her airway. Only a few more seconds, and she would need to breathe. But—damn the human body—she couldn't stop now, not yet. Farther, farther … could she get into her esophagus? If she kept going, would she eventually reach her stomach, where she could pull the food out herself? She would need to breathe; her lungs craved oxygen. This attempt would end like all the others.

One more push. Her finger had invaded new territory, and at last she tasted the warm acidic mixture as it moved into her mouth. So this was how it felt.

She cried again. Salt stung her eyes, and she blinked, knocking the tears into the toilet bowl. She'd never liked throwing up.

Her breath was unsteady and hesitant. Her heart could have leapt from her chest. She coughed, and more tears slid down her cheeks. Was this the way it would always be now?

Her bathroom mirror showed tear-stained cheeks and bloodshot eyes. Her legs felt close to giving out as she leaned against the sink. Her hands were shaking again. Stefanie thought of that day during psychology when she had tried to free herself from that extra bowl of cereal. Had Ms. Olson known? Had she been able to tell? Stefanie longed to talk to her. She wanted to sit there and explain everything to the one person who just might care. Her reflection shook its head. No, she couldn't talk to anyone. That would ruin all her work. She was lighter now—it wasn't just the pounds, it was her spirit, too. This "New and Improved" Stefanie. If everyone knew her plan, they would make her eat breakfast. They would look for her at lunch. And dinner. Yes, tonight, she had finally found the solution. If they knew, they would take that away too.

Ms. Olson would be worried. Stefanie knew that what she had done wasn't normal; it was what "those" girls did—the gaunt ones with sunken, lifeless eyes. She could imagine herself joining their cover girl group, with their hair and make-up just so, for a group shot. Textbook. But no, there was no reason for concern. It was only one time; she didn't really have a problem—not yet. Those girls were crazy; she wasn't. She was only losing weight until she was happy with herself, only dieting until she was no longer fat. Those girls were still starving even when their bodies were obviously emaciated. That was the difference. Stefanie thought back to the first night when she had heard the "bones" song. That was when she had decided to diet reasonably, not to cut out entire meals, let alone all meals. So maybe she had gotten a little carried away. So what? She was losing the weight. She was successful. That was the important thing.

She remembered the beginning: every meal that she had missed, every muffin or piece of chocolate that she had passed up, every time she answered "fine" while dying to cry, "Hurt, angry, frustrated, sad!" She remembered every moment from Laura's phone call that first night to when she had pressed her forefinger to the back of her throat for the first time.

There was only one detail missing: When had this diet become all-consuming?

− 9 −

*S*he was so smart. Her parents would never catch on. Why was the water running for so long this morning? Why didn't you stay at the table after dinner? Why have you been spending so much time in your room doing homework? These were questions her parents would never ask. They were trying to give her space, like the books about parenting teenagers said. Her mother had a shelf of them—a stack she tried to keep discreetly away from Stefanie's view. As if Stefanie didn't know. The experts seemed to agree. Don't overcrowd your teenager with your questions, or they will shut you out. But if you appear too detached, they will feel unloved. The task of the teenager was to be responsible for herself. The task of the parent was to make sure she earned it. Now that Stefanie was older, her parents assumed she was like all teenagers. *She wanted the extra freedom; she wanted the independence; she wanted them to remain aloof when friends came to the house ... that's what they thought. But was she like the others, really?*

The soap bubbles were washed down the drain, and with them went the vomit from Stefanie's hands. She had done this so many times that it had become routine. Every night she purged, and every night she washed the remnants down the drain. It was just what she did. Her fingers were cracking and dry from being washed so frequently, and her nails were brittle. There were white lines across her nails—a vitamin deficiency, she had once been told—but she didn't really give a damn. Who cared about stupid nails anyway? What day was it now? She had lost count a few weeks back. Did it matter? She hadn't set a time limit when she started, and she didn't have one yet. She'd know it was time to stop when she'd lost a few more pounds. She would be thin *and* the center of attention.

Thinness would bring happiness, and happiness was the goal. She wasn't happy yet, so she supposed she wasn't thin yet either. She figured she'd know when enough was enough.

Tuesday, February 27th. Annabel would be waiting, and Stefanie was still standing in front of the mirror in her underwear. She didn't have time for sit-ups and leg lifts, so she would compensate with an extra hundred later in the day. Over the back of her bedroom chair, Stefanie found the pair of sweatpants that she had thrown there the previous afternoon. She slipped them on and welcomed the cozy softness of the fleecy interior against her skin. She had been wearing pants under her uniform skirt for weeks now. Not because she was cold, at least, not always because she was cold, but because she hesitated to subject other people to the sight of her disgusting, jiggly thighs. She wanted to be able to see her knee caps and maybe that shinbone also. Sure she'd lost weight, but not enough, not yet. And no one could see her until she was satisfactorily skinny; she wouldn't allow it. But at least she was able to feel her hip bone—sharp and pointy—about three and a half inches below the bottom of her ribs. Ahh ... She could breathe more deeply now. Her ribs stuck out even more if she breathed deeply. And she liked that.

It was lunchtime again. Another day, another missed lunch, but Stefanie didn't get hungry anymore. Her friends would be sitting together at their usual table in the cafeteria, but she didn't care. It wasn't important. She had grown used to the empty hallways and the familiar sounds of teachers' voices as they ran through lessons with the other girls. The student-painted murals kept her company, and sometimes, as she stared at them, she thought about the girls that had worked on those walls in years past. Had they been tall or short? Skinny or plump? Had they dieted too? Had they been happy?

Recent artwork had been arranged along the walls as well. The seventh grade was learning about stereotyping in the media, and their collages donned the walls of the first-floor corridor. While Stefanie waited for the minute hand of the clock to move, she stared at the eclectic pieces. From several of them, Barbie and Ken look-alikes encouraged the viewer to lose more weight. Losing weight was a popular theme even among the younger girls. The media's messages were identical and unmistakable: one more pound, one more pound. This far-ranging consensus made it easy for Stefanie to shake her head when Annabel, Laura, or Julia asked her to join them for lunch. She had to lose one more pound, one more pound. Stefanie wasn't sure why, but it seemed that after the initial flurry of newfound popularity that had followed her first noticeable weight loss, their invitations had fallen off. Perhaps they'd grown tired of asking and being turned down. Or perhaps they'd grown tired of her.

Other people, girls she might have enjoyed becoming close to, sometimes stopped in front of her on the way to lunch and asked if she was going downstairs. The first time someone had asked, Stefanie felt a surge of happiness. Someone wanted to sit with her! But she hadn't been able to say yes. She'd already had breakfast that morning, and that was already too many calories. Later, it occurred to her that they weren't asking her to join them after all; they only wanted to know if she was planning to eat. People had begun to notice all right. The attention and accolades had begun to sour. Did they think she'd turned into a freak? They talked about her weight loss in quiet whispers when there was no new gossip. They stepped over her outstretched legs on the way to lunch and continued walking. "Don't even ask. You know she's not going to go." It had become a generally accepted fact that Stefanie Webber didn't go to lunch anymore, ever. Self-righteous dieters warned her that what she was doing was dangerous. But Stefanie dismissed them. They were probably just jealous.

One day, just as they reached Third Avenue on their walk to school, Annabel told her that people thought she had an eating disorder. "They talk about you," Annabel had announced. "They talk about what they see, and they don't like it. They say you look like a skeleton."

But that was just talk. She didn't look like a skeleton—she was reminded of that every time she passed by a mirror. And why were they so certain that she had an eating disorder? Wouldn't she know? That was what she had said to Annabel: she would know, and she didn't have a problem. Annabel had shrugged noncommittally and said she didn't know what to think.

Out in the hallway, the wall was solid behind her back, and Stefanie succumbed to the inexpressible weight that pulled on her. Her shoulders sagged, and her head listed to one side. She was sitting by Ms. Olson's door again, hoping that her teacher would come out and start a conversation. She didn't want to talk about anything in particular—there was nothing to say—but she wanted to talk. She wanted to hear Ms. Olson's voice rise in that slight crescendo that told Stefanie she cared, that she belonged.

She pressed her back against the wall until she felt the pressure on each vertebra. It was a good feeling. Stefanie liked it when she was reminded of protruding bones—it reinforced her progress. Ms. Olson had said, "Feel free to come and talk to me," so why couldn't she? She tried to imagine what Ms. Olson would think if she walked in unexpectedly. Would she be disgusted? Probably. Would she be concerned? Yes. Would she be confused? Yes. Would she worry? Yes. Would she overreact? Yes. Yes. Yes. Yes. It wasn't fair to get Ms. Olson involved in her problems. Stefanie forced her spine into the wall until her vertebrae began to hurt. Even if her teacher *had* volunteered to talk, she couldn't do it. Suddenly, the silence became unbearable. She was going to scream. The ticking clock could have been a jackhammer, and Stefanie covered her ears. Was that ringing normal? She didn't think so. And where was everyone?

They were all at lunch. Even the girls who dieted sat with their friends and snacked on saltines and salads. But Stefanie couldn't risk going to the cafeteria. She could never sit so nonchalantly in that forbidden zone, surrounded by leftover muffins from breakfast and sprinkle cookies for dessert. She might eat, and then she would be ruined. One cookie, and she wouldn't stop. One cookie, and she would go back to being "Stefanie Webber, the bright but undisciplined student." Ms. Olson would never talk to her then.

While the other girls, the non-dieters and the dieters alike, sat around the cafeteria and discussed their favorite teachers and least-favorite subjects, Stefanie gathered her textbooks and headed for class. Recently, it had been taking longer to get up the stairs; she was so tired.

The hallway turned on its side, and Stefanie reached for the wall to steady herself. "Fluorescent lights will do this," she told herself and waited for the dizziness to subside. A blackness obscured her vision, and only patches of color were visible beyond the dark cloud—tans, browns, blacks, and greens; she knew they represented the carpet and stairs and lockers, but she couldn't make out their definite shapes. She closed her eyes to block out the chaotic hallway, and the colors stopped mixing. The swirling waves were gone, and she felt safe and in control again. The wall felt sturdier, and she was confident that the room wasn't truly in motion. Everything was almost back to normal …

Voices echoed in the stairwell, and Stefanie opened her eyes. The room was right side up again. The lockers and stairs had resumed their appropriate shapes. Everything was back to normal. Stefanie picked up her backpack and began the hike up the stairs to English. She felt better now. She had just gotten up too quickly, that was all. There was nothing to be concerned about. She was fine—thinner and fine. Never better.

- 10 -

Stef, I'm concerned." Annabel looked at Stefanie as the two of them sat on the sidelines by the volleyball court. It was the second rest Stefanie had taken that period—only fifty-two minutes—and Annabel was surprised. Stefanie was no great athlete, but she was a good sport, an enthusiastic participant, when it came to team play. She didn't usually get a note from the nurse to excuse her from class. She didn't usually like sitting on the bench. It was better to be out there, breaking a sweat despite the air conditioning, showing the younger girls who walked through on their way to class how volleyball was supposed to be played.

Annabel was talking, but Stefanie wasn't really listening. She was staring at the white blur of the volleyball as it bounced back and forth across the net. She sighed as she bowed her head and rested her forehead against her arm. She knew she should be out there jumping and spiking, burning those calories, losing that weight. But her head felt too heavy. Could she make it lose weight, too? Was that possible?

"I'm worried. Really, Stef, you're starving yourself. You need to eat something. I feel like a bad friend just watching you diet. We've learned about it in school so many times—you have all the symptoms."

Watching the ball had grown old and Stefanie turned her attention back to her friend. Or was she her friend? She hadn't been around very much lately. Annabel tapped her leg against the ground. One, two, three, four; one, two, three, four … Stephanie counted the taps. Annabel was nervous. Stefanie knew this was an intervention, another topic they had learned about in school. Step one: do research about the suspected problem. Step two: confront the friend. Step three: talk to a guidance counselor if the problem seems unresolved.

After their talk, would Annabel consider the problem resolved? Unlikely. Annabel didn't like to be contradicted. So who would Annabel tell? A parade of teachers marched through Stefanie's mind, and she mentally passed judgment. Who could she tolerate? Mr. Maloney—no, too new; Mrs. Smith—too old; Ms. Montarescu— too serious; Madame Bordot—too French; Ms. Olson ...?

Stefanie decided it was time to talk. "I know this is an intervention, Annabel. I've done the readings too, and I know how these things work." Stefanie's cold words echoed in her ears with more severity than she had intended. "There's no reason for you to be concerned. Look, I'm here, and I'm fine. Please don't tell anyone that I've been skipping breakfast and lunch. It's not such a big deal, I promise." Stefanie wondered if she had been heard; now it was Annabel who was watching the volleyball.

"If you have to tell somebody, tell Ms. Olson ..." Stefanie's voice rose at the end of her sentence. If Annabel had been listening carefully, she would have detected the note of desperation.

Stefanie stared at Annabel's profile, waiting. Her features were soft, flowing into each other, and she was prettier than Stefanie had remembered. In the last couple of months, her blonde hair had grown long, and it formed gentle waves around her shoulders. The only sign of Annabel's distress was that her eyebrows wrinkled in the center and she played with her tongue, twisting it around inside her mouth. Why wasn't Annabel saying anything? What was she thinking? What was she deciding? Was she ever going to speak again?

"Are you going to tell anyone?" Stefanie looked away. She couldn't meet Annabel's eyes. She let the question hang in the air. She needed an answer.

"No." Annabel didn't look over. "Not yet. You've been eating dinner because your parents make you. That's something, at least. So I'll wait."

Stefanie nodded. She wrapped her arms around her knees and looked down at her stomach and arms. Skin sagged off the bone, and Stefanie pinched at it. Fat. She was disgusting, a regular butterball, a failure at this game of dieting. She felt empty and alone. "There are ways to lose weight even if you do ingest food." Stefanie's voice broke, and the last words were barely intelligible. Her face was blank and uncaring, apathetic, but underneath the facade of indifference she was close to tears.

Without looking up, Stefanie knew that Annabel's eyes were fully locked on her face. Was Annabel beginning to understand? Looking at Stefanie, she stammered, "You can't exercise that much—you'd have to spend hours in the gym."

It was obvious that Annabel was trying to convince herself that everything was all right. Stefanie shook her head. "There are other ways ..."

What was she doing? Stefanie's heart was beating fast—did she want to tell Annabel the truth? That she counted calories obsessively. That she stood in front of the mirror and looked for new bones every night before bed? That if she found any new bones, the day was a success; if not, it was a failure? Did she want Annabel to know that she threw up her food, that she wanted her parents to think that she ate it?

She was doing what people with eating disorders do. She'd been throwing up, exercising, and counting calories for a while now, and she didn't plan to stop anytime soon. She wanted to see bones. When the room spun, she secretly enjoyed the flip in her stomach. It proved that she was successful. But none of these things was normal. Intellectually, she knew that. Did that mean she had a problem? Did that mean she had an eating disorder—that she was one of those girls? Did that mean she needed to get help?

Annabel's face was beginning to reflect a gradual comprehension of what Stefanie was telling her. Her mouth moved slowly, forming the words for all her unanswered questions, but it was inaudible. Annabel's usual smile had been replaced by a grimace as she realized the implications of what she had just heard. Annabel raised her eyebrows in a question and Stefanie knew what she wanted to ask.

Almost involuntarily, Stefanie nodded. She was admitting to purging, a secret she had thought she would keep forever.

The ball bounced off a sideline nearby and skidded toward Stefanie. She ducked. The gym teacher was dismissing the class. The girls scrambled for the locker room, the echoes of their voices ricocheting off the walls as they scrambled for the doorway.

Stefanie was still so tired, almost too tired to move her mouth, but she needed to know. "So are you going to tell?" Before Annabel spoke, Stefanie knew what the answer was. Annabel would tell. It was an unwritten law—the third step of an intervention. It was the reaction that Stefanie had expected.

Annabel stood and looked at Stefanie as though she was seeing her, really seeing her for the first time. "I have to get going. I have a math test next period. Take care of yourself, OK? Just take care of yourself." She headed for the locker room.

"The shinbone's connected to the knee bone; the knee bone's connected …"

Stefanie closed her eyes and took several deep breaths. She tried to imagine her chest heaving in and out as her lungs expanded. She was exhausted, completely exhausted. She had seen the internal conflict in the crinkles of Annabel's forehead. To tell or not to tell. Annabel had declined to answer Stefanie's question, but she knew Annabel would tell. Stefanie had confessed to something considered a disease in psychology; it couldn't be kept a secret. Why had she continued the discussion? She had known what the outcome would be—she had to have known. Why hadn't she stopped before she had incriminated herself? Had she wanted Annabel to tell? Stefanie opened her eyes and stared into the empty gym. She didn't know the answer, but maybe.

A crack ran across the white ceiling from one corner to the other, stopping only when it reached the teal molding, the quietest of signs that the great building at Park and Eighty-third was gently settling. Like a tree bending with the wind, adapting to change, unfearing.

Stefanie imagined that the crack was trying to escape, trying to break free from the perfect whiteness of the ceiling, perhaps trying to become teal. She liked that crack for its loneliness and its desire to be different. And they had become companions—even friends—spending time together each sleepless night while she tore at her sheets and threw her pillows on the ground.

Time was stagnating. One lingering minute followed another, and the sun still did not appear. Why was it taking so long? Why was it making her suffer?

If only the day would begin. Once the anticipation was over, Stefanie knew it wouldn't be so bad. What could Ms. Olson do? Had Annabel gone to her yet, or would today be the day? Annabel had done what she could: reasoned with her, shamed her, tried to make her see. But she couldn't make her eat. Stefanie was stronger than that. She sighed and waited. Another minute passed as she lay in bed. And another minute … and then another one …

Finally, from behind the plaid curtains, the sun cast its light on the street below. Stefanie slid out of bed and shivered when her feet touched the carpet. She was forced to surrender the warmth of her blanket. As she steadied herself at the bathroom sink, her teeth chattered. Even her scalp felt cold. The telltale signs of another long night were etched into her face. There were two grayish rings around her eyes, and the lids were puffy from crying. She was so tired, yet why couldn't she just sleep?

Stefanie had lost track of the days. One waking hour melted into the next, and still sleep would not come. Every morning she wiped the dried tears of frustration from her face and went to school; every night she lay in bed and stared at the crack that tried desperately to escape the confines of the ceiling. Maybe one day they would flee together when the darkness became oppressive and her pillow was wet beneath her cheek from her tears. That was the fantasy she entertained.

An hour later, she found Annabel waiting at their usual corner. The sun was fully awake and shining brightly. Stefanie pushed past an elderly lady with a walker to join her friend; she wasn't feeling particularly charitable that morning. Under the weight of her heaviest coat and her backpack, Stefanie struggled to keep up with Annabel's pace. At each corner, she mentally counted how many more blocks they had to walk, but the initial count of six dwindled too slowly. She was soon lagging nearly seven steps behind. Annabel was walking more quickly than usual. Normally, they chatted during these walks, but that day they were silent. Neither knew what to say, so they just walked along, with Stefanie trying hard to concentrate on the back of Annabel's blue quilted jacket. Occasionally, when she caught up at the corner while waiting for a light, Stefanie was bold enough to glance over at her friend. Annabel's eyes were fixed on the ground in front of her, and Stefanie didn't want to break into Annabel's thoughts. She was busy with her own anyway. The silence was deafening.

Soon they were at school. Stefanie was alone but waiting—waiting for what she knew would come. Had Annabel done anything yet? The classroom felt familiar but strange. Stefanie took her seat. She bit her lip and stared at the door to the classroom. Where was Annabel? Where had she gone? They had entered the classroom together, but then Annabel had run off, a purposeful look on her face. Was she telling now? Why couldn't she have waited until later, at the end of the day? Stefanie had made a mistake. A big mistake. She didn't really want Annabel to talk to anyone: not her teachers who would be disappointed, not her friends who would be disapproving, not her parents who would be distressed. She had had it with the lot of them. They had eyes, didn't they? But they all had looked right through her all along, long before any of this had started. What difference did it make now? Stefanie laid her head on the desk. She wanted to be left alone. All she wanted was to curl up in bed and never come back to school—away from the temptations of food. She wanted to …

Stefanie could hear Ms. Olson's voice on the other side of the closed classroom door. Stefanie's hands groped for her ribs under her uniform and the sweatshirt and turtleneck that she was allowed to wear as long as it matched the plaid skirt. She relaxed. For a moment she felt elated. The ribs were still there. She was going in the right direction—toward happiness.

With a squeak, the door to the classroom opened, and Stefanie raised her head. Annabel stepped into the classroom, but her vacant gaze didn't reveal anything. Stefanie couldn't get her to make eye contact. Had she told?

The plastic seats around Stefanie were beginning to fill. Laura had arrived. The room was getting noisy. Talk of boys and homework assignments. There was a Spanish test today, and clusters of her classmates were frantically trying to conjugate a set of irregular verbs. No one talked to her anymore in the few moments before homeroom. They thought she was strange and unsociable because she didn't go to lunch. It didn't matter anyway. Alone at school, she got a jump on her homework. And the more homework she finished at school, the more free time she had after school for the gym and sit-ups. All in all, the system had worked well enough.

Stefanie craned her neck and stared out the window. The East River looked cold and gray, and a barge floated languidly along, letting the current carry it. That cold water could wash over her limbs and make her numb. She would feel no pain, and everything around her would just fall away into blackness. She saw herself sinking. One big breath … and under … down … down … down. She wasn't afraid.

Having fled the confusion of the classroom for the relative peace of the hallway, Stefanie paused to wait for the black dots in front of her eyes to dissipate. The white walls of the hallway were stark and agreeable. There were no murals in swirling colors and Stefanie had often thought of them as her model. Unadorned was the ideal. Unadorned with pictures, just as her own body would be unadorned by excess flesh. It was something to aspire to.

And then someone was tapping her shoulder, interrupting her reverie. Ms. Olson was standing in front of her, extending a white piece of paper.

Stefanie unfolded the note in the silent safety of the ladies room, in the stall farthest from the door.

> Stefanie,
>   Come by today. I'd like to talk with you. How
> about one forty-five?

With her eyes closed, Stefanie sank to the floor. She had sat in the same position over a month ago, and it felt comfortingly familiar. That first morning was when it had all begun, but now everything was wrong. She could feel the new gap between the elastic of her underwear and her hip bones, and she realized that it hurt her tail bone to sit on the hard tile. She ran her hand down her stomach. Flat, straight, almost—if she let herself hope—concave. Things had certainly changed.

Now her stomach jumped into her throat, and her heart was pulsating; was she going to be sick, or was she just scared? What would Ms. Olson say? What had Annabel said? Stefanie's hands were back around her torso. She wrapped her hands around her rib cage and tried to force the two index fingers to touch each other; it was her way of measuring. She was closer to being good enough than ever before, but not quite there yet. She still had a little way to go.

Ms. Olson wanted a meeting. But what could she possibly have to say?

Homeroom had ended. Stefanie could hear other girls outside the bathroom door gathering their books. It was first period. The hallway would be crowded and overwhelming. Standing, she braced herself and waited for the dizziness to subside.

Like that first morning when Stefanie had gone to unlock the stall door, her hands were still shaking. A meeting ...

Was she nervous ... or excited ... or finally relieved?

- 12 -

The door looked impassive, and Stefanie wondered if she could open it. Maybe she would be trapped out there, standing in the middle of the hallway, while Ms. Olson sat at her desk, grading papers and waiting for her to arrive. Was that feasible? Would Ms. Olson forget? Could she foil Annabel's plans and avoid this meeting? Did she want to?

Her mind raced, searching for a safe thought to land on. She had to make a decision: She would either go in now or turn away. The thumping of her heart would most certainly betray her presence within seconds. But she could only wait, listening to the emotional and rational voices in her head, the two personas, fight for supremacy. The emotional voice cried to be thin. She begged for her freedom and held up a diet article, "The Top Ten Ways to Lose Weight that You've Never Thought Of." She wanted Stefanie to read and be inspired. She wanted her to turn away from the door and leave Ms. Olson in peace. The rational voice told her to put her hand on the doorknob. This voice was reciting from the psychology textbook: "Anorexia nervosa, with a mortality rate near 9 percent, should be treated immediately. Don't wait to get help." What would she do? Which voice would she listen to?

Maybe she would give in, ask for help. Maybe she would eat. Maybe she would stop dieting …

Stefanie sent a ripple through her thigh by hitting it.

Bzzz! Wrong answer! She wasn't thin enough yet. She couldn't afford to gain any weight. She shouldn't talk to Ms. Olson. She needed to focus on her diet; she didn't have time to fool around. The Barbies in the magazines had been right. She needed to diet. She needed to exercise. She needed to throw up sometimes. Why didn't anybody understand that?

The rational voice started in again: *An eating disorder ... a disease with a mortality rate near 9 percent.*

Out of every one hundred girls who developed the disease, nine would die. Many more would never fully recover, eternally besieged by thoughts of calories and fad diets. Could she be one of those girls? Would she always check the nutritional analysis on the back of the box? Or would it be worse—would she be one of the nine?

The brass doorknob turned in her palm. Stefanie pushed open the door and took a few steps into the room. For now, the rational side had won.

"Come, sit," Ms. Olson had turned one of the desks around so that it faced another, and she beckoned for Stefanie to join her. Stefanie stood in the doorway, frozen. Was her heart still beating? Would her feet still move? She wasn't confident that she could walk, even if she tried. Maybe it would be safer to just stand still.

"You don't have to be scared of me."

Ms. Olson's voice beckoned her, soft and encouraging as she had hoped it would be. Stefanie took a step forward. She didn't fall. She could make it. Only a couple more feet, and she would be safely supported by the chair.

"What's been going on, Stefanie? I heard some pretty worrisome things from Annabel. But I didn't call you here only because of her. I was going to talk to you on my own anyway; you haven't been yourself lately. I want you to tell me what is happening." Ms. Olson watched Stefanie's face as the girl digested her statements.

What had Annabel said? Would her teacher believe her if she said she didn't have a problem? Could she tell Ms. Olson that Annabel had lied? Why had she come in? The hallway had been much safer. In here, she was vulnerable. She couldn't escape; she was trapped.

Ms. Olson was waiting for an explanation, but Stefanie couldn't give one. She didn't know what to say. How could she begin to describe the emptiness inside of her if she didn't know why it existed?

She couldn't say that everyone had praised her for losing weight. She couldn't say she was finally getting results. Those were the excuses that all girls made when people confronted them. If she said these things, she would be falling into a trap, reciting from a script of things not to say. She didn't want to let on that she had noticed she was losing weight—that she was doing it on purpose. She couldn't mention Laura and the competition that she had invented. And Ms. Olson would never understand that she avoided the hallway near the cafeteria for fear that she would be overcome by the scent of the food and succumb to that gnawing hunger.

It seemed wiser to say nothing. Ms. Olson just waited.

The bright morning sun had been replaced by the half-hearted rays of midafternoon and the light glanced off the candy bowl on Ms. Olson's desk. Stefanie stared at the candies while her teacher stared at her. How had she ever indulged in that chocolate? What had she been thinking? That bowl was a virtual incubator for calories, grams of sugar, and saturated fats.

In their silence, Stefanie imagined herself eating them during class, stuffing handful after handful into her mouth. There wasn't even enough time for her to chew and swallow; she reached to catch the pieces as they tumbled from her mouth. She didn't want to lose a morsel. In her imagination, one bowl was empty; Ms. Olson filled it again, and she continued eating. As Stefanie gorged herself on their sweet gooey richness, she could feel her thighs expanding and her stomach distending, but still she shoved in the next handful. She had lost control; she couldn't stop.

The daydream embarrassed her, and she turned away, hoping that Ms. Olson hadn't seen the desire in her eyes.

"Stefanie, I need you to tell me what has been happening with you."

Her voice was soothing and concerned. In that moment Stefanie believed that this kind teacher might be the only person in the world who really cared about her. Ms. Olson was the one person who hadn't always looked through her. She had noticed when something was wrong. Stefanie thought back on that first morning when Ms. Olson had tried to draw her into the conversation. This teacher hadn't let her slip away, and she wasn't going to let her now. Stefanie knew that something had gone wrong. Maybe she had gotten carried away; maybe she had taken the diet a bit too far. Sometimes when the room spun, she did get scared. Sometimes she didn't really want to die. What she was doing was sick. Maybe *she* wasn't sick, but her actions were. Ms. Olson could see that. She wasn't blind. If she was going to be helped, Ms. Olson was the only one who could do it. Stefanie wished she could thank Ms. Olson for caring.

Her eyes filled with tears and, almost imperceptibly, Stefanie's head nodded in assent. She would tell Ms. Olson the truth; she didn't have the strength to resist.

They talked well into the next period until Stefanie's mouth was dry. She didn't have the ability to utter another word. What would happen now? What would Ms. Olson's reaction be? What action would she take? Would Ms. Olson hate her now? Stefanie wasn't even sure what she had said. A chilling thought suddenly swept through her mind: *what if Ms. Olson decides to tell my parents?*

A car alarm went off outside, and Stefanie looked down at her sneakers. Crossing one leg, she tugged at her laces and methodically retied each bow, though they hadn't come loose. A string was dangling from the hem of her skirt, but she couldn't get it off. When at last she gave up, there was a pink line where her hand had grasped the thread. Shaking off the pain, Stefanie surveyed her teacher and waited.

Ms. Olson's hands were folded on her desk, and the look on her face was calm. Stefanie wondered what she was thinking.

All right, Stefanie thought. She could deal with this. She could tell her parents it wasn't true. She would say that she had only wanted to find out what Ms. Olson's reaction would be. It had been blown out of proportion. It was only a game, a hypothetical situation, a figment of her overactive imagination.

But then she thought about her journal—the goals, the purged dinners, the regimen sit-ups and leg lifts, the sleepless nights—all her secrets set down with the meticulous precision of a jewel cutter. Oh God. If her parents ever read what she had written, Ms. Olson's story would be substantiated. There could be no denying the truth.

– 13 –

They'd always been a close family. Not as close as Julia's, but close. They had taken picnic basket suppers to Central Park to hear the symphony on summer nights and had enjoyed mugs of hot cocoa at Rockefeller Center following winter afternoons of skating. They had occasionally read aloud in the evening and had played board games at the kitchen table when the cable went out and there was no TV. They had fought, like everyone does, but love had moved them over the rough patches. They had always apologized, and life had gone on.

Not this time. Stefanie pulled her arms inside her jacket and tried to forget where she was going. Maybe if she got lost she would never have to hear the anger in her mother's voice or see the disappointment in her eyes. She was scared of that face, scared of the way it made her feel, the fracturing of something inside her, the numbness, the anger at herself for causing that face, and the anger at her parents for being angry.

Each tile of the lobby's floor brought her closer to her apartment, and she dragged her heels, taking baby steps. With her toe she traced the outline of a black diamond tile as she waited for the elevator to arrive. She watched the illuminated numbers above the elevator. Each one went out, and the next one was lit in succession: 1, 2, 3. The door opened.

"Have a good evening," Freddy the doorman said with a smile. Freddy, who had known her since the days she had run barefoot through the lobby, was waiting for her to step from the elevator toward her apartment door.

"You too, thank you. Good night."

Stefanie waited until the faint whirr of the elevator's motor had disappeared, then she leaned against the door and pushed. It opened slowly, heavier than Stefanie remembered.

Standing in the center of the front hallway, she listened to the silence of the house. Were her parents out? Had they missed the message from Ms. Olson? Did they know yet? Was she safe?

She could check the answering machine and delete any messages. She could check the caller ID and delete the missed calls. Her parents would never know Ms. Olson had called, and Ms. Olson would think her parents didn't care. It was the perfect plan. Brilliant. Shrewd. Ingenious. Deceitful.

"That you, Stef?" The silence was pierced by the sound of Madeline Webber's falsely cheerful voice. Stefanie turned toward the kitchen. Her mom appeared in the doorway.

Nothing moved. Was she still breathing? Had she died? Was this all a dream? No. Her rapid heartbeat reminded her that she was still alive. It wasn't a dream, just the beginning of a game, and her mother was waiting for her to make the first move.

Why didn't her mother yell? Why was she just standing there with a bottle of olive oil in her hand, dressed only in the oversized T-shirt that she wore for cooking? What was she waiting for? Anything would be better than silence. Why didn't she say how angry she was?

Stefanie's index finger and thumb encircled her wrist. Where was that newest bone? Still there where she had left it. Nothing had changed. She would be OK. The circle of her fingers inched up her arm. How far could they go? A quarter of the way ... a third of the way ... halfway ... halfway up her forearm. Her fingers still touched. Had she gone farther than the day before? Maybe a few millimeters. A few millimeters of progress.

Somehow that piece of good news settled her. But she couldn't just stand around, waiting for her mother to throw the first punch. She needed to do her exercises. She had to make up for the neglected ones that morning. She had to get away to the safety of her room, where she could close herself in and push those abdominal muscles beyond their capabilities. Standing there, just waiting for her mother to make a move, was wasting precious time.

She had to take her chances; they couldn't stand there, in the front hall, all evening. Someone had to yield. Stefanie moved toward her bedroom door.

Checkmate.

"I think we need to talk."

The hallway became a vacuum as four oriental-papered walls closed in on her. As she struggled for breath, Stefanie was certain that there wasn't enough oxygen to support two life forms. She'd die if she didn't get away, but her mother was gaining on her. What now? Would her mother tell her what a disappointment she had been? Would she disown her? Stefanie could imagine herself curled up in a cardboard box on Lexington Avenue. She'd be cold and wet and hungry, very hungry. Her parents might come by occasionally and throw some coins in her direction. They might let her take some of her books to pass the long, tedious days or bring some of their finished newspapers for her to insulate her makeshift cardboard home. They might bring her a new sweater on her birthday or give her leftover eggnog at Christmas. Or they might not even do that. Maybe she wasn't worth that much attention.

Something was holding her up. Stefanie's eyes were closed, but she could smell her mother's favorite perfume: Lily of the Valley. At times, she had found this smell overwhelming—when she hugged her mother good-bye just before they left for the party of the evening—but now it didn't seem so sickeningly sweet. The smell was muted and comforting. Stefanie breathed deeply, trying for air, inhaling the familiar aroma. Her mother's long, toned arms were supporting her. There was no screaming, no reprimanding, no disowning. There was only a hug. She was wrapped in the embrace that she had longed for, with no danger or fear or sadness. This wasn't what she had expected. Where was the screaming? Why wasn't she angry?

Stefanie gave a soft, involuntary sigh, as though her nervous system had waved a white flag of surrender, no longer on guard, utterly and completely relaxed. With her head resting in the arc formed by her mother's neck and shoulder, Stefanie could only feel sadness. Her mother seemed fragile, breakable. Why had she done this to her parents? Hot, sticky shame ran through her. She recognized the feeling in her stomach, the quick-pull-over-the-car sensation that filled her from her scalp down to her pinkie toe. It was the same one she had every time she opened the back door and tossed her dinner in the trashcan. It was the same feeling she had every time she knelt over the toilet bowl after a meal. Her parents deserved better. They deserved a better child, a better teenager, a better daughter. They deserved Laura's pretty face and Julia's enthusiasm. They deserved Annabel, the way she could play sports all day long and never get tired. They deserved a daughter who was intelligent and independent, athletic and fearless. They deserved the perfect daughter, someone they would be proud to be seen with on the street. She was a disappointment, and bless them for not even showing it. In the fish-bowl world of New York's Upper East Side, Stefanie knew countless parents who wouldn't have bothered.

She pulled away in embarrassment. Where her head had been, her mother's shoulder was wet, and Stefanie knew that she was crying. A droplet of salty water rolled across her lip. Her mother still hadn't said a word. Stefanie waited, feeling very small.

As the sun dropped below the East River across town, Stefanie suddenly remembered her new friends from the gym downstairs. As Stefanie and her mother sat together on the couch, Stefanie wondered if they were asking each other what was keeping their youngest member. Her mother began to talk. She had been worried; she had noticed the changes. She had known that something was wrong even before Ms. Olson had picked up the telephone. Everything was going to be OK. They would get through this. She had already called a therapist, and Stefanie was set with an appointment for later that week.

They talked more that night than they had in over a year. She didn't deny Ms. Olson's accusations; she didn't even try. For some reason, she couldn't. Shadows began to dance and grow longer on the walls. As the room gradually darkened and neither moved to turn on a light, they were close again. They just sat. And they cried together.

Was the game over? Stefanie was going to get help. Her mother had already talked to a doctor, and she was going into treatment. Would it be painful? Would they make her feel worse about herself than she already did? Would they hurt her in any way—either physically, by prodding her with needles and drawing blood, or emotionally, by confirming all the thoughts in her head that told her she was a lousy human being? She hoped not. Would they make her eat? She assumed yes. Was this the end? Had all her hard work been for nothing? Anorexia nervosa—it was a disease, a disease that she could die of, and she had known that all along. Why had she ever begun? Why had she been so stupid? And now, why, after everything, didn't she want to give it up. It was important. Too important.

"The shinbone's connected to the knee bone, the knee bone's connected to the thighbone, the thighbone's connected to the hip bone …"

The perturbing chorus echoed through her ear drums. She was hearing the song all the time now. Shinbone … knee bone. Faster … faster … faster … They sang continually faster. Was this the end? Had she actually gone crazy?

They were still going to have dinner that night. Stefanie could smell it in the kitchen, cooking even as they sat on the couch together.

"Things will get better, Stef. They've already started to turn around. We're going to get you eating again."

Stefanie looked into her mother's hazel eyes. They were optimistic, hopeful despite the tears, but Stefanie didn't understand why. She didn't plan on giving up all the work that she had done. She didn't plan to let them take all that away from her.

The room was completely dark now, and the timer went off in the kitchen. Her mother led her toward the kitchen, and Stefanie flopped onto her chair. She was too tired to move. But she still didn't want to eat.

Shinbone ... knee bone ... shinbone ... knee bone. Faster ... faster ... faster ...

- 14 -

Two leather sofas. An oak coffee table or maybe maple. Off-white walls and landscape paintings. Framed pictures of sunsets over water. A fish tank with tropical fish, the kind that she had kept as a little girl. Twin towers of magazines rising from either end of the table. It was just like every other waiting room that she had ever sat in. The same monochromatic environment, the same sterile furniture. The layout might be different, a couch placed here rather than over there, but the feeling was still the same. Stefanie always felt out of place on waiting-room chairs. She couldn't help but feel watched, even if she was the only person in the room. It was as if she had come into the office perfectly healthy, then just from sitting there she would inevitably become sick. The very existence of the place would make something wrong with her.

She wondered who had last sat in her place. An anorectic? A compulsive eater? Maybe a manic-depressive? Or someone with obsessive-compulsive disorder? She had probably arranged the magazines into those perfect piles. Stefanie pulled her hand away from the top magazine, hesitant to disrupt the fictional person's careful work.

It had been two days since Ms. Olson had talked to her mother. Two hazy days in her memory in which she went to school, wandered to classes, and did her work without really caring or thinking about the motions. There was no pretense that she was eating anymore. She'd just stopped, and there was nothing that her parents could do. Not until they brought her to a "specialist." Annabel and Laura knew what had been planned because, after all, parents talked—the doctors, the therapy, the appointments—and Julia could probably have guessed that something was going on, but Stefanie neither confirmed nor denied their suspicions. It didn't matter what they thought, and it didn't matter what they said. She didn't care.

The buzzer sounded, and a young man quickly entered the small room, taking a seat on the other couch. Stefanie wondered what his problem was, but, when their eyes met, she looked down at the floor and dug her fingernails into the palm of her mother's hand. Why did she have to stay there? Her heart's rhythm sounded uneven, though she knew it wasn't really; her mouth felt sawdust-filled and dry. And her mother was so calm. She just sat there, waiting for Stefanie to be summoned inside. She wasn't scared. Her mother wasn't even anxious. Her father was at the office, or at a conference somewhere in Manhattan. He hadn't wanted to come, or maybe he just hadn't been welcome. He had been cautious around her lately, not really saying much, sometimes hugging her, sometimes walking into her room when she cried. But not talking. The sight of him made her scream, though she didn't know why. He had learned quickly to stay away.

A drop of sweat inched down her side, running over the ridges formed by her ribs. Stefanie squeezed her arms against her body and exhaled as the trickle caught in her cotton bra, beneath the (now-loose, once-tight) oatmeal-colored T-shirt and blue Nike sweatshirt. Soft, sterile Muzak played in the background, but Stefanie wished for the bones song. She needed that encouragement. She needed to think about each bone in her body that was covered by fleshy tissue. She needed to imagine that flesh disappearing, the pounds melting away, oozing to the ground and sliding off the scale. She didn't need to sit in a therapist's office. Determination was essential—if she wasn't determined, how could she ever succeed? And she needed faith in the power of restricting, the belief that she could lose the remaining weight. Just a little bit more—she couldn't say how much yet, just a little bit more. But without determination and faith, she would be tricked. She would be induced to eat; she would gain back all the weight. That couldn't happen.

"Stefanie? Madeline Webber?" The door opened, and a woman dressed in a long black skirt with flowers embroidered around the hem and a coral sweater walked toward them, her hand outstretched. "I'm Katherine Grant. Please, come in. I'll meet with both of you first, and then perhaps I can get to know Stefanie a little better, one on one."

It was already starting. This young, thin creature standing in a doorway was already trying to seduce her. She couldn't have been more than thirty-three years old. With her long hair tied back in that slightly off-center half-ponytail. The way she didn't quite walk but more like floated across the floor, leading the way to her office. She was a fraud—already trying to make her fat. She wasn't a qualified professional at all, with that falsely calm demeanor and cheery disposition. She was only acting. Role-playing. Pretending to be a therapist. Pretending to help people. She probably couldn't even spell the word *help*. She certainly wouldn't make Stefanie feel better. They would go back into that room and chit-chat about what worried the Webbers, how Stefanie had changed, what the family dynamics were like, but eventually her mother would leave. Then they would sit on the couch like partners, and this lady would try to convince her to eat. She called herself a therapist, but Stefanie knew what she was—a traitor, an ally of the calorie army, a spy sent ahead to clear a path of attack. But Stefanie was on to her games, her tricks, and her promises.

Next to her, Stefanie felt the couch's cushions rebound as her mother stood and extended a hand. "Good to meet you, Dr. Grant. Thank you for seeing us."

Katherine Grant gave Stefanie a warm smile and motioned for them to follow. Ah ha! She appeared so sweet. She was setting a trap. Stefanie would be lured by the sickening kindness, and then— Boom!—she would find herself trapped in a cage, just waiting to die. The brass plate on the door read: Dr. Katherine Grant, PhD— PhD! Did those engraved letters give her the right to invade people's thoughts? Did they give her the authority to change people's minds? Was it even ethical for her to try? Could she actually succeed?

Stefanie felt her mother's hand pulling her up out of her seat and toward the open doorway. It occurred to her that, if she didn't move, if she refused to stand, her surroundings might just disappear. Maybe she would wake up, and it would all be a nightmare. Stefanie didn't yield easily, but the grip tightened. Stefanie felt the painful pressure of her mother's emerald wedding band against the bones of her hand. She had to go in.

Allowing herself to be led by her right hand, she dug her left hand against her hip. It was hard to find the bone beneath the folds of the oversized sweatshirt that hung across her bony shoulders and ballooned around her waist where there seemed to be no stomach left at all, but there—finally—there it was, just the same as always. She thought of the *Motivation* CD at home in her stereo and hummed the bones song to herself. She had to go in; but she didn't have to listen, she didn't have to talk, and she didn't have to change.

Dr. Grant sat in a recliner; she and her mother sat opposite her on a big couch with giant suede pillows; Stefanie made note of their softness. The room was predominantly cream-colored with certain splashes of color here and there—a hunter green throw rug in the corner, a red afghan draped over the back of the couch. Stefanie looked at the diplomas—large, framed, and displayed prominently. Dr. Grant had graduated from University of Michigan, then Fordham graduate school. She was licensed in various forms of psychotherapy, which was evident from the framed certificates, and had obviously had extensive training. But beyond reading what the words said, Stefanie had no idea what they meant. She didn't know what Rational Emotive Therapy was or Cognitive Behavioral Therapy or psychoanalysis, and it didn't seem like anyone planned to explain it to her.

There was silence in the room as each waited for someone else to begin.

A substantial desk stood in one corner of the room, and Stefanie studied its contents, looking for clues to this lady's personality. Across the top shelf above the desk, there were psychology books:

treating eating disorders, dealing with trauma, ending sexual abuse in the home, a guide to antidepressants. There were workbooks for obsessive-compulsive disorders and compulsive overeating. A stack of file folders rested on the desktop—patient folders, Stefanie guessed. It was a sizeable pile. Did Dr. Grant see all those patients in one day? What were the people in those folders like? Were any like her? Maybe she wasn't alone. She wanted to flip through those pages, explore the people this doctor had seen, and perhaps discover the identity of the person who had so scrupulously organized the magazines in the waiting room. The rest of the desk was empty, save for a recent *New York Times* bestseller, hidden slightly behind a cup of pens and a bag of Swedish Fish in the corner. Candy? Would she have to eat it? Stefanie wondered. Would the candy be some kind of twisted test to see if she really had an eating disorder? Would Dr. Grant force it down her throat when she refused? Would the refusal seal her fate: therapy for life or until she gained the weight? Swedish Fish. Not so very many calories but every little bit counted. She couldn't eat the candy; she couldn't and she wouldn't.

Dr. Grant was watching her intently, watching her twitching leg, how she fidgeted in her seat, how she looked at her mother before speaking, how her fingers played with the fraying edge of her watch-band. "So, Stefanie, would you like to tell me why you're here?"

That was a stupid question.

Stefanie pulled at a loose thread poking out from the end of her sleeve. One of the perfectly spaced stitches came undone. If she kept pulling, more would follow, and the whole thing would fall apart, one thread at a time. Stefanie released the thread and tried to steady her eyes on Dr. Grant. The question hadn't been rhetorical; she was waiting for an answer.

Both her mother and the doctor were staring at her. Four eyes trained on her face … waiting for some answer, some explanation. Stefanie shrugged. "My parents found out that I wasn't eating very much."

There. She had answered. They couldn't expect her to say anything more than that. She wasn't going to incriminate herself. As long as they didn't ask her directly about throwing up, exercising, or dieting, she would be fine. She'd tell the truth, but not unless directly asked. She'd play a game of semantics, and tell them what they asked for but nothing more. Inwardly humming the bones song, Stefanie looked into Dr. Grant's dark eyes. She could still be strong.

"I see." Dr. Grant's voice was calm and even, "Mrs. Webber, why don't you step outside. I think I'd like to talk to Stefanie alone for a little while."

Her mother was standing and moving toward the doorway. Stefanie could see that she forced herself to smile at Dr. Grant as she passed, but moments later the smile was gone. Her mother was abandoning her, leaving her to sit in this strange office, surrounded by Swedish Fish. How could she do this? Madeline Webber turned when she got to the door, but Stefanie looked away. They wouldn't lock eyes. She wouldn't allow her mother that comfort. Weren't parents supposed to be supportive of their children? How could her mother just leave? Didn't she care?

The door to the office closed, and Stefanie leaned back, ensconcing herself into the pillows of the couch.

Dr. Grant moved a couple inches forward in her chair and clasped her hands together. "So you weren't eating. What else?" Her head cocked to one side, almost affectionately, and she looked into Stefanie's eyes; the cadence of her voice was one of concern and interest and trustworthiness. The words washed over Stefanie, and she felt warm inside her cocoon of pillows. Dr. Grant didn't move. She didn't blink, and she didn't smile. She didn't laugh at Stefanie's stupidity, or tell her that she was crazy for coming to therapy when she was clearly not sick. Her dark eyes had flecks of blue in them. If Stefanie allowed herself to look more closely, she could see the blue flecks, mixed with an exotic tinge of yellow. Dr. Grant was watching carefully, but not intrusively. Stefanie caught herself wanting to explain it all. But she didn't know where to begin.

Stefanie looked down at her feet. Did this lady really care, or was she just pretending to be interested? Was there some secret in her past that allowed her to care, to relate, to empathize? Or was she just a really good actress? Another stitch of the sweatshirt came free as Stefanie formulated a response. It was a sort of extreme version of the old adage: Think before you speak. That way, people could never reproach her for speaking rashly. It would be harder, though not impossible, to say something that she would later regret. But she didn't want Dr. Grant to disapprove of her, or think she was silly, or assume that her family was overreacting.

"Sometimes I throw up." There. She said it. She placed her hand against her side and pressed hard, anticipating a reaction. Would Dr. Grant hate her now? She pinched her skin and felt the ribs underneath. It was a small comfort.

"Tell me what you're thinking right now," Dr. Grant's voice was composed as she watched Stefanie's roaming hand. "How do you feel today?"

Another question that she couldn't answer.

Sad … numb … empty. What should she say? She could pick one randomly, but it wouldn't be what this lady was looking for. Dr. Grant wanted the truth—and Stefanie didn't know what the truth was.

One Mississippi, two Mississippi, three Mississippi … she counted the seconds like her mother had taught her. One minute … two minutes … three minutes … one hundred eighty Mississippis …

The floor was covered by a carpet of cream-colored pile. Behind her a wall of windows looked out on Central Park West. It wasn't rush hour yet; Stefanie could tell because the taxicabs that passed by the ground floor office window all had their yellow lights illuminated. When the hour was up, that would have changed. Stefanie and her mother would most likely take the cross-town bus home at Eighty-sixth Street. It would be impossible to get a cab in the twilight. Maybe they could leave now? Stefanie turned her gaze back to Dr. Grant. She was still waiting for a truth that Stefanie didn't understand.

What was she feeling? What was the answer that the doctor was looking for?

Four minutes ... five minutes ... three hundred Mississippis. How much longer could this go on?

"This must be hard for you. I know you don't want to be here."

Was she being patronized? How much were her parents paying the doctor to make fun of her? Stefanie shrugged and gave the loose string on her sweatshirt another tug. She shifted on the couch so her feet could reach the floor and tapped her foot. Why was she here? When could she leave? Couldn't Dr. Grant see? She didn't want help. She just wanted to go home.

"I'm sorry that you've been forced to come here, Stefanie. But I'd like to help you," Dr. Grant tried again.

"The shinbone's connected to the knee bone, the knee bone's connected to the thighbone, the thighbone's connected to the hip bone ..."

She ignored the kind words and hummed the song to herself. Strength. Strength. Strength. She wouldn't be helped. She wouldn't be helped. She wouldn't be helped. Strength.

Dr. Grant was standing up. "All right, it was nice to meet you, Stefanie. I'll see you next week."

Stefanie was out in the waiting room now. It was over. She had survived. Her mother put down her magazine. "How was it?"

"Fine."

A cab had just pulled up to Dr. Grant's building as they stepped outside. A girl in a blue pea coat was counting out change. Next victim, Stefanie thought grimly. As the car turned onto the Central Park Drive, Stefanie slipped on her headphones. Next week she would be back there, again trying to answer those questions—those stupid, pointless, naive questions. She wouldn't be anymore prepared to give satisfactory explanations than she'd been today. She hadn't lost yet. And Dr. Grant hadn't won.

~ 15 ~

Therapist appointment Number One: *She asked boring questions. I don't know how to answer. And "doctor" has mushroomed suddenly into an entire team of them. Doctor's appointment Number One: today. Psychopharmacologist's appointment Number One: tomorrow.*

She capped her pen and shut off the flashlight. The dim glow disappeared, and Stefanie was left in the quiet darkness. It was that time of night when one day has disappeared, but the next hasn't quite arrived to fill the emptiness.

Stefanie felt a comfort in being nowhere. Her chest rose and fell rhythmically, her breathing strained and painful, replenishing the oxygen supply that had been used up exercising. She had done a hundred extra crunches tonight, on a whim—almost compelled to do more, as if to prove her obstinacy. She welcomed the burn as she felt her stomach muscles tighten, and she smiled when her quads began to cramp. This was the point. This was the goal.

Stefanie thought of Laura and Annabel and Julia, asleep in their nearby bedrooms down the block or just uptown. She envisioned them peacefully in their beds, their chests moving slowly and deeply with the pulse of sleep. What had they done that afternoon? While she had been sitting in a shrink's office, where were they? Who were they hanging out with, and what would they have thought if they knew where she'd been today? Stefanie turned over onto her stomach and rubbed her cheek against her cool pillowcase. It would happen again and again. While they went on with their lives, hers would be filled with doctors and therapists and psychopharmacologists—who even knew what those were? She would sit in waiting rooms, staring at mindless teenybopper magazines, while the others did their homework, attended a sports practice, or met at Starbucks for iced coffee or white chocolate mochas. It hardly seemed fair.

Appointment Number Two: the Fifth Avenue office of Dr. Megan Adler, across the street from the Met. They were standing in the bright midafternoon sunlight after yet another school day of anxiety and attempts to avoid any traces of food.

Stefanie chewed on her lip as her mother pressed the buzzer and announced them collectively as "Stefanie Webber." Madeline Webber had finally gotten her wish—switching Stefanie to a female doctor (it was just *time*, she said) after a lifetime of visits with the man who had watched Stefanie grow from five pounds to one hundred twenty-five pounds. Dr. Adler had come highly recommended, but Stefanie didn't want to change. Why now, at this most difficult time? This so-called doctor would put her on the scale and judge her. Then they would all see what a mistake they had made. She could imagine the empty medical chart filling up quickly with disapproving words and criticism. It wouldn't read "Anorexic." It would read "Obese." The word made Stefanie's stomach contract, with the slithery sound of the *s* hanging over the *e*'s in rolls of fat.

The doctor was late. She and her mother were sitting in cushioned wooden chairs, while her mother completed Stefanie's history for the New Patient Information form. With a promise of "The doctor will be right with you," the receptionist disappeared, and Stefanie spotted a bowl of M&Ms on the counter. Why was there candy everywhere in this world? Didn't anyone know about the artery-clogging saturated fats that were in each crunchy, chocolatey morsel? Didn't anyone understand how tempting that was?

If only it were over … Stefanie tapped her foot against the leg of her chair and wiped at the reopened split in her lip.

Dr. Adler appeared, followed by another teenager, who coughed deeply and reached for a tissue. Dr. Adler was a small woman with a mischievous smile and a glint in her eyes. "Feel better. Call me if it gets worse. You can come back in, and we'll go from there. Don't forget to get that prescription filled." Dr. Adler walked a few steps toward the door with this other girl, and then turned back, her attention now on the Webbers. A gust of wind blew in through the doorway as the girl left. Stefanie envied her freedom.

"This way, please. You can both come with me." Dr. Adler shook her mother's hand and headed down the hallway toward her office. Stefanie didn't trust her. She was clearly an enemy, wearing a white lab coat over black pants and a pink cashmere sweater. Her mother had hired this woman to fatten her up; Dr. Adler couldn't possibly care about Stefanie. If she did, she wouldn't have agreed to meet with them. If she did, she would have known that Stefanie didn't need a therapist, that she didn't have a problem.

They were ushered into a spacious office and given the preliminary "It's nice to meet you" lecture. Dr. Adler explained her practice—adolescent medicine. She dealt primarily with girls, though there was the occasional guy. She talked about her training. Then she talked about her treatment philosophies surrounding eating disorders. Hers was a team approach, and she believed that various professionals would have to be involved to conquer anorexia or bulimia. She had had extensive experience with eating disorders and knew Stefanie's school well. She liked to work more directly with the patient and less directly with the parents, and everything—within reason—would be kept confidential. Madeline Webber cringed at this but was assured that, given the patient's critical health, at this point she would be involved in all aspects of her daughter's care.

Stefanie wanted to scream. The whole discussion seemed so impersonal. They were talking about her as if she wasn't even in the room. Her mother was explaining Stefanie's dieting history, but she was getting the details confused. She hadn't started with a goal in mind. It didn't start because she thought that people would like her better if she were thinner. That hadn't been the point, but she didn't want to open her mouth to correct them.

"Well, I think that's all for now. Mrs. Webber, you may step outside now. We'll call you when we're finished." Dr. Adler smiled, and Stefanie almost smiled back, relieved that at least this part was over. She didn't know what would come next, but she hoped that it would be better. It wasn't.

She fidgeted as she stepped on the scale in Dr. Adler's exam room. She was uncomfortable and cold, standing there under fluorescent lights that made her skin look shockingly sallow. Beneath the hospital gown, she could see the tips of her pelvic bones. She moved to see her bones dance, to watch as they moved beneath the thin layer of cotton. Dr. Adler had to ask her to stand still. As she slid the weights along the balance, Dr. Adler watched Stefanie closely. Her face was not concerned. Stefanie was sure she'd seen patients much worse than her. She'd probably seen patients whose heart rates were so slow that they could have been dead. She'd seen the girls from the psychology textbook after they'd passed out in their apartments. Standing on the scale, trying so hard to read her new doctor's expression, Stefanie felt naked and exposed. She knew that Dr. Adler could see her ribs jutting out from her sides, and the kneecaps that now hurt when she lay on her side in bed at night. There were bruises on her shins in places where she didn't remember getting hurt. One day they had just appeared.

Dr. Adler read out the number from the scale, and Stefanie could feel goose bumps running the length of her arms. The hair stood on end. She stepped down off the scale and could feel the tears start to build in her eyes. It wasn't low enough. She was a failure even at being anorexic.

"How many calories do you allow yourself to eat in one day?"

Stefanie settled herself on the examining chair and pulled the robe tighter around her frail body.

Some days she wasn't allowed to eat anything at all. Some days she ate a handful of grapes in the afternoon. How much was a handful of grapes? A hundred calories? She'd call it a hundred just to be safe;

she didn't want to give herself credit for eating less than she really was.

"One hundred calories." She didn't mention that that was only on some days, that mostly she didn't eat anything. She didn't tell Dr. Adler that sometimes she threw up the grapes when she retreated to her bedroom to "do homework."

"One hundred calories? Seriously? That's not enough. You can't live on one hundred calories a day."

Stefanie didn't understand why Dr. Adler seemed so shocked. One hundred calories seemed like plenty. Dr. Adler was acting like it wasn't. But she didn't need to eat more than that; she was still fat. If she ate more, then she'd never lose weight. Then again, Dr. Adler was on her mother's side—the side whose only goal was to turn Stefanie into a 2000-pound whale.

Dr. Megan Adler kept her word to Stefanie's mother and moments later called Madeline Webber back into the room. They talked, once again, as if she wasn't in the room, but Stefanie didn't really care. She wouldn't listen. She didn't like this doctor. She wouldn't eat more. In the dark recesses of her mind, she was already planning to avoid eating dinner.

Next she saw Dr. Mary Mollani, the psychopharmacologist, who asked the same questions that Dr. Grant had asked: "How are you feeling today?" "Why are you here?" "Tell me, how did this all start?" "Did something traumatic happen in your life that set the diet in motion?" The second time around, the questions sounded even stupider. Stefanie didn't want to repeat the same information. She knew she could have kept the plan a secret for longer. She could have let Annabel think that everything was just fine, but instead she had betrayed herself and given up her secret. It was embarrassing that she had let herself get caught, that she had given in.

Dr. Adler thought she needed to eat more—one hundred calories a day wasn't sufficient. Dr. Mollani thought she needed antidepressants—SSRIs she called them. She had even left that office holding a flimsy white piece of paper that read Zoloft—75 mg in nearly illegible script.

Dr. Mollani had prescribed it to lessen the anxiety and depression and to help Stefanie cope with eating. But both doctors knew nothing. If she ate more, she would gain weight. If she took antidepressants and they made her more willing to eat, then she would also gain weight. She didn't want to give up the competitive edge that she had finally gained. Besides, antidepressants were for crazy people. Stefanie didn't want to become that stereotypical twentyish woman on Prozac—the woman who was cheerful and laughing to a point that was unnatural. She'd rather be unhappy.

Three appointments in three days. If only that had been the end of it, but there was more to come. Grant, Adler, and Mollani—all wanted to see her again. And regularly. On the bulletin board in the kitchen, the calendar's boxes were filled with appointments, all for her. What was the point? Sometimes she thought she didn't have a problem, and sometimes she knew that she did, but it didn't really matter anyway. She didn't want their help. She didn't need to get better. Nothing was wrong with her that anyone else could fix.

The week before, she had been normal. She had gone to school and done well. She had been involved with the school's literary journal. She went home after school if there was no meeting. She didn't sit in doctor's waiting rooms more than once a year. She had never talked about how she was feeling or why she was feeling that way. But now, all that had changed.

Now she was a diagnosis. She would be weighed once a week at a doctor's office. She would take antidepressants. She would be forced to put words to feelings that she didn't understand and didn't want to understand.

Stefanie opened her diary, wrote down her goals for the next day, and turned off the light. Everything was certainly different.

– 16 –

"Stop by today. We should talk."

"You've got to eat more."

"Why don't you join us for lunch?"

"You'll end up in the hospital if you don't start eating."

"Would you rather die and be skinny or live and be average?"

Ms. Olson … Laura … Julia … her mother … Annabel … They didn't know what they were talking about. Laura was jealous because she was being beaten. Julia didn't really care. Her mother was just parroting what the doctors said; Annabel was only asking more stupid questions. What was the point of living if she had to be average?

It was lunchtime again but unusually quiet. The freshmen were on a field trip at the botanical gardens, studying biology; the juniors were at a college essay writing workshop. Usually, when people passed her in the hallway, Stefanie tried to read their expressions to see how many of her secrets they knew. Laura and Annabel and Julia all knew where Stefanie disappeared to in the afternoons, but they didn't really talk about it. She didn't give out much information. When Annabel asked how things were going, Stefanie just gave her a terse, "Fine," and moved on. Beyond her friends, it wasn't clear how much her classmates knew or suspected or guessed. Gossip spread like wildfire within this building—she'd seen the chain in action, maybe she'd even taken part in it—but had anyone gotten her story right? As silence swept through the hallway, Stefanie realized how very alone she was. The only noise she heard was a faint hum of movement from the first floor, where the girls ran back and forth to the cafeteria. What might they think, Stefanie mused, with some pride, some anger, if they knew she had all these doctors now, that she'd become a project? Or that every morning before coming to school she swallowed a cream-colored happy pill? Perhaps that would make her exotic and mysterious. It might give her cachet, stature, that she'd never had before. People might even be a little bit afraid of her. She'd seen it before with cliques of bullies or tough girls—fear could move you up in the social hierarchy. Maybe they would simply pity her, the sophomore who had gone crazy, and stay away, watching for the next bit of information that they could glean and then passing it along to anyone willing to listen.

Tuesday. Tuesday of her third week of therapy and weigh-ins. She'd be seeing Dr. Adler that afternoon. Stefanie slid one hand to the waistband of her skirt. It sat squarely on her hips now, or maybe a little below. She knew she had lost weight—twenty-five pounds—but that still wasn't enough. She had to lose more because she wasn't happy yet. She had gotten a taste of what it felt like to see the numbers on the scale drop, and she wanted to keep going. When she looked in the mirror, she looked worse than ever. She assumed that she had just grown more sensitive to the contours of her unacceptably large body. She must try harder. Maybe after thirty or thirty-five pounds she would be able to see the difference. Or maybe forty or forty-five … She felt for the bones. The other hand encircled her wrist. Her index finger and thumb crossed. She pushed further, how much smaller could she go? Since the day before, how much more pronounced was that bone, the one that protruded from the outside of her wrist? This was the easiest of her ritualistic tests, the least conspicuous. And she felt calmer.

If a teacher walked by, she would get in trouble. Her Discman would be confiscated. Her *Motivation* CD would find a new home inside a teacher's desk. But it was worth a chance. Most of the teachers were at lunch anyway, and the eerie silence was strident.

"The shinbone's connected to the knee bone; the knee bone's connected to the thighbone; the thighbone's connected to the hip bone …"

Stefanie's heart beat faster as the music picked up speed. Could she induce her own heart attack? Was this how the nine died, those nine girls in one hundred who did not recover? She placed her hand over her heart to track the beat. It was an odd salute, as if she were saluting the names of her bones. It seemed irreverent, yet almost appropriate. She wondered if those other girls had felt the same way.

Minutes later as the lunch period ended, Stefanie's heart was still racing. It was a strange sort of high that took her at odd moments of the day. A sudden burst of energy and then a crash; she might not be able to keep her eyes open during math. But who needed to learn the formulas anyway? She didn't need to know what the trigonometric function of an angle was. It wasn't going to make her happy. She already knew what would, if only everyone would just let her get there.

Math … English … science … doctor … home.

She was so tired. Her feet dragged along the concrete, and in the low light of evening, Stefanie watched for the sparkles in the cement. They were like stars. Of course, living in New York, no one actually saw stars, but as a little girl she would look out the window with her mother and name the constellations that were out there somewhere, miles and miles away. And she would make a wish, a wish and send it into the deep blue darkness. Just knowing the stars were there, even if she could not see them, made Stefanie feel safe. Now as she trudged home in the disappearing light, she knew that dinner would be on the table and that her parents would be waiting. Could she stay out here all night and just fade away, become part of a stone wall or the base of one of these tall buildings? She could trade comfort for frost, food for disappearance to be safe from the terror of confronting the world on her parents' terms. Where she wouldn't have to see anybody, and nobody had to see her. She could become only an observer, a sidewalk fixture, barely even a real person. She wouldn't have to think or eat or talk. Dumb, mute, and blind, she could sit on the cold street. Was there a star out there on which she could wish for that?

But her feet carried her into the warm lobby of the apartment building where Freddy the doorman wished her goodnight, and she smiled back. She was neither alone nor invisible, and, upstairs on the table, a warm dinner was waiting.

Three cubes—no, four—of chicken, three asparagus stalks, two slices of red pepper, and a spoonful of rice. She couldn't eat all of that ... she wasn't that hungry ... it was too much. Stefanie began to count the grains of rice, moving them slowly around her plate. There were more than the night before. She scraped a thimbleful to the side of the plate. The fatty edges of the chicken cubes joined the rice, along with a burnt piece of red pepper and a hard morsel of asparagus. This was the untouchable pile—just enough so that she felt certain she was skimping, but not so much that her mother would be suspicious. They didn't make a fuss unless she was obviously restricting. It was a matter of choosing their battles, as Dr. Adler had once put it. As long as she made it look like she was eating, she was basically home free. What could they do? She was supposed to eat more every day, and she would tell Dr. Adler that she was. Who could contradict her? Her parents didn't know what she had been eating. She cut the rest of the food into squares as her parents began to eat. After two glasses of water and a calcium pill, she was finally ready to begin eating. Her father was nearly ready for more, and her mother was watching as Stefanie reached for more water, as she tore off more chicken than fat and moved it to the side of the plate, as she cut her food into precise pieces and finally chose which item to eat first. They had each been cast in specific roles. She was the problem child. Her mother was the policeman. Her father was the bystander. This was the nightly routine.

She wasn't allowed to throw up anymore—not that it had ever been acceptable—but her parents hadn't known before. Now, when she pushed back her chair from the table, four eyes swiveled to watch. They didn't trust her anymore, so she couldn't just sneak off. They would follow; they would waylay her with questions: "How was your day? How was school? Therapy? How did the math test go? Did you see Julia or Annabel or Laura?"

"Just a day ... OK ... the usual ... average ... no, no, no ..." So many questions that she would never make it to the bathroom in time, anyway. Twenty minutes was a small window for success.

She lived by this time frame; someone at school had once told her that after twenty minutes, purging could accomplish nothing. And it wasn't worth it. Her parents knew to watch for the red indentations on her index and middle fingers. They knew to question her on the nights when she allowed herself more than her usual meager portions, correctly assuming that she planned to purge away the guilt later. They had learned some of the tricks of the trade; they were on to the shortcuts of the game.

Two hours later, after she'd kissed them both goodnight and had retreated to her purple bedroom, in the dark, behind her closed door, she resumed her sit-ups and leg lifts. She moved stealthily toward her evening's goal like a tiger tracking a kill until her muscles ached and she could barely get up off the floor. And down the hallway, her parents remained blissfully unaware of it all. The intervention was working, they comforted themselves. They had bought the best care available, and she was eating again. They had seen it with their own eyes. But Stefanie was having none of it. She hadn't admitted defeat; she had only changed her strategy.

There were lines across her cheeks in the pattern of the wooden floor. Stefanie tried to move her neck and winced in pain. Her left side ached where her hip bones had suffered the weight of her body without the cushioning softness of a mattress underneath. Without looking at the clock, she knew that it was morning. She was awake now.

Vaguely, Stefanie remembered. It had been during the final repetition of leg lifts when she had needed to stop. But she couldn't. Not yet, not now, not after so much work. She wouldn't stop, not until she was finally happy. So she had kept going, pushing through that final set, though her body protested and her head had started to spin. And she'd finished, finally, then added an extra two lifts to compensate for her sluggishness. But then she hadn't been able to move. Even with the help of her arms, she couldn't sit up. Her eyes had rolled back in her head. It had hurt to right them. It had been a struggle. The room twisted and turned, an amusement park ride when you've already had enough. Her computer desk was spinning. Her book shelves were upside down. The world was not at all what it should have been.

She wouldn't make it into bed that night. It had looked so far away. Now, in the clarity brought by morning, Stefanie could see that she was only two feet from the edge of her mattress, but that had seemed impassable the night before. So she had slept on the floor.

She listened for her mother's footsteps in the hallway, uncertain of the time. She needed to get up. She needed to get moving and dress for school. She needed to continue through the day as if nothing had happened. She had only been tired. Once again she repeated the mantra that she had said seeing Dr. Grant: Nothing is wrong.

But something was. Last night had been different. Now, thinking about it, Stefanie chewed on her lip and took a deep breath to calm her pounding heart. She still felt shaky. That had never happened to her before; she had always felt in control of her body.

She rubbed her cheeks vigorously to send some color into them and started toward the kitchen for breakfast—one handful of Honey Nut Cheerios. She was sixteen years old, still a child. She was immortal; she couldn't die. Nothing was wrong, not like her parents and the doctors and her friends all thought. But the dull ache in her hip reminded her of where she had spent the night. Stepping out minutes later into the February chill, she was just a little scared.

~ 17 ~

The paper crinkled as she eased herself back up onto the exam chair. She shivered, grateful that she had been allowed to change out of the thin purple gown. Dr. Adler's pen jumped across the page, writing down the newest number: her present weight. Stefanie scanned the sheet over her doctor's shoulder. She wouldn't be one of the nine after all. The balances of the scale had come to rest at the same notches as the week before. She hadn't lost even an ounce.

"OK, Stefanie." Dr. Adler's face was impassive. "You didn't lose this week. That's good. But you didn't gain either. You need to make the numbers move, and you need to do it now—by next time. You must gain weight."

Stefanie looked away, embarrassed because, in her own mind, this number signaled a failure. She didn't want to gain weight. She didn't want to stay the same. She wanted to be thinner. She wasn't, so she had failed. Stefanie clenched her teeth. "I'm doing what you said. I'm eating more."

"You must put on some weight by the next time. It's non-negotiable. Any questions?" Stefanie shook her head, and the doctor stepped to the door. "Mrs. Webber, you may come in now."

They stood there discussing her as if she weren't in the room. Dr. Adler was offering advice about eating what foods and when: try ice cream or an Ensure or cranberry juice, and Madeline Webber's mind was absorbing it all to remember for later. It was ammunition for her mother to use against her. Even her parents claimed to be fighting the so-called eating disorder. Dr. Adler, Dr. Grant, Dr. Mollani, her mother, her father, Ms. Olson, her friends … all versus Stefanie. It wasn't fair. The sides weren't equally matched.

But it was always the same way. Dr. Adler would perch on the edge of the swivel chair and speak to Stefanie, though what was said, only Madeline Webber heard. Stefanie would sit on the raised exam chair and watch her mother's face for a reaction; she rarely cared about Dr. Adler's "advice."

"I'm concerned that the present treatment is proving ineffective, and I think perhaps that inpatient hospitalization may be required. In a hospital setting, Stefanie, you will benefit from added support and highly regimented meals. What I mean by that is three meals a day and additional liquid supplements."

Stefanie's fists and tight lips betrayed her determination. She was already eating. Already, she was eating too much. She wouldn't eat more at home, and she wouldn't eat more at any hospital. Why did they think that anything would be different?

"And if you don't eat what they give you, they'll put a tube in your throat or in your nose and feed you the calories that way. It's not fun. So you'd do better to eat what you need to, and you'd save yourself a lot of trouble if you could do it outside of a hospital." Dr. Adler tried to make eye contact, but Stefanie stared at the wall behind Dr. Alder's head; she wouldn't give her doctor the satisfaction of looking into her eyes.

"Stefanie, this is not a failure on your part." Dr. Adler played with the gold band on her ring finger, twisting it around. "It only means this disease is too hard for you to fight." She lowered her hands to her sides, as if suddenly self-conscious, and instead picked up her clipboard to make notes on what she was saying. "It only means that you need more support than we can give you. It's been a month now, and you weigh less than when you walked into my office. I cannot just continue to write down your ever-decreasing weight every week and give you a pep talk. Hospitalization is required in some cases. This is only to help you overcome an illness, the same way that hospitalization would be necessary if you were having an operation."

Meaningless words, meaningless words, Stefanie was sing-songing to herself. Didn't Dr. Adler say these same things to girls before her?

It was all just a routine. Dr. Adler didn't really care what happened to her. Stefanie was only another one of the patients. And how many of them had actually been admitted? Besides, she was different. The other girls had starved themselves down to seventy pounds. Stefanie looked back at the scale. She was no fool. She had weighed in today at just over one hundred—a regular whale. She didn't have a problem. OK, so maybe she had carried the diet a little far, had done things a little too quickly. But hospitalization was completely unnecessary. She would gain the weight when she wanted to. The hospital would look at her and turn her away. "Come back when you're seventy-five pounds, little girl. We don't treat fat girls like you." She didn't fit hospital criteria, and she didn't look like the girls in the psychology textbook, either.

"… until next week. If you haven't shown me that you can gain weight at that point, then I'll have no choice but to admit you to a hospital."

Stefanie pulled at a hangnail on her left ring finger and shifted her jaw from side to side. "I'm eating what you told me to. It's not my fault that I'm not gaining weight."

She looked to her mother for support but met only a lifeless stare. Her mother was not going to agree with her; it was written in the lines of her face. Why? Why couldn't her mother come to the rescue now? Why couldn't she tell Dr. Adler that the hospital wasn't the right plan, that it wasn't going to fix anything, that it wasn't going to help? But she wouldn't. Madeline Webber had changed over the past month. She cried behind her closed door at night, and she watched her daughter when she slept sometimes. Dr. Adler's ultimatum had not been a shock. It was like they had discussed it, like they were double-teaming her, ganging up on her. Stefanie could have screamed out at the injustice of it. She wished she could claw the doctor's pseudo smile right off her face.

"I'd suggest drinking Ensure to help you increase your calories. It's the easiest way."

Stefanie shook her head. No high-calorie milkshakes. No supplements, no added calories. No way, no way. She wasn't drinking those cans of Ensure that had mysteriously appeared in the refrigerator a few weeks back. Not if she wouldn't even take calories from real food. She was prepared to be adamant, insolent even.

"But you can eat anything you want, really. Cookies, doughnuts, candy, ice cream. I've known people who have eaten a pint of Häagen Dazs every night just to maintain their weights."

She could eat anything that she wanted. Anything that Stefanie and Laura had placed on the forbidden list weeks ago was now allowed—encouraged, even. She was supposed to eat junk food. A kind of breathy laugh was filling her body. She wanted to smile, to laugh out loud. She felt giddy. The prospect of such freedom seemed almost too much to handle. *Anything.* That sounded better than Ensure. And she might even consider ice cream.

– 18 –

The supermarket. It was Stefanie's paradise—her Mecca. It wasn't like the school cafeteria, where if you stopped to look at what the salad bar had to offer before making a decision you held up the line, and where people stared at the amount of food on your tray. Here she was just the average shopper, trying to decide what to buy. No one had to know that she didn't actually plan to make a purchase. Aisle upon aisle of food: frozen, dairy, meat, candy, cereal, cake mixes, cookies, potato chips, fruit, vegetables, canned food, cheese, sauces and dressings, drinks, ice cream. Since she'd begun her diet, she'd discovered the joys of wandering the aisles methodically, one after the other. She could imagine herself biting into an orange and having the juices fill her mouth; the sweetness of the candy; the crunchiness of the cereal and granolas; the creaminess of the yogurts; the saltiness of the hams, salamis, and tortilla chips. If she looked but didn't touch, if she fantasized but didn't act, then everything would be OK.

She would hum the bones song quietly to herself to keep strong. That was the trick. Then she wouldn't actually need to eat any of the food that she saw. She could pretend. And pretending was almost as good, nearly as satisfying, and certainly a lot safer.

Her mother had stopped beside the ice cream freezer. Aisle three. To the right were the cake batters; to the left were the sprinkles and toppings for sundaes. In front of them, a multitude of flavors, many more than Stefanie remembered. Chunky Monkey, Phish Food, Mint Chocolate Cookie, Cherry Garcia, Everything But The …, Half Baked, Chubby Hubby. Mentally, Stefanie calculated the number of calories in a serving of each flavor. Too many … too many … too many … too much fat. Anything above twenty calories was too many, so which could she pick? Her mother was waiting for her to decide. Apple Crumble, Peanut Butter Cup, Limited Edition: Festivus, Southern Pecan Pie, Brownie Lover's Delight, Cookie Dough, Raspberry Sorbet …

Raspberry sorbet …

Sorbet was healthier than ice cream …

Stefanie reached for the red container, but her mother redirected her hand. "Not sorbet. Dr. Adler said ice cream. We're not going to buy sorbet."

Stefanie grimaced. There would be no escaping. She was stuck swearing to herself that she would eat only the tiniest portion. Stefanie wrapped her hand around a frosty container of Cookies and Cream. It seemed safe enough, and she'd always liked Oreos, anyway.

They got in line at the cash register. The cashier swiped the credit card and handed the plastic bag to Stefanie. Ice cream had been her favorite dessert, and she hadn't had it in months, but now, she didn't even want it. As they started home, the hard container knocked against Stefanie's legs, and she muttered a silent prayer, asking for the strength to avoid eating the ice cream. She'd give the faith thing another chance. Maybe God would help her continue to lose weight if she asked again. Or maybe her mother would forget about Dr. Adler's stern instructions. Maybe the ice cream would be forgotten. Stefanie would know what she was supposed to do, but, without a reminder, she wouldn't eat the prescribed serving. She wouldn't have to.

~ 19 ~

No one forgot.

A generously sized ceramic bowl was placed in front of her on the kitchen table, ice cream obscuring its yellow bottom as the white substance slowly melted. Stefanie bit her tongue trying to quell the hunger pains that besieged her stomach. That absolute creaminess ... the chocolate cookies ... the slightest crunch mixed with smoothness. The contrasting tastes would mingle on her tongue and leisurely proceed down her throat, chilling her esophagus along the way.

It all sounded so good. In theory. In reality, she couldn't eat that ice cream. She just couldn't. After all her hard work, she wasn't about to cave in now, no matter how they fought her, wished for her to fail. That night at dinner, her parents had threatened her again with the hospital, with tubes down her nose or in her throat, with a loss of freedom, with a summer spent in a psychiatric facility. She tried to block them out. None of those promised events would ever happen. And she wouldn't let them see her fail. But that was what they wanted. Now two pairs of eyes looked back at her with concern. They were desperate for her to eat only one spoonful, to make some sign of progress, to somehow demonstrate that she could, and would, eat.

In her hand the spoon felt heavy, perhaps even too heavy to lift to her mouth. Stefanie's eyes swelled with tears. This wasn't fair; none of this was fair. Didn't they get it? The spoon traced shapes through the surface of the ice cream. She picked out a piece of chocolate cookie and held it in the spoon. She laughed to herself; it seemed that suddenly everything was a joke. She thought of her parents, frantic with worry. They loved her, but that just wasn't enough anymore.

"You're only hurting yourself, Stefanie. Just try to eat. Or else we'll do it; we'll send you to the hospital. You won't leave us any choice."

Her mother gently placed her utensils on her plate—the perfect picture of a lady. "You must know that we side with Dr. Adler on this; what she says goes."

Her father picked up the baton now. They made a pathetic tag team. "We can't prevent it, and we won't, if the time comes for you to be admitted to a program." Her father had taken to speaking in these generic terms, without feeling, without emotion. Just as though he was on the verge of closing another business deal.

Nothing was funny now. Stefanie's salty tears mixed with the sugar from the ice cream. She hated these talks with her dad. Would he ever be able to understand how she felt? Would he ever be able to relate on a less superficial level? It wasn't likely.

Deep breath. She knew that her parents would lock her up if Dr. Adler gave the command. They had already said that they wouldn't sit by and watch her kill herself. So, she had to do it. Slowly, the spoon made its way up to her mouth, and she tasted the sweetness and the creaminess. Even the chill of the ice cream seemed to have a taste, a good one. Stefanie caught herself about to smile—it tasted good!—and began to cry instead. Damn it, damn it, damn it all. She didn't want to enjoy this. She couldn't enjoy this. If she did, she might not be able to give it up again. And she had to give it up.

With each mouthful, she cried harder. Her parents didn't speak; they only stared at the spectacle of their daughter, who they barely recognized now, slumped over her bowl of ice cream mush, a little girl throwing a tantrum they couldn't quiet.

She hated them. She hated Dr. Adler. She hated Dr. Mollani. She hated Annabel, Laura, and even Julia. She hated the way the skin on her stomach was pinchable and the way it folded if she leaned over far enough. She hated the food that was in front of her, and she hated that they were taking away her chance at happiness. She hated the pigeons that cooed outside the window in the early morning, waking her with their mating harmonies. She hated the sun and the moon and the clouds. She hated the world.

The last bite of ice cream. Two hundred and fifty extra calories. She didn't want to stay inside her skin. The flesh was tightening around her body, around her throat, and strangling her. It pulled tighter, and Stefanie wondered if she might burst. She wanted to scream, to run through the apartment, to break things. Why were they doing this to her?

Tears cascaded down her cheeks into her empty bowl. Cautiously she ran her hand along the outer rim, picking up the excess vanilla with her fingers. She didn't want anyone to know that it hadn't been so bad, really. In fact, she'd enjoyed it as much as she'd ever enjoyed anything else, except stepping on the scale after eating stringently all week.

Her father smiled. It was the type of smile that screamed: *I'm going to say this because I read that it's the right thing to do.* There had been a lot of those smiles lately, coupled with a significant number of books on his bedside table. "Honey, I just want to tell you that we're proud of you." Uh-oh. He was reading from the script again. "We know how hard this disorder is to fight."

For weeks now, after she'd said her goodnights only to begin her bedroom guerilla war of crunches and leg lifts, her parents were reading *What to Do When Your Child Has an Eating Disorder, Anatomy of Anorexia, The Secret Language of Eating Disorders.* It was all a lot of bullshit.

The enjoyment was forgotten. She didn't want to hear what he had to say. She didn't want them reciting prefabricated homilies out of books. They seemed to have forgotten that she'd read the books, too, long before they had even had the sense to do the reading or ask questions. "Praise your daughter and tell her that you recognize what a difficult time this is for her." She could see the words so clearly on the page. "Encourage her with praise. Let her know that you support her." That was what they all said. Why did they just throw the stuff back at her without even varying the wording? They couldn't possibly be proud. And they couldn't possibly understand. They could never understand.

It would have been better left unsaid. But no, her father used those iron-on words with that forced smile and brought her back to the reality of a harsh white kitchen and an empty bowl of ice cream. Yes, the momentary enjoyment was gone.

"Stop. Don't talk." The words flew across the table and landed hard, deep within her father. She could see the pain on his face, but she couldn't stop. She found herself screeching. "You don't know what you're saying. You don't understand. You're not me." The sound of her hysterical voice hurt even her own ears, but it was too late to stop now. Her hands flew to her burning, crimson cheeks, and she pulled at the hair on her head. "Don't talk to me like I'm a case in a textbook. I'm not. Just because you read something doesn't mean that it applies to me. I'm going to my room."

She hiccupped once through her tears and tried to draw in a deep breath. Instead she ended up coughing—and feeling bad. Her father hadn't deserved that. She knew she'd overreacted. She knew he was only trying to help. But she wanted his help to be good enough, and it just wasn't. She wanted him to wrap her in his arms and tell her that she would always be thin—that she always had been. She wanted him to call her Skinny-ma-link again and complain that her butt was too bony when she sat on his lap. She wanted him to save her from herself. She wanted him to step down off his pedestal and become emotional. She wanted so much from this man. She wanted him to just read her mind. But at the same time, she just wanted him to leave her alone—forever.

And so for five out of seven days, Stefanie ate the ice cream. The other two, she said she was tired and went to bed early. She had put off eating the ice cream until late at night many times, but each time she had been compelled to give in to her parents, who were watching her like goddamn hall monitors. It was a nightly battle between wanting to please her parents and wanting to please herself.

With each new bowl of ice cream, Stefanie pleaded to be exempt from the "dessert torture," as she had taken to calling it. She argued that she would choke on the food, that she was physically unable to swallow. She claimed that if she took one more bite, she would throwup. She demanded to know why her parents hated her so much, why they were making her go through all this. She tossed guilt and blame around as if they were bouncy balls, and she did her best to make her parents feel sorry. They deserved to feel as bad as she did. She cried harder and louder and grew more cautious about portions. She estimated which part would have more calories—the chocolate cookies or the vanilla ice cream—then she tried to sway the proportioning by digging through the container, dishing out only what she was willing to eat. Her parents knew all about the tricks she was using. They had just about given up. Stefanie wasn't sure if this was what she really wanted. She wanted someone to believe in her sometimes. But it didn't matter. They no longer reminded her of the possibility of the hospital. They no longer begged her to eat. All three of them knew that those words hung silently in the air, palpable, menacing, stifling. But no one wanted to give them a voice anymore. Tuesday was looming, under a week away now. Then they would all know what was to happen. There was no use hashing and rehashing what was out of their control. So the words just stuck in their throats like cotton balls, choking them, tormenting them, making even light conversation nearly impossible. Their exchanges were reduced to stilted pleasantries and polite civilities. Even her parents' relationship—usually so grounded and complementary— floundered under the strain. They had small fights now over silly things like the set of silverware used at dinnertime. And by the time they fell into bed at the end of the day, there was no energy left to talk. Stefanie was foremost on their minds, and there was no time left to dedicate to their relationship.

Every meal was a showdown.

"Here's your food ..."

"Don't want it ... Not hungry." She sat in her usual chair at the kitchen table, pulled her knees up to her chest, and wrapped her arms around her legs. Her mouth was set in a straight line, and she didn't make eye contact with anyone. She wouldn't give them the satisfaction of seeing her squirm.

She could sense, without even looking, that her mother had taken a deep breath and steeled herself for the battle. The chicken Parmesan—the highest calorie meal possible, Stefanie noted angrily—sat on the table and gradually grew cold and rubbery. When she couldn't resist anymore, Stefanie took a bite. She chewed slowly and then put down her fork. "I'm done. Thanks." Her mono-tone voice was the horn that began the war.

"You have to eat more than that."

"No." She looked at her father to see what his reaction would be. He hadn't spoken yet, and she rejoiced momentarily. Maybe she'd finally trained him not to speak.

"If you're not going to eat, then you can go straight to bed. You're not well enough to be out of your room. No school tomorrow. You're a liability to them, and they won't have you unless you're eating. What if you fainted on the stairs?" She picked up the plate and headed for the sink. "Go ahead, Stefanie. Get to bed."

"Shut the fuck up!" The hysterical note in her voice surfaced quickly. "Stop it! Fine. I'll eat it. Give me back my plate. I'll eat it. I'll eat it. But I hate you."

Madeline Webber bristled at the pure abhorrence in her daughter's voice. Where had they gone wrong? What could she and Stefanie's father have done differently? Their daughter had become a monster ruled by unfathomable demands that she continue to lose weight. For a moment, she didn't like her daughter anymore. Why was she doing this to them? And why was her husband so ineffectual? Why was everything so new and strange? Stefanie had always been such a good little girl; now she seemed possessed by the devil. She wanted to shake her daughter—make her realize what she was doing to herself, make her eat the stupid chicken Parmesan, make her eat the ice cream, make her give up the stupid dieting game in which she'd gotten tangled. But she couldn't do any of these things. They wouldn't do any good. Instead, she slid Stefanie's plate back across the table. The force of her frustration went into the plate, and Stefanie had to catch it before it tumbled over the edge.

"Eat on your own. I'm finished."

Stefanie watched her mother disappear into another part of the apartment and looked at her father. His attention had shifted back to the television and the stock charts that sat in front of him on the table.

* * *

Her bed shook as her small body was rocked by sobs that she just couldn't stop. She had eaten half the dinner. Then she had been full and couldn't stand anymore. All she could do was cry. So she had cried long and hard. Cried until she was too tired to continue, and then the tears gradually slowed. In the next room she could hear the television and wondered what her mother was watching. If she'd been able to see through walls, she would have known that the television was only background noise; her mother, too, had been crying.

She heard the door to her bedroom creak, but she didn't move to see who it was. But she could smell lily of the valley. As her mattress sunk down under the weight of her mother and a hand landed on her shoulder, Stefanie tensed. She and her mother were inexplicably tied to each other by mutual exhaustion, despair, and uncertainty. The war had reached a stalemate. She'd always loved having her back rubbed. She'd delighted in her mother's hugs long after her peers had recoiled from their own parents' touch. The soft smell of fabric softener that pervaded her mother's comforting sweaters still made her want to bury to face in her mother's arms. But she couldn't accept it. She didn't deserve it. She had been a bad daughter.

"Please, Mom, just let me die. Please, I can't do this anymore. I can't get through another day. Just let me be. Just let me disappear. Let me die."

"Stefanie." Her mother's words were low but firm as she sat on the bed next to her emaciated daughter. "We know how hard this is for you. We know that you struggle. And we love you. We will always love you. But we will not let you die. I will not watch my only daughter starve to death. We are going to help you."

"No. Don't send me away. I don't want to go to the hospital. I don't want help. I don't need help. I don't want to eat anymore. I just want to die."

Her mother's eyes filled with tears, and her face showed the pain that Stefanie's words had caused. "We're going to do whatever it takes. We've told you this before. We'll put you in the hospital if necessary. But that's only because we love you. I want my happy Stefanie back."

Her mother didn't get it.

"Help me, please, help me!" In her frustration and anger, she was screaming nonsense now. Her parents couldn't help her; she didn't even know what kind of help she wanted. "Let me out of my skin. I'm going to burst." Tears choked her and garbled the sound of her words. "Why can't you just let me do what I want? Just let me not eat. The hospital isn't going to help. I'm just going to starve again when I get out. You'll be throwing your money away, and me with it."

She'd never really been hysterical before, but those nights she came close, exhausted from fighting. She was tired of ice cream. She was tired of being a troublesome child. She was tired of causing problems. She was tired of disappointing them. She was tired of disappointing herself. She was tired of giving in. And she was tired of starving, but she was not ready or able to just give it up.

~ 20 ~

The dull sound of her foot tapping against the wood floors kept up to the rhythm of her heartbeat. Her mother sat to her right; her father across the room. Why had they both come? There was no reason for them both to have come. Her father should be at work, not sitting in a wooden chair in a doctor's office—her doctor's office. He'd never come before, why should he start now? Stefanie wanted him to go home. This was her domain. They had a ritual—her mother, Dr. Adler, and she. She knew what to expect when it was just the three of them: weigh-in, discussion, conference. Within forty-five minutes they were in, out, and back in the apartment. She felt a slight prick of guilt. Why didn't she want him there? There had been a time when she couldn't get enough of his company—their Saturday morning breakfast dates, the evenings when she used to curl up with her head on his shoulder to watch the Yankees or the *Friends* reruns her mother refused to watch, having seen them so many times. They laughed together at all the same parts, deep and loud, until tears came to her father's eyes. And she had always felt important while "helping" him with his evening work. They looked through stock charts together, and she exclaimed over the companies whose prices had risen steadily in the recent months. She asked what companies he had bought recently and told him what she thought of each one in her own naïve, pre-adolescent way. While he valued companies for their price per share or their earnings estimates, she looked at it from a consumer perspective. "No, I don't like McDonald's anymore. Burger King has better fries." He might not always have taken her advice, but he always listened to it. And he always explained what he did—how he chose, what he was looking for—teaching her to do math that she wouldn't see for another four years. She knew more about call options at the age of twelve than most grownups. He loved her; she knew that. But now, at the sight of him in her territory, she felt enraged. She didn't want anything to be different. The same was good; the same was safe; she knew what to expect from the same.

She kicked again at her mother's seat and wished that they weren't sitting there, waiting to be seen. It was Tuesday. *The* Tuesday. Judgment Day.

"Come with me." Dr. Adler's characteristic refrain startled Stefanie, and she momentarily stopped her tapping foot.

She wouldn't smile. She wouldn't talk. She would go in there; step on that scale. She would do what they asked and no more. They would see that she hadn't lost weight, and she would go home. There would be no hospital.

Shoes. Sweatshirt. Pants. Shirt. She wrapped the exam gown around herself, leaving it loose enough to mask the ribs that stuck out haphazardly from her sides. This was the so-called moment of truth, and Stefanie shuddered. Water was dripping from the faucet, and she leaned forward to turn it off. She had heard of girls who drank water to fabricate the feeling of satiety. That was one way to avoid eating; she'd tried it once, and it had worked well. But she couldn't stand the sight of her distended tummy, even if she knew it was just water-weight. And she had heard of girls who "water-loaded" just before weigh-ins, adding instantaneous, phony weight. There were cups by the sink; maybe there was still time to try it— just that added ounce of insurance. The flow of water increased with each slow turn of the knob but then, abruptly it stopped. There were girls that did those things, but those were the really bad ones—the ones that persisted in the game for years and never recognized there was a problem. It would be stupid for her to try it. She didn't need the insurance. She'd been eating ice cream all week; she didn't need to add any more weight. Dr. Adler was waiting just beyond the bathroom door. She stepped into the room and forgot the dripping faucet with the paper cups; the hospital wasn't even a remote possibility. She was confident.

The balances slid past the 75-pound mark and came to rest at 110—too high. Then 107—too high; 105—too high; 101—almost; 100—too low; 100.5. Dr. Adler took her hands off the balances and waited for the needle to stabilize. Stefanie tried hard not to fidget—that had been her weight the week before also.

"One hundred point five." Dr. Adler wrote the number in her chart. "You didn't gain any weight this week, Stefanie. It's just too hard for you to do. I can see that. Inpatient hospitalization is going to be necessary. There is a bed for you at the hospital downtown, the Barrett Institute. It's been reserved, and they are expecting you. I'm going to call your parents in and tell them my recommendation."

What? It was so sudden. Stefanie felt the room constricting, tightening around her body as if she were in the grasp of a venomous snake. Her hands had turned cold and clammy, and she tried to wipe them dry with the robe. She was simultaneously burning up and freezing. Suffocating—someone was pushing down on her shoulders from above. She couldn't breathe. This had to be a joke.

"Any questions for me first?" Dr. Adler paused on her way to the door.

She was serious?

Sure, she had questions, but she didn't want Dr. Adler to hear that crack in her voice. She didn't want Dr. Adler to sense her agitation. Why was this happening to her? What was the hospital going to be like? She'd be locked up with psychopaths and tormented; how would she survive? Was she really a mental case? Images from *Girl, Interrupted* flashed through her mind: straitjackets, wild eyes, insane people. How long would she have to stay? What would they do to her? How much weight was she going to have to gain? Would her parents be allowed to visit? Would she be in a room by herself, with no one to talk to? Would she start talking to herself? Would this force her to recover? Would she leave looking haggard, drained, and exhausted, with blood-shot eyes that held only a vacant look? There were lots of questions that she wished she could ask, but she felt mute, incapable of forming words. All she could do was shake her head.

Her body began to tremble, and she heard a voice she didn't recognize—it sounded like a trapped animal. It was hers. She was becoming hysterical, more hysterical than she had been during those nights of ice cream torture. She was pleading with them for another chance, but no one was listening. Why wouldn't they listen? Didn't they care that she could eat on her own? She'd been eating more these past couple of weeks—maybe not enough, but more. Why couldn't they see that? She still had school to attend. She might flunk out or be held back. And then what? Did they think the Ivy League would have her then? Didn't they care that the hospital wouldn't be able to help her? Couldn't they see that there was actual physical pain inside her heart at the thought of being sent away? Didn't they care that she didn't need help, that she wasn't really hurting herself? Didn't they care that they were taking away her chance of being happy?

"It's time now. We want Stefanie to realize this is not a failure on her part, but it's time now."

Dr. Adler had made a recommendation, and they were going to follow it. It was that surprisingly simple. It was what they had always told her would happen. A doctor's word was a doctor's word, and that made it infallible.

Four minutes later, cold air blew past Stefanie's ears as she bolted from that stuffy, overcrowded, hateful doctor's office and ran down the long East Side block. She was running away. She didn't know where she was going, but she couldn't stay where she was. She would lose everything.

"The shinbone's connected to the knee bone, the knee bone's connected to the thighbone, the thighbone's connected to the hip bone ..."

"I won't go. I won't go. I can't go. I can't go." Stefanie chanted the words to herself even as that same old chorus echoed through her head. No. She wouldn't go; how could they make her? She would sooner die than be sent away. The fear and the anxiety were gone.

She wasn't scared, and she wasn't confused; she knew what she wanted. She was only angry.

Her breath was coming in short gasps now. She hadn't run this much in a long time, and a yanking pain in her side told her that she would need to stop soon. But she couldn't. If she stopped she would be giving in—her mother was gaining on her, running down the block after her ... trying to catch up ... trying to stop her.

The corner of Park Avenue, red light. Stefanie stopped running. The cars sped past her, but just beyond their blur she could see her apartment building. It was like the recurring nightmare that she'd had as a young child: she was running for safety, but couldn't quite get there. In her dream, she was always shot, stabbed, or caught just before she reached her doorman. Should she keep going and cross the street now? She could almost imagine the scene: car horns would screech, taxis would swerve toward the corners, amblers would run for the shelter of apartment buildings. "Hello, operator, 911 please. There's been a car accident." She could hear the emergency phone call. But maybe it would be too late. Maybe God would save her— claim her back and cradle her in the clouds of heaven. Would it hurt?

She had waited too long. The traffic light hadn't changed to "walk" yet, and her mother was standing on the corner next to her. Her father was still back at Dr. Adler's office, paying the bill, but her mother had followed behind her. It was too late to run for it. Her mom would grab her. Finally, the light turned green, the cars stopped moving, and Stefanie's feet resumed their beat against the concrete. She hadn't quite been caught. Her mother hadn't tackled her yet; she was still a few steps in front of her pursuer.

Into the building, through the lobby, past a woman with a small dog, walking in the opposite direction, into the elevator with Freddy—up, up, up. Where was she going? What did she think she could do? Her mother was following her, going through the same motions that she had gone through only moments earlier. Running for the elevator, panting, pressing the button furiously, the edges of her mouth strained into a kind of look that Stefanie had never before seen. Her mother was coming for her, but Stefanie didn't think about the future. She didn't plan for when her mother would invariably corner her in the back of the apartment—nowhere to hide, nowhere safe, nowhere to get away. She couldn't think about logistics. She couldn't see through the blanket of tears that clouded her vision. She couldn't think. She couldn't plan. She could only concentrate on getting away. It didn't matter how.

The familiar bathroom tiles were still cold, and Stefanie threw herself onto the floor, waiting for the chill to seep into her bones, waiting for the cramp in her side to go away, waiting for the tears to subside. She'd run all the way home—more than she'd run in months—and her body was protesting.

Madeline Webber didn't knock. She just opened the door and walked in. Stefanie screamed for her to get out, but her mother stood her ground. She sat down on the tile with her and tried to soothe her.

Stefanie cut her mother off. "I won't go. You can't make me. It's not going to help me. I'd rather die. Just let me die. Let me do what I want to do. I can't get better until I want to get better, and I'm not ready yet. You promised you would give me a chance. Give me one more week. How much damage can I do in a week? I've been eating. I won't go. You can't make me."

Stefanie gulped for air, and her words slurred together. She slapped the tile floor as though by beating it she could make her parents conform to her will. "How could you let this happen? How could you agree to send me to the hospital? You never had to listen to Dr. Adler. You could have said, 'No, I'm her mother. Stefanie does not need the hospital.' You promised me one more week to get myself together. You promised. What happened to that? You lied to me. You lied."

Her mother finally spoke. "This is a tough battle. But, sweetheart, we're proud of you no matter what happens. And we'll stand beside you. We always will—"

Those, stupid, stupid textbook words!

Where had *he* come from? Stefanie covered her ears and tried to kick the bathroom door shut as her father now tried to enter the tight little room. "You don't know what you're talking about!" she lashed out at them both. "You never have! You only talk to me with those stupid textbook words! Don't you think I know? God! What's the matter with you? Try showing emotion for once! I don't want you here. Get out! Get out, now!"

Her father took another step closer, and Stefanie shrieked, "No! Get him out!" She struggled to hide behind her mother's body.

He left the room.

Stefanie continued to beg. "They didn't tell me … they didn't warn me. I never understood. I don't have to go because I never got a chance. I deserved a warning. They weren't serious. Why is this happening?"

As Stefanie screamed and writhed on the floor, Madeline Webber tried to protect her daughter's skull from bouncing off the tiles. She knew her mother had never seen her like this before and didn't know what to do. Stefanie knew she was scaring her mother, but she didn't care. Her mother wasn't helping. Why couldn't she just do something? It didn't matter if she was scaring her mother. Her mother deserved it.

"I won't go. I won't go. It's not fair. I just want to die."

A man's voice joined the high-pitched fray, saying, "Stefanie, get yourself together. We have to go now; they're expecting you at the hospital. This is *not* an option. We will not oppose Dr. Adler's recommendation. We can't ignore her; she is the doctor. She is a trained professional." Her father had joined them in the bathroom again.

"I'm not going." Stefanie's voice rose in an emotional crescendo, her voice reached its highest possible pitch. "Leave me alone." She closed her eyes, attempting to block out the images of her parents, hoping they would be gone when she looked around again. They weren't.

The room spun. Her heart's rapid palpitations scared her. It wasn't supposed to beat that quickly. She couldn't breathe. A heart attack?

Her temples throbbed with the noise of her own sobs echoing off the white and blue tiles. She couldn't speak; frustration and anguish engulfed her body. Somehow, she had expected to get away with it. When she couldn't, she thought she could run away from it, and, when that failed, she thought she could talk her way out of it. But now, fatigued, she could only cry, trying to make them understand.

"It's going to be OK. Take some deep breaths." Her mother's long, soft arms slid around her thin body, and Stefanie relaxed into the embrace—spent, but still breathing heavily.

She hoped that it was over. She almost believed that it would be over. Maybe they finally understood. Maybe they were finally going to give in.

"Stefanie, it's time to go. Wash your face and come with us now; or we're going to have to call an ambulance or carry you to the car. Take your pick."

Her mother's voice was firm; her parents hadn't changed their minds. Stefanie pulled away but didn't have the energy to resist anymore. An ambulance? Physically transporting her to the car? Would they take her bound and gagged? Nothing she could say would make a difference.

"Five minutes. Just five more minutes." She was desperate.

All of a sudden, the hospital had become very real.

- 21 -

The blue plastic bracelet read: *Stefanie Webber—admitted March 13, 2001.*

Cold metallic discs had been connected to her chest moments before. An electrocardiogram, they'd called it. She'd watched the machine spit out data in series of lines that she couldn't read. It was still light outside, but getting darker. Stefanie played with the buttons on her Nike digital watch and noted that it was four o'clock. School had gotten out early, but not that early. The three hours that had passed since she left the school building seemed like they had taken days, weeks maybe. Three hours ago, she had been happily leaving school, going to a doctor's appointment. Ten minutes ago, they had walked through a door labeled Barrett Institute Psychiatric Hospital. It had all happened so quickly.

She had been in the taxi with her parents. Now she was inside a mental hospital. She looked at the directory on the front of the intake desk and noticed that eating disorders weren't the only disorders handled here. Axis I disorders were housed on the second floor, east wing. Axis II disorders were grouped together on the third and fourth floor of Tower Five West. There were other labels: eating disorder unit, drug and alcohol rehabilitation, schizophrenia, mania, depression, teens, seniors. At the end of the hallway, Stefanie caught sight of a nurse holding a patient in a blue and white striped gown firmly by the shoulder, leading her around a corner. To where? She could hear noise at the far end of the hallway and wondered who was there. Doctors? Nurses? Interns? Visitors? Patients? Crazy people?

"Please come with me ..." Some nurses' aid led Stefanie away without a smile and the next time Stefanie realized where she was, she found herself alone in a room. Her parents were back at the desk, signing papers. Were they signing her life away? Would she return only to find that her parents had gotten tired of her and decided to disown their problem child?

A heavyset lady positioned a stethoscope on Stefanie's back, and Stefanie flinched under the touch of the nurse's hands, certain that each finger was feeling the rolls of excess blubber on her torso. The tension of the blood-pressure cuff increased around her upper arm. The nurse murmured something under her breath and made a note on the chart. Stefanie lay on a cold, hard table. The nurse prodded her stomach. Stefanie tried not to cry out in pain as her spine pushed against the metallic surface. Next, she stood with her back against the wall and let them measure her height: five four and a half. She answered the questions they asked slowly, contemplating each response. Could she plead the Fifth Amendment and remain silent?

Age? Sixteen. *Birth date?* December 14, 1985. *Time of first menstruation?* March 11, 1998. *Time of last menstruation?* January 15—this year. *Highest weight?* 128. *Lowest weight?* Just over 100—her present weight. *When did the anorexia first begin?*

This was too much. Who had said that she was anorexic? Since when had it become anyone else's decision? This was America—innocent until proven guilty. But they were sentencing her already. She wanted a trial; she wanted a judge; she wanted a jury.

When did the anorexia first begin? She wouldn't answer—not that it would make any difference.

~ 22 ~

ower 3 North. She would never forget those first five minutes, not as long as she lived.

One, two, three, four … Stefanie counted the curious sets of eyes that stared at her from the plastic couches. Eight, nine, ten.

There were ten of them there. Ten of them. And her.

They had moved from the examination room down an unpleasantly conspicuous, whitewashed hallway to the nurses' station. Stefanie's father stood in the doorway. He was waiting for a short, pudgy nurse to file the paperwork and unlock the door marked 507. *Five-zero-seven*. Home sweet home. The last in a line of identical doors: 501, 503, 505, 507. The only inconsistency was on the other side of the hallway, where there was no door, only an empty space and numbers to right of a door frame that read 500–508. Not very welcoming. At least ten beds were scattered across the floor of this room.

Stefanie had taken her mother's hand as they waited and now grasped it tighter. Without the pressure of her mother's fingers against them, her own hands would be shaking. She didn't want to ever let go. If one finger loosened, she might lose them; her parents might walk out that heavy, locked door at the entrance and not come back. They might forget about her or decide that they liked it better without her home; certainly, daily life would go along more smoothly. The hold on her mother's fingers had become the hold on her life—the harder she squeezed, the more likely she would be to return to her apartment that night. Couldn't they all just walk out of there together? She would eat if they just went home, really she would.

"Don't leave me. Please, don't leave me. Don't do this to me." The words were more whisper than sound.

Madeline Webber squeezed Stefanie's hand and tried to keep her face composed. "It'll be OK." What exactly did OK mean?

There was a strange smell, like an unidentifiable cleaning solution mixed with—and masking—the putrid smell of old socks. It couldn't quite be labeled good or bad. Colorful posters, obviously assembled from cutouts of magazines, displayed chirpy, upbeat messages: "You can do it!" "Beat this thing!" "Food is your friend!" "Eat that cookie!" sporadically broke up the solid white of the walls. There were pictures of average weight but still-beautiful women sprinkled among the posters, women they were supposed to look up to and strive to be. Stefanie wondered who had put up the posters.

Everything was clean and square and unfriendly. No soft edges. Straight lines. It was not like home. Though she saw no heart monitors or respirators, she knew it was a hospital. It felt like a hospital. That bare, minimalist approach to decorating. Nurses wore funny, brightly colored shirts that no one would ever wear outside, at least not in her right mind. The air was suffocating, humid with the tears that had been cried here and the imperviousness of the walls, jaded by all that they had seen. The Barrett Institute's Eating Disorder Unit. She didn't like it.

And there *they* were, sitting there in what was apparently the common area, on plastic couches, the television turned to *Oprah*. If only she could close her eyes and block out the entire scene, but she knew she would look stupid. She had to keep her eyes open.

One of the ten was off to the side, under the watchful eyes of an intimidating black woman. She was small and looked to be about fourteen. It was hard to tell by her prepubescent body. Her hair was wispy and a dull brown, like dirt on a misty day. Her legs were tucked under her, and her eyes were watery. The way she caved in her chest, displaying her protruding collarbones, made her look cold. The girl waved secretively and smiled in Stefanie's direction. The black woman—whether she was a nurse, babysitter, or matron, like in a prison, Stefanie couldn't tell—looked up from her newspaper, and the girl averted her eyes again, looking down at the letter she was writing. For a moment, Stefanie allowed herself to wonder what this girl's story was.

The eyes on the couches continued to watch her. They seemed to be inspecting her, everything from the size of her feet to the length of her hair. Even her parents appeared to be under scrutiny. These girls watched the way she clasped her mother's hand, pushing the emerald-stoned wedding band into her palm as if, through physical pain, she might know that she was still alive. They watched her mother's cold stare, rolling eyes, and long, breathy, exaggerated sighs, betraying her irritation at having to wait. The way her father stood—slightly hunched in a blue cashmere sweater that someone in the office had given him for Christmas; the way he just stood there, waiting to sign the release forms—even his infamous joking had stopped. And the way her own shirt hung on her shoulders and her Hard Tail pants hung on her hips. They were taking it all in, making their assessment. When one girl whispered something to another behind her hand and got a nod in return, Stefanie guessed that they were talking about her. Her eyes followed the line of couches around the room, and she took in the other girls. *That one was so thin. Did she think she needed to lose more weight? That one could be nice—she had a comfy pair of flannel pajama pants with teddy bears on them. The one with the designer jeans and skin-tight shirt was definitely not someone she wanted to hang out with for any prolonged period of time—except maybe to find out where she had gotten the shirt. Laura would like it, and her birthday was coming up. Why was that girl sitting by herself at the end of the hallway? Why was that one clawing at her wrists and bouncing her legs—didn't anyone else notice? Why were they watching her like she was a freak show?* She was thankful when one of the inhabitants of the couch closest to the television finally moved, diverting some of the attention.

A tall girl stood and smiled. Her most striking feature was her long curly hair. Mentally, Stefanie assigned her the name "Curly." On the television set, Oprah talked to two young children, illustrating for viewers how they could help their children through the difficulty of a divorce. Stefanie's mind roamed: Oprah had lost some weight; she looked good, but amethyst purple wasn't really her color. "And we'll be right back …" The camera panned out, and a commercial for Tide detergent came on. Curly began to dance slowly to the music from the commercial, testing the awareness of the woman engrossed in her newspaper. When the woman failed to look up, Curly increased her speed. On a couch nearby, a girl with a sharp jaw and stone-cold gray eyes had a tube in her nose that was connected to a tall IV pole and a bag of creamy liquid. Curly do-si-doed halfway around the pole and returned the opposite way. Stifling a laugh, she stamped her foot like a cowboy and looked in Stefanie's direction.

Madame Newspaper looked up from her reading. The dancing ended with one stern look. Curly took her seat again, and that show was over. The other patients went back to watching the family at the nurses' station. They were still watching her—judging her. She wanted to disappear. She didn't want them looking at her. Turning away casually, out of feigned teenage boredom, she hoped that if she didn't stare at them, they would reciprocate and look away also.

There were names next to the numbers on the doors: Becca, in black box-letters, zigzagging across the paper; Dana, written in neon pink and turquoise bubble letters across yellow construction paper cut in the shape of a cloud; Francesca, written simply but surrounded with cutouts of handbags, lipsticks, and high-heeled shoes; Madeline, written in simple pencil against a white background; Ellie …

The short, pudgy woman who had kept them waiting appeared suddenly from behind the door to the nurses' station, "Hi. My name is Linda. I'm not a nurse, but I'm part of the staff here." She spoke in a detached kind of way, slowly and deliberately, as if she had done this a thousand times before. The sickly girls of Tower 3 North were only part of her routine. Stefanie would have bet that she didn't even notice them anymore, wasn't even horrified. "You can come with me now." She led them in the opposite direction, back toward the now-locked door through which they had entered the unit, "This will be Stefanie's room." Linda turned the key in the lock and opened the door into another hospital room—just like all the others, Stefanie was sure.

The walls were white. There were two beds, two desks, and two dressers—all the light, plywood-colored generic brand that she remembered from sleep-away camp. The bed was unmade, and stamped across the center of the mattress were the words *Barrett Institute* in large block lettering. *So that she wouldn't run off with the mattress?* There was a small heater and one window, which looked out onto city streets and a small courtyard far beneath, that was surrounded by a fence topped with barbed wire. The window too, had reinforced metal screens and large black wrought-iron bars. There was a very long drop for anyone who tried to climb out these windows.

Linda stepped into the room and held the door open behind her, motioning for the Webbers to enter. "She doesn't have a roommate yet, but we're expecting another new patient tonight."

She was carrying Stefanie's bag at her side and dropped it on the twin-sized camp bed farthest from the door. "Please open your bags. It's policy that we conduct an inspection."

Open her bags? What was this—airport security? They had no right to touch her things. It was personal. This was a violation of her civil rights.

But apparently it wasn't. Linda dismantled the suitcase, unfolding each item of clothing only to refold it sloppily and drop it on the other bed. She opened the flashlight—which Madeline Webber had included as a reading lamp for midnight sleeping difficulties—to check the battery compartment. She confiscated the razor and the tweezers. "You can get these back later, once you've been granted privileges."

Privileges? Stefanie wanted to grab them out of the Linda's hands. These were her belongings. And now she would have to be granted permission to use them?

The last few items were removed from the bag and placed on the bed. Linda confiscated the tie to her blue bathrobe and sent the soft, down pillow home with her parents. "There, I'm finished now; you can get this back in twenty-four hours." She indicated the bathrobe tie and left the room.

The bed wasn't even soft. Stefanie buried her head in the hospital's pillow and wished that she could have kept her own. But that was against the rules. No shorts, no tank-tops, no stuffed animals out of the rooms, no tweezers, no razors, no scissors, no water, no cell phones, no headphones in the rooms, no spiral notebooks, no cameras, no "inappropriate" magazines ... She used the pillow to stifle a scream. There were so many things she couldn't have here; there were so many rules. Meanwhile, her parents silently arranged her clothing in drawers.

"Mr. and Mrs. Webber, I understand your concern for your daughter but I'm going to have to ask you to leave momentarily. It is almost time for dinner, and Stefanie must attend, along with all the other patients." Linda had returned to the doorway of room 507.

They stood, and Stefanie flung herself into her mother's arms. She was hysterical again, looking around for some way of hurting herself or anyone else. They couldn't leave her like this! This place was a prison! The unit was five stories up, above a Manhattan sidewalk, but the windows were still bolted shut to prevent them from trying to escape, as if they were criminals. Failing to eat was not a criminal activity, for God's sake. This place—Stefanie's eyes swept the room. The beds were cots. She had been given only a thin cotton blanket, two sheets, and a flat pillow. The couches in the common area were plastic. Why was she being punished like this? She'd never make it. She wouldn't get used to it. And they were dumping her here, like a piece of forgotten baggage.

They were walking out the door now. Her mother kissed her lightly, and her father repeated his irritating refrain: "We're proud of you."

What did they have to be proud of? Their only child was in jail.

She tried to hold on to her mother's hug, but Linda was watching, hovering over the good-bye scene, just waiting to close and lock the door. She let go, and her parents left. Linda got her wish. The door closed solidly. There was a click as it locked. It seemed like a bad version of a Hollywood movie.

The pillow met her head, cushioning it against the force of her body as it fell against the mattress. Stefanie shuddered and wondered if God might take pity on her and somehow remove her from this hostile world where no one cared about her.

Her parents were gone. They'd turned their backs and left her, just like that. They'd probably stop off somewhere nice for a bite of dinner before going home. She could imagine them ordering a nice bottle of wine and toasting—to what? To Stefanie's good health? To their success at resolving their little problem?

Stefanie gave a long sigh, her rib cage heaving as she slowly exhaled. She wouldn't be getting out of that door any time soon—not even if she tried.

This was happening. As much as she'd told herself that it wouldn't, it had. It was.

And now, Linda was standing at the foot of the stairs, calling out the alarm: "Dinner!"

~ 23 ~

*H*eading toward Linda's bellowing voice, Stefanie took one long, hard look at the place that had suddenly become her home. First, she saw the huge, heavy white door that locked automatically upon closing. Stretched out from there was the hallway with all the bedrooms and the posters. Then the common area with its vinyl couches and *Oprah*. Another hallway shot off from the common area and also ran the length of the unit, essentially parallel and identical to the first one, but without bedrooms. There was only one doorway—no number on the wall next to it—and apparently only one room, with four wooden tables.

Stefanie followed after Linda and the other patients. Linda was their shepherd, and they were her little lambs, following with hunched shoulders and slow, careful steps. What would happen if she turned around and went back to her room? Should she test it?

Stefanie turned. A woman that she hadn't seen before was watching her. "It's that door," she snapped. "Follow the others. Stay with the group."

Checkmate. Again. Another loss. Recently, it didn't seem to matter who her opponent was; she just couldn't win.

"You, new girl, right there. That's your seat." Linda pointed to the table closest to the door. There were three chairs, two occupied, one empty. A Dixie cup sat at the empty seat, filled with a white, foamy liquid. That was her place. At the other seats, clear plastic containers held the patients' dinners. Eventually, she too would have a plastic container labeled with her name, marking her seat. But tonight there was only a white paper napkin with Webber hastily scribbled on it, almost illegibly, and that one Dixie cup. She could see that the others had more, but one cup was bad enough. Foamy, creamy, fattening, sugary, frothy, thick, white liquid. *Ensure.*

Dr. Adler had been telling the truth. This was her dinner. And she was going to have to eat it.

From the next table over, Curly turned and tapped Stefanie's shoulder. "It gets better. Don't worry. Just drink it. And then get 200 milliliters of juice, and you'll be fine. It doesn't even taste that bad, really. We've come to like it." She motioned to the group of girls that sat at her table.

"Ms. Johnson, turn around and face your own food. Keep your hands in front of you. I don't want any tricks from you tonight." Linda's voice surprised Stefanie. Her tone was harsher somehow and less caring than the one she had used back in Room 507.

Curly obeyed the command and resumed her own eating in small, precise bites.

"Natalie Jefferson, I don't want to see you cutting the food up so small. Normal bites." Linda had quickly moved on to harassing someone else.

Curly turned carefully around again and, shrugging her shoulders, smiled. It was a nice show of camaraderie.

"Drink that … then get juice …"

Stefanie was grateful for Curly's advice, but how could she do it? The whole room smelled of macaroni and cheese—the chosen meal for the evening. She couldn't eat with that stench. She couldn't even be in the room; she'd gain weight just by breathing.

At the other tables, the girls were going through their rituals. Stefanie noted that there were about twenty patients in the room. Some secretly cut the food into small bites while avoiding the gaze of the vigilant Linda. Some took big mouthfuls, as if in a hurry to finish what they could and remove the tray from view. Some mixed the food together and ate it, unable to tell one item from the next. Others pushed the elements of the dinner away from each other, dividing their plates into quadrants for each food group, being careful that they didn't touch in the process. They looked around to see who had gotten the most food and who had gotten the least. Each counted the grams of fat and number of calories that she had to eat, either mentally or with her fingers under the table. Stefanie recognized the scowls on their foreheads as they added the numbers from dinner to the totals from breakfast and lunch. They were checking to make sure that the hospital hadn't made a mistake and inadvertently—or intentionally, you never could tell—served them more than the prescribed amount of food.

There was a table near the door where the girls didn't have trays—where they dished out their own portions and decided what they would eat. Their bodies weren't quite as skeletal, and there was some life behind their eyes. Jealousy was hurled at these girls from all corners of the room. In the social hierarchy that Stefanie could already see emerging, a seat at this table gave you high status. These patients had freedom.

She studied the girls at her own table. They were the lowest-class citizens: the newcomers, the failures, or the deviant ones. They swirled their cups around as if the *Ensure* was wine and they were the connoisseurs at a tasting. She smiled. They held their Dixie cups about three inches from the plastic and slowly poured their dinners back and forth between the container and the cup, watching as a layer of bubbles formed along the surface if they poured at just the right speed. Sometimes it splashed over the edge, but their napkins quickly moved in to soak up the spilled liquid—one less drop to drink. Linda reprimanded them from time to time, but invariably they returned to their rule breaking as soon as her head was turned toward the other side of the room.

No one talked. Except for the occasional comment from Linda or the sound of someone pouring juice or biting into an apple, the room was silent. Was it because they weren't friends, or because they were preoccupied? Or was the silence just another rule, as though they were Trappist monks locked away in some mountaintop seminary?

Stefanie looked down at her own Dixie cup—still untouched. She couldn't procrastinate any longer. It sort of tasted like a vanilla milkshake, but less creamy. She swirled this first taste around in her mouth and let the sweetness wash over her tongue. It coated the roof of her mouth and the insides of her cheeks. Thick. Caloric. She took another sip. And another. And another. How many calories were in this little cup? This ... plus juice, Curly had said. Could she do it? Did she even have a choice? Another sip.

"The shinbone's connected to the knee bone, the knee bone's connected to the thighbone, the thighbone's connected to the hip bone ..."

The song jumped into her head like a Pavlovian response. The stimulus was food. She couldn't eat it. She'd conditioned herself not to. But now she had to; there were nurses and other people watching, and she didn't want to make a scene. She wished they would leave. She tried to drown them out, but it didn't work. She tried to distract herself by watching the other patients, but nothing seemed to help. All she heard was the music of the song, and all she felt was her imploding stomach, obviously shutting down to prevent food ingestion. Deep sigh. And she shook her head, as if through violent movement she might be able to dislodge the song from its player in her head.

Stefanie tilted the remaining liquid back into her mouth.

"Twenty minutes."

Curly turned quickly and, in a hurried, almost-frantic whisper, explained why Linda was calling times. "We have thirty minutes to eat. That way we can't take too long—we can't make eating a meal an all-day process. They call twenty minutes as a warning. Ten minutes left. Hurry." She broke off and focused on her own food. Linda's gaze had just returned to their side of the room.

In the time it took for Curly to explain, the dining room had responded to Linda's call. The girls with trays began to eat faster, and the noise level picked up. At Stefanie's table, the girls poured themselves glasses of juice from the small refrigerator by the door.

"Two hundred milliliters of juice for you too, young lady." Linda's eyes fell on Stefanie, and she pointed to the refrigerator.

Apple, pineapple, grape, cranberry, prune, or orange juice. There was a pitcher of water, but it wasn't for her. She poured herself a glass of apple juice.

"Thirty minutes. Time to report."

Another call and another flurry of action. The girls took their final bites and stood, forming a line in front of Linda. What were they doing now? The ritualistic behavior of this place confused Stefanie, but she fell into line with the other girls—assuming that, if everyone else was doing it, she probably had to also.

"Portion of macaroni and cheese, one glass of juice, one apple, portion of broccoli, portion of salad with one-half dressing; restrict one-half dressing. Three hundred fifty milliliters of Ensure, two hundred of pineapple juice."

Linda wrote quickly on the pages of a binder. She made a note of what each had restricted (declined to consume) and how much of it. She wrote what had been ingested and in what quantity.

It was Stefanie's turn, and she stepped forward. She was reminded of the scene in the *Sound of Music* when the children introduce themselves to Maria in march-step to their father's whistle. Stefanie felt like she might throw up and wished that she could just die right there where she stood. *What the hell was going on? How had she landed herself in this stone-cold place with these sickly skeletons and these hard-assed wardens?*

The girl before her had restricted half of her macaroni and cheese and her apple. Recording that entry, Linda had shaken her head and warned her. "If you continue this way, you'll get the tube." The girl didn't seem to care, as she raised her shoulders in mock bewilderment. She practically skipped out the doorway, a smile just beginning to turn up the corners of her chapped lips, and Stefanie wondered at her obstinacy.

"Step up, next. What's your name, again?" Linda seemed impatient, frustrated perhaps that her evening was being spent writing down portion sizes and otherwise keeping an eye on spoiled, skinny teenagers.

"Stefanie Webber," she said in a soft voice and wondered if grabbing a napkin to blot her bleeding lip on her way out was a possibility.

"First night, huh. How much you have?" It was said in a tough-guy tone that Stefanie was unused to.

How much was in one Dixie cup? She didn't want to make a mistake, but she didn't know. "One cup of *Ensure*; two hundred milliliters of juice."

"One cup? That's two hundred milliliters—remember that for next time. No restrictions yet? Good. If you can keep that up, you'll get out of this place. Next."

Was she trying to be nice? Or was she mocking her, assuming that Stefanie would fail? It didn't matter. She was confused. And full.

Her stomach hurt from the unexpected nourishment. The body had gotten used to starvation. In the morning, she would be incrementally heavier—on her way to a place she didn't want to go.

Day: March 13, 2001. Meal one: over.

- 24 -

Curly's real name was Sarah Johnson. She was eighteen and had been dieting for five years. For the past two weeks, she had called the Barrett Institute, Tower 3 North, her home. She'd never been there before, but this was her third hospitalization. As she put it, she was a veteran. She was also friendly.

"It's sitting time. You better take a seat, or the warden'll get on your case." Sarah pointed to Linda, who had rejoined them in the common room, and patted the seat next to her. "My name's Sarah, by the way. And you are?"

"Stefanie." She wasn't sure how she felt about Sarah. It was a little early to be socializing with them; after all, she didn't plan on staying there for very long. It was only a matter of time before they all realized that she wasn't actually skinny and sent her home.

"This is sitting time. We always have it for one hour after meals. You sit here on one of these lovely vinyl couches and make yourself at home. Write, or read, or relax." Sure enough, as Stefanie looked around, she saw the *Seventeens, Elle Girls, Nanny Diaries,* and personal journals come out, appearing suddenly in all corners of the room. "Or sleep if you want. Some people do, their medicines make them tired. What you can't do is move around." Her voice lowered in a conspiratorial way, "It burns calories." Her voice returned to full volume. "Personally, I like to talk." She shrugged apologetically. "Hope you don't mind."

"No."

She didn't know what she could say that might interest the older girl, but she didn't mind the idea of conversation—but only if Sarah would initiate. It was sitting time, apparently, so Stefanie sat. She curled her legs up underneath her and noticed that Sarah had done the same. She couldn't help but inspect the girl's legs: her bony knee-caps jutted out from underneath baggy flannel pants. Stefanie studied her own legs. If her knees were the same way, she couldn't see it.

"Been sick a long time?"

Stefanie shook her head. God, why couldn't she answer like a normal person? Her heart raced inside her chest, and her palms were sweaty. She had vocal cords, why couldn't she use them? She was hesitant to share her story. Surely it wasn't as bad as the others' stories. And she was the new girl, an interloper of sorts; she should want to make a good impression. Stefanie willed herself to speak; otherwise this girl would think she was a fool.

"No, not too long. Just bad these past couple of months." It was all she could manage.

Why had she admitted that she was sick? She wasn't sick—not by the standards of this place, anyway. She had skipped a couple of meals and thrown up occasionally; it wasn't any worse than other girls. Everyone dieted. It had been a mistake to say anything. She wasn't sick. It was a title she hadn't earned. Sarah was skinny, and she wasn't. Period.

But Sarah nodded sympathetically. "It's no fun, this thing. Me, I've been sick for five years. And they just keep putting me back in these places ..."

Stefanie was confused. Sarah hadn't disagreed with her or acted like what she'd said was facetious. Stefanie was sick. She was in a hospital, and, evidently, she deserved to be there. To Sarah it seemed like that was all there was to it. She acted like Stefanie had every reason to be there—as much as Sarah herself did, anyway.

"But they're not so bad actually; you get used to 'em after a while. The first one scared me shitless: got the tube and everything, and one of the other patients beat me up. I stayed healthy for seven or eight months after that. Never thought I'd be back again, and neither did my parents. We even had a party to celebrate." She paused, as if to gauge Stefanie's reaction. "I was fifteen at the time, but by the middle of junior year, I was back in a different program. It wasn't so bad the second time around: didn't have as many rules, and no one bothered to watch me. I guess they just didn't care. There were too many patients there, anyway; the nurses were out-numbered. That second time, I wasn't half as scared, and now I'm fine. The wardens don't even intimidate me anymore. Each place is different and has different rules, but you learn to adjust. You learn to work the system. You know, get around the rules, make mischief." Sarah smiled as if imparting some secret knowledge, "Got any questions—come to me."

She certainly was chatty but warm and self-effacing too, and Stefanie couldn't help but like her. Maybe they'd become friends.

The other conversations, which had masked the sound of theirs, dwindled, and journals or paperback books disappeared. The hour had passed, and the patients began to move around the room. Slowly, as if waking from a deep slumber, patients stood to test their limbs. One flicked on the television, and they all moved in to watch it.

"We're not allowed television until after dinner," Sarah explained. "Except for *Oprah,* and sometimes the morning talk shows. We're supposed to be reflecting on life, or why we're grateful for our bodies—crap like that. Or go to group therapy, where we talk about our problems—it's meant to give us a sense of camaraderie. It's all shit, if you ask me. Camaraderie is better formed when we're just sitting around talking or playing board games. Or we're supposed to be meeting with a doctor or talking to a therapist. Stupid things that only take up time and never help anyway. That's why they're all so hungry for TV," she giggled at her inadvertent pun. "It's our connection to the outside world."

Stefanie wandered over to the window. Outside, the sky had turned a murky shade of navy blue, lightened by passing clouds. The strangeness of the evening sky complemented her feelings of displacement. Everything felt still and expectant, a moonless night that could very well be a prelude to snow. What were her parents doing now? Eight o'clock. They'd be finished with dinner and probably watching TV, too. Stefanie tried to run through the program listings in her head, but her mind was slow. Were they talking about her? Did they miss her? They'd always been a trio, a three-legged stool. When had she veered off their steady axis? How had she come to find herself on this very shaky path?

Stefanie pushed the curtain back and stared down at the street. Linda was watching closely but didn't say anything. The spindly trees that popped up from manicured and tended plots in the concrete looked haggard and forlorn in the March cold, as though winter had already been a long fight and they just wanted out of the ring. There weren't many people outside, she noted. Lighted windows climbed the facades of older apartment buildings, shining holes of light against a dim background; people were inside on a night like this.

Laura, Annabel, and Julia would be at home studying. Spring vacation started next week, and they had two weeks off. Her entire school would be scattering to ski condos or the pink beaches of the Caribbean. But first there would be exams to take, and it would be a punishing week. Spring break was the reward. She knew her friends would be looking toward the following week with excitement and expectation: Laura for Aspen, Annabel for London, and Julia for Palm Springs. Meanwhile, her own family's Colorado vacation had been spoiled.

Stefanie wondered if she would survive the night. Did her friends at home even know where she was? What would her mother tell them if they called? What would she be telling the school tomorrow? Idly, Stefanie wondered if there would be a surge in her number of e-mails once the news spread. As though her classmates were naive enough to think she'd been allowed to take her laptop with her to the hospital—assuming that they even cared to write.

Stefanie glanced away from the window and shielded her eyes from the surprisingly bright light of the room. They were nice here—at least Sarah seemed to be—but it just wasn't the same as being home. Her sheets, her bedroom, her stereo, her necessities. What was going to happen to her? Looking back out the window, her breath formed a crystallized circle of whiteness on the glass. Deep breath and out—to make the circle bigger. A second circle appeared next to the first.

Sarah had joined her at the window. "I stood here my first night, too. The first night's always the hardest. You're new; you don't know the routine; you're lost and confused and don't believe that any of this is really happening. I know the feeling. Tell you what—our rooms are still locked ..." She paused at Stefanie's surprised expression. "Oh, you didn't know about that? Every night until nine. It's to keep us from isolating ourselves or sneaking around behind closed doors. Let's play a board game. It's what we do here to pass the time. Lot's of time ... And they've got them all here—more games than cans of Ensure. What do you think?" Sarah's mouth turned upward in a half-smile.

The rooms were locked until nine o'clock? It really was a prison. She'd never survive this. "OK." She grudgingly nodded as Sarah pointed to a stack of board games in the corner of the room that Stefanie hadn't noticed before. "I'll play."

They'd just pulled the game of Life from the middle of the pile when Linda's voice interrupted the silence, "Commodes ..." Linda stood next to an open door at the end of a shorter hallway. Behind her, Stefanie could see bathroom stalls and sinks. She'd forgotten about bathrooms ... she hadn't even realized there wasn't one in her bedroom. But it made sense now.

Sarah was standing up. "Commodes. You better come if you've got to go. They won't open again until bedtime, and, when Linda's on duty, you don't want to ask for special favors just because you didn't think you had to go earlier. Especially with her. She's worse than the others; she doesn't take—how should I say it?—kindly to requests."

Stefanie followed after her. She didn't imagine that she would want to ask for any special favors, from Linda or otherwise.

At the doorway, Sarah pointed to a white container with "Stefanie Webber" written on the side. "That's you, right? You're lucky. You only have a hat; I'm on commodes. Because I was a purger, they don't want me to throw up and be able to flush it away. That means I have to pee in this," she held up a pink plastic, circular pot and headed toward a closed-off room. "I do the other stuff in here too. You just pee in the white thing. Rest it on the rim of the toilet seat like this." Demonstrating in mime, she showed Stefanie how to set the hat so that it was like a cup to pee in that you didn't have to hold because the rim was sandwiched between your butt and the toilet seat. Even Sarah, whom Stefanie would have bet wouldn't be easily embarrassed, blushed. "They were supposed to have told you all this." She seemed to be apologizing for her flushed cheeks and single, girly giggle. "Then, when you're done, look to see how much there is. And report it. Tell Linda how much you peed."

Stefanie noticed the gradations on the inside of her hat. Kind of like a measuring cup. There were lines along the inside of the cup, so she could tell just how much urine had landed in the plastic receptacle. Measured in ccs. Sarah couldn't be serious. This was degrading. She wasn't sick. She was going to use a toilet, just like normal people. The common area had emptied, and all the patients were standing in one long, single-file line. Waiting for their moment to step up, claim their commode or hat, and disappear into a stall or that other little room where Sarah was now. This was crazy. They locked the bathroom and expected her to disregard her dignity.

Sarah had to use the pink commode. That was worse—Far worse.

Because Sarah used to throw-up ... but so had she ... had someone made a mistake?

"Young lady, hurry up. None of us have all day."

The stall was small and uncomfortable as Stefanie tried to arrange her hat. She certainly wasn't going to tell anyone that there had been a mistake, that she needed a commode. That would have been stupid. She just hoped she was doing this right. How had Sarah held it? Had she lifted up the toilet seat first, or left it down? Thankfully, it only held one way—with the toilet seat down. What if it fell into the toilet? Everyone would laugh. Linda would yell. She would die.

Flush down toilet ... record amount ... wash hands ... back out onto the unit.

When she left the bathroom and took a deep breath of the still-stuffy air, Sarah was waiting at the table where they'd left the board game. "Don't worry. That's another thing you'll get used to. We're not even embarrassed anymore. It becomes second nature. And you're pretty good for an amateur. I've heard stories about girls dropping hats in the toilet the first couple times. One girl did it eight times before the nurses got annoyed and made her use a commode instead. Compared to her, you've got real skill."

She stopped and looked straight into Stefanie's eyes. "And you'll survive; people here usually don't die from fear. Other things maybe," she said and giggled again. Disgusted and increasingly terrified, Stefanie hoped she was kidding. "But, anyway, it's your turn. Better spin, or we both might die of old age before we ever finish this game."

~ *25* ~

*S*tefanie was middle-aged and Sarah had passed the half-century mark in the game of Life when a bass chime echoed dully through the hallway. It wasn't like the doorbells that Stefanie was used to at home, with their high-pitched rings that tormented the canals of your ears until you ran for the door, if only to halt the sound. This bell was more of a deep-throated groan, a warning for those outside: Enter at your own risk.

It was Sarah's turn, but she paused before spinning the dial and looked toward the door. "Now what?" she said as she grimaced. "It's too late for visitors. They have to leave by eight."

Linda had said that there would be another new patient arriving that night. Maybe the person ringing the bell would be her roommate. Stefanie had scarcely formulated the thought before the atmosphere of the room had changed.

Where, moments before, people had been sprawled across furniture or engrossed in the WB's Tuesday night line-up, young women were now alert and sitting at attention. Someone had lowered the volume on the television, and many had closed their reading materials. Everyone was watching the door. Occasionally someone hazarded a whispered guess at who was standing outside, but no one ever said anything in response. They just didn't talk much, these girls. So far, frivolous conversation didn't seem to exist at the Barrett Institute.

It felt strange to sit there with Sarah and watch Linda amble slowly toward the door. This time, Stefanie was one of them. Only three and a half hours earlier, she had been the one entering the room. Now, she felt herself studying the incoming family. There were two young children—ten or eleven. Why would any parent bring his young children to a place like this? And an older, slightly stocky man with graying hair and a broad forehead and a girl, maybe her own age. The father looked tired; his arms hung loose at his sides, and bags sagged woefully beneath his eyes. He looked like he was crumbling under the pressures of responsibility. Maybe he didn't have anyplace else to leave these two young children.

Bones, bones, bones. Knit Juicy Couture pants hung low enough to expose the elastic of her underwear—GAP—, Stefanie noticed—and the upper curvatures of her hip bones. Her once-white sneakers looked too heavy for her thin legs to lift, perhaps making it impossible to walk. And her wrists, which stuck out at the ends of her sleeves, looked like the twigs from one of those sickly Manhattan trees. The girl shivered, obviously cold, though the heat was already on. The eyes from the couches just watched. Stefanie's first urge was to feed her—feed her a lot and often.

"A mortality rate of nine percent ..."

This one looked like death might not be so far away, if not from malnutrition then from fright.

Stefanie wondered if she should stop staring. Perhaps she was being rude. But the girl wasn't paying attention anyway; she was watching the ground intently and answering her father's occasional questions with only the slightest movements of her head.

Was this going to be her roommate? They were going to sleep in the same room and share the same mirror? The mirror—what did that girl see when she looked into it? Did she see the same obese funhouse image that looked out at Stefanie every day? Did she see the same grotesque rolls of fat that jiggled when Stefanie walked? No, she must see the bones jutting out from her sides. She must see that she couldn't continue to lose weight. She must realize that she was skinny—the ultimate skinny.

But how had she done it? How could she have gotten so skinny without anyone noticing? What were her tricks? How had she fooled the doctors? Had she lied? Or had she simply not had a friend intervene? Didn't matter. She was the winner; she had played the game until she couldn't go any further.

Stefanie wondered if she could do that when she was discharged. Could she beat the system, as Sarah put it, and get that thin? It was about more than being skinny. It was about being the best; it was about acknowledgment. She remembered that first day in the cafeteria when she had competed against Laura. Now she wanted to surpass this girl just as she surpassed Laura. She wanted to surpass them all. They were all thinner than she was: Sarah, the girl with the tube in her nose, the one that had cut her food into tiny bites. They had all held out longer. They hadn't given up and admitted defeat so soon. To beat them, she was going to have some work to do.

Linda's soft and pleasant voice was back. "Ah, here you are. The Stones, right? We've been expecting you. Follow me, you'll be in room 507." She led the family to the same room where Stefanie had taken up residence.

The sideshow was over. The girls relaxed, and the volume was turned back up as journals, books, and magazines reappeared. Sarah spun the dial, and the needle landed on five. "Your new roommate, it looks like. Well, *she's* a project. Could she be any thinner? Needs meat on 'em bones. Whatcha think?"

Stefanie shrugged and spun the dial. It was too soon to tell. And she didn't know what to think anymore.

– 26 –

She would never be the most talkative—not even later, when they had known each other for months. It was just her nature. Lily Stone was guarded, careful with her words, a perfectionist even with her speech.

She didn't talk much that night. She wasn't exactly hostile, but Stefanie had struggled just to discover her name.

Nine o'clock came, and a petite older lady who introduced herself as Lucy the RN unlocked the bedroom doors. Stefanie watched as the room emptied, and the other patients suddenly sprang to life—liberated from the uncomfortable vinyl couches. No one stayed in the common room past nine. They got tired of sitting, staring at a pointless screen as if it were life outside those walls. They were tired of watching other girls struggle or cry over the pages of their journals, even though they had done the same moments earlier. They were tired of being watched by the "wardens." Topics of conversation: diets, calories, weight-loss stories, family complaints, commiseration about being sick, and the unfairness of the Barrett Institute's arbitrary rules, were exhausted quickly over the course of the day, and few if any had the energy to make small talk. The mini-cliques formed during the day broke up and dispersed; everyone knew that these friendships were a necessity, brought about by shared experiences and a common enemy. So now—regardless of the early hour—each member of their isolated community gathered her belongings and trekked back to her tiny room, grateful for the variation in scenery. Even Sarah said goodnight and retired. And Lucy took over the television now, changing the channel until she found the nine o'clock news.

Bedtime came early at the Barrett Institute.

Self-consciously, Stefanie changed into her T-shirt and boxer shorts. She raised her shirt over her head with her arms already into the next one, with her back to the door. She wanted her body to remain secret. She didn't want this skinny girl to see the fat and blow her cover. The Stone girl was probably already staring at her, disgusted, ready to ask for a new room, ready to explain to Sarah and the others what a hideous sight she had seen.

But when Stefanie looked over her shoulder, her roommate was also facing the wall. Apparently, neither one of them had wanted to be seen changing.

"Should I turn out the light?" Stefanie asked. Lily was already curled up in the bed near the door, and she hadn't said a word yet, besides her first name.

The floor felt like a layer of ice under her bare feet. The darkness of the room made it impossible to see, and Stefanie moved carefully to her bed.

As she collapsed onto the mattress, she felt it sag where the springs had grown soft. "I'm Stefanie," she said, trying again. "It's my first night here, too." Her voice quivered under the weight of those words. *I'm Stefanie. And I have an eating disorder.* Isn't that what they did at AA? So she was really there. Her first night in the hospital. How many more would there be?

"I know. Nice to meet you." The girl turned toward the wall and pulled her legs closer to her chest; Stefanie watched the small lump under the covers move.

The sound of the soft voice was startling. It trembled, uncertain which pitch to hold. So her roommate was also struggling with the same overwhelming fear and uncertainty.

The sheets were cold, and Stefanie shivered, surrounding herself with the thin cotton blanket. She missed the downy softness of the quilt on her bed at home. She missed her pillow and her mattress and the sound that the pipes made when the heat came up through her radiator. Mr. Whiskers was with her, but tonight he was of little comfort. She tried to snuggle against him as his fur grew wet with slow, salty tears. She couldn't seem to stop. Stefanie could hear Lily's deep breathing, and imagined her own chest rising and falling in that same pattern.

Breathe in … breathe out … breathe in … breathe out … and soon Stefanie closed her eyes against the blackness. Finally, she slept. Slept until the sound of raspy cackling shook her awake.

"Good morning, ladies." The high pitch on the end of "morning" was impressive. "Time to get up." Another chortle on the word *up*, and the wake-up call grew more distant, moving down the hallway.

In an instant, noise could be heard up and down the corridor.

What on earth was going on? Were elephants dancing? Was there a fire? A bomb scare? The travel clock that her mother had thought to pack read six thirty. Why was she rousing them at this ungodly hour? It couldn't possibly be time for breakfast yet.

Lily appeared just as confused and perhaps even more scared; they glanced at each other questioningly. Neither of them knew what they were supposed to do.

Sarah's appearance, moments later, was a welcome aid that first morning. As she arrived in the doorway, she laughed at the two roommates, "Careful, your faces might freeze that way." Stefanie could only guess what she had looked like; maybe her face revealed the terror and confusion that she wouldn't let her mind acknowledge.

"Get out of bed sleepy heads. Big happenings are going on. You gotta strip down out of your underwear, get into the gown that they gave you last night, pee in a hat—or in a commode if you're special like me—and then get weighed. It's everyone's favorite part of the day. And hopefully all before the line gets too long. It gets cold out there if you're only in a robe."

Thank God for Sarah!

Five minutes later, uncomfortable and shivering slightly in thin cotton gowns that didn't close in the back, Stefanie and Lily joined Sarah outside the weigh-in room.

"Thanks a lot. Because I spent time explaining the routine to you two lazy-bones, I'm the last one here. Now I've got to wait on a long line."

"Sorry—"

Stefanie didn't want to make any enemies on the first morning, but Sarah just laughed.

"God, you're gullible! I was already late by the time I came into your room. People move quickly in the morning, mostly 'cause they've got to go to the bathroom. So what's with your roommate?" She motioned to Lily, who had positioned herself off to the side, against a wall, where she couldn't be easily seen or talked to.

"Sarah, you're up. Quit the yacking and get on in here." Sarah disappeared behind a door at the summons of Lucy the RN, the one with the raspy voice.

"No underwear—got it off, right? Let me see."

The words floated out from where the door hadn't quite closed all the way, and Stefanie's head gave an imperceptible start. It was too early in the morning for this kind of torture. They were going to weigh her *every* morning—Every morning. Just to see if she had gained weight. One pound, two pounds, three pounds … she could feel it settling already. They were going to make her into the heaviest person in the world—and the least likeable, the least intelligent, and the least successful.

Stefanie could already see her failures mounting as Sarah came out of the room crying. Lily was called in next.

− 27 −

Over the next couple of hours, Stefanie would learn that tears were common in Tower 3 North. Tears when people gained weight or when people lost weight. Tears when girls had to eat or when they misbehaved and lost privileges. Tears when they were treated harshly and during therapy. Tears during family visits. In fact, if crying was a way to burn calories, then the girls had it made. Lily could even be counted on to burst into tears unprovoked.

In Stefanie's case, tears came when she went looking for Sarah not long after that first day's weigh-in and learned that she'd been put on bedrest—locked in her room until she gained weight.

Bedrest had been the cause of Sarah's tears earlier that morning. She hadn't gained weight. She had to stay in bed. She couldn't move. Bedrest meant no socializing, no dancing around IV poles, no board games, no television, no walking, no movement, no companionship. You were lucky if anyone remembered to wheel you to therapy. For Sarah it would be torture. For Stefanie, it would be a warning, an introduction to hospital life. Watching Sarah, even for one night, was a learning experience. If she didn't want confinement, she'd have to watch her step.

Breakfast was at eight thirty. The hallway filled with the pungent odor of maple syrup; And even before entering the room, they all knew that it was going to be a difficult breakfast.

Stefanie watched as the others felt for their bones, reassuring themselves in the same way that she did that they were still there— that they weren't fat. It was apparent that no one wanted to accept those trays of food or sit around those tables. Breakfast alone tallied up to more calories than she ate in an entire day, and she wasn't going to put up with that.

Not that she had been given a tray.

At the table where she had sat the night before, there was the Ensure again. That same, foamy whiteness. This time Stefanie discovered that she, too, had a plastic container with her name on it. Officially, she had joined the ranks as one of them.

200 milliliters of Ensure, 200 milliliters of juice ... Stefanie remembered the amounts from the night before and, making up for Sarah's absence, passed the information along to Lily, who seemed to have gotten lost during the three-step journey from door to table.

"Ms. Webber, who do you think you are ... getting too big for your britches already? You been here one day, and you forget what it's like to be new; leave the new girl alone. Ms. Lily, you just drink your supplements, listen to the doctors, and you get out of here. You got it?"

Linda was back, and, before the early morning caffeine hit her bloodstream, she was even more ornery than usual.

Easily intimidated, they stopped the conversation, and Linda moved on to another poor soul, berating her for having folded her napkin the wrong way. Lily's chin quivered, and she ignored the rest of the room, focusing solely on the drink in front of her. Stefanie's eyes wandered. She couldn't help it. Today, without the uncertainty, she could watch the other patients even more closely.

The one called Natalie sat at one of the two tables with trays. Her large brown eyes stared at her food as if it had been laced with cyanide. Across the table, the same expression appeared on the face of another patient. Her long, tapered fingers were painted raspberry, and she cut her food in such a way that everyone could see the flashes of color on her nails. She wore a Michael Stars cap-sleeved shirt, fitted close to her body, and tight Diesel jeans. It was as close as she could get to disregarding the dress code: no shorts, no tank-tops, no showing clothes (supposedly to protect them from the competition of displaying their emaciated bodies) without actually breaking any rules. Sarah had said her name was Francesca. To Natalie's left, a girl with thin hair and a chipmunk face sat with her back to Linda, voraciously eating the food that had been set in front of her. That was Dana, with her wavy reddish-blonde hair that, when healthier, would have gently framed her face. Stefanie could tell that she had once been pretty, and she remembered how Sarah had described her as the recovered one. There was a fourth girl at the table, but she had pushed her chair as far from the others as possible and didn't seem to be a part of the scene.

Her attention was caught, and she watched these stick-figure teenagers as they dined. Dana looked at Natalie's tray. Natalie looked at Dana's tray—which was all but empty. Francesca looked at them both.

With slow, deliberate motions, Francesca unfolded the wax paper that wrapped her pat of butter. Natalie slid her knife under her pancake and braced it with her fork. Francesca, the only one with a clear view, glanced quickly at Linda. What were they doing? Was this another strange ritual, like cutting food up into miniscule bites or eating slowly?

A nod of her head and, in an instant, Francesca's tapered fingers, nail-polish and all, disappeared under the table and returned to rest on her tray. Her hand still held the wax wrapping but no butter. Her first instinct said the floor, but somehow Stefanie knew it wasn't there. That would have been too obvious. Instead, it had been stuck to the underside of the tabletop.

And Natalie's plate no longer held a pancake; Dana's did. Her eyes wide and innocent, she had flipped it over to Dana, who was cutting it quickly, using this addition to her meal to sop up the extra syrup that thinly coated her plate. If Stefanie had turned her head, she would have missed it. Linda did. The girls exchanged secretive smiles, and everything continued as if nothing had happened.

Would she soon be doing these things too? Was this why Sarah had been put on bedrest—because she had been cheating? Did it happen all the time? How had she missed it the night before? And why would Dana eat the others' food? Did she want to gain weight? Evidently she did. Evidently she wanted a one-way ticket out of here. Evidently she wanted to go home. Tears immediately rimmed Stefanie's eyes. She thought about her parents, the pancake breakfasts she might have been enjoying now, about moving on and getting back to life. Dana evidently wanted to move on. Why couldn't she? She watched the girl finish her breakfast, she saw her bring a syrup-topped finger to her mouth and delicately lick it. She tried to imagine a heavier Dana, who didn't seem to care that a future outside this place virtually guaranteed that. Stefanie paused, and considered what the two shared. Obviously, each wanted to be happy again. But how could Dana expect happiness to come from living life with people who always judged her as fat? Stefanie understood Dana's desire. But she was certain the Ensure that sat in front of her wouldn't get her to happiness. It wasn't possible. It couldn't happen.

"Twenty minutes." Linda looked at Dana's tray. "You're eatin' slower than usual, missy. What's the catch?" Her eyebrows were raised in suspicious warning.

"There's no catch, Linda, really. I'm just enjoying my food, same as always." Dana smiled, but Linda gave her a look. Stefanie turned and kept her eyes focused on her own table. She didn't want to be told off a second time, not with Linda in that mood. And there were only ten minutes left. She had drinking to do.

Deep breath. Deep breath. She could do it. She could do it. Just bring the cup up and take a sip. There, not so bad. Not bad at all. Think about something else … anything at all. Think about the walls, lovely white walls. Think about the posters—colorful posters. Think about her journal—perfect empty journal, just waiting for words. Think about the world outside: yellow taxicabs; the M31 downtown bus that she had always taken to Sweet Life, a candy store near Chinatown; the empty potters along Park Avenue where, in another month, there would be tulips blossoming. Don't envy the ones who played games, trading food or hiding it. *They were the sick ones.* And she'd never *really* been sick.

"Hi, I'm Stefanie. What's your name?" Stefanie turned to the girl she had begun to associate with an entirely matching wardrobe and who had been assigned the seat next to her. The girl's face looked pale against the purple velour that she had chosen to wear that day, and the color highlighted the purplish rings under her eyes. Stefanie wondered how old this girl was, but the anorexia made it hard to tell. Everyone in the room looked like young children, frail and weak, and yet old, haggard even, aged beyond their years. Age was no longer an identifying characteristic. None were older or younger; they just were. They just didn't think about it.

"Sorry, I couldn't hear you. What did you say?" Maybe, Stefanie thought, if she could only make conversation, she could keep her mind off the food.

The girl ignored her.

"So what's your name? How long have you been here?" Stefanie tried the fourth girl at her table, clearly the unit's resident Goth. Initially, she'd been intimidated by the dark eye-shadow, black baggy t-shirt over dark jeans, leather bracelets with spikes, and dog tags around the girl's neck, but Stefanie figured that disturbing conversation would be better than no conversation.

The Goth smiled, but before she could answer, Purple Shirt Girl cut her off. "I'm Ellie; that's Becca. OK? Consider all introductions over. And now, shut the hell up. We're not looking to attract attention."

Becca's friendliness had been stomped out. Ellie controlled her, though the dark exterior said it should have been otherwise. Becca wouldn't talk if it didn't suit her tablemate. Rebuffed, Stefanie poured the last bit of Ensure into her mouth and swallowed. With the empty cup back on the table, she assessed the amounts that Ellie and Becca still needed to drink, wondering if, perhaps, she was being just a little bit too compliant by drinking her entire meal. The other girls didn't seem to be hung up on finishing—they didn't really seem to care if restrictions were written down in the book. Stefanie considered restricting at the next meal; maybe she didn't have to do exactly as the nurses said. Becca's container was empty and the cup had only a gulp left, but Ellie's container was nearly half full.

How did she plan to drink all that, plus the required juice, in seven minutes? She'd have to chug it, and she didn't look capable of that. First she'd have to stop pouring it back and forth between the container and the cup, but that would be difficult to do … the action had become so ingrained. She probably couldn't stop, but she'd have to—or else What?

The answer came seconds later.

A drop of Ensure splashed onto the table as it sloshed into Becca's empty container. Now her container was half-full, and Ellie's was empty. So that was how it worked. But how did Linda miss so much? The sound of the liquid against the plastic had been surprisingly loud, and Stefanie couldn't understand how Linda hadn't heard. It had been so obvious. Ellie had just reached across the table and poured her breakfast into Becca's container. And Becca drank it down, and Ellie smiled. As if it was perfectly normal. Normal. They'd been awake for all of three hours and already there was lying and cheating. What would happen as the day went on?

Stefanie was staring, and she knew it. But she couldn't help herself. Ellie held up a finger to silence her and mouthed a silent thank you to Becca.

"Ms. Rebecca, Ms. Newberg." Linda's voice yanked Stefanie from her astonishment. "Separation, now … for forever. You two will never speak again. That's enough!" She was livid, screaming so that Lucy stuck her head in the door to see if help was needed.

"No, Lucy, I've just caught our two little bitches causing trouble again. Swapped supplements this morning. But I got it covered. The rest of yous, record." She refused to acknowledge the perpetrators, except to spit a few last biting words in their direction: "You two'll be dealt with later. Expect restrictions."

"This is bullshit." Ellie's temper flared. "What the hell are you saying? Threats, huh? Well, you'll hear from my father about this; he's a lawyer, and we'll sue. I know the justice system. Take me to court if you think I'm guilty. Innocent until proven guilty. You've got no proof. We've done nothing wrong."

She ran with her emotions, sparring effortlessly, but Linda was ready. "I don't need no proof. I'm an eyewitness. I see you thanking each other, and you must think I'm stupid. What more proof do I need? You been spouting off at the mouth too much fer a young lady. No off-unit privileges for Ms. Rebecca. No socializing for Ms. Newberg—CO. Starting now."

So this was what happened if you were caught—CO: constant observation. It meant you were watched twenty-four hours a day, seven days a week. It meant a room change to the large room with no door, where the light from the hallway shone in your face all night, and you shared a room with more than one person. During the day, you stayed near the on-duty staff member and didn't talk to anyone else. Sarah had explained it the night before. It was worse than bedrest.

So there it was, Learning Experience Number Two: don't get caught hiding food. Not ever—not ever. Not ever. Not ever. The other patients didn't understand that, or maybe they were too sick to care. Stefanie remembered how she had told everyone at home that she wasn't sick, but they hadn't listened. She wished they could see what passed for normal behavior around here. At least she got enough nutrition to think straight. They certainly didn't. They were wasting away to nothing, and, still, they wouldn't eat. She wondered whether this would happen at every meal.

– 28 –

With Sarah on bedrest, Ellie isolated, and Becca on closer, if not constant, observation, the hours passed more quietly. Lacking any alternative occupation, Stefanie was getting to know the other patients, just by watching.

Natalie looked like a bird and whined like a left-behind puppy, complaining about every rule—only to break them later with an apathetic disregard. Dana was the unit's poster child for successful rehabilitation, their valedictorian, who gave motivational talks about the perils of unhealthy eating almost hourly. Her message was largely lost on Francesca, who flaunted her thin thighs and emaciated torso at every opportunity, making Stefanie want to scream. *Who did she think she was anyway?* A slightly removed but integral part of the dynamic was Riley: the only guy on the unit and Francesca's bosom buddy. It was obvious in the way that he agreed with her every word and let her put her feet in his lap that Francesca had seduced him. She was clearly unable to stop chasing men for a second—even as she sat in the hospital with a life-threatening disease. Riley was a sad creature really, used and manipulated by a girl who didn't even have a personality. Then there was Lane McInerny, the girl who spent her time at the end of the hallway, away from the group. She was unlike the other girls who passed the time sharing their stories or the patients who played board games, laughed at the perfect lives they saw on television, and moaned when the anorexic models strolled across the television set for their cameo appearances. She didn't take part in the back-rubbing that occurred in the tearful aftermath of visiting hours or the clandestine hugs that were shared with at least a modicum of sympathy and understanding. No one knew her history or why she was there. No one really cared. If you weren't willing to be part of the group, they weren't going to come to you. Lane was a mystery. And Madeline, the one with the same name as Stefanie's mother. She slept in the dorm, too, and never spoke a word—not even when spoken to. Her eyes seemed glazed over, as if she weren't really alive at all, but just a shell of a person. What had she been like before? What had the others been like? Had any of them had the same kinds of cravings for pizzas, boyfriends, and flawless skin as normal girls? Or had they always been freaks?

With Sarah out of commission, Lizzie, the fourteen-year-old she had noticed on her first day, took over her role as the resident joker. She had finally been released onto the unit, deemed fit for interaction with peers and no longer a danger to herself. Away from Madame Newspaper, Lizzie, the youngest of them all, was outgoing and friendly, even more than her first cautious wave would have suggested. She lay on the couch with her head hanging over the edge. A "head-sit" she called it and laughed. A couple of people rolled their eyes; they were trying to read, or write, or meditate, and Lizzie was distracting. But Stefanie liked her instantly. She wanted her conversation and gaiety and welcomed the diversion.

"D'you want to play cards? I have some in my bag." The girl certainly wasn't inhibited.

Stefanie nodded, and Lizzie went to retrieve her set of cards.

"BS? Spit? Rummy 500? Poker? Crazy Eights? Your pick." Lizzie obviously knew her way around a deck of cards.

"Rummy 500." That was the only card game that Stefanie knew. An old babysitter had once taught her to play.

Lizzie shuffled while Stefanie waited, hoping she hadn't forgotten the rules. Lily moved closer. When she dealt, Lizzie didn't even ask. She just made three piles of cards and pushed the third toward Lily. And for the next hour, they played cards. Group therapy wouldn't begin until later, so, for the time being, they dealt and played and dealt again.

Stefanie was beginning to feel that this was all they did here at the renowned Barrett Institute: play games, write in journals, and run fingers along the bones of rib cages. Individual therapy would happen two or maybe three times a week, depending on how dire the situation would be. Group therapy was an hour-long diversion approximately two times a day. Occasionally, the nutritionist came to talk with a patient, but that was infrequent—only if the patient was new or if a major adjustment had been made to her menu. Stefanie had only seen the nutritionist on the unit once—the time she had come to tell her that eventually her diet would consist of 2,200 calories a day. The rest of the time, the patients were on their own. On their own, that is, until it was time for the next meal or round of Ensures. Six times a day they traipsed into the dining room, ate and drank all that was set in front of them, reported to whichever nurse was on duty, and then sat for the mandatory hour. Stefanie's mind often wandered to thoughts of her friends and her family. What they were doing, what they were thinking about, where they were, if they missed her. But she was never bored for long. There was always someone crying, or fighting with a staff member, talking on the phone, or exercising secretly in the corner. And, unlike at home, it was never hard to find someone to talk to.

The sun shone in through the windows. She and the other girls sat in the bright spot on the carpet, and Stefanie could feel the warmth soaking her skin like a warm shower of light. For the moment she wasn't cold, and she wasn't scared. She stretched her legs out in front of her and looked at Lizzie and Lily. Lizzie was pretending to peek at Lily's cards, and, drawn into the game, Lily gave her a shove.

"Stay back, cheater. Even if you could see my cards, I'd still beat you." They were the first light-hearted words that Lily had said since she'd arrived, and she was almost smiling.

Stefanie laughed. This wasn't so bad. Not *really,* anyway. Things were looking brighter.

"Commodes."

Bathroom call. The card game was abandoned as they rushed for the door. Even using the hat didn't seem quite so distasteful, at least at the moment.

And then:

"Ensures; supplements."

Maybe not so fast …

That was something that she would never get used to.

No matter how many times she had to drink it, it didn't get easier. Six times a day, six milkshakes, six times the calories of an eight-ounce can, six Ensures. Disgusting. Cold, thick, liquid traveling down her esophagus and into her stomach. It would pass through her intestines, and her body would absorb the nutrients. Yeah right, nutrients—calories and fat were more like it. The warmth of the sun didn't penetrate the dining room windows, and Stefanie shivered with every sip she took. Lily was sitting next to her, but Lizzie wasn't in the room. She didn't have to drink supplements anymore, only her three meals a day. She wasn't severely underweight. What was the criterion for severely underweight? Lizzie was shorter than she, but much lighter too … proportionally, they must be about the same. But the doctors didn't think so. That was why Stefanie was sitting on a hard wooden chair next to Lily, and Lizzie was downstairs doing head-sits. It didn't make sense.

But then again, she didn't get to have an opinion. She wasn't entitled. She was nobody. She was a patient, in their minds a sick person who didn't know how to take care of herself. And she wasn't even an adult. She was still just a minor under her parents' jurisdiction, and that meant that she had no rights, Not here anyway. They assumed that everyone was like Becca and Ellie, or Natalie, Francesca, and Dana—liars and sneaks.

After the morning's auspicious start, time began to crawl. The midmorning hours through the afternoon typically seemed to be the hardest part of the day.: some meals over, enough still stretching out in front of them. It was the time when their feet were most firmly planted in the reality of the Barrett Institute's purpose; when the emphasis on weight gain, not playground, was the most deeply felt. She could sense it in the way the others withdrew. Where before the talking had been minimal, now it was nonexistent. Lily cried quietly in the corner. Lizzie righted herself on the couch and resumed a letter that she had been working on—one of those letters you write but don't send, one of the ones that the therapists advised writing. Dana drew pictures, while sleeping bodies sprawled across the couches and even on the floor. They slept, or drew, or wrote to escape what was happening. To pass the time. To avoid their thoughts. But Stefanie couldn't sleep, or write, … or read.

She went looking for Sarah.

Room 511 was comfortable. Sarah slid over to make room and took off her headphones. Stefanie could hear the muffled sound of the Matchbox 20 song *Unwell* as the tinny melody rose from the earpieces. Sarah had been here long enough to have the privilege of going each morning and retrieving her discman from the locked cabinet next to the bathroom. It occurred to Stefanie that her own personal box of outlawed items was untouched in the closet, locked up until god-knows-when. She listened carefully to the words of the song, not knowing when she would next hear music, and joined Sarah on the bed, momentarily surprised that no one had noticed when she just disappeared. Then again, she didn't really feel bad about being forgotten; for once it was useful.

Sarah had decorated as best she could with the minimal number of items that were allowed. Posters and collages gave some color to the room, and she had pictures taped above her bed, like this was camp or boarding school or even college. Stefanie didn't know what to make of it. She didn't know if she should regard it as a positive attitude or her resignation. Stefanie leaned in to look at the Scotch-taped photographs. People with the same smile and eyes. People with the same hair. Some were older, some younger. Sarah pointed to each and gave Stefanie a brief bio.

"That's my mom. And there's Grandma before she died; it's an old picture. She had a stroke when I was eleven and died a week and a half later." She pointed to another picture that was blurry and out of focus. "Those are my cousins, but you can't tell because my dad was taking the pictures. He's a real joker." She laughed at a picture of her father hanging upside down from a tree limb by his knees. "Guess that's where I get it from."

There was another picture on her nightstand, but this one was in a silver frame. "That's Edward. My boyfriend. God, I miss him." Sarah's voice drifted away, and Stefanie looked toward the dresser. She couldn't help thinking that, if she'd had a boyfriend or even just a friend, she wouldn't have ended up in a place like this. Then again, what did she know? From where she'd started, no guy would ever have looked twice at a whale like her. Notebooks lined the dresser. Ah, journals, Stefanie recognized. Sarah had kept a journal every year since the age of thirteen, when she'd first started dieting. And she'd brought them with her, though she wasn't sure why.

Pictures, books, CDs strewn about the bed—it was almost like being home. Sarah didn't seem at all uncomfortable here.

"Now you can't expect to come in my room and not give me the scoop. How's your first morning going? You're surviving, obviously. Met any nice people? Anything else that I should know about? Any traumas or vomiting or restraint use?"

Trauma? Restraint use? Vomiting? She hadn't seen any of that. Were those things common? Would she know about it? Where could they do it? Not in the bathroom certainly; the door was always locked. Not in the wastebaskets; there would be nowhere to dispose of the evidence. Closets seemed unsanitary—wouldn't they smell? Not even out the windows; they were locked too. And she hadn't seen anyplace where someone could hide. And restraints? What about restraints? This was an eating disorder unit. They weren't murderers, and this wasn't the psycho ward. They didn't need to be chained down or put in straitjackets.

But apparently Sarah didn't really want an answer, at least not that second. "You're hanging out with other people, right? Don't be one who holes up in a corner and doesn't talk. You might as well make some friends. You might be here a while, by the look of you— no offense meant."

Offense? *By the look of you?* What was Sarah talking about? *She* wasn't thin. She barely had any weight to gain at all. *She* wasn't *obviously* emaciated, not like Sarah.

"Lizzie's cool. I hear she got off CO today. She's been here, like, forever. Seven weeks now, according to the nurses' gossip, and she hasn't been allowed to socialize normally with us yet. Still you can tell she's a cool kinda chick. And Lily, your roommate. She's the quiet type, but with potential. If you can draw her out. The others I'm not so sure about. Madeline came on the same day as me but hasn't said a word yet. Dana hasn't been here long, but she doesn't seem to want to hold on to her eating disorder. Natalie's a complainer—don't hang around with her. And Riley's cool, if Francesca the Leech would leave him alone for just one second."

Sarah was making up for lost talking time. She'd been alone for too many hours already, and it was only eleven forty-five am. Stefanie revealed the gossip from that morning, and as Sarah listened, she wondered if Sarah would survive bedrest.

"Stefanie Webber." A new voice called from somewhere nearby. They had finally missed her.

"Quick, get out in the hallway. That's Jules, one of the med school volunteers. They're in training. They come here to watch us, talk to us, observe us, *learn* from us. She's nice, but you'll still get in trouble for being in here. They check up on each patient every half hour and make a note of your location and what you're doing. Hurry. Just say that you were lending me your markers." Sarah held up a package of markers that were under her pillow, "I'll show her these if she asks."

Stefanie retreated quickly to the hallway and joined Lizzie and Lily. Within minutes it was lunchtime. More food.

~ *30* ~

*D*ay *One Hospitalization: 99.6 (less than at Dr.
Adler's office). Day Two Hospitalization: 101.5*
*Madeline spoke tonight. She's getting bolder, coming out
of her shell.*

Day Three Hospitalization: 102.1

Two and a half pounds in three days. And she was still sitting
at the Ensure table. She wouldn't get real food until the next day:
Saturday. It was the start of her first weekend at the Barrett Institute.
She hated the doctor, Dr. Gray, for making her wait so long. They
had spoken only once, after the assessment meeting in which the
doctors schemed together and decided which patients would get
which privileges. Dr. Gray had emerged all smiles, handed Dana
a signed pass that would allow her to go to the cafeteria once a
week, and patted Stefanie on the back. "Sorry, sweetheart." The
words seemed to drip with sugary condescension, and Stefanie
longed to remove the hand from her shoulder. "It won't be so much
longer. Can't get the order in until the weekend starts. You'll have
to wait until then. It's not so bad anyway, just like a milkshake.
And you're gaining weight nicely." *What was that supposed to mean?*
She already knew she was fat; he didn't have to assure her of this
fact. Assessment meetings were on Thursdays. Either you got your
requests granted for sharps, unsupervised bathroom, unsupervised
showers, changes in a caloric prescription or you didn't; there were
no appeals and no explanations. The doctors emerged from the
weigh-in room, where they could talk without being seen or heard,
and passed their judgments. Then they disappeared. Dr. Gray
had not reappeared after that moment, and the image burned into

Stefanie's memory was of a white lab coat heading toward the door without looking back.

Three days down. She envisioned a long highway stretching ahead of her with mileage markers whizzing past. One. Two. Three. How many more? Thank God Sarah would be off bedrest tomorrow. Stefanie had been sneaking into her room occasionally, staying only very briefly so they wouldn't catch her and add on to her sentence, like they did in prison when you broke the rules. She'd also passed the time playing cards with Lizzie, who was a wiz at Rummy 500. And she and Lily had become closer ever since she started talking; that was two nights ago. But there had been no real excitement, nothing to break the tick-tock steady routine of the ward. Rumor had it, however, that a new patient was coming in today. Whispers and squeals tumbled through the air as each patient wondered what the new girl's story would be.

Group therapy was always held in the same room at the end of the hallway, beyond where Lane usually sat. It was a big open space where the couches and chairs were arranged in a homey semicircle. An unused piano sat off to the side, tucked away into a corner; an emergency exit and art closet broke up the monotonous white of the walls. They perched on the edge of chairs uncomfortably, tapping their feet incessantly, believing that this would burn calories. Occasionally, Dr. Franz, the usual group moderator, would order their legs to be still, but even that stillness would last only a minute. The urge to move was too powerful to resist—not that they really tried. They were supposed to share their difficulties, fears, and stories during group, and troubleshoot when problems arose.

But Stefanie hadn't really witnessed any of this yet. There were a few girls who talked—Lizzie, Becca, and Sarah, when she was allowed to come—and there were some who remained silent. Stefanie had spoken maybe two or three times, enough so that no one could yell at her for being uncooperative but not enough so that anyone would really know about her. She was just getting used to being one of them, and she didn't want to expose herself as the fraud that she was—the fake anorexic girl.

The other day, when Dr. Franz had asked about fear foods, the discussion had become animated. But when asked to discuss why there were fear foods, their eyes went back to wandering the room. Dr. Franz no longer had many hands in the air, waiting to be called on. Sometimes Stefanie wondered if these doctors—Dr. Franz and Dr. Katz, her therapist—ever got tired of playing to a crowd that was perpetually hostile. Sometimes she thought that she should comply more readily, answer the questions, drink the Ensure, get *better*, just to make their jobs easier. But she might have been the only one who had ever had this thought, and she had never acted on it.

So these all-unit meetings remained a kind of distorted merry-go-round that never stopped and changed only slightly between the comings and goings of patients. Some days they felt like being more difficult than others. It was like they had formed an alliance: all of the patients versus the staff members. These were the fun sessions. On other days, they sat quietly and let Dr. Franz lecture about the importance of changing thoughts in order to change behaviors. An hour after the meeting had broken up, not one girl would remember what they had discussed. Perhaps it was from lack of nourishment to the brain, but more likely because they just didn't care. They weren't really there to be helped. *Were they?*

Today was a boring day. Group that morning had been the same as always—royally unproductive—but when the girls' minds wandered, they had something to fill their thoughts: the new patient, the next member of their elite squad.

"Her name's Abigail Lexington." Stefanie heard the conversation between the nurses as she waited at the office door to request her hard-won headphone privileges. "Yeah, another one. Rampant these days. This one'll be in the dorm. The empty bed that's already made." The rumors were very rarely wrong around here, but this one wasn't just rumor: it was fact. Stefanie waited to hear more. She wouldn't mind another patient. It would be someone new to talk to, someone new to make friends with. The more the better, so long as this new one wasn't too skinny.

"She'll be here before lunch. Her parents are bringing her in. She'll be on CO for a day, just to test her. She's a swimmer, so watch for exercising. That's her obsession."

The door opened, and Lissa Perry, the program director, walked right into her. Ms. Perry was a tall woman, exceedingly thin—to the point where Stefanie wanted to feed her a can of Ensure—and intimidating. Sarah had said that she appeared once a week to run Unit Common Time, where each patient was given the chance to bring up any problems that she was having with communal living. It was a meeting that reminded Stefanie of cabin time at sleep-away camp. Other than that, Lissa Perry was unknown to the patients. She swept through the hallway once a day in her long, A-line skirts and Bobby Brown makeup: coral lipstick, golden eye-shadow, and rosy pink blush, and basically kept the unit running. No one was sure what that job really entailed, but supposedly it was important. She didn't talk to anyone, and no one talked to her. Among her and the patients, there seemed to be mutual terror.

Stefanie feigned a smile and forgot what she was doing at the door. "Sorry. I don't remember what I needed." She laughed at herself and recoiled, still wondering if she and Abigail would become friends.

Abigail was your typical athlete, but much thinner. If Stefanie had been asked to describe Abigail before the girl even arrived, she would have been able to do it. It might not even have been a challenge. She was five foot seven inches tall with straight brown hair, highlighted golden, that hit just below her shoulders. Her legs were long and her torso was short, making her already thin legs look even thinner.

There was no fat on her body. Not an extra ounce anywhere. It was too hard to see the color of her eyes, but the way they flitted around the room yet refused to look down at the floor showed nervousness and determination. That same look Stefanie imagined had been in her own eyes on that first night. Obviously, Abigail didn't want to be there either.

Stefanie felt sorry for her. She didn't know that once you were in, you couldn't leave without completing the program. It was already too late for her to turn back.

The hand of Spit that they were playing, in the minutes between group therapy and lunch, had stopped abruptly with the entrance of the new girl. They scanned her body. They looked for obvious bones. They looked into her eyes—did they seem scared or hostile? There was a distinct difference. They looked at her posture. Would she like some encouragement and advice? Could they be friends? Lizzie was used to this routine, but Stefanie and Lily were still new to it. Stefanie had only seen Lily, and Lily had never seen anyone admitted.

"Her name's Abigail. She's an exerciser," Stefanie whispered, her voice low and her mouth shielded by her cards. "I heard Lissa talking about it in the office. They're putting her on CO."

"That's bad. CO, and it's only her first day. Stinks to come in on that. Takes forever to gain any trust around here, and CO doesn't help any." Lizzie shook her head, speaking from experience, and put down her hand of cards. "I'm tired of Spit. Let's play Rummy 500 this time. Won't do us any good to try and talk to her—not for a few days at least, and not in here where they'd see us anyway. She'll be in the dorm with me. Maybe I can try to help tonight. But anyway, Ladies,"—she always used the term "ladies," as though Barrett was some sort of fancy finishing school and they'd just aced Fingerbowls 101—"let's get back to our card game. Nothing better to do, it's not like we can make friends."

Lizzie was right. Abigail was confined to a seat across the hallway from Ellie, and the two were watched all day. No one could talk to them, and they couldn't talk to each other—not that Ellie would have been such great company. Their only reprieve would come during a bathroom break, when they got to retreat into a stall and close the door. They were watched even on their way down the hall and as they stood in line.

It would likely be some time before Abigail would get to meet any of them. Lizzie spoke to her that first night, but only briefly before she was called away and reprimanded. It was only long enough to try and offer some solace, though she didn't know if it had helped.

~ 31 ~

They guessed that Abigail won the nurses over. They weren't sure how she had done it, and she never did explain. But the next afternoon, Abigail appeared in the common room without either Jules or Morgan, the other daytime volunteer, on her heels. Lizzie confessed to being jealous. Lily got shy—she'd been restricting and was sure that the staff was disappointed in her. She didn't want to talk to someone who was on their good side. They might think that she was trying to corrupt the angel. Stefanie wasn't sure what to think. She wasn't inherently outgoing. And this girl was *so thin*, she looked like she might break. It was embarrassing to think that Abigail might be disgusted with her and the additional pound that the scale had registered that morning. But Sarah, who had finally been released from her bedroom confinement, was her usual hearty self, and, within the hour, Abigail had been dealt into the latest hand of Rummy 500.

In fact, by day seven, their little group—Sarah, Lizzie, Lily, Abigail, and Stefanie—had become inseparable, if such a concept could even exist under the circumstances. Secretly, Stefanie had to admit that as much as she would have liked to go home, now that she was part of a group, the place really wasn't so bad. The card games had allowed the girls to open up to each other. It had taken awhile, but Stefanie had found that friendships were possible even in this most unlikely of environments.

It was information she would have liked to pass on to Naomi, another new girl who had come just before lunch. By that evening, the girl had thrown up twice. And although Naomi had been told that she'd get an NG tube if she didn't stop, the girl had said she couldn't help it—that she'd gotten to the point where she purged automatically, without even forcing it. Naomi was one of the sickest ones here. Unlike the other purgers, she hadn't even bothered to go behind the TV, when no one was watching, or in the corner behind the art cabinet, where it was sheltered. Maybe she'd heard that if you tried to hide like that and got caught, you'd get CO.

That throaty gag cut Stefanie's reverie short as Naomi's guts spewed across the floor for the third time that day. Both times before, it had happened the same way. First she gagged. Then she put her hand up to her mouth. And moments later, the sound of liquid splattered against the floor. It didn't make a difference whether it was on the linoleum or on the carpet—the smell was the same, and the sound was only slightly dulled on the carpet, where it took even longer to clean up. The first time, Stefanie had made the mistake of watching. She'd had trouble not vomiting herself. The second time, she didn't watch but heard it instead, and that was almost as bad. Now, she hadn't been quick enough to close her eyes and had been a witness to the heaves that brought the last bit of food out onto the floor. Each time she did it, Naomi had been made to clean it up, but that didn't seem to stop her. She only scrubbed the floor again and reinforced the antiseptic smell that never seemed to fade.

Now Naomi was standing with her hand clapped across her mouth and was staring up at the ceiling. Probably willing the vomit back into her stomach. It was sad to watch. There was a resigned look in her eyes, as if she knew what was going to happen, and she just couldn't fight it. As if she didn't care that within five minutes she would be back on her knees, washing the floor.

Stefanie tried to help. "Naomi, try not to think about it, OK? Think about something else. Look at the ceiling. Keep your head tilted back, and think about anything except for the Ensure," The pitch of Stefanie's voice changed suddenly from low to high. She was acutely aware of sounding like some new remix of Alvin and the Chipmunks, but she inched closer and fixed her eyes on Naomi's face, determined to offer whatever support she could. "Just keep it down, and you'll be fine. It feels rotten now, but it'll get better. They told me that the first night I was here, and I just rolled my eyes. I didn't believe them. But I'm still here, and they were right. It really isn't so bad. You get to know the other patients, and you form a kind of support group. Some of the nurses are mean, but, if you don't bother them, they won't bother you." She continued talking until Naomi righted her head, and she could see her gray-green eyes and ostrich-like neck; she looked strange—pinched and skeletal—but, with a few additional pounds, she might have been pretty.

Stefanie stopped. She had been babbling. Maybe she'd gone too far. This girl probably just wanted to be alone. She didn't want the help of a failed, fat anorexic. And she was intruding on her space. Stefanie backed away from the chair slowly—as if quick movement might scare the thin creature. She'd done enough damage; she wouldn't do anymore.

"Thanks, that helped. Your talking took my mind off it for a minute. I'm OK now. I'm Naomi, by the way."

Stefanie stopped moving away and took a step closer. "I'm Stefanie." She already knew the girl's name; she had used it when she had first started talking. But Naomi probably didn't know hers. "Glad to help. That's sort of the way things are here. We have to help each other. Otherwise none of us would make it."

She'd included herself in the group. She'd referred to herself as one of them. Just like that first night, when she had admitted to Sarah that she was sick. Would Naomi notice? It was a presumptuous statement to have made. Certainly, if Naomi looked hard enough, she would see the layers of fat and know that Stefanie Webber would make it on her own. Of course she would; it wasn't a problem if you weren't sick. And she didn't need to be here in the first place. But Naomi didn't react. She just gave a shaky, grateful smile. Stefanie smiled back.

"What game are you guys playing?" Naomi was addressing Stefanie but watching Lizzie and Sarah as they wrestled over the deck to determine whose turn it was to deal. Sarah gave a final tug on the cards, and they came out of Lizzie's hands. Sarah heard the question and answered for Stefanie. "About to play Rummy 500. I'm just getting good—after a week of sucking." She started to deal. "Should we count you in?"

And just like that, Naomi became a part of their small group. The sixth member.

*S*he might have felt disloyal …

But Laura, Annabel, and Julia were all on vacation. They were gone for a week or more, and, when they got back, they would be tan and relaxed and ready for Spring Term. They weren't going to give up Vail and Cancun and Paradise Island just to sit by their phones and talk to her once a day. They were going to ski and soak in the sun and drink strawberry daiquiris—virgins they told their parents, but sneaking the real stuff when they weren't watching. They needed a vacation from her. Even Julia, who hadn't really been involved in the intervention, seemed tired of dealing with her. Toward the end, Julia had talked only long enough to remark that Stefanie was too skinny, and then she had drifted away again. They weren't going to call or come visit—not that Stefanie could really blame them and not that she really wanted them there—but, somewhere in the back of her mind, she couldn't help thinking that it would have been nice.

So what did it matter if she had made some new friends? Lizzie, Lily, Abby, Naomi, Sarah and Stefanie. They'd formed a group. The doctors called them the six musketeers of Tower 3 North.

Stefanie had been there eleven days now and was beginning to settle into the routine. It happened slowly, but she got used to drinking cans of Ensure and waiting for commodes until two hours after meals, after which time purging would be useless because their bodies would have already absorbed the calories. She woke up automatically now, earlier even than when Lucy called for them, and she and Lily were usually the first in line to wash up and use the bathroom. She was comfortable wandering the hallways in her fuzzy leopard-print slippers, and she didn't worry what people would think if she isolated herself and cried. There were no limitations put on her range of feelings; they'd all been there and done the same thing in those hard moments. They knew not to take it personally.

She'd been promoted to trays of real food: burritos, cheese blintzes, hamburgers and French fries, cookies, ice cream sandwiches, though still with supplements in between—still three times a day. It had felt nice to chew and have the Rice Krispies crunch in her mouth that first morning she'd been given real food, when she had sat at her tray with a sense of accomplishment.

They played card games incessantly, inventing some of their own when the old ones got tiresome. Ellie sometimes screamed at them to keep the noise level down, but she was just moody. They'd lower their voices for a minute, then forget, be shushed, and break out into giggles. And when Stefanie called her parents in the evening now, she still begged to come home, but the desire wasn't so great. She'd make it here, if she had to stay. And if she cried, there was always someone there to rub her back when she had to hang up the phone.

Now, it was time for group—the big excitement of the day. The schedule for today read CBT: Cognitive Behavioral Therapy. It was the most frequently scheduled group, scheduled four times a week, with varying topics each session. It was the part of their recovery program where they challenged past beliefs—that they would get fat by eating—and tried to look rationally at their problems—that they were underweight as it was, and their bodies needed fuel to survive. As if any of them believed that. It didn't really seem so overwhelmingly helpful, but Stefanie had to go anyway. Personally, she had felt good about the previous day's Assertiveness Training with Dr. Franz, the therapist at Barrett who always seemed lost and whose hair stood out in a poof of brown curls, but the groups rotated on a cycle. She didn't know when she'd get that again.

Today, Dr. Katz, Stefanie's therapist at the Barrett Institute, was leading the discussion, and she was holding up a large pad of white paper, which she placed on an easel. The discussion du jour was Eating Disorders: Punishments and Rewards. A fancy name for the typical pro/con list. It was meant to show the patients that eating disorders were not worth the trouble.

Stefanie wondered if Dr. Katz could succeed. After all, being thin meant being happy, and wasn't happiness worth anything?

"Who'll start?" Dr. Katz waited while they chose seats. Distracted, Stefanie wondered if all hospital therapists had curly, frizzy hair, and she thought about what Dr. Katz and Dr. Franz would look like with straight hair; it was hard to imagine. The curls were definitely what made the outfit. In a perfectly pressed khaki suit with clean, straight edges, Dr. Katz might have looked refined even, if it hadn't been for the hair. Stefanie whispered for Lily to look, and together they grinned widely and squeezed each other's hands to keep from laughing out loud. Therapists were a strange bunch of people.

Becca was always the last to arrive because she sauntered in, purposefully late just to assert her independence. And Natalie barely preceeded her; she had been late to group so many times on account of phone calls, that her phone privileges—which allowed her to call anyone, whenever she wanted, as long as it was on her own time not the hospital's—were close to being revoked. Stefanie was usually prompt. She didn't see any reason to put off the inevitable. She had tried that once before, when she got hysterical the day she was admitted. It hadn't worked then, and she knew it wouldn't now. It was just easier to do what they asked.

"Come on, throw some pros at me. I know you all have them." Dr. Katz took in the circle.

Stefanie fidgeted in her seat. She could feel those eyes resting on her, and wished she could melt into the hard chair that hurt her tailbone. Those first few moments of group were always the hardest. No one wanted to speak. They just sat and looked around. They crossed and uncrossed their arms, then their legs. Ellie fanned herself with her hand and announced that she was having "Ensure sweats." They—meaning the hospital—were re-feeding her too quickly and causing her to get overheated as her metabolism sped up with each meal. The doctors just ignored her; they wouldn't enable her bad behavior by giving her the attention that she was craving. No one else spoke, but their eyes said more than their words could have. At the same time that Dr. Katz surveyed the group, the group surveyed itself: assessing its members, exchanging nervous glances, waiting together for someone to say something to end the silence that rang in their ears.

"Fine, I'll go. Pro: My boyfriend, Ed, likes me better when I'm skinny," Sarah began. Stefanie thought of the silver picture frame on Sarah's nighttable and wondered if this were true. Had Sarah just imagined it, or had Ed ever said anything? She couldn't remember what Sarah had said about him. She had said that she loved Ed. How could she, if he was superficial enough to only care about the size at the back of her jeans?

"He always said that I was too fat. Now he'll go out with me," Sarah continued. "He takes me out after classes, and he spends the money that he makes at Pizza Hut just to make me happy. We met at school, and he never liked me before. But now, well, our relationship is just so much better."

"Good, Sarah, thank you for your honesty." Dr. Katz's voice was calm. Trained. Unemotional. "Now, let's think about this. Would Ed really not like you if you weren't emaciated? Would he really—"

Sarah interrupted, and Dr. Katz let her continue. "Then again, con: I seem to have conformed to fit his idea of a perfect woman. He wants a model for a girlfriend, not me. And yet, I'm trying to give him what he wants." Sarah looked confused.

Dr. Katz looked pleased as she divided the top sheet of paper in half. She labeled one side Rewards and one side Punishments and made a note of Sarah's points. "Good for you, Sarah. You're already starting to challenge that voice inside of you that only sees the pros and ignores the potentially fatal cons. I liked that you thought about what you were saying as you were saying it, and you weren't afraid to contradict yourself. You're right: being skinny for Ed is a pro and a con. Isn't it possible that Ed would love you even at your target weight? And if not, why are you starving yourself for someone else?"

Many heads nodded in agreement, but Sarah didn't look convinced.

"Who's next?" Dr. Katz again took in the group, but this time a few hands went up in the air, volunteering to talk. "OK ..." Her voice trailed off as she thought about which girl to call on. "Lizzie, why don't you take a turn?"

"It makes them all feel bad for me. They ask if I'm OK and stuff like that. They spend time with me."

Who? Who was Lizzie was talking about? What was Lizzie like at home? Why was she starving herself? Was she looking for happiness, or did she have another reason? Why were all of the patients in the room starving themselves? She knew that they were and for how long they had been and how seriously ill they had made themselves, but Stefanie suddenly realized that she didn't really know that much about her new friends. Their identities were based on their eating disorders: Abby was the overexerciser; Lizzie was the one who had been on CO; Sarah and Naomi were the purgers; Ellie and Becca were the deceptive ones. She'd spent eleven days at this place, but beyond these few simple facts, what else did she know? Who were these girls?

"... And it dulls the pain." Lizzie tucked her feet under her body and rested her head in her hand. Her voice had softened, and her words had become barely audible.

Pulled out of her thoughts, Stefanie noticed that Lizzie's knuckles and knees were extremely bony. She wondered how she could sit like that. Didn't it hurt? Her eyes followed the thin line of blue vein under Lizzie's skin down to the side of her ankle. There were a couple of scars along the ridge of her foot, near her Achilles tendon and up onto the ankle. Making eye contact, Stefanie smiled. Lizzie didn't smile back. She just laid the palm of her hand over the scars and continued to stare at the ground.

Generously filling the silence, Lily took the floor. In her quiet voice, which was barely audible when she spoke to a large group, she explained how she would get recognition at school if she were thin.

She didn't get enough attention just for being a good student. "I'm at the top of my class, but it doesn't even matter. Nobody cares. It's like I'm not even there—like I don't exist."

She wanted more to her personality than grades. "Why must I always be a stupid number on the top of a test? They're all waiting for me to make a mistake, I know it. If I were thin, at least I'd have something else going for me. I'd be more than a GPA."

Besides, her mother would have *wanted* her to diet. Her mother had dieted until the day she had died, a few years before.

"On her death certificate it doesn't say cancer. It says malnutrition. Starvation. She starved herself to—death." Lily paused before the word death, and her voice broke when she went on. "All my life, she was dieting. I tried to get her to eat sometimes, but I thought she was beautiful. She was my mom."

As the group dispersed back to their common room stations, Stefanie thought about all she had learned. She hadn't challenged any particular belief with a pro/con list, but this had probably been the most informative CBT session yet.

What else didn't she know? These were the people that she had been living with, sitting with, eating with. These were the people that she cried with, and with whom she tested for protruding bones. In the time that it took for the sun to set eleven times, they had become her family.

Curiosity gnawed at her, and Stefanie wished she could know their stories. It had never occurred to her that she didn't really know it all, but suddenly the world seemed different. A pang of guilt stabbed at her stomach, and she wondered how she had lived in the same room with someone for so long and never found out that her mother was dead. It had seemed strange that only her father would have checked her into the hospital and that he would bring the younger siblings, but she had never thought to ask. And Lizzie was so good at taking care of everyone else, but what was she concealing behind the smiles? And the others—were they showing their true selves, or were they all in hiding? Back in the common room, she picked up her journal and wrote down what she had learned that day. Their blunt statements had been startling, and she wished she could have known more. There was more information to find out; it was just a matter of time. And patience.

− 33 −

She didn't have long to wait. As much as she was curious about the others, they appeared to be just as curious.

Saturday nights were always more laid back. The weekend staff was generally kinder, more like hired babysitters and less like jail-keepers. They were more interested in reading the *Glamours* and *Redbooks* that they'd brought for distraction than in patrolling this group of privileged, sassy, self-absorbed waifs, as the Monday-to-Friday staff considered them. For the patients, it was a time when these otherwise blacklisted magazines—prohibited because of their emaciated models and potentially triggering pictures—infiltrated their cloistered existences. When left in plain sight, every fifteen or twenty minutes—so the staff could locate each patient and note her behavior, or when they took a patient who had been granted off-unit privileges to the room just outside the door to the unit, where movies could be rented out each day for use on the units—the temptation was almost too great to resist. The first weekend Stefanie was there, Becca had stolen a *Vogue,* which she had then passed along to Francesca in exchange for five dollars. Just where Francesca's money came from, Stefanie didn't know, as all her money had been confiscated upon admission. What use would she have for it in the hospital anyway? But the girls were evidently desperate enough to ogle the advertisements for Prada, Marc Jacobs, and Chanel that they were willing to risk suspension of courtyard privileges or the opportunity for autonomy that could only be had when not on CO. Over the course of those two days, the magazine had migrated, passed hands, smuggled into rooms under sweatshirts. They had poured over the models' stiletto-thin bodies, looking for bones or lines of definition around muscles, whispering pledges to each other, promising to look like that as soon as they got home. Occasionally they exclaimed over the injustice of life. If these emaciated skeletons were allowed on the runways, why were they locked up? The models were much skinnier. And then on Monday, when they returned from the weekend, the doctors wondered why there had been more restrictions.

But that second Saturday, after Naomi had entered Barrett, Francesca ran out of money, and Becca's entrepreneurship came to an abrupt halt. After that, there was little or no distraction.

"Let's do something. I'm bored." Abby was lying on her back with her hands across her stomach. "It's too quiet here. I need to move. That last Ensure's just sitting in my stomach turning to fat. Come on, there has to be something we can do."

"You're the active one—the one who knows all the games. Make a suggestion." Sarah tossed her journal at Abby. "Come on. I'm bored too, but I don't have any ideas."

Stefanie rolled lazily onto her back next to Abby. Where were her hip bones? She reached for her sides instinctively. For an instant, the combination of alarm and disgust that gripped her nearly pulled her out of the evening's torpor. She'd gained so much weight in those eleven days that she cringed every morning when she got on the scale. Her jeans didn't fit right anymore. Her relatively new size ones pinched around her stomach and hugged her thighs more closely than she would have liked. Could the others tell? Did they know that her numbers had crept steadily upward? Stefanie inhaled sharply, forcing her stomach to contract. Holding her breath, she tested again. There they were, thank God. She could feel the ribs and, higher up, her rib cage.

Abby started the conversation. "OK, tell me about yourself, Sarah. That should take up some time, since you're never lost for words." Abby giggled, righted herself, and tossed Sarah's book back to her.

"OK then. What should I say? My name is Sarah Amelia Johnson. I'm eighteen years old. I love writing in journals and watching movies."

She sounded like they were sitting in a circle in the middle of a cabin somewhere deep in the woods, playing bonding games. It reminded Stefanie of those getting-to-know-you exercises that they did at school with new teachers to help them put a face, perhaps even a favorite hobby, with a name. Stefanie tried not to laugh.

Putting down her assigned make-up work for school, Lizzie joined the conversation. "No, no, no. Not that kind of stuff. You sound demented, like this an AA meeting or something. Tell us the interesting stuff. You know … Why you're here … how long you've been sick and why … stuff like that."

For someone so young, Lizzie was unintimidated by the older girls. Sometimes it even seemed like the older girls were more hesitant than their youngest counterpart. Sarah grinned mischievously, "Oh. Well then, that's a different discussion. I'm here because I've been sick since I was thirteen years old—five years. There, two answers in one."

Lizzie stuck out her tongue, momentarily showing her immaturity. "OK, but you've only answered my easy questions. *Why are you here?*"

"*Why?* Lizzie, what kind of question is that? I don't know why. Who in this room knows why? Do you know why?" Naomi moved in closer and Abby pushed herself up on her elbows, as Sarah turned the question around and asked it of Lizzie. They were all masters at avoiding this question and were curious to see how Lizzie would respond. It was a loaded question.

Lizzie shrugged. "I've got some ideas: I hate looking like a woman."

Francesca, who was sitting on the couch behind them had overheard the comment and had opened her mouth in the shape of an O. It was as if she couldn't believe what Lizzie had said, but at the same time her head was nodding—barely, almost imperceptibly, but still nodding.

"I don't want to be one. I don't want to have boobs, or get my period, or ever get married. I don't want men to look at me funny and hoot from car windows when I walk down Fifth Avenue." Lizzie made a face, lifting her upper lip in disgust and crinkling her nose.

"So what's starving got to do with it? You're still going to be a woman, even if you don't eat anything." Lily's voice was kind, but her words were harsh. Stefanie remembered reading about the causes of eating disorders and how some girls developed them to stave off puberty. At the time she hadn't really been sure what the phrase meant, but now she had a strong feeling that Lizzie was about to explain it. She wanted to understand. Flashing a quick, somewhat-coy smile in Lizzie's direction, Stefanie was simultaneously grateful to Lily for asking the question and yet angry with her for being so blunt. *What was it that made people hostile when they didn't know something—or couldn't understand?*

Lizzie wasn't put off. "The solution is to starve. If I don't eat, well then, I'm smart enough to know that I won't look like a woman. And at least that's something."

She looked at Lily for a reaction, and Lily spoke, barely audible. "Maybe that's part of it—not wanting to grow up." She was staring into the air just above Lizzie's head, and her eyes seemed unfocused.

"OK fine, I'll break the silence." Sarah jumped in to fill the void with speech, "I want to be my own person. I want my parents to get off my back and let me live the life that I want to live. I want to move out and move in with Ed—we want to get married. But *no!* They've always tried to control me." Her tongue ran over her chapped lips, and, wetting them, she paused for a moment as the nearly visible waves of anger passed over her. "When I was ten, I wanted to sleep over at a friend's house more than anything, and they said no—said we had plans. We didn't." She rolled her eyes, editorializing. "The next weekend, I asked the same question, got the same answer. When it continued for over a month, I finally gave up. I never did get to have that sleepover. And that's only one example. There are tons more." She paused again, gathering steam. "There's more that I want. I want Ed to love me like I love him and to look at me the same way he looks at the swimsuit models in *Sport's Illustrated.* I want him to be happy to see me every night. I want him to tell my parents to burn in hell because we're moving in together, and he can't imagine living without me. I want to please him and make him proud. I want—"

Abby had been right; once Sarah started, she just didn't stop. Finally, Lizzie cut in. "OK, motormouth. It's Lily's turn." By this point, Stefanie was paying full attention. Here was the information that she had been craving.

"Me?" Lily spoke cautiously. "I don't know—I just want to make my mother proud of me. Nothing special. That's it." Her voice was flat and nondescript.

Stefanie wouldn't settle for that. This was the girl she was sharing a room with. She deserved to know more about her than that she wanted to please her mother. She wanted to know what Lily dreamt about in bed at night, what foods scared her the most. She wanted to know the progression of each of her friends' diseases, and she wanted to know if they really wanted to get better. She hadn't thought about it before—she had been caught up in all the similarities—but they were all so different. She wanted to know why Sarah wasn't Lizzie, and why Lizzie wasn't Abby. And then she wanted to know what it was that held them all together. What had landed all of them here, together?

"Sorry girl, you gotta do better than that." Apparently Sarah was thinking the same thing.

"Really, it's not that interesting. I don't want to bore you." Lily seemed to be waiting for reassurance, because when Stefanie, Naomi, Lizzie, Abby, and Sarah moved in closer, she managed to continue, though her voice shook under the weight of the words. "My mom died two years ago. She always watched her weight. I want her to be proud that I know how to eat healthy also. She was so careful—especially toward the end." Her words were halting and slow but because she could see they were all still listening, she continued. "She wasted away to nothing. And I had to watch."

Naomi rested a hand on Lily's shoulder and murmured, "Oh sweetie …"

Suddenly Lily's face turned red, as if she'd something sinful, and she couldn't seem to get her next words out fast enough, "I mean, my dad's great, but he's just not my mom. He tries hard. He does so much for us." She was covering for him. "I love him and all. He's just not around that much."

Naomi's hand was still on Lily's shoulder, but her eyes were beginning to fill with tears. Lily looked at her and stopped, afraid to make it worse, but Naomi nodded and urged her to continue. "No ... don't stop. Say it. You gotta say it. I know how it feels."

Stefanie wasn't convinced that this was a good idea and Lily looked uncertain herself, but it had become obvious: now that she had started, she had to finish. It would have been like opening Pandora's box and not waiting until the end for Hope to fly out. Everything had to be let go. "He doesn't have enough attention to go around, really. And what he does have goes to Campbell and Andrew, because they're younger. Not that I blame them. I can deal with it. It's hard for my family. My dad has to work so hard. The insurance company won't always pay, and this place is expensive. I don't know how all our families do it. I get what attention I need at school—from the teachers because of my grades and from the other kids because of my diet." Laying her palm over Naomi's hand, she squeezed hard and continued slowly. "I need the diet because ... well—I know I'm being selfish—but sometimes the grades just don't feel like enough." These last words tumbled out of her mouth, and two tears raced each other down the slope of her cheek.

Ellie and Becca were staring from across the room as if their little cluster on the floor was a freak show, and Terry, the one man who worked on this unit, raised his eyebrows in their direction but decided to leave them alone. It wasn't like he hadn't seen tears before. Becca opened her mouth as if to comment, but he silenced her with a glare and a flick of his pointer finger in her direction. She closed her mouth again.

Stefanie nodded. She could understand. Sometimes she felt the same way: that grades just weren't good enough. They didn't get her friends. They didn't get her invited to parties. They didn't make people talk to her on the phone at night—unless they were calling for homework help. And she wasn't even as good a student as Lily. She could tell that much just by watching. She had imagined that Lily got all the attention; she was always reading a textbook or doing math problems. She had imagined her being the teacher's pet, the class favorite, the most popular girl. It had made sense that Lily would get more attention because Lily was smarter. But still that hadn't been enough. Stefanie could definitely understand.

Lily stopped, and Stefanie started where she had left off. "I know what you mean. I don't get nearly the attention that you must get for your grades—mine are nothing special—and that's all the recognition that I ever get. Maybe the occasional pat on the back and the 'Good work, Stef!' but it's just not enough. Maybe it'll never be enough. God." Exasperation filled her voice with breathiness. "I just want to be happy."

Stefanie blushed and bit down on her lip, but not hard enough for it to bleed. She'd never said those things out loud before. Those thoughts had been confined to the pages of her journal, and she'd never expected to share them with anyone—much less a group of five girls.

It had been an hour since this new tell-all truth game had started, but there still seemed to be more to say. In the beginning, the explanations or comments had proceeded reluctantly, but now they were comfortable and happy to share their most secret desires and needs. There was a trust between them. Each had already told their worst— so that anything that came after wouldn't be so awful, so hard to say or face.

Naomi gave Lily a hug, looking closely at the nurses to see if they were watching. "You're not the only one who has—or had—a weight-obsessed parent." She shifted slightly on her butt, as if maybe her tailbone had started to hurt from the hard floor, and blinked once. "My dad's the same way. He counts calories on everything. He was my biggest dieting resource. He's the only man I know who eats sorbet instead of ice cream."

Abby laughed but nodded at the same time. "He's not the only one. My dad's the same way!" Together they rolled their eyes, and Stefanie was relieved that her father was not this type. He watched his weight, certainly, but he was more of an exercise fanatic than a calorie junkie. For that, she was suddenly thankful.

Naomi wasn't finished. "He's not around much either—for different reasons probably, but we have that in common also, Lil. The workaholic, middle-aged, type A personality: that's my dad. And whatever time he does have to spend at home, he's always going to the gym or the squash courts instead. That's his biggest passion—squash. You'd think his biggest passion might be his kid, but no, it's squash. He couldn't care less about me." Her voice was quivering with hostility, and Terry was watching again, conscious of the mounting tension in the room. The other patients had gone silent; they too were listening to the tone of Naomi's voice and watching her facial expressions. As the other patients looked on, Naomi's eyebrows furrowed, and her eyes narrowed. "He never cared, no matter how hard I worked to please him. The pressure to please Daddy Dearest was always there, but nothing was ever good enough."

Naomi finished, and no one quite knew what to say. Lily was still holding her hand, but it had gone limp. Naomi fidgeted, looked at the ground, and began to tap the floor with the toes of her right foot. Abby was the only one who hadn't shared a story, and Lizzie poked her arm. The two of them had bonded over the shared injustice of sleeping in the dorm. "Tell 'em about pressure, Abs."

"I was just thinking about that, Liz." Her voice had grown more quiet than usual, and she seemed far away. "But it's not really such a big thing."

Sarah jumped at the opportunity. "You started this whole thing. You gotta share too. And we've all talked. It's not like we're being shy. Just tell your story." Stefanie laughed. Sarah certainly didn't have the virtue of patience.

"It's hardly a story, but OK, if you insist, I'll tell. So I'm a swimmer. When I was three, my parents used to call me their little fish, and I guess I just grew into that title. I've been swimming since I was two, and I've always loved it. Now, after years of practice, I'm finally the number-one swimmer on my school's swim team."

Sarah pushed Abby, and she fell from her balanced position on her elbows. "I'm so close to hitting you—no story? What the hell have you been smoking? Why the hell are you here? You've got something to work for; you've already got a place in the world and a reason for living. That's better than the rest of us poor slobs can say for ourselves!"

Stefanie thought of taking issue with the "poor slobs" bit, but she kept her comments to herself. Abby continued, ignoring Sarah's interruption. "Anyway, we've been to the States before, and I had a chance to go on to the Eastern Division meet this year. But then I got sick, and now we don't know if I'll be able to go. My coach was fuming when my parents told him that I wasn't going to be at practice for the next couple of weeks. He really wants me there; he needs me, he says." She took a deep breath and swallowed, the action of her throat visible beneath the icicle-white skin. "I don't want to disappoint him. He pushes me so hard to be my best, but I'd never have gotten where I am today without him. I know I'm going to let him down. I have to stay in shape, and these stupid rules forbid exercising. I have to get out of here if I'm ever going to have a shot." She shivered, as if the next thought was almost too hard to handle. "Or he'll have to start looking for a replacement. He doesn't like to lose."

"It's a sob story—just tragic. I'm so sorry that you're the best swimmer in the world. Poor little overachiever. I'll light a candle for you at church." Sarah pantomimed lighting a candle with a glowing stick and laughed raucously at herself. Lizzie smiled.

Abby reached over and took Sarah's journal, using it as a paddle to land a perfectly aimed blow on Sarah's backside. One of the negligent nurses finally looked up when they heard the sound of hardback cover against vertebrae. "Ladies, don't make us come over there. You don't want our wrath tonight."

That was the end of the conversation. As Stefanie lay in bed that night and went through her usual checklists—testing to see which bones still stood out where and which bones needed to be recovered once she got back home—she thought about their little group. There were so many connections between them all. Inattentive parents, the stress of school, trying to please people, pressures: the themes were all the same. When they talked, they could have been telling each other's stories—the emotion, the fear, the confusion. No wonder it seemed like they understood how she felt; they did. Where others looked at her with confusion or frustration, these girls looked at her with compassion and sensitivity. They really were the Six Musketeers. Stefanie's eyes wandered until they rested on the golden moon outside her window, high above Manhattan, and, as her hands traced the topography of her body, she wondered if they were all lying on their beds at that moment, feeling for the same bones.

– 34 –

After that night, things changed. They talked more often as they played cards and occasionally stayed by the couches even when their rooms were open. It didn't seem as important to get away anymore. And Stefanie got the impression that they were all more honest. Now when they talked, it wasn't about their favorite classes at school or what their favorite foods had been. They had real conversations; they talked about their feelings, about home, about family, about fears and desires.

She liked talking to them. She realized that it was no longer those girls and her, but us girls. Gradually, Stefanie had come to the realization that she had been sick. *Had been.* They'd shared in all the injustices of this psychiatric hospital and had bonded over those experiences. They were forever connected in a way that Stefanie had never felt before. When she cried, they knew why. When she closed her doors in the evening against the prying eyes of the wardens, they all knew that she was exercising. When she took as long as possible eating the food in front of her, they knew that it was a tactic for unsuccessfully avoiding the inevitable. They said she was still too skinny, but they couldn't see. Maybe they were just being polite— maybe their views of everyone else were distorted. Maybe she had been sick, but not now. She couldn't believe them when they told her that she still needed help. But somehow it didn't matter. The friendship between them wasn't based on what each girl weighed; they all understood each other. She knew what they were feeling, and they knew what she was feeling. She reminded herself of that whenever she felt that old competitor rise to the surface and think, "I can be thinner." Connection. They had become her closest friends. She told them things that she wouldn't have said to anyone else, and sometimes she didn't even have to tell them: they just knew.

And as the days inched into the end of Stefanie's second week, they only got closer. True, they were in prison's equivalent but joked that it was just Get-Fat Camp. They created games and played them enthusiastically. They invented alternative identities for the cans of Ensure.

"Hamburger today, Abby?"

"Yes, thank you, Lizzie; but make mine with cheese and bacon—and a tomato."

Those frothy drinks became everything from Salisbury steak with A-1 sauce to ginger and brown sugar-glazed salmon to French fries or Oreos. Then they had chugging contests behind the backs of the staff—gulping down the Ensure and slamming the cup down onto the table when the last drop was gone. And when the other patients or the volunteers looked over, they just tilted their heads back and laughed like hyenas because they knew they couldn't get in trouble for not restricting.

For the first time in months, it seemed like everything was going well—or as well as could be expected. Stefanie had been granted privileges: permission to use sharp objects, unsupervised showers, unsupervised bathroom, courtyard, off-unit activities, and Wednesday Morning Cafeteria Breakfast.

Wednesday Morning Cafeteria Breakfast. Stefanie had progressed faster than most. Stefanie had done what she was told and had been rewarded. She'd gained weight steadily, with only one minor slip-up (restricting a piece of what she considered rotten fish), and the doctors had been pleased. Sarah still had supervised bathroom. Lizzie was still sleeping in the dorm. Abby had finally been granted unsupervised showers and bathroom, but only after days of pleading. Naomi was still being watched closely after those first days when she purged and restricted; the medical staff had hesitated to consent to anything. So she was lucky when permission was granted to allow her to join the others for breakfast on the other side of the big, white, eternally locked door. It had been a celebration of sorts. An outing, even.

"Hi ho, hi ho, it's off to eat we go. To eat and play and try all day, hi ho, hi ho, hi ho, hi ho." Abby skipped down the hallway and dragged Lily with her. And Lizzie ran to keep up, while the others followed more sedately behind.

The cafeteria was down two floors in the elevator, across another hallway, around a corner to the right, another corner to the left, and then straight ahead. It was off the unit.

The smell hit them as soon as they turned the last corner. It wasn't specifically recognizable but rather a concoction of various scents that mingled together to form a haze over Stefanie's senses. She thought she could smell maple syrup, pancakes, waffles, and coffee. Bacon, eggs, coffeecake muffins, and cinnamon buns. Whatever it was, it smelled good. Stefanie's mouth watered, and, as they walked side by side, she heard Naomi give a little squeal. They were all excited.

They couldn't go by themselves. Jules, who worked early on Wednesday mornings, followed them closely. And they couldn't choose just anything. It had to be at least equal to the number of calories that would have been on a tray upstairs. But still, in a sense, they were free.

Inside, there were even more choices than she had anticipated. There were bagels and cream cheese, yogurt and fruit, and granola bars, oatmeal, and grits. There was even a whole wall of cereal, more cereals than she could even remember. There were so many colors; the patterns of the boxes made her pleasantly dizzy, as if she had spun in the grass with her head tilted up toward the sky too many times on a summer day. There were so many things to choose from, so many delightful things to eat. It was as good as the supermarket.

And then there had been the interns: med-school students getting credit for hours spent in work experience. Three young doctors in white lab coats, their stethoscopes and ID tags hanging lazily from their strong necks, sat at a nearby table. The girls tried to suppress their giggles as they watched the men dig into plates piled high with food they still resisted. The antiseptic banality of the hospital setting and reality couldn't contain them here. One meal would lead inexorably to the next, but now, as the girls laughed, stole looks, and conspired to casually bump into the young men as they returned their trays to racks by the exit, it was clear that the interns would provide a conversation topic for quite a few hours when there was nothing better to do. More important, as they collected themselves and dutifully followed Jules upstairs, they could remind themselves how good it had felt to act like normal teenage girls.

− 35 −

*I*f only that could have lasted. True, somehow, things were easier to take here. As much as Stefanie hated to admit it, Dr. Adler had been right: to eat, she had needed the assistance of the hospital. It wasn't going to change things when she got back home, but she liked that, for the moment, the decisions were taken away from her. She had to eat. There was no wavering. There was no ambiguity. And she had to eat what was placed in front of her. There were no alternatives—higher calorie, lower calorie—there was no guilt. She didn't have to think that the food could have been avoided or that she had been weak to eat it. She hadn't had an option. Eat or tube. Eat and be discharged, or restrict and be held. It was all so simple.

What she didn't like was the ten pounds she had gained in the eighteen days that had passed. She would do something about that just as soon as she got home. She'd always known as much.

She wondered what the doctors who were so happy with her would say if they knew that every morning when she stepped onto the scale, she clenched her teeth and planned to diet again. It would only be a couple more weeks, and then she could do what she wanted. She'd lost the weight once before; she could do it again. The doctors didn't know that, of course. So they had trusted her—maybe too much.

Stefanie closed her journal. The green leather cover wasn't perfect anymore. It had scratches running along at odd angles, and on the back there was a stain of black ink where her pen had slipped. Perfection destroyed. The poor journal had been through a lot. Gently, she tucked it into her paper bag—her survival kit for the long days out in the hallway once the bedroom doors were locked. She buried her face in Mr. Whiskers' round tummy and tried not to look around. She read what she had written.

It's funny how fast things change here. One moment we're all doing great, and the next ... well, you know. As fast as you can start doing well, that's how fast you can stop.

She knew what was going on; it had been going on for the past couple of days, but she didn't want to see. It was one thing to know what you were going to do when all of this was over, but this was something else entirely.

The sound of nylon—windproof material that wasn't meant for contact against a wall grated on Stefanie's nerves. But Lily didn't seem to care. She pushed her back into the wall, willing her legs into action, and the legs and butt of her Abercrombie and Fitch pants made that awful noise—like sandpaper against metal. Or maybe that was just because of what the noise meant: wall squats. This was Lily's chosen form of exercise when the doors were still closed early in the morning, and she could get away with it. She'd done it the past few mornings now, mixing in sit-ups and pushups late at night. And Stefanie couldn't watch.

"Breakfast!"

For once, she had been saved by the call. They'd go in to breakfast, and the exercising would end. But to Stefanie, it just wasn't fair. If she couldn't exercise, then they shouldn't either. Not that she had ever tried.

Breakfast that morning consisted of cheese blintzes with strawberry topping and a glass of milk. It looked surprisingly good and tasted even better. It was sweet, but not too sweet; filling, but not too filling. It was slightly warm against her tongue and the roof of her mouth. She'd known breakfast would be decent. Once she'd stopped convincing herself to dislike the food, she'd discovered the meals here were more than decent, delicious even—although those words stuck in the back of her throat. It took courage to say them. She couldn't give in and corroborate the fact that she was recovered. And yet, the food was good, and she didn't hate it. Maybe she was supposed to, but she didn't. Occasionally she looked forward to meals; occasion-ally she was even hungry.

"What do you think she'd do if she caught me hiding food?" Sarah's question was obviously rhetorical; she knew the answer. They all did. "I can't believe they're serving this to us. I mean, look at this!" She scrunched up her napkin and threw it at her still-full plate, "Cheese, cholesterol, fat—you can't get any less healthy. And these floury, pancakey shells? You wouldn't catch me within twenty feet of them at home."

"Shh, they'll catch you. This isn't a good idea. And don't you want to be healthy?" Abby asked. "You need to eat to be healthy." She didn't care if the question had been rhetorical.

"Healthy? Who needs it? I've been sick for so long now that I'd rather stay this way. It's easier. I kinda like it."

Stefanie understood. She didn't always want to eat; sometimes she wanted to stay sick—if she was in the mood to even admit that she was sick. And sometimes she wanted to be sicker, as bad as Sarah or Naomi or any of them. As sick as she was, sometimes she wanted to be worse; she still wasn't good enough. And with her weight gain, she was falling behind. They all understood what Sarah was saying, but, still, Sarah was breaking the rules. You weren't allowed to talk about food, weight, or calories in the dining room. Ever! And you weren't allowed to hide food.

"The shinbone's connected to the knee bone, the knee bone's connected to the thighbone, the thighbone's connected to the hip bone ..."

The song popped into Stefanie's head, and she couldn't shake it away.

It was rude of Sarah to talk like that. She wasn't supposed to say those things. They might upset someone. Shinbones ... knee bones ... hip bones ... stupid, stupid, stupid. Stefanie bit her lip; she was upset. It didn't offer much comfort when, peripherally, she could see that Sarah had spilled a good two sips of milk and had wiped away a fairly significant portion of the cheese with her napkin. How was Sarah any different? Why was she special? Why didn't she have to eat?

Stefanie wished she could make Sarah stop cheating. She even felt a strange urge to turn her in. She'd just pull Jules aside and whisper what she'd seen. Sarah wouldn't be able to fool around anymore, and Stefanie wouldn't have to be envious. But she couldn't do that. She couldn't turn Sarah in.

That morning, Lizzie had left one third of her tray: one cheese blintz and half the strawberry sauce. She reported calmly and tucked a knife into one pocket. What did she need with a knife? Stefanie knew that Lizzie was not allowed to use scissors or tape or razors, but she didn't know why. And she'd never thought to ask.

"Step up now, Miss Abby. Let's keep the line moving ..."

"One glass milk, one cheese blintz."

"That's it? Restrict one blintz, strawberry sauce?"

That's it? Stefanie would have liked to echo those words. Abby was doing it too? Abby, who wanted to swim at nationals? What could she be thinking? This was just more stupidity.

Naomi did it too: she handed back her half-filled plastic container without even contemplating the partial tray with half portions of each item that had her name on it. Stefanie understood the fear of the partial tray. Unlike a full tray, it was just additional calories that hadn't been figured in to the daily amount of Ensure, and, for that reason, it was strictly optional. They had all been through the partial tray stage, except Naomi. Sometimes Stefanie just wanted to pull her along, perhaps force the food down her throat. But still, she could understand her friend's hesitancy. That was comprehensible. But the restriction of the Ensure just wasn't. Naomi had been doing so well; after those first couple of days, she'd barely restricted. And now this. Lily was the sole member of the clean plate club. And that was only because she had exercise to fall back on as soon as they were allowed into their rooms. They were all screwing around.

Stefanie felt a surge of warm, energizing adrenaline rush through her veins. Or maybe it was jealousy.

Her own tray was nearly empty. She should have left more. She hadn't enjoyed it; she tried to convince herself. But she'd eaten it, and that was just as bad.

It's OK. It's OK to eat.

She tried to believe it, but couldn't. They were already so much thinner than she, and they weren't eating. Why was she? She was a whale already. She'd only become bigger.

"Step up. We don't have all day."

Linda's words jolted Stefanie back into reality, and she stepped up and recorded—and promised herself she'd do better the next time.

"The shinbone's connected to the knee bone, the knee bone's connected to the thighbone, the thighbone's connected to the hip bone ..."

After breakfast, she requested her headphones: another privilege she had recently been granted, and listened to the *Motivation* CD for the first time in days. And she prayed, once again, to lose more weight.

It could have stopped. They could have just gone back to the way things were: eat, talk, laugh, go home. That was how it should have been, but it wasn't. Instead, it was restrict, cry, refuse, stay sick. It was what the others chose, and Stefanie went along. That they were hurting themselves didn't matter; she wouldn't be left behind.

And the numbers on the scale began to fall.

Every morning before she got up and every night when they'd turned off the lights, Stefanie thought about that old statistic. Nine in one hundred would die from the disorder. They were all struggling. Would they be some of the nine? There were no signs of turning it around, none at all. They all continued to restrict and work out and hide food. And now, Stefanie lay on the floor and exercised right alongside Lily. They stayed up late into the night, doing crunches on their beds, listening for the footsteps of approaching nurses. Though the footsteps came close and Lucy's head appeared occasionally in the doorway, they were never caught, so the workouts continued. It was then, as they spent more and more time on their backs and Stefanie grew more and more competitive with Lily, that she knew for certain that she was, and had been, sick.

I have anorexia nervosa.

The pen jumped as she tried to hold it against the page. It hadn't been easy to write those words. She hadn't wanted to, but even if she wasn't the thinnest person here, she knew they were true. She was sick. She was anorexic. And with that realization came another worry: could *she* be one of the nine? It was the same old question that had occurred to her late at night in her own bed in Apartment 8B, as she lay staring up at the crack in her ceiling. But she'd never really concentrated on it before. It had only been a fleeting thought. Now it seemed more possible than ever. The questions writhed in her head. Could she be one of the nine? Would she ever recover?

The nurses started weighing Sarah, Naomi, and Abby backward, believing that the steadily increasing numbers had scared them. That only made them worse. Abby and Naomi became convinced that they had gained five to ten pounds overnight. Sarah withdrew.

"Please leave me alone. I don't want to talk anymore … No, please back off … don't wanna talk about it."

Those were the only words that Sarah spoke anymore. The doctors had tried to give her more Prozac to help with her depression, but she rebelled and stopped taking her medicine entirely. The punishment: another afternoon confined to her room.

Stefanie was lying on the floor with her legs straight up, leaning against the wall. She looked up at her feet and ran her fingers along the creases on her ribs. She searched for the tip of her sternum, then into the dip that was her stomach. Rib cage walls rose up on either side, forming the side of a crater. She'd put on weight. Her ribs were less prominent, and it didn't hurt quite so much to lie on her tailbone. She tested it: yes, she could still feel that little useless bone at the end of her spine, but only if she wiggled around a bit.

Were Lizzie's thighs smaller than hers? Did her kneecaps seem more pronounced? Did her ribs stick out more, reaching closer to the ceiling?

They were lying in the same position next to each other, like a pair of bookends.

Lizzie tried to touch the floor with her toes by lowering her legs back over her head, and one flared cuff of her jeans tumbled away from her ankle. A flash of crisscrossing scabs and a large Band-Aid was exposed before Lizzie had time to notice and right herself.

The scars on the ankle that day at group; the scabs and Band-Aid; the restriction of sharps; that smuggled-out knife. Stefanie stared at her own scar-free ankles. She'd obviously missed something important. "Liz, what happened to your ankle?" Stefanie's voice quaked, and the rest of the room seemed too quiet, like they were alone in a vacuum. She was half-afraid of the answer.

"Oh, that's nothing. I just scraped it getting out of bed this morning. Haven't you heard the rumors by now? I'm just clumsy."

That wasn't an answer. The cuts were too red; there were too many of them. She would have had to rub her leg back and forth against the edge of the bed just to accomplish half of that damage.

"Come on, Lizzie." She tried to make herself sound nonchalant. "There's something you're not telling me. You didn't get those scrapes from the edge of the bed. I really don't think so."

"You don't want to know. No one wants to know. Don't try to tell me that people care. No one cares that sometimes I'd just like to die. I may be young, but I've been around. I know how it is." Her voice was hard. Tried and tested.

"What are you talking about? Of course we care. And you are young—too young to believe that you've got the world figured out. I am too. You can't know it all yet, and neither can I." As she said it, Stefanie realized that it was true. She didn't know the world as well as she thought she did. There was the possibility that her self-absorbed friends and lonely apartment might just have some softness around the edges. But she didn't want to think about that. Had she hated it without reason? No. Couldn't be. It was easier to believe that she had been right.

Lizzie leaned her back against the wall, and Stefanie followed her lead. She didn't know what Lizzie was going to tell her, but she wanted to be ready.

"Here. See for yourself." Lizzie pulled up one pant leg.

Stefanie cringed. Maybe she had expected this, but she still didn't know what to say. The scars that she had seen that day during group were only the beginning. They stretched up Lizzie's leg, halfway to the knee. Little pink and tan lines: a tic-tac-toe board etched into flesh. Some were thin; others were as wide as quarter of an inch. Some came in sets of three, perhaps where a razor had hit the leg. And others that she guessed had been fast and deep with a thicker, sharper knife—like the one her mother used to cut hard cantaloupe—hitting the soft, pliable, warm skin with a precision that was obviously calculated and painful. Most of them looked months, maybe years old, but there was the one area where Stefanie had seen the Band-Aid. She didn't know what the red sticky plastic hid, but around that point, there were the obvious markings of stressed, punished skin. Pink, magenta, and deep fire-engine red: the new cuts on Lizzie's legs covered the entire red end of the color spectrum.

Stefanie was both repulsed and dumbfounded. "Oh my God, Lizzie. I don't know what to say."

"See. I told you, you wouldn't. But don't worry, no one ever does. My parents didn't. They just denied that I did it; they bought into the clumsy story wholeheartedly. Then again, that was before I became part of the system—before my mom left us and my dad got arrested. I don't tell anyone. He was a cocaine addict."

Stefanie's throat was dry, and she knew that her chapped lips were in need of immediate Chapstick. All she could do was look into Lizzie's soulful eyes and hope that she knew her friends here loved her. In the sheltered world of Manhattan private schools, this didn't happen. If it did, it certainly wasn't talked about, just swept away as simply as one might sweep away a cobweb at the start of spring cleaning. Why wasn't someone else there who might know what to say? Where were the other four musketeers? One for all and all for one—but the others weren't there. She was alone with Lizzie, in over her head, fumbling for even one word to say.

Lizzie didn't seem to care if Stefanie responded or not, because she just kept going. Maybe she felt like she had to keep going; maybe if she stopped she would explode. Stefanie had felt that way sometimes. Things piled up, and you just had to let them go.

"My new family, my foster family, put me here. Only two months after I moved in with them, they saw the scars and took me to the psychiatrist for a consultation. The next day I was checked in here. They kept my sister. She's the good twin: the one without issues, so they wanted her. They never really cared about me, or had time to, I suppose. And if they did, I never had time to feel it." Lizzie turned away, her blue eyes shining with unshed tears. She pulled her pant leg down. "You won't want to talk to me now, not now that you've seen and know. Just leave now, since I know you're going to. No one ever stays. I'm crazy. I'm not worth having as a friend. I should just die and save a lot of people a lot of time and money. So just leave. I won't be hurt."

Stefanie wouldn't leave. Lizzie had never shared this with her, maybe with any of the musketeers. She didn't know what to say, but she had to say something. This was serious, really serious. Lizzie was a cutter. Lizzie wanted to die. Really die, as in dead, gone, and final. What did that mean? And how could she help? She felt overwhelmed by her powerlessness.

"I'm here, Lizzie, and I do care. I promise I do." There were words coming out of her mouth, but Stefanie didn't know why. She didn't know what she was saying or how. And yet, as she heard her own words and saw Lizzie's face, now damp with tears, she thought maybe she was close to saying the right thing. "You can't continue this. Lizzie, I do care. We all care. Please, don't do it anymore. Please stop. You'd been doing so well. Where is the knife from the other day? I saw you take it, and I know you still have it. Will you give it to me? Please, for once, choose to be safe. Give me the knife, and I'll return it for you next time we're in the dining room. And if I get caught, I'll say that I took it by accident. I don't know how I'll explain it, but I'll find a way. We do care. We don't want you to die."

Lizzie's crying weakened. "OK. You win. You can have the knife. I'll give it to you tonight, once they've opened the doors. It doesn't matter anyway. It wasn't sharp enough."

Stefanie couldn't expect more. She was choosing to live and choosing to be safe. It was a hard decision. As she lay in bed and finished her daily journal entry, the words echoed loudly in the silent pauses between Lily's deep breathing, and Stefanie realized they all needed to choose. They all needed to fight. Her words, if anyone bothered to listen, would be clear to all of them.

She sighed, turned off the light, and fell into bed. As she drifted off to sleep that night, Stefanie felt better knowing that the knife was tucked away in the top drawer of her dresser beneath her New York sweatshirt, with Lizzie a safe distance down the hall under the watch of the dorm monitors.

~ 36 ~

With all that had happened, it would have seemed logical that the girls would call Barrett Institute home for a while longer. But they weren't being held. The first to go would be Sarah, leaving on her fourth Tuesday: twenty-one days after Stefanie had seen her dancing around the NG pole on that first afternoon. The others would follow close behind.

Only a little over a week after they'd all struggled so badly, Sarah would be sent home, free in the real world again. She was still too thin, but she said that she would work on the weight on the outside, that the hospital had done all it could for her. The hospital agreed. There were discharge meetings and relapse prevention meetings. They diagrammed prospective menus for her to follow and talked with her therapist from home. She started taking Prozac again. And she said that she would be OK. She promised.

That last weekend, they stayed close. If they'd drifted apart during the time that they'd struggled, no vestiges of those days remained. Every now and then a smack of worry hit Stefanie when she thought about Lizzie and the knife that she'd safely returned to the dining room the day after Lizzie had surrendered it. A wave of panic had crashed over her body the day that Lizzie was approved for sharps and requested a razor to shave her legs. But nothing happened, and everything seemed OK.

They were on a roller coaster, careening around corners out of control. One bend brought them closer to home and freedom, and the next sent them down into pits of ambivalence, where it didn't matter if they ever recovered. They all lacked the power or courage to grip the steering wheel and take control; they were just along for the ride. They never knew where the next turn would find them: The

Jungles of Denial? The Mountains of Bliss? The Sea of Confusion? The Valleys of Despair? They were traveling without a road map, going wherever the road led them.

For the moment, they were in the Isles of Contentment. They'd turned a corner at the end of the week and were safely pushing onward, toward Sarah's departure.

"Abby, your go."

They were playing cards again, the day before Sarah would walk out the doors and hopefully never return. They'd exchanged home and e-mail addresses and cell-phone numbers, and they'd written good-bye notes, drawn pictures, and replicated the posters for Sarah to hang up on her wall at home to remind her of the friends that she had left behind. They'd all but said their good-byes. Sarah had even admitted that she'd be sad to go home. She didn't want to stay, but she almost didn't want to leave.

Sarah's parents were scheduled to arrive on Tuesday around lunchtime. They weren't Sarah's first-choice pickup, but Ed had to work. He couldn't get off until five. And Sarah got the feeling that he didn't really want to see her anyway.

"He'll think that I'm fat. He's not going to love a fat girl," Sarah moaned as she stretched out on the couch.

"He's not going to think you're fat because you're not. You said it yourself yesterday, and the day before that, and the day before that: you still have more weight to gain. You're not out of the woods yet. You've still got work to do." Naomi had taken the big-sisterly approach to handling Sarah: blunt and up front, not hiding behind euphemisms or friendly conversation.

"Stop it. I'm fine. Never been better."

Stefanie scowled. Sarah did have a lot of work to do. She'd been restricting until just days before, and in Stefanie's eyes she wasn't ready to go home. But Sarah didn't see it that way, and neither did the hospital. She was being discharged willingly, not AMA—against medical advice like people sometimes were.

"Ed's not worth it if he doesn't see that skin and bones is unhealthy. He's not right for you then. So just dump him." Stefanie could hear the pitch of Naomi's voice rising as she got more and more frustrated.

"Is it my turn yet?" Abby leaned toward Stefanie and nudged her on the shoulder, unaware of the progress in the game. Had she been paying attention, she would have seen every card that her friend was holding.

"Hey, keep your eyes on your own cards." Stefanie drew her hand in closer to her body, until the cards lay against her chest.

There was an ache in Stefanie's stomach when she thought of Ed looking Sarah over like a piece of meat. Sarah Johnson didn't deserve such treatment. But she couldn't see it for herself, so she was walking right back into the problem.

Naomi laughed as she said, "Abby, it's been your turn for the past hour, and we're all waiting on you. Well, maybe for the past minute ..."

Abby blushed. "Sorry, my head drifted off into the clouds. Will we really keep in touch once we're all gone? I mean will you really write to me, and e-mail me, and call me? I don't want to leave this place if that's not going to happen."

Lizzie was impatient. "Look, we'll still keep in touch after we all leave this dungeon—really. But right now, if you don't discard, we'll never leave, and we'll never have the chance to keep in touch. Because we'll be here forever." Lizzie never liked to wait, especially if she thought she had a chance to win.

"But still, you never know. Let's make a pact. Right now. Right here, the six musketeers. Let's promise that we'll always stick together no matter what. Friends forever—but more than that even—support forever."

Lily made an exaggeratedly pained face at Abby. "My ears! My ears! My English teacher would say that that is so clichéd. If we were a story, she'd mark us with a big, fat, red X. And she'd take off five points for such mushy sentiment."

Sarah smiled. "You'd better watch it, or I'm gonna sneak a look at your cards while you're so busy contradicting Abby." Sarah liked to tease Lily because they were so unlike each other. Sarah had missed so many days and weeks of school that, even if she wanted to finish out high school, she'd likely need to be home-schooled. Lily was Little Miss Scholar: she hadn't missed a day of school since the fifth grade and had never been late with an assignment until this year's hospitalization.

"Yeah, yeah, yeah, I know. Keep your beady little eyes to yourself. This is a winning hand of cards, and you're not getting a sneak preview." Teasing Sarah back was just one of the ways that Stefanie knew Lily was slowly making progress. At least now she was speaking.

"So who's in?" Abby's hand still held an extra card that she was meant to discard, but she was obviously waiting for an answer.

Naomi was the next one to question. "Do you think that's possible? It seems against human nature. Who sticks together forever? It's just not realistic. People move on, no matter how much you try not to. No matter how much you want things to be the same. We can say we'll always be friends, but there are no guarantees. Think of camp friendships, or vacation friends. How many of them do you still know? I've lost touch with all of mine. Those friendships just don't thrive in foreign soil, away from where they began."

Lizzie nodded. "I'm with Naomi. Survival of the fittest, just like in science class. Don't get overly trusting because then—*bam*—you're dead. People that you want to care never do. That's just the way life is." The words didn't surprise any of them; nothing less could be expected from Lizzie.

"Some of us are certainly cynics." Stefanie uttered her first words of the conversation. Personally, she was inclined to agree with Naomi—it just didn't seem possible. And she definitely agreed with Lily; the statement was clichéd. But there was no real reason for them not to try. If it didn't work, it didn't. If it did, then all the better. They'd all taken bigger risks; those were what had landed them in the hospital. She felt surprisingly self-aware. They'd tried to starve.

It was a slow form of suicide. That had been a risk. Compared to that, making a pact wasn't a risk at all, even if it didn't work out. She wanted to try it. She liked the idea of support forever.

"What's the harm in trying? Can it hurt us? Abby's got a good idea, and I say we go for it. And Sarah's leaving tomorrow, so we've got to do it now", urged Stefanie.

There wasn't much of a debate. With hugs all around and a carpe diem from Lily the Latin scholar, the six musketeers made their pact. They'd always be friends, they agreed. They'd always offer support. Sarah would leave in a day, but she'd call them every evening. And when they all got out, they'd talk online and go see movies together.

Abby finally discarded. "I'm happy, guys. I'm glad we got that out of the way. A pact lasts forever. Now where was I? Oh yes— Gin." The game had ended and Abby had won, but the others didn't mind.

The next day, around the same time, Linda's call sounded the alarm and they were called to lunch: Sarah's final meal.

Once again she assumed her place at the free foods table where she got to choose her own food and dish out her own portions. The Six Musketeers were in the middle of the meal, in the middle of a conversation, when her parents arrived. Sarah looked around, then down at her plate. She hesitated as if she didn't really want to leave, but, while her parents gathered up the brown paper bags with her belongings, she said her good-byes and finished her peanut butter and jelly sandwich and glass of whole milk. It was time.

Stefanie had thought that it would be easier. This should be a good thing: one of them was ready to go out into the world again. They were succeeding. They were recovering. They would never again look like the emaciated waifs that she had seen that first Tuesday, three weeks before. But it didn't feel good. She was jealous that Sarah was leaving her behind. She was angry that Sarah was moving on before she was ready. She was sad to be losing a friend. A familiar emptiness filled her stomach, and she wasn't hungry anymore. She remembered feeling this way before, when she woke up one day and realized that she had lost touch with Julia and she didn't know why.

Sarah met her parents at the door to the dining room, and Stefanie joined the line of girls waiting to give Sarah her parting hugs. Linda and the other supervisor were more lenient than usual, perhaps under the scrutiny of Sarah's parents or maybe because, deep down, they had some compassion. They chose not to enforce the rule of sitting at all times during meals, and they were willing to allow physical contact, which had theoretically been prohibited since the beginning. Stefanie embraced Sarah and held on. This was the first person who had made her feel welcome in this place. This was the person who had assured her, time and again, that she did belong. Now she was leaving, but Stefanie could still feel the fragile rib cage beneath her clothes.

"Stay safe, Sarah. For us—for me. Eat. And forget about Ed. Take the control from your parents some other way—rebel if you have to, but don't hurt yourself. In the long run, you only give them more control. Please …"

"Don't worry, Stef. I'll be fine. Take care of yourself. You'll do great, and we'll see each other when you get out. I promise." Sarah's voice sounded confident; Stefanie gave her one last squeeze and stepped away.

"You'll do good, guys. I'll talk to you soon. We'll do lunch." She giggled, but her parents didn't find it funny and the joke was cut short. She was on her way out the door. "OK, better be getting outta this hellhole. Parting words of advice: Be healthy. Take each day as it comes. Take it one tray at a time."

- 37 -

One tray at a time. That became their new motto. As each meal was placed in front of them, they tried to see only that meal—not the meals that stretched out down the long line of hours and days in front of them. They hoped that what everyone said was correct: that it did get easier.

"I'm leaving tomorrow! I'm leaving tomorrow!" Abby danced along the hallway and flopped down next to Stefanie. "I'm leaving tomorrow."

Stefanie had been attending discharge meetings too. If she didn't restrict, she would go home in two days. She'd been there only a few days longer than Abby, so it made sense that they should both be thinking about going home. But Abby had been restricting. How could Abby be going home sooner than she was? If Sarah hadn't been ready, then Abby certainly wasn't. Abby had been spending a lot of time on the phone with her coach lately, and his goal was to have her ready for division sectionals—if she could get out and get in shape by the deadline. Maybe they didn't know it or they couldn't see it, but Stefanie didn't think it was a smart idea, strategically speaking, if the goal was Abby's long-term health.

"Are you ready?" Naomi had been listening to their conversation.

"Sure. They won't let me leave if I lose, so if I don't then I guess that shows that I'm ready. Besides, Coach needs me. This is what we've been planning for, what I've trained so hard for. And there will be a lot of scouts there—college recruiters. I've *got* to be there."

Was the coach sacrificing Abby's health? Did he care about her, or only his stupid championship? And why didn't Abby realize that she still needed more time at Barrett? It was so blatantly obvious. Stefanie wanted to smack her into seeing reason.

The tiles in the shower stall were cold and wet as Stefanie stepped under the water. There was a limited amount of warm water, and, with its occupant flaunting the fifteen-minute shower rule, the stall next to her had been in use for more than twenty-five minutes. Abby's showers were the longest of anyone's in the unit. Stefanie couldn't imagine what she did in there for all that time. Stefanie was clean after only five minutes. What could Abby be doing?

"Disgusting." Abby's voice drifted out from behind the shower curtain as the water went off. One thin, bare leg appeared, followed by an arm, and then Abby's whole frame, wrapped in a blue terry-cloth towel.

"What's disgusting?"

Abby pinched at her stomach. "The water. It tastes like chlorine. I feel like I'm showering in a goddamn swimming pool." Her finger found a small pocket of skin, and she made a face. "And I'm so distended."

It tasted like chlorine. But how would she taste the water? Or, better question: why? Stefanie looked at her.

"It's a hint that my coach gave me a long time ago: 'Abby, drinking water adds weight.'" She mocked her coach's baritone voice. "He wants me out of here, and so do I. I'll do whatever I have to do—even if I hate the taste."

"How can you do this? Isn't it cheating? Is he trying to get you healthy, or is he just trying to win?" They were still standing in the bathroom, wrapped in towels, but Stefanie had to ask.

"Honestly, Stef, I'm kind of scared to go home. I don't want to relapse, but I have to get back to swimming. Coach Klay wants me to do this, and he's been there for me for a long time. He's been my coach since I was ten—training me for the varsity team before I could even do the butterfly. And my parents say I need swimming as a spring board into a good college. Stupid pun, but it's true. I'm not smart the way you and Lily are."

As the girls began to dress, Abby looked around suspiciously, as though she were expecting eavesdroppers, and her voice lowered. Stefanie leaned forward to hear her.

"I always thought that I wanted to swim, but I don't. Not anymore really. I don't want to go back. And I know I'm not ready, but I don't have a choice. The doctors have spoken to my coach more than to my parents. The people that I call Mom and Dad have pretty much backed away. So he takes the reins and assures them that he's trained to watch for this type of thing, and he'll keep his eye on me. He swears to them that I've learned my lesson and that I'll be fine. He's told me to drink as much water as I can get, not knowing—or caring to know—that they regulate what we drink. He just tells me to get more somehow and to eat salt, lots of salt, because it will make me retain water. Now I know that it's true, and it's why I'm leaving so soon."

Abby led Stefanie down the hall until the girls were out of earshot. Then she stopped and looked at Stefanie. The two girls stood, eyes locked, waiting, until Abby finally spoke. "And just so you know, I'm not an idiot. I am scared. It doesn't really feel right. I don't want to die …" her voice cracked. "But at least I'll make him proud—and them proud—and maybe do something for myself, so I'll have a good future. Maybe I'll swim my way into a scholarship. We'll all meet up again in the Ivy League: you and me and Lily. It'll be great."

So Abby knew. She wasn't ready, and she wasn't fooling herself. She'd gotten herself trapped, and there was no way out. She was going home the next day, and her face would show only smiles. She'd pretend that she was happy because she was supposed to be, and maybe she'd even convince herself that she was, but Stefanie knew the truth. Abby was scared to death. She was scared of Coach Klay, scared of disappointing her parents, scared of competing again, and scared of swimming—the sport that she hated and loved at the same time. *One tray at a time.* Stefanie wrote the words on an index card and handed it to Abby just before she walked out the door the next day. "Remember this. And one meet at a time. You can always drop out. Everything will be OK. You'll go to college with or without swimming. And no one is going to like you any less if you stop."

Parting words.

And then it was Stefanie's turn. Two days later, at ten o'clock, she'd be set free, released into the sea of living, breathing people five floors below. She'd wander back out into New York City as if nothing had happened and go back to school the next day. She'd walk with Annabel, console Laura, and try to manufacture encounters with Julia—just so that they would stay her friends. Just more of the same.

As she stepped onto the scale for a final time, she shrugged and took a deep breath. Fifteen pounds. She had gained fifteen pounds in a month's time. But it would be OK, because she could go back on her diet now. She could go back to being healthy. She'd cut out the ice cream sandwiches that had periodically surfaced as evening snacks, and she's stop drinking milk or juice with every meal. And she'd definitely stop drinking Ensure. Little changes would make a difference in her weight. She could be thinner and happier. Everything would go back to the way it had been.

Good-byes had already been said. Lizzie had been picked up by her foster family only minutes before. After eleven weeks at the Barrett Institute, she was finally going home. Sarah was gone, and so was Abby. Only Naomi and Lily were left, and they would be in a relapse prevention planning group when the Webbers arrived to take home their daughter. They'd hugged already and reaffirmed the pact. They'd always stick together. Then they'd parted ways, and Stefanie had waited for her parents to arrive.

The common area was empty except for Madeline, who still sat immovable and silent, and Dana, who was looking for a marker that she had lost the day before. It was lonely and strange, not at all like her memories. There were bad ones, but good ones too, strangely enough. Board games and card games, ogling young interns, Ensure chugging contests, make-believe cookouts and hamburger fests, *Oprah,* videos, weekends, talks—and promises of eternal friendship.

She'd fought and screamed, and only condescended to come voluntarily because her parents had threatened, but now she was halfway sad to leave—not that she'd ever admit that to anyone.

The antiseptic smell that had become so familiar dissipated when she stepped out the door with her parents on either side. She turned around and looked back at the couches and the television, hoping to find Lily or Naomi running toward her. No one was there. She hadn't really expected them to be, but nevertheless she was disappointed.

The door closed in her face as Linda wished her good luck and relocked the dead bolt. She was an escapee from a maximum-security prison, but her friends were still inside. It didn't seem right just to leave. And, without her mother's firm grip on her hand, an "I can't believe I had to do this to you; I'm so sorry" hold, she doubted whether she would have been able to.

But it would be OK. They would meet up again on the outside. Four of the six were already out. They'd talk that evening or the next day, and the others would join in—most likely within a week. They'd promised to stay friends. And they'd all do well. Sarah would get better, and so would Abby; and Lily, Naomi, and Lizzie were well on their way. She might diet a little bit more just to lose some of the weight, but nothing would happen to her. Because she'd never been as sick as the others, she wouldn't have to give it all up—yet.

How were Sarah and Abby doing now? She hadn't spoken to them in days. How had Lizzie's first morning home been? And what would Tower 3 North be having for lunch?

The blue awning of the Barrett Institute receded in the background, and Stefanie looked forward, down the street ahead. The wheels of their taxi moved swiftly over familiar streets, speckled with black spots of gum and the occasional Starbucks coffee cup. Mohammed Daniel—or Daniel Mohammed, she could never remember which name came first on the NY Taxi and Limousine Commission licenses—honked his horn impatiently and navigated around a Third Avenue bus. It was like she'd never left. She was going home. She'd be back in her own bedroom that night with Mr. Whiskers tucked under her arm, the stereo on her dresser, and everything familiar in place. She could picture the entire scene as if she were there that minute, but going home seemed strangely unnatural.

Should she call first? Or e-mail? Or write? Where was Sarah now? Had Abby started swim practice yet? Was Lizzie getting along with her family?

She looked around with awe, seeing it all so differently than she'd ever seen it before. This was her city, her New York, but she felt detached from it. Tall buildings. Street-side vendors and the smell of their sickly sweet peanuts, pumped full of excessive calories. Delicatessens. Subway and bus stops. Dog walkers. People, people, people. The sights were familiar—she'd walked this block many times—but they weren't welcoming. She could have been in Iowa and felt less out of place.

It had felt strange just to walk out the door and into the sunlight.

- *38* -

Wednesday, the fourteenth of April, was a cold spring day when tulips poked their heads up through the flowerbeds and decided to go back to sleep. Stefanie empathized. She didn't want to get out of bed.

Backpack packed? Yes, as of the night before. Appropriate uniform? Yes—plaid kilt with collared shirt. Textbooks? Yes, she'd gone through her room twice, looking at the pile of homework that Annabel had carried home for her and the books that had gone unopened for so long. They looked odd and alien to her, and she couldn't remember reading them. Her psychology book was on her desk, and she fingered the worn pages but decided not to open it. Homework done? Yes, most of it—as much as she had been able to do.

Everything else was ready, but she wasn't. She'd chosen to return right away—her parents had wanted her to wait out the weekend and acclimate—but she had refused. Now she wondered how she could go back. Everyone would look at her strangely, noticing how much weight she had gained, how her gelatin-like thighs bulged. They would peer at her from behind their textbooks, stare at her butt as she climbed the stairs between classes, and decode her entire being for signs that they would hash and rehash among themselves.

To her face, they would smile and nod, smug in their assurance that they had won. "Hi, Stefanie! Good to have you back. You look great!" Then they would turn away, and she would be as she had been before: the girl with potential but no discipline. She had refused to be normal, and, God, how she had tried. But she had failed miserably. Everyone would be able to see that. Now she was neither invisibly normal nor spectacularly thin. Now she was just another plump piece of mediocrity, a girl recently released from a psychiatric hospital, a freak show, and everyone would see that.

"The shinbone's connected to the knee bone, the knee bone's connected to the thigh bone, the thigh bone's connected to the hip bone ..."

She was out of bed but panicking. The sun shone into her eyes just a little too brightly. Mr. Whiskers was somewhere under the bed, in the dust that had gathered during her absence. She'd forgotten about the crack in her ceiling, but now she looked up at it, as if finding a lost companion. The little crack darted and twisted in imperfect veins, splintering, running together, jumping apart. She traced the lines with her eyes, shielding her face from the sun with her hand.

Her school clothing was all there, as it had always been: cleaned, pressed, and free of static cling, lined up in her closet. And she had managed, slowly, to get dressed. Victoria's Secret bra and underwear first. Then the light blue Gap polo shirt. And shorts for under her skirt. As she pulled these up, it occurred to her that they were unnecessary: a part of the gym uniform that Stefanie wouldn't be allowed to wear until Dr. Adler had given the OK to return to physical activity. Next her blue, green, and white plaid skirt, then the socks with blue stripes to match her shirt, and her same old pair of sneakers. Standing in front of the mirror, she flipped her head upside down and brushed the underlayers of her hair. Then, shaking her head to get the hair to fall smoothly, she stood back to survey her appearance and assess what damage had been done.

She exhaled slowly, her lungs quivering as they released the air. She had gotten fully dressed, but she had nothing to wear. She couldn't go dressed that way. She couldn't. It was too humiliating. The waistband of her skirt was tighter than it had been. The button pulled more than it had, and the wool itched where the waistband of her shorts had previously prevented wool-to-skin contact. The sleeves of her polo shirt hugged her upper arms more closely, and she had to tug on them to make the openings wider.

"Stef, everything OK? It's almost time to go."

As her mother's voice echoed around the corner from the kitchen, Stefanie barely had time to catch the lamp that had begun to fall when she knocked into it, her arms flailing. Damn! Who to blame? Her mother for annoying her with the false cheerfulness in her voice, or herself for being so fat and clumsy? She yanked at the tight areas. There. There. There. How would she fix this? Why didn't the wool and polyester blend give more? Why wouldn't the damn material just stretch?

Maybe even her socks were smaller—and her shoes. No, that was the eating disorder talking, as she'd been told again and again, ad nauseum, at the hospital. Her shoes shouldn't have been any tighter, and she halfway knew they weren't. But everything else was, and she only hoped that no one would notice. She couldn't think of anything that would make it better, anyway, and moments later she was running out the front door.

Freddy the doorman didn't detect the difference. Neither did Mr. Firenze, the bachelor investment banker who lived on the sixth floor and was just entering the building after what she could only grimly suspect was a late night with a Kate Moss clone. The resident homeless man that lived on Eighty-fourth between First and Second and who was just waking up didn't detect a difference, and neither did the children she saw every morning, as they waited for the school bus. Not the dog walkers. Nor, even—surprisingly, miraculously—Annabel.

They hadn't seen each other for four weeks. Annabel had never bothered to come to the hospital, but she had called the night before to find out if they could walk together, and Stefanie had agreed. It was all part of a normal day. Now Stefanie could see her from the corner: her jacket pulled in tight around her while she waited in front of her building. She looked cold, but Stefanie knew why she was waiting outside. Annabel's eyes were trained on her as she walked out her front door and down the street. Annabel took a few steps closer, Stefanie slowed, and Annabel came to her. As much as she wanted to look Annabel in the eye, she couldn't. Her eyes darted from left to right and then down to the ground, resting on Annabel's face for only a second. Her friend was smiling, but the smile looked painted on and she didn't say anything. Stefanie looked up Park Avenue and wondered how long they had been standing there.

Finally their eyes met. Stefanie's were cold and gray; Annabel's a chestnut brown. They hugged briefly, and Annabel welcomed her as they turned toward school. A dog barked down the street as another dog rounded the corner. Ambulance sirens went off in the distance, and a car alarm was tripped by an unsuspecting pedestrian who had walked too close. The early morning city was busy and noisy: like a stopwatch had snapped the Upper East Side into activity. But the girls' conversation was all slow motion, stilted and lacking. A sense of déjà vu took over. They were back a couple of months, back on February fourteenth when they'd walked together knowing that— for one of them—it could be the end of the friendship, and—for the other—it could be much more serious. Even the coolness behind the sun's facade of warmth reminded Stefanie of that morning.

Annabel kept up the conversation much of the way to school. "Courtney got yelled at yesterday by Ms. Montarescu. She skipped doing her homework for the fourth day in a row, and of course Ms. M. wanted to know why. So Courtney said that she was just having some trouble concentrating. Yeah, right. It's tough concentrating while watching reruns of *Friends* and *Dawson's Creek*. She's obsessed. But Ms. M. didn't buy it either. Oh, and guess what! Madame Bordot is going out with Mr. Maloney—they're a couple. Can you imagine anything more gross? Their poor children will need therapy for life."

Stefanie faked a smile and kept walking.

"And Taylor, Diane, and Ali decided to play a trick on Mrs. Smith, so they turned her clock ahead, and for the rest of the morning she let out every class she taught twenty-five minutes early. She didn't catch on until she went to lunch and saw the clock in the cafeteria. And Laura got back from Vail last Friday, so she missed that first week of school, too. Let's see, what else?" Annabel paused as Stefanie just stared in wonder. The girl hadn't stopped long enough to breathe as she offered a play-by-play of everything that had happened since March thirteenth, even though none of it really made a difference anyway. They were only filling time. Filling the space that remained stale and empty between them. Ruefully, whatever her hopes might have been, Stefanie had to conclude that their best days were behind them. Nothing had changed—or had she?

As they dropped their coats in the locker room, Stefanie took in the stuffy air and shuddered when the warmth hit her lungs. She couldn't be here yet. She couldn't see people. She couldn't do this. She wasn't ready. She wasn't ready for all that this day would entail: friends, teachers, classes, homework, meetings, hallways—lunch. She wasn't even close to ready.

Yet here she was, back in school. Someone, somewhere, had made a mistake. But where, then, was she supposed to be? Certainly not back at Barrett. Wasn't there anywhere she could feel comfortably alive, thin, and freed of herself? What would they say when they saw her? How would they react?

She couldn't do this.

Surprisingly, no one in the entire tenth grade made any direct reference that day to her prolonged absence. The day passed smoothly— too smoothly. But what could they say? "Gee, you've put on some weight." "What happened to you?" "You're looking chunky." "We needed another student in this class, but a whale will do just fine." "How's the swimming been with that permanent flotation device around your middle?" "How about a doughnut? Oops, I forgot you don't eat those."

"Stefanie, it's so nice to see you back," Ms. Olson said when they passed each other in the hall. "Stop in later. I'd like to find out how things are."

She'd almost forgotten what her teacher's voice sounded like, but there it was again. Warm, caring tones almost forced her to acknowledge that she was welcome someplace.

It was the first reference anyone had made to her about having been gone. They all knew where she had been but had chosen to ignore it. On the one hand, she felt grateful—she didn't really feel like talking. On the other hand, Stefanie almost wished they would ask, that she could just talk on and on about what she had been through. She'd lived purely on Ensure for days. She'd peed into something called a hat. She'd been unable to shave her legs for nearly a month. And she'd cried hysterically and pulled at her ever-tightening clothes daily.

In a month's time, she had seen things that none of her classmates would ever be exposed to in the chambers of their safe, privileged little lives. She'd befriended a depressive. She'd counseled a cutter. She'd seen four-point restraints used on patients throwing tantrums. She'd heard alarms sound all over the building, sending nurses' heads snapping up and guards running—burly security men who were hardly necessary to contain the meager one-hundred-pound terrors who inhabited Tower 3 North. Vomit on the floor, stark white walls, deceit, fighting, and threats had all become part of her world.

So much of her wanted to scream about her experiences from the rooftops. But they didn't want to hear it, or, even if they did, they didn't ask, so she didn't tell.

It felt like she'd been gone much longer than a month. Her classes had gone on without her, and they'd had homework assignments, tests, and papers due. With each additional period, the to-do list that she had begun in the back of her notebook grew exponentially. Her teachers offered extensions and extra help, and they tried to reassure her that she'd catch up. In class she sat farther back in the room so that she wouldn't have to feel the eyes of the other students boring into her back. Her mind wandered.

During history class, her thoughts carried her back downtown to Tower 3 North. She wondered what her Barrett friends were doing at that moment, and she found herself jumping up to go to the bathroom at just the right time for commodes. She halfway expected her teacher to call out, "Ensures!" and lead them off into another room, but, instead, the lecture on the War of 1812 continued.

And the day continued. Stefanie went in and out of familiarly strange rooms and stayed after each class to talk to the teacher about how she would catch up. Trying to remember her schedule, she ran up and down stairs panting and aching, and she realized that she had gotten terribly out of shape. As she passed girls in the hallways that she had known since kindergarten, she wished she could run and hide. She just knew that they were staring at her—judging her and wondering why she had ever been hospitalized, because she certainly wasn't skinny.

Finally her first day back was over. But by the end of it, she was physically and mentally exhausted from the effort that it had taken just to make herself appear natural and unselfconscious.

She'd survived school, but she hadn't had lunch. That night, she skipped the gym workout but did the sit-ups and leg lifts. She recorded the numbers in her journal, tucked the book into her nightstand, set the alarm, and turned off the stereo, pausing the *Motivation* CD in midspin. It occurred to her that she should feel guilty—this was clearly against the rules—but her mind flashed to Abby, swimming her heart out, burning thousands of calories, still working out. If Abby didn't have to stop, she shouldn't have to either. No one had to know. During dinner, her mother watched her eat: carefully and deliberately cutting her food into small pieces and bringing one bite after another up to her mouth. Her father offered her seconds, but she refused. After dinner, her parents waited to see whether their daughter would purge.

It was like a silent presence in the room when they were there: a ghostly assembly. They were careful around her, didn't ask too much of her, were afraid of overwhelming her. In an effort to make things normal, they all gathered in the living room after dinner. Her mother leaned back on the couch and began to snore softly. Her father collected his mail and turned on the Yankees game. And when Stefanie said goodnight and went to bed, they were both too tired to monitor her anymore. Now they were asleep down the hallway—just like old times. They'd had to let her go. Their daughter was a stranger to them, a mirage of what she had once been, broken and changed. And they'd had to get away; they didn't know how to relate to her anymore.

Lying in the darkness of her room, her legs and stomach muscles became a painful reminder of the rules she had just broken, and she once again felt the choking grasp of loneliness.

W elcome back. You can come with me." Dr. Adler's voice was filled with the tenacity of memory, hardly as warm as Ms. Olson's, as she led her from the waiting room with its counter and the M&Ms to the exam chair with the crinkly paper slip … the thin cotton gowns … the floors that didn't look much like a doctor's office. But, then again, this was Fifth Avenue. Stefanie went over each familiar thing in her mind, tracing the angles and curves and projections in her mind's eye, so that she wouldn't have to look at her doctor.

"How are you? I see your mother didn't come with you today. You brought yourself. That's progress." Dr. Adler cocked her head to the right, gave a slight smile, instantly made silly by the eyebrow that involuntarily rose with the corners of her mouth, and waited for an answer. She wore her white lab coat and held Stefanie's chart, glancing over the old notes. Her eyes finally focused on Stefanie's face and stayed there. She didn't look away. It wasn't a stare of hostility— or particularly warm hospitality. It was more like detachment, clinical preoccupation, interest in Stefanie as a patient and nothing else.

"I'm fine." Stefanie's eyes met Dr. Adler's, and she forced herself not to let them wander.

What answer did she expect? They weren't buddies. They weren't pals. This was the lady who had sentenced her. For the past month, Stefanie had been locked up because of her. And now Dr. Adler wanted to be friends? Just like that? Stefanie tightened her mouth into a straight line and promised herself that she wouldn't talk. After all, she was angry, right?

But somehow, Stefanie wasn't angry. There was actually something comfortable about this office now. She almost didn't mind sitting and shivering while she had her blood pressure taken and listened to a warning about the dangers of calcium loss.

"Really?" Dr. Adler looked skeptical.

"I'm OK. Not great, but certainly OK," she added quickly. That was stupid. What was she doing? Why was she saying anything? Hadn't she learned her lesson? Speak and you get hurt, stay silent and you're safe. She'd talked to Annabel and Ms. Olson and had been sent away; if she'd only kept her mouth shut maybe she would have been closer to happiness. Wasn't that what she had learned from this whole experience? Don't volunteer information unless it's demanded of you—and even then, be careful for Christ's sake! If she had learned her lesson, then why on earth was she talking now? Couldn't she just have said, "*I'm great, thanks for asking. Never been better!*"?

Dr. Adler didn't seem surprised by Stefanie's improved demeanor. Her distant professionalism broke for an instant, and she smiled. "So you survived, huh? I said you would. Well, anyway, you look great."

Stefanie rolled her eyes and raised her eyebrows. "Sure, whatever. I feel disgusting."

"Yep, classic symptoms. You'll feel disgusting for a while, but you just have to trust us. We're your team, and we're not going to let you get fat. And slowly, it will begin to feel better. You'll begin to feel better."

Yeah right. She knew what she looked like; the doctor was only trying to spare her feelings. "Can we please lower my target weight?" Stefanie felt like she was asking for a reprieve.

"Tell you what, why don't we talk about that in a month or so, when your weight has stabilized again and you've gotten your period back and things are looking good? We can discuss that then." She held out a lavender gown. "Why don't you put on this lovely shade of purple, and we'll get you on the scale. We still need to keep an eye on your weight. You're not out of the woods yet, my dear."

Music to her ears. *She wasn't out of the woods yet.* She was still sick. Thank God. She was still a member of the Eating Disorder Club. People might still worry about her; they still might want to talk to her. She wasn't just average yet. She still had something special.

The number had dropped, and her heart leapt. It had been a little over a week since she'd been out of the hospital, and she'd lost almost four pounds. It wouldn't keep going that way. She'd been warned about an initial weight drop at the hospital, as her body stabilized and was no longer taking in all those extra calories through the Ensures, but there was still hope. She was four pounds lighter already, and she was only cutting out the most menial amounts of food.

As she handed Dr. Adler her credit card and signed the bill, Stefanie grinned euphorically. Her mouth stretched into a smile as she cheerfully pulled open the heavy door leading back to the outside world. She turned around to look back at Dr. Adler. With her voice high and animated, she said, "Thanks. Have a good night."

Imagine what she could do if she cut out more food.

The appointment was over. The fading light traced patterns across the sidewalk, as the sun lowered in the sky. Fifth Avenue was crowded with rush-hour travelers returning home after work. Stefanie sidestepped an elderly woman with a cane. Dr. Adler's inadvertent good news propelled her through the evening throng as she darted across Madison and raced up Park.

At home, dinner would be waiting, and she was hungry. Hungry, yes, but not famished. She wouldn't be willing to eat just anything—nothing scary like pasta or starch. She'd eat only a negligible amount of protein to avoid all those calories and fat. If cutting out a measly few hundred calories had taken off four pounds in a week, imagine what cutting out more could do. And neither her parents nor Dr. Adler would be the wiser because Barrett Institute had never reported week-by-week specifics; all that money spent and Dr. Adler was totally unaware of exactly how much Stefanie had managed to gain.

Later that night, however, Stefanie could barely keep her eyes open and it was just after nine. Why was she so tired? She reached over to turn her music up and settled down again with her graphing calculator and math book. The computations made no sense. She tossed her pencil down. There was no way she was going to get this work done. Maybe she'd just start her workout now.

Her mind seemed fogged, smoky, hazy. She knew if she didn't give herself a rest, if she continually pushed the way she had been, for one more sit-up and one more set of leg lifts, she would always be tired. Any sane person would suggest that she go to bed early, skip the obligatory exercises, and get some much-needed sleep. Any sane person would listen to that advice. Her mother said it didn't surprise her that she was so tired; emotional stress could do that. Any sane person would give in and give her body what it wanted. But Stefanie couldn't. Or maybe she wouldn't.

She couldn't sleep anyway. She could lie there for hours and count sheep, or grams of fat. She could talk to herself or to the crack in the ceiling. She could cry. But it wouldn't do any good. Her eyes just wouldn't close. It didn't matter how tired she was.

And she wasn't sane. As the days progressed and she still hadn't heard from Sarah, or Lizzie, or Abby, she felt more and more crazy. She was torn between maintaining her perfect image and doing what she wanted. People wanted her to eat, but they didn't understand and they didn't care to. She wanted to starve, but she didn't want people to know how twisted and confused she was inside. She didn't want them to see her cry. With each bite of food, she believed that it would be harder to stop eating, and she wanted to spit out what was in her mouth. But a napkin would only hold one mouthful, that much she knew. And getting rid of one bite wasn't an effective method. But she had no other options. So she just went crazier and crazier. She pushed harder at night, with her bedroom door closed and the stereo on just loud enough so that she could hear it when she lay on the floor. She panicked after dinner and cried into Mr. Whiskers' tummy. She wished that the weight would just melt off again, and she despaired because she'd never be thin enough to be happy. She'd never be good enough.

Alone in her room or in the hallways of school, her old tricks returned. She continued to skip lunch at school. She continued exercising. She didn't try to maintain her weight; she tried to lose. She had to prove that she could still be thin. She had to prove that she could still be skinny enough to be respected and content.

Had she ever been sane? Had she been crazy when she went into the hospital, and then gotten sane, only to go crazy again? She'd been locked in a psychiatric hospital because she was committing slow suicide. She still wasn't eating. Had she ever been healthy? Even when she didn't want to restrict, that old voice inside her head—the sick voice that had wanted to turn away from Ms. Olson's door and never ask for help—urged her on. And if she lacked the willpower to resist, what about the others? They'd been so much sicker than she had been throughout the entire ordeal. Stefanie remembered Sarah's chipmunk cheeks, swollen from too much purging, Abby's water-loading, and Lizzie's crisscrossing scars. She'd never been that skinny, not compared to them. So if she wasn't eating as much as the doctors thought she should, what were they like?

Nine in a hundred will die.

Nine. Every time she heard it, the seriousness of that number hit her with renewed force, as if she'd forgotten how big it really was. Every time it surprised her, taking her unaware. Nine. There were six of them. And she hadn't heard from any of them yet. Would they be part of the nine? Would they ever fully recover?

It seemed too soon for anything to have happened, but what if something had? Would she know? It didn't seem likely. They hadn't been in contact yet. Why didn't they call? Why didn't they keep in touch, like they'd promised to? What good was a pact if they didn't adhere to it, if they didn't even try?

The thoughts circled inside her head. Why this? Why now? Who am I? Who are my friends? Her parents begged her to sleep. They didn't understand that she was trying. They thought that it was so simple, but she'd only be able to if she could turn off her mind. And that was a task she hadn't mastered yet.

- 40 -

*S*he slipped out of bed early and closed the front door quietly behind her, leaving a note on the kitchen table. She told her mother she was meeting a classmate at seven o'clock to exchange biology notes for the days she'd missed. It was a white lie, but it was harmless enough. She stepped outside and breathed in deeply. It was still nearly dark out, but she didn't care. The streets of New York were pleasingly calm and serene at this time of morning, and she wandered without purpose. She walked past the fire department, the For Rent sign where the all-night diner had once stood, and the Tasti-D-Light. She passed Blockbuster and D'Agostino's, where she'd bought mint chocolate cookie ice cream a lifetime ago. Ice cream. It had been awhile since she had had ice cream. She'd promised herself that she would never have it once she got out of the hospital. But if she allowed herself to really think about it, she realized that she missed it. She adjusted the collar of her suede jacket so the soft fuzzy lining rose against her neck, warding off the early morning chill. She thought with some longing about the minty chocolate taste and the creaminess of the sugary, frozen dessert. She kept walking.

She didn't really want any ice cream. She couldn't possibly want any ice cream. It was much too early. Of course, that was only an excuse. She knew that it didn't really matter what you ate at a given time of the day. They'd taught her that at the hospital, and Dr. Adler had reinforced the theory. She could have steak for breakfast or a turkey sandwich; she could have pancakes or waffles for dinner. And the world would still rotate on its axis.

Lack of sleep combined with the long, aimless walk left her drained. She didn't want to have to drag herself through the school day, but now it was too late for her to return home, and turning up at the nurse's office to request to be sent home would only raise a red flag in everyone's mind. No, she didn't want that. She glanced at her watch. Twenty minutes before class, that should be enough to recoup some strength—at least enough to get upstairs for pre-calculus and maybe enough to make it through Latin afterward.

The thought occurred to her that she'd skipped breakfast and that perhaps some food would give her the boost of energy that she needed. But she wasn't willing to eat. It didn't matter that her stomach grumbled for the entire world to hear. It didn't matter that the light from the streetlamps had blurred momentarily when she'd walked down Third Avenue earlier. She remembered these feelings. What was it that they had said at Barrett? What had Dr. Franz explained during CBT? Whatever. She didn't care enough to give it any more thought, and she dropped her head into her arms. There weren't that many classes before lunch. She just had to get through them, and then she could sleep.

Classes came and went. When they were over, Stefanie couldn't have recalled what they were about, even if a gun had been pointed at her head. She tried to pay attention, to absorb the love poems that they were reading in Latin and to contribute to the discussion, but her mind wandered. Food, Barrett friends, school friends, parents, doctors, teachers, homework, sickness, health. She had trouble sorting even one thought from the others, and it was impossible to pay attention to work with all that was going on in her head.

And then it was lunchtime again. Annabel was standing before her with her hand outstretched and her eyes darting to the door where Laura stood waiting. "Come on, Stefanie. Don't go down that road again. Come to lunch."

Annabel's face looked hopeful. She was trying really hard. They all were. They hadn't forgotten her after all—and hadn't evidently damned her either. They had, in fact, rallied around her, in part out of curiosity, in part protectively. Stefanie felt bad that she hadn't been more grateful. Even Julia had been around more—until she started restricting again, and then Julia had returned to Taylor. But it had been a nice interlude. A caring word here, a helpful hug there, and she hadn't even thanked them. And she didn't want to go to lunch either.

"No thanks. I'm not so hungry. I'll see you later."

Annabel shrugged. "OK, suit yourself. I'll be downstairs if you change your mind."

She'd asked every day for three weeks—every day since Stefanie had first come back. And every day Stefanie had said no. In the beginning, Annabel had pushed hard, urging her to join them, sending Laura over to try when Stefanie refused. Now it seemed that her pleas were a little less persistent; Annabel gave in more easily and seemed less confident about asking. She seemed to be following Julia's path, but at least she still asked. She was still trying. Stefanie wished she could show Annabel how much that was appreciated; she wished she could say yes—just once say yes.

She just had to stop thinking. She only had to put her books back in her backpack, stow it all away in the cubbies, and follow Annabel downstairs. She just had to wait in line and pick up some food and rejoin her friends. It was so simple. But she couldn't yet. She hadn't been in the lunchroom in a long time—not since before she'd gotten sick. And she wasn't ready to return. If she did, she'd be giving something up, something she wasn't yet prepared to sacrifice.

Three girls walked down the hallway, looking at her, scrutinizing her body, trying to unlock her secrets.

"Is she still anorexic?"

"I don't know. I mean, she was in the hospital for it, wasn't she? So I guess she should be better now."

"But she's still so skinny. And she still doesn't go to lunch."

"She's definitely anorexic. I heard it from Chrissy. Her sister, Taylor, is in Stefanie's class. She missed a month of school because she was in a psychiatric hospital. And she still never eats."

The conversation wasn't meant for Stefanie's ears, as she sat in the hallway, doing her math homework, but she heard it anyway.

Rumors—if you could call the truth a rumor. Maybe the proper word was *gossip*. They talked about her behind her back. The whispers were meant to go unnoticed, but they never did. Stefanie heard them all, everything that was said about her, or somehow she found out. Once Carrie, a sometimes friend, had confessed that everyone knew, that she was the topic of conversation around the lunch table, that some people thought she was just plain weird. Carrie's words hadn't been particularly tactful, but that was the way things usually worked. Words that were spoken somehow had a way of returning to the one person they weren't meant for.

"She must be still sick. I heard that it was really bad. She still looks like death. And it's not normal to never go to lunch."

"What's the matter with her anyway? I know it's supposed to be a sickness and everything, but really. I think she's just looking for attention."

"Yeah, like in death."

The words reverberated through Stefanie's head, and she wondered if they even knew she was sitting right there. If so, why would they talk like that? Who gave them the right to decide what she looked like, or how sick she was? The other girls spoke for her, and she lost the power of speaking for herself. The disease became more theirs than hers; they owned it, they talked about it, they made guesses about it. The truth wasn't important, but the gossip was. No one cared what she had to say. But why would they pass judgment on her right in front of her face? Not that she really cared. They were going to make up their own stories about her anyway, so why did it matter if she said anything or not? She didn't want to waste her breath. Besides, there was a kind of twisted enjoyment that came from listening to these conversations. She was still skinny. She was still considered anorexic. She might have given up her voice, but she hadn't had to give up her title—or her identity. She was still sick. And everyone could see that. She felt powerful, and a pulse of pride ran from her heart through the extremities of her body.

Anorexic: it was a title that she both loved and hated. She loved it for the uniqueness that it gave her and hated it for the life that it had taken away. Those girls had been stupid, but they had also been right: she didn't want to lose the attention she'd gained by being sick. But then, she also wanted to be normal again. She was tired now, tired of always being tired, tired of counting calories, tired of not eating the foods that she liked.

She wanted to eat Oreos. She wanted to eat lots of pasta with Bolognese sauce—she could imagine the bits of meat mingled with the tomato and the way the leftover sauce was perfect for dipping bread. And she didn't want to experience the suffocating feeling that overwhelmed her whenever she had to turn down an invitation. She wanted to go out with her friends. She wanted to sleep over at their houses and not worry about having to eat. She wanted to gorge herself on chips and salsa and late-night pizza, and stacks of pancakes and home fries in the morning, and she wanted to feel OK doing it. More than anything, she wanted to be normal. Normal but skinny, a contradiction in terms.

She still didn't feel ready to give up what restricting gave her. She wasn't ready to go back to being plain old Stefanie Webber, who had never been good enough, who'd been hidden away for too long in plain sight. She wasn't ready for her friends to withdraw again—or her parents. She bet they were just itching to return to the forefront of their old social scene, the one they'd enjoyed before she'd embarrassed them by abusing her body, by lying, by deceiving, and by landing in the hospital. She wondered if their social cachet had been hurt forever. They had once been so happy living their lives. But she wasn't ready to permanently sacrifice the chance of happiness that she'd been chasing for so long.

Both arguments—the illness and the cure—were equally strong, leaving her caught in a conflict between two lifetime adversaries. In the beginning, she'd hated to label herself anorexic, but now she didn't want to give up the claim. She still couldn't say it out loud, but just knowing it gave her a sense of accomplishment. It was a daily battle, and she never knew which side would win. Sometimes she was prepared to continue restricting until she'd finally reached that elusive goal of happiness, and other times she felt ready to give up because it just wasn't worth it.

So the gossip both pleased and angered her. A fifty-fifty split. She liked what they said, but on the other hand, why did they have to talk at all?

"Whatever, she'll do what she wants to do. I guess that's the way things go in this world."

Stefanie didn't even know the speaker, but she had gotten it just right. She would do what she wanted. She could starve or not, and it was her choice: not Dr. Adler's, not Dr. Grant's, not her mother's or her father's. It was *her* choice. She just had to make one. But that was the part that left her struggling and disoriented.

"The shinbone's connected to the knee bone, the knee bone's connected to the thighbone, the thighbone's connected to the hip bone …"

She hummed to herself and watched the talkers move on down the hallway, probably toward lunch. Her parents believed that she was cured, but the doctors weren't as stupid. Because she swore that she would try harder and then only lost more weight and because she couldn't articulate what her goals were, the doctors had labeled her ambivalent. But she wasn't ambivalent; she was just confused. They could ask her what she wanted until they were all blue in the face, and she still wouldn't have an answer. All she knew was that she wouldn't be going to lunch that day.

~ 41 ~

"You've got mail." Finally.

Thank you, God. Thank you, thank you, thank you.

There had been a drought in God's responsiveness the past couple of days. She hadn't heard from any of them in weeks. Why didn't they write? Why didn't they call? Why didn't they stay in touch? What had happened since they had left the safe sterility of Tower 3 North? Did they really care?

Had Sarah and Ed eloped and run off to Las Vegas? Had Lily and Naomi ever been discharged? Had their transitions home been smoother than hers? Was Abby still swimming? Or had her coach bullied her beyond her capabilities and then abandoned her? Had any of them ended up back at a hospital? Had Lizzie finally cut too deep? Had a heart attack claimed an innocent life too soon?

She'd prayed every night for a word: just one word.

She needed those friends more than anything else that she could think of, except maybe being skinny. She didn't want to lose that hospital life, and yet she could feel it slipping from her grasp. She was already beginning to forget what they looked like, what they sounded like, why they had been friends in the first place. Her life had settled into a routine, but that routine wasn't the hospital one. It felt abnormal. At some point, Ensures, commodes, and group therapy had become the usual.

Classes, cafeteria lunches, and homework had become strange. She was lost in a world that had once been so familiar, and she needed those friendships to ground her. They could hold her steady as the wind blew her from side to side. Stefanie longed to feel whole again. But her two worlds had to intertwine before she'd ever feel better. Both were who she was, and she couldn't forsake either.

"You've got mail."

They were the words that she'd been waiting to hear. SAJ83: it was Sarah's screen name. Sarah had written her. It should have been the most natural thing to read the e-mail. But now she didn't want to click on the little digital mailbox with the waving red flag. She'd been waiting so long; she was half-afraid to massacre the anticipation. She wanted to make it last just a little bit longer.

Her heart was pounding. Click.

> *Hey there, Girlie.*
>
> *How's it going? Good here. I'm thinking of moving out, maybe moving in with Ed. He's been great since I've been home—only eyed one girl when we went to Roosevelt Field Mall over the weekend. Sure is an improvement. And she wasn't even that skinny.*
>
> *So how ya doin? Enjoying normal life again? Still eating, right? I am too, though those doctors must be on crack. I don't need 1800 calories a day. That's ridiculous. So I'm just not following it. But don't you worry about me—the doctors sure don't. I'm not even being weighed weekly anymore. So we're all good. And I talked to Abby. She lost the weight she had put on right after she got out. Her coach was happy. He said it makes her speedier. She's aiming for nationals sometime next month. Well, that's about it, dearie. Write when you get a sec.*
>
> *Love Always, Sarah*

It sounded just like her, and Stefanie smiled. Inside and out of Barrett, her friendship felt good. She let her eyes dance over the words again, soaking up all their meaning and implications. This was what she'd been waiting for.

She'd finally heard from Sarah. But with each subsequent reading of the e-mail, she lost a bit of that initial enthusiasm. There was something in her friend's words that pulled at her stomach and made her uneasy.

It was obvious. Sarah shouldn't move in with Ed; Sarah should eat her recommended amount; Sarah should be weighed. But none of those things were happening. Why couldn't Sarah just do what she was supposed to do? Given her track record, had she ever really gotten any better? Stefanie was beginning to doubt that. And 1800 calories? Sarah, who still needed to gain weight and who had sworn that she could be trusted, was eating less than she was, and she had already reached her target weight. What did that say about her? Stefanie had thought that she'd cut back satisfactorily, but maybe it hadn't been enough. If Sarah was cutting back even more and believed that that was fine, then what would Sarah think of her? Click.

> *Hey Sarah,*
>
> *So you think you might move in with Ed, huh? Is that a good idea? I mean, should he be eyeing ANY girls at the mall, even if they aren't skinny? And how was the decision to stop the weigh-ins made? Is it really in your best interest?*

She didn't want to sound like an old lady or, worse, a mother, but she had to say these things. If Sarah was really her friend, then she was just going to have to take it. Stefanie pushed her chair back from the computer and read over what she had written. It wasn't too critical, not really. She didn't want to come off as an obnoxious little twit. She was only being honest and asking questions that she hoped Sarah would consider.

> *Me? I'm just fine. School's okay, and friends too. They're being really good about everything, surprisingly good. In fact, so are my parents. They're still worried, but it seems okay. They're trying to let me take it one day at a time and adjust to everything. So all in all? Well, home again,*

and enjoying it, though I miss you guys. I thought you'd never write to me, but I'm so glad you did. Thanks. Write back soon. Don't be a stranger. Love, Stef

Click. Your mail has been sent. OK.

Boring maybe, but that was good enough. What did Sarah expect? She couldn't just invent some exciting new life, could she? A boyfriend and a brand-new, size two wardrobe.

So she sent if off, knowing that even her real situation wasn't exactly the way she had described it. She could have said more. She could have written about how she'd cut back her own food intake. She could have written about how she was listening to the *Motivation* CD again. She could have written about how her parents assumed that everything was going fine when it really wasn't. She could have written about skipping lunch and limiting the time that she spent with her friends. Or she could have written about the two different people who lived inside her head and fought over whether or not she should recover. But she didn't write any of those things. She had chosen not to. Sarah didn't need to know, and Stefanie didn't really want to say.

Saying how much she had been allowing herself to eat would seem like an admission that she was still failing, that she wasn't doing enough to stay sick. At least it would seem that way to Sarah, whose unconditional commitment to thinness didn't seem to have wavered. Stefanie had said just enough not to be rude, but she wouldn't say anymore. Clearly, her first experience with the pact of "friendship forever" wasn't exactly what she had expected.

Lily wrote a couple of days later, but this time, when the message appeared in her maibox, Stefanie wasn't excited.

Dear Stef,
I miss my roomie. It's strange to sleep at night without someone in the bed next to mine. Campbell's a good sleeping buddy and she loves our pajama parties, but she

doesn't put up with the sit-ups. I hate it when she looks
at me with those big hazel and gold-flecked eyes and begs
me to stop—she's smart, and she knows what I'm doing.
She says she hated it when I was gone, but seriously, I'm
doing well. (Sarah would say "good," right?) Anyway, I
went out to dinner with my dad, Campbell, and Andrew
once last week. They were really supportive. I know if
I'm going to get over this, it'll be for them.

So I thought we were going to "stick together," oh,
Miss Supporter. What happened to that promise? Don't
tell me that Naomi was right. Prove her wrong. Long
live the clique! Ha, ha. Write me back. Love, Lily

This was a better letter. The instant comfort and supportive energy that Stefanie had expected from Sarah was there. It had always felt like that with Lily. There was hope. Lily was doing well, and presumably had the motivation to keep working toward recovery. Lily would fight for her life. It didn't look like she would ever be one of the nine. It looked like she'd recover.

Before she wrote back, Stefanie went into the kitchen. Her mother was sitting at the table with the *New York Times* crossword puzzle, and Stefanie bent to peak over her shoulder.

With a smile, she kissed her mom on the top of the head, and took a Granny Smith apple from the refrigerator. After a letter like Lily's, it seemed acceptable to have a mid-afternoon snack.

Her mom blew her a kiss as she left the room and called after her, "I'm proud of you, honey." And for once, Stefanie didn't cringe at the words. This wasn't so bad.

She wished every e-mail that came was like Lily's, but they weren't—the majority were more like Sarah's. Abby wrote next, pointing out how superbly the pact was being upheld and wondering why they didn't write more often. Stefanie wished she could point out that they were all struggling—except maybe Lily—but what relevance did that really have?

Lizzie's AOL wasn't working, but she had left a note for Stefanie with Freddy downstairs. She was adjusting fairly well, though her foster family still looked at her wrists every time her sleeve inched up. They were in almost-daily contact with her therapist. Her weight was being very closely monitored since she'd lost eight pounds, and she had cut herself a couple of times since she'd gotten home (she didn't specify what "a couple" really meant). And Naomi had just written to tell them all she'd decided to take the semester off from college and not return for the final few weeks. She'd already missed too much anyway, and she was going to work on getting herself back together emotionally and physically. But poor words were better than no words, Stefanie decided. Contact was the key.

Just hearing from them brought back some sense of really living. When she opened their e-mails, she didn't feel numb anymore. She knew that she was alive because there were people out there talking to her. She had something to look forward to when she returned from school every day, and she had somewhere to turn when she didn't know what else to do. They were different from her school friends because they understood. They empathized and commiserated and exchanged stories. And she rarely had to explain more than once. They just got it.

– 42 –

Finally, Stefanie was beginning to settle into a tolerable, if not comfortable, routine. The six musketeers e-mailed fairly regularly now. She did her homework every night and went to school every morning. She was finally caught up in all her classes, and she had even taken the exams that she had missed. At lunchtime she retreated to her old homework corners, and at home she resumed her old exercise regimen. In general, when she placed Mr. Whiskers on her pillow in the morning and gave him a parting kiss on his worn-out snout, she knew what to expect from the day.

Time was passing, the seasons were changing, and the weather was getting warmer. Along Park Avenue they had planted the yearly array of tulips, and splashes of color were beginning to brighten the islands in between the rushing cars.

It was another morning, another walk to school. Annabel was at her side. Her backpack wasn't particularly heavy, the sun was shining unusually brightly, it was quiet, she'd been caught up in all her classes for a week now, and there were no tests scheduled for the next four days. Stefanie breathed an easy, contented sigh and realized that the air really wasn't cold anymore.

"So how was Dr. Adler yesterday?"

Stefanie stumbled over a grating on the sidewalk. She hadn't known that Annabel even knew the name of her doctor, much less when the appointments were. "It was OK." The response was slow and wary, as if she didn't quite trust what she was saying—or hearing. Had her mother told her? "I supposedly need to get more calcium in my diet. Then we talked about my blood work that came back two days ago—my estrogen levels are really low. She doesn't really care what my weight is, though I've been losing somewhat steadily. She just wants me to get a period so that my bones will start growing denser again."

Stefanie had volunteered more information than she would have liked, but Annabel still seemed interested, like she really cared. This was something new.

"What's it like, Stef? I mean, you never talk about it. Tell me about the hospital and how it feels now."

Where was the Annabel that she knew? This wasn't the boy-crazy girl that had abandoned her for the more popular kids. This wasn't the Annabel that had appeared over the past three years; these questions weren't only rhetorical. They were genuine questions. And Annabel really wanted an answer.

"How it feels now? I don't know, kind of numb, I guess. Sometimes it's OK; sometimes it's not. Sometimes I think I made all this up—that I was never sick. But then I don't eat, and I wonder what the truth really is. I can't always remember what it felt like to be at the hospital, but sometimes I want to go back. I'm supposed to be fixed because I went into the hospital, but I don't feel fixed. My parents want me to be, and I want to be—for them. But sometimes I feel like I'm going crazy—like I just can't stand to be inside my own skin."

She paused for a minute to calm her shaky voice. "It's not as easy as just 'eat this and get over it.' It takes more work than I'd ever imagined. It's not fun, and no one really understands." She looked over at Annabel to see if she was still listening. She was.

"And I know I walked myself right into it." She rubbed her eye, as if to get rid of something that was clouding her vision. She hoped that Annabel didn't know she was rubbing away the tears before they had the chance to fall.

"Stef, stop it. Don't say that. You know what they say." Annabel had apparently been doing some reading. "It's not your fault that any of this happened to you. It's not. You didn't ask for it. And you didn't deserve it. You didn't cause it to happen." She gave Stefanie a firm hug then held her back at an arm's length. "Sometimes bad things happen to good people, and you just can't explain it." Annabel stopped, unsure of herself. "Look, I don't know what I'm saying. I'm not a shrink or a doctor or anything like that, but I've done some reading too. I've been to the Web sites. I know that it hurts. You can't blame this on yourself. Eating disorders don't ask to be invited into your life. They just arrive. They show up at your doorstep uninvited, and once they're in it's like trying to get a bad houseguest to leave. You didn't ask to get an eating disorder."

An eating disorder. Stefanie flinched at the words, and her first reaction was to deny the perceived accusation. She didn't have an eating disorder. She never had; she never would.

But Annabel didn't even know the half of it. Of course she had brought this upon herself. Annabel didn't know about the sleepless nights that she'd spent listening to the bones song or studying the pictures from the psychology textbook. She didn't know about the admiration that Stefanie had felt for those girls, for their strength and determination. And she didn't know about the prayers to God to help her lose a lot of weight. Annabel couldn't see that it was her fault; but it was. She had wanted it; she'd even chosen it.

"Are you eating now, Stef?" Annabel asked.

"Um, yeah. The hospital makes you eat; that's how I put on so much weight. For me, the amount was 2500 calories a day or more. You start out drinking Ensure, and then they work you up to food. By the end, I was eating three full meals plus three Ensures daily. So, yeah, I was eating."

Somehow she knew she was stalling, that she didn't really want to answer that question.

"And now?"

"Sure, I'm eating." Stefanie smiled, trying to make light of the situation, hoping that Annabel would accept her response as casually as she had offered it. "Maybe not as much as at the hospital, but I don't have to eat that much. I'm not supposed to be gaining weight anymore. So I've cut back a little bit, like not having as much starch because that's the most fattening, but nothing major." She looked over at Annabel. "Really." She gave her friend's arm a little squeeze. "I'm doing OK."

"Why'd you do it? Weight doesn't make a difference anyway."

"That's easy for you to say, when you're just naturally thin, and you never eat anything that isn't low in fat and nutritious. Just look in your kitchen. You mom keeps the place stocked like a diabetic supermarket or a gourmet health-food bar."

"Stop it. I eat a ton. You know that. I eat more than everyone else in the cafeteria. And I have fat just like everyone else. I'm no supermodel."

Yeah right. What fat was Annabel talking about?

Her friend bent over to pinch a roll from her stomach. "See."

It was a pitiful showing.

Annabel released the thimble-sized bundle of skin and rubbed at the red spot. "Ouch. It hurts."

Point made. "It only hurts because you're pinching pure skin. If there was any fat at all, it wouldn't hurt." Stefanie smirked, knowing she was right, but inside she wasn't happy that Annabel had been wrong. It would have been preferable for Annabel to actually have some fat.

"So why then did you start?" The girls had stopped walking now and had turned to look at each other with a new intensity.

Stefanie wasn't sure if she wanted to tell Annabel the truth—if she even knew what the truth was. But they were having such an honest discussion, and she hesitated to end it. "Truth, Bel? I don't know. I think I just wasn't happy—I'm not happy now—and I was—am—trying to find that happiness by losing weight." She paused, not sure if she should continue with what she had been about to say.

They stood at the corner, and the street sign read York Avenue. They were getting close to school, and, if she didn't talk now, who knew when there would be another chance. She searched her friend's eyes, looking for a sign that no matter what she said today, she would be safe.

"I guess I just wanted some attention—from my parents, and our teachers—" Stefanie hesitated. She couldn't say "you," so instead she said, "everyone, and anyone. I just wanted someone to care about me."

There. She had said it, out loud.

Annabel shook her head slightly. "God, Stef. I don't know what to tell you. I want so badly to help you—to make you better, but I just don't know what to do. I don't know how to help, but I want to. I feel like a failure as a friend. How could I not have noticed sooner? I feel so, well, guilty. I don't want you to hurt, but I just feel so powerless. I'm so sorry."

As they resumed walking, rounding the corner by school and reaching the front door, the conversation came to an end. But for once, Annabel didn't run off to find her new friends. She gave Stefanie another, more cautious hug, and they walked upstairs together. It was more than they'd said to each other in months.

− 43 −

*I*n high school, things changed quickly. If you looked away, you might miss it. Nothing could be taken for granted; everything was transient. Old friendships transformed themselves into hostile alliances or tentative acquaintances—even open hatred. And sometimes time—and experience—healed breaches once thought to be permanent.

Stefanie and Annabel talked on the way to school now, and, while Annabel usually did most of the talking, she was willing to listen as well. The days were good. Stefanie talked to her school friends in school and her hospital friends at home, by phone with Lily and by e-mail with the others. She ate breakfast at home before school, a snack when she returned home, and dinner. She hadn't been to the cafeteria yet, because they didn't stock her afternoon snack: an eight-ounce cup of Dannon regular yogurt—Fruit on the Bottom, apple-cinnamon flavor preferred. She was losing weight steadily but still eating. She didn't have to lie about her surprise when she stepped on the scale every Tuesday. It was a shock to see the numbers continue to drop, albeit slowly, at a quarter or maybe half a pound, per week. And while she was tired often and crabby, things were definitely getting better. There were actually mornings when she didn't wake up and dress only to get back into bed, wishing that the sun would detonate. In the dark of night, she didn't usually imagine her own funeral anymore or pretend that her bed was a coffin. And she didn't stare toward her wide windows, thinking about a body falling against the concrete below, with quite the same urgency. There were days when she even looked forward to the English muffin or bowl of cereal that waited on the kitchen table to fill her empty stomach.

It was just before lunch, and Stefanie was sitting in her usual place in the hallway, excused from PE because Dr. Adler still didn't want her burning extra calories. She was copying problems out of her math book, which was lying open across her thighs, and trying not to listen to Ms. Olson's voice—it would only make her wish she were part of that class also, the other psychology section.

$X \times Y = 75$; $Y \times 3 = X$; $X - Y = 10$; find X and Y. She didn't really care about the math. She'd been working for forty minutes straight without allowing her eyes to wander, and she didn't feel like solving yet another algebraic equation.

Her thighs. Was it the lighting? They didn't look quite so big. Not at all really. Had she really lost some weight? She turned her leg, the outline of her calf muscle was clearly visible. She couldn't find any of the fat that had tormented her for so many days. She wouldn't admit it to her friends from Tower 3 North, but she thought she looked pretty good. She wondered if her body image was finally becoming accurate. Dr. Grant and Dr. Adler had both said that it would happen eventually. Why had she resisted for so long? They'd been right. She didn't need to gain any weight, but she didn't need to lose any either. She was already skinny. The realization felt good.

"Come to lunch with us, Stef?" It was the customary refrain; this time Laura was asking. They were all eating together—Julia had even forsaken Taylor to join them.

Stefanie glanced up. She hadn't heard the classrooms empty, but they had. It was time for lunch. Why shouldn't she go with them? She looked just fine. She'd already put her math homework away; she couldn't concentrate anyway. She was hungry. She wanted to be with her friends—her friends. They were better friends than she had given them credit for. Maybe, just maybe, losing weight wouldn't really find her happiness. It hadn't so far. Maybe she'd just have to find that on her own. Taking them up on their offer would be a start. It might be fun, and one lunch wouldn't make her fat. She was thinking clearly enough to know that.

But as she had contemplated accepting their offer, she'd taken her eyes off her thighs, and, when she looked back down, the view had changed. Where lean muscle and bones had been seconds before, fat covered her legs. They were bigger than they'd been yesterday. She knew it with a sudden certainty that made her throat close and her chest tighten. She must have miscalculated her calories at dinner the night before. She'd have to make up for that later, maybe even get down to the gym.

She knew the way to get rid of it. Restrict. Starve. Don't go down to lunch. If one dinner had put on so much weight, imagine what a cafeteria lunch would do.

"No, thanks. I'll see you at English. I've got some work to do. It's taking me longer than usual."

Laura gave up and joined Annabel and Julia, who were waiting at the top of the stairs. Stefanie watched them go downstairs and wanted to join them. If only she'd never given her thighs that second glance.

But she had.

"**I** don't understand it. What the hell is wrong with me?" She sunk back into the pillows of the couch and rolled her big toe around in the plush carpet.

"What do you mean, Stefanie? Can you tell me what happened?" Dr. Grant was sitting in her recliner again, a notepad on her lap and a cup of coffee on the table in front of her.

Since she'd been out of the hospital, the two of them had developed some kind of a relationship. It was a little more than a tolerance. Despite herself, Stefanie had come to trust this thin woman with the Swedish Fish on her desk. Twice a week she sat in this office— almost willingly—and groped for the words to describe how she was feeling. Dr. Grant was good at listening; Stefanie would have to give her that. The questions might be dull and stupid, but Dr. Grant heard her when she spoke, and she didn't interrupt.

"They invited me to go lunch, but I said no. Julia was going, and Annabel and Laura, and I was just sitting there in the hall all by myself. I can't go to lunch. I'm too disgusting and fat … But I'm tired of this. Why can't I just be normal? Why can't I eat without obsessing over everything?" Her voice was high-pitched and whiny but Dr. Grant didn't seem to notice.

"There's nothing wrong with you, Not fundamentally. You have a disease, and you have to take your medicine—food—in order to get past it. But getting better is possible."

Stefanie rolled her eyes.

"I promise. I'm not going to let you go without getting you better."

"But I deserve it. I deserve to be sick, don't I?"

"Where's the proof for that?" Dr. Grant settled back into her chair, ready to write down what Stefanie said.

"Oh, I don't know. I just do. No one cares about me, no one loves me. I might as well be dead." She paused, waiting to see how Dr. Grant would respond, almost testing her. Would she react? Would she contradict her? Would she say that she cared? Would she ignore that last statement and pretend that it had never been said?

"Do you have thoughts of death, Stefanie?"

She nodded. Dr. Grant wasn't ignoring it, and just that fact made her feel, somehow, more secure and less out of control. "Sometimes."

"Do you think of hurting yourself?" Dr Grant had stopped writing and was watching Stefanie's face for a reaction.

"Sometimes."

"Do you have a plan?"

"No."

"Do I have your word that you'll call me if you ever do feel like hurting yourself? You'll call me immediately—before you act?" Dr. Grant put her pen on the table and took a sip of coffee. "Things will get better. You're depressed right now, but you'll get past this. You'll feel better. We just have to keep you safe until you do. So I need you to promise that you'll call me if you're thinking of hurting yourself."

Stefanie nodded, afraid that she might cry. Dr. Grant had passed whatever little test she had been giving: she hadn't just ignored the statement about death. Stefanie was relieved to know that she would be safe from herself until the worst was over.

"Now, why don't we talk about what happened at school today? Why don't you tell me why you don't deserve to go to lunch?"

"I don't know. I can't articulate it. I just don't." She didn't know how else to explain it, and she was too tired to try. The session was almost over anyway.

"Come on, dear, you can do better than that. I know you have the words in there somewhere. Just try. What are you thinking right now?"

Stefanie stared at the ceiling as if the answer might be scrolled across the sky. What was she thinking? There were too many thoughts in there swirling around in her head; she was lucky to distinguish even one from the rest of them. And every time she got close to isolating one particular thought, her internal editor popped up and ordered her to stifle the words. He didn't want her divulging her secrets. She shook her head, trying to knock the self-editor down. He fell momentarily, and she heard herself speak. "I'm thinking about how much I just want to be normal. No, I still want to be special, but I hate this. I hate my skin. I hate myself. I hate going to school like this. I hate watching my friends do things together, and I hate knowing that the only thing that stands in between them and me is a preoccupation that I just can't shake. I don't want to die. I want to eat again. I want to be happy."

Her hand rose to her mouth; she was surprised that she had spoken. Had she said too much? The self-editor was back. She'd been bad to say those things. She should have been more careful. She should have kept them inside, safely locked up, where they couldn't spring out into the open.

"Those are some strong feelings."

Stefanie had almost forgotten that Dr. Grant was in the room, but, called back to reality, she nodded. "Uh huh."

"Well ..." Dr. Grant finished writing her sentence and looked up into Stefanie's tear-filled eyes. "If you want to be healthy again," (Stefanie noted the use of the word *healthy* rather than *normal.*) "you can be. We'll get you there. It will take some time, but you'll get there. Just keep wanting it."

"I'm just so tired of this."

"I know," she said as she smiled, rolled forward in her chair, and rested her hand on Stefanie's knee. "But I promise you, it will get better. Trust me. What you're going through isn't any fun. You're conflicted, confused, anxious, and depressed on top of it all. I wouldn't want that combination; it doesn't feel good."

Realizing the session was ending, Stefanie sat up straight on the couch and picked up her bag. Silently, she removed her wallet, unzipped it, and handed Dr. Grant the check for that session. She gave a half smile, but one tear landed in her lap. "Promise I'll feel better?" She stood and so did Dr. Grant.

"Yes, I promise. You've already made progress. You're talking to me now."

Stefanie giggled as she opened the door to the waiting room. "Yeah, I guess. Thanks."

The door closed behind her, and Stefanie wondered if she wanted to have made progress. The anorexic voice and the healthy voice stopped wailing in her head for just a moment, and, left alone in the silence, she thought that maybe progress wasn't such a bad thing after all.

– 45 –

"Stefanie, phone call. Are you done with your food?"

"Yeah, thanks, Mom. I'll take it on the portable. By the way, good dinner."

She knew it was Lily. They'd been talking once a week for the past month and a half. They had agreed that it was better to hear each other's voices. They got a better sense of what the other was really thinking: it was too easy to disguise your words in an e-mail.

"Hey, Lil."

"Did I interrupt dinner? Your mom sounded angry."

"Oh, no. We were just finishing up. My mom's just tired. It's not you at all; it's me. She's just tired of living with the eating disorder. So how's it going?"

"Um, questionable." Lily sounded shakier than usual. As if maybe she'd been crying.

"What does that mean?"

Lily wasn't having an easy time. While the others just sort of stumbled along, doing somewhat less than perfectly, after that first note, things for Lily had gone downhill quickly. She had passed out in school two days before and had been sent home. Because of it, she had missed what she said called the "biggest history test of the year." Her father hadn't been around. He'd been driving back and forth to Connecticut to meet with the insurance company about payment for Lily's expensive doctor bills. Stefanie had wondered how they all paid for the hospital and the doctors and the therapy, but they didn't really talk about those things. Medicare stopped paying; insurance didn't cover it. The unspoken financial burden that many of the patients of Tower 3 North faced daily came up, but they didn't ever harp on it.

For Lily, this meant that Campbell and Andrew became her responsibility in the afternoons. During the school day, she worked incessantly, trying to get her work done before four o'clock when it would be time to walk her siblings home and help them with their homework. During boring math lectures, she had taken to laying an open book on her lap and reading as she pretended to listen. She wasn't eating lunch: there was just too much work to do, and to take even twenty minutes out of the day was completely unthinkable.

As Lily talked, she sounded tortured by perfection—by something she was striving for but could never attain. Nothing would ever be good enough for Lily. She could get straight A's and still not be happy—they weren't all perfect scores. She could score a 1600 on her SATs and still not be happy, because testing wasn't everything in the college process. Whatever she did well, she nullified with another fault. It wasn't enough to be a good big sister; she had to protect her siblings from every injustice that they might face. If she took time out to finish her own homework, she berated herself for not spending more time with Campbell and Andrew or for not cleaning the kitchen before her dad got home. To Lily, perfection was everything. It was the thing that motivated her and pushed her to work harder. It was the thing that made her so successful, but it was also her biggest weakness. It was a source of frustration, because, in her eyes, she was always a failure.

Often, she didn't finish her homework until midnight, and then she exercised in her room until one or one thirty. Only then did she let herself collapse into bed for a meager four hours of sleep, at which point the exercising would start up again. She quizzed Campbell before the fourth-grade spelling tests and made up her own quizzes to test Andrew's comprehension of fifth-grade math. The whole time, she was trying to keep her grades up, focus on college visits, and practice SATs. It was like she was on a never-ending treadmill—always running, always trying to catch up with the next thing that she needed to do.

As she talked, Stefanie could hear that she was tired. Lily's voice gave that away, but there was also a hint of hysteria there, behind the exhaustion. Listening to her was enough to make Stefanie appreciate her own household, where her mother was usually there to hold her hand, and where her only obligation was to get better.

"I'm exhausted, Stef. I just can't keep myself together anymore. I'm falling apart at the seams. Campbell needs me for math tonight, Andrew needs me for social studies, and I can't concentrate enough to remember what one-third plus one-fourth is, or the name of Michigan's capital. I can't remember what I'm supposed to be doing anymore. I'm coming apart again." Lily was crying now, hard, racking sobs.

"Lil, what's really going on? There's something else, something that you're not telling me, isn't there?" Stefanie could guess what that might be. She could almost visualize Lily's hands as she held the receiver, the fingertips of her other hand running along her ribs for comfort, like they'd often done back in room 507. "You don't have to tell me if you don't want to. But, if you do, I'm here to listen"

"You don't want to know, trust me. You're going to hate me, but, God forgive me, I've broken my promise. And now I've got to go. I'm … I'm …" Her voice choked back more tears and then faded.

"What?" The wind had been knocked out of Stefanie, and she gasped for the breath to form additional words. "What do you mean? Where are you going? What's happened?" She had visions of Lily on life support or in a coffin, the same wooden coffin that she'd imagined herself in, or clutching her chest with two hands, trying to fight the pain of a heart attack. *Nine in one hundred die. Nine in one hundred.* "Tell me!" she demanded. "Tell me, Lily. Goddamn it."

"They want me back in the hospital—my therapist and medical doctor. They want me back there tomorrow. Right after I go to school to talk to my teachers and find out how to keep up. They think it's reasonable, that I can do this, but it's not. It's going to destroy any chance at a decent college. Two hospitalizations during junior year doesn't look good. But I have to go. And I have to go tomorrow."

On the other end of the line, Stefanie waited, assuming there was more. There was.

"I'm scared, Stefanie. I restricted too much, I guess. I'm almost back to my admission weight, and, if I go lower, they'll tube me. I'm a fucking failure."

"Oh, Lily. What happened?" Stefanie sighed. Had she been pretending too? Lily was the one who wasn't supposed to stay sick. That first e-mail had been so good when all the others had been filled with words of struggling and faith in the disorder that they all held onto so fiercely. But Lily's had been different. Lily's was hopeful, and now Lily was going back to the hospital. She was the last one who Stefanie would have expected.

"Look, Lily, it's going to be OK. I promise. Everything is going to be OK. You're not a failure, and everyone will understand that. You'll go back to the hospital and get yourself together again. The stress got to you, that's all. Next time, things will be different. Maybe this is what needed to happen for you to get it right. You can do this, I know you can. You just have to believe that you want to—and you have to know that we're all here for you. Me, Lizzie, Sarah, Abby, and Naomi—all of us. I'll call you at the hospital; I still have the number."

Stefanie smiled, hoping that Lily would hear it in her voice and use it to bolster her determination. "Here's what we're going to do." She kept her voice even, forcing a calm she didn't really feel. "We're going to hang up. You're going to remember that I care about you and think of you every day. You're going to forget about everything else except getting well. And I'll be here in case you need me. If you don't call, then I'll call you at the hospital in a couple of days."

"OK." The tears were gone, and Lily's voice now sounded small and far away.

"OK. Good-bye."

"Bye."

And Lily was gone. Stefanie returned the phone to its cradle in a daze. She'd said all the right things to Lily but hadn't necessarily meant them all. Of course she cared about her. She'd call and write and do whatever she could to help—that was also true. They'd stick together forever because that had been the pact, and because Stefanie still wanted Lily's friendship. But did this mean that Lily was a failure? Not quite, but what she'd heard had made Stefanie angry. Why did Lily think that starving herself, removing herself emotionally from the lives of the people around her, was doing any good? It seemed selfish. Stefanie wanted to shake her.

Starving took a conscious effort, and Lily had been making it. She could blame her mother's death or the stress of babysitting her siblings or the media or school or college, but even Stefanie could see the obvious. Anorexia had a grip on her, but she wasn't even strong enough to admit it. What was that called? Denial.

− 46 −

*L*ily ... Lily ... Lily ...

"The shinbone's connected to the knee bone, the knee bone's connected to the thighbone, the thighbone's connected to the hip bone ..."

Lily ... Lily ... Lily ...

One more. Just one more. She was so close. Lily would be able to do it.

The CD skipped as she finished the last repetition and let her legs drop to the floor. Sitting up would be too much work. The room was a little hazy around the edges, a little out of focus. And she felt sick to her stomach. Her stomach ached from sit-ups and was still distended from her afternoon yogurt.

Maybe it was catching.

Lily struggled and then, like a cyclone, swept up the rest of them as she passed through town. One powerful gust, and they bent, like fragile trees snapping in the path of the storm. They struggled too. Was it Lily's fault? Or did these things just come in waves, each period of difficulty moving in independently from the ones around it and independently from what had come before?

She sat up, but the room spun. She decided not to stand just yet.

It wasn't easy for any of them. Now when they talked online the troubles came out. Sarah was depressed again. She suspected Ed was cheating and that she'd start to lose weight but couldn't seem to make herself eat. Abby was swimming her heart out, pushed— in Stefanie's non-expert opinion—too hard. But worse, Lizzie had gone to watch her at a meet and had been scared for Abby's life when she saw the girl's bones protruding beneath her Speedo bathing suit. And, as before, Naomi's issues were predominantly with her father, who steadfastly refused to accept there was a problem and wouldn't go to family therapy, so nothing changed. And Stefanie? She didn't make it easy to tell. If you'd asked her parents, who saw her eating regular dinners, and her various doctors, who saw her regularly but at intervals, she was OK—with the exception of Dr. Adler, who had resumed the careful monitoring once Stefanie had lost a significant amount of weight.

Occasionally, Stefanie would have at least half agreed with their willfully hopeful assessments. But on most days—on those days when she'd completed a baker's dozen of leg lifts and sit-ups and thought to run to the bathroom after every meal; when she seriously thought about going back to purging because it seemed to be the easiest way to accomplish all she wanted—she knew otherwise. Dr. Adler wasn't so easily fooled, and neither was she. For the others, it was enough that she was eating something. It was enough to know that she'd completed the hospital program. That was enough for them; that made her healthy, regardless of what the truth was.

What was the truth? Stefanie would lie in bed at night waiting for sleep to come and thinking on that good talk with Annabel and her first alarmed, careful e-mail to Sarah. She thought about that day in the hall at school that she had had that flash of insight about the way she saw her body—or failed to see it. All those moments seemed to be leading her away from this sick, sad place she'd been dwelling in for a time. They were sporadic and always brief moments to be sure, but she had glimpsed what her life on the other side might be like and had believed she could summon the strength to get there. So what had happened to her and Lily and the others? Were they like lemmings, all fated to go over the side together?

She missed talking to Lily. It wasn't the same now that they communicated over a pay phone and were limited to fifteen minutes, during which the operator would continually interrupt to ask for more change. Having been there, Stefanie knew that Linda would press the emergency call button and have you physically hauled off the phone and strapped down with two- or four-point restraints if you went over the allotted time while someone was waiting to make a call. So she didn't press Lily for too many details and never felt quite satisfied when she hung up the phone.

Lily talked about the changes that had been made at in the hospital in the two months since they'd been discharged. Jules was still there, but Morgan, the nice volunteer, was gone. They'd changed the menu, and the food wasn't half as good. She was rooming with someone she didn't really like—a girl named Emily who was bipolar and depressed. This time around, Dr. Katz was not on service. They'd rotated back to mean old Dr. Gray. The other major change at the Barrett Institute had been the altered visiting hours. Now the same non-parent/non-guardian visitor could visit only twice a week: meaning that she'd barely seen Campbell and Andrew during the two weeks she'd been there. But as much as Lily talked and made the whole experience sound more like prison than the first time, Stefanie couldn't make herself believe it.

It was funny how memory could do that: mutate to remember only selective parts of an experience. Looking back, Stefanie remembered only the good parts. She remembered enjoying the food and making friends; playing cards, drawing pictures, and talking. At Barrett she'd felt more comfortable with the people around her than she'd ever felt in her life. And when, occasionally, the bad memories resurfaced, she dismissed them as minor annoyances, like mosquitoes on a summer day.

It didn't matter what Lily said. Despite what she was told, Stefanie's anorexic half, which pleaded for Stefanie to stay sick, wished that she were the one back inside the white walls of that penitentiary.

Lily was the successful one. Stefanie had been trying to restrict, but Lily had done it better. There was always someone better—someone sicker. Why couldn't she get back her hospital weight? Why had her willpower waned? Why could Lily still do it?

While the room slowly stopped spinning, Stefanie's mind raced. Why did she want to stay sick? What was so glorious about the title "anorexic"? What did it really gain her? And why, when she knew that the real answer to this last question was that it didn't win her anything—not friends, not unconditional love, not happiness—did she still cling to the belief that it did?

"Stefanie, it's time for dinner, honey. Please come join us." Her mother knocked on the door but didn't open it, and Stefanie finally pulled herself to her feet. Her parents were completely unaware that she was struggling, but, even if they had known, they would have waited for her to come to them for help. All the books said this was a delicate and important point in the recovery process that made the patient feel trusted and empowered. Yeah, right. She would never ask—not as long as everyone else was still sick. She wouldn't be left behind—not while Sarah and Lily and Lizzie and Abby still starved. She refused to be alone.

"How was school?"

"Any tests today?"

"How's Annabel? And Laura?"

"How was Dr. Adler today?"

"What's the funniest thing that happened at school today?"

They fired questions at her in an attempt to jumpstart a conversation, but she didn't feel like responding. One word, or two—Fine. No. Fine. Fine. Fine—and a look of exasperation would be sufficient. Eventually the questions stopped, and Stefanie was allowed to retreat inside herself again. Her parents would only push so hard before they gave up and talked exclusively to each other.

Nine in one hundred will die. Nine in one hundred. The statistic replayed itself over and over. Where were they all? Where was Sarah? She hadn't heard from Sarah in a couple of weeks, and she was the one who Stefanie worried most about those days, knowing that the doctors had said if her weight didn't remain stable it was very likely her heart would give out. Sarah couldn't ever purge again, that's what they had said. And Stefanie knew she had been. The thought scared her.

Her mind spun. *Sarah can't purge. Sarah can't purge—but I can.*

She'd thought about it every night after dinner, when she walked past the bathroom on her way back to her room. Every night. But she hadn't acted on it. Not yet.

It would feel the same as always: Her fingers crawling down the back of her throat, coming into contact with the dangling ball at the back. Her teeth, the sharp incisors, scraping against the knuckles of her index and middle fingers as she pushed back farther and then farther, and moved the fingers around. Flushing the toilet a second time and watching the remnants disappear, pulled under by the funnel-shaped pull of the water. The burning throat that she only noticed once the toilet was safely flushing and she had swished out her mouth. Red eyes. Shaky, sandpapery hands where the harsh lye of the soap had already begun to dry out her skin.

She'd asked herself earlier why she bothered to restrict any-more—why any of them did. She couldn't say that the answer was any clearer. But she did restrict, or she tried to. And she hadn't that night at dinner, so she'd have to take another route. The detour had led to her bathroom.

– 47 –

The end of the school year was quickly approaching. Annabel, Laura, and Julia were constantly talking about their summer plans. Julia was going to New Hampshire to work for Habitat for Humanity during the month of July, and then she was taking off with her parents for a cruise—someone was celebrating a twenty-fifth wedding anniversary and they were having a family reunion; Laura was going to Switzerland with her church's choir, where she was going to tour by day and party by night. "And," she said proudly, "learn to speak French fluently." They'd all laughed, but with Laura you never knew. She might just be able to do it. Though the others' summers were exotic, Annabel's was by far the most confusing. She was going to California to spend some time with an aunt there; she was horseback riding and playing tennis in Arizona; she was going to a writing camp at one of the colleges in Maine; and she was taking sailing lessons out in the Hamptons. Stefanie's head spun just thinking about it.

She was doing nothing. Her big plans consisted of the same old doctor's appointments and therapy, and sitting home on her butt trying not to burn any calories. She listened to her friends talk and silently wondered why they were so lucky. She wasn't allowed to go anywhere. She understood why: they were afraid that without super-vision she would stop eating again, but it hardly seemed fair. There were things she wanted to do. She had been supposed to go with Annabel to the writing program. She might have spent a weekend with Julia in Arizona and maybe invited Laura to spend a week with her in the country, once Laura got back from Switzerland. But all those plans had been cancelled. She wouldn't be going anywhere or be doing much of anything.

The test calendar in the classroom showed only one and a half more weeks to go and only two more final tests. Summer excitement buzzed through the hallways, and the corridors were less crowded as most upperclassmen fled the building in exchange for the sun during free periods.

Stefanie and Ms. Olson had been talking occasionally. Her teacher sometimes pulled her aside after class, or sometimes joined her in the hallway for a moment or two between classes or before lunch. She assumed Ms. Olson knew that she wasn't eating lunch, but she didn't mention it. She asked how Stefanie was, and she asked about summer plans, and she gave Stefanie her e-mail address and said to please write. Stefanie had held on to that piece of paper with the address on it all day, and then deposited it safely in the top drawer of her nightstand when she got home. She wouldn't use it, at least not right away, but it was nice to have it. She was flattered that Ms. Olson had given it to her, but a voice inside her head screamed that if she ever dared write, Ms. Olson would hate her forever—that she'd only been acting nice and hadn't really meant what she said. It chided her and demanded to know why she could be so stupid as to think that this teacher might actually care about her. But, despite believing that voice, Stefanie didn't throw the little rectangle of white paper away. She decided to keep it, just in case.

Eventually the last tests were taken, the test calendar came down off the bulletin board, and the teachers' moods lifted, knowing that end-of-the-year comments they had left to write were the only thing that stood between them and two months of freedom. And the last Monday arrived, complete with its ritualistic cleaning of lockers and recycling of books. School wouldn't officially end until Thursday, but classes were over. They wouldn't need any books. That afternoon, although the weather was damp and cold for early June, Stefanie agreed to walk home with Annabel, both of them weighed down by bags full of junk that had inevitably collected in the bottoms of their lockers. As they turned the corner and headed down the next street, Ms. Olson tapped Stefanie on the shoulder and gave her a firm hug.

"I'm proud of you. You've worked hard this year. Have a great summer. E-mail me, OK?"

Stefanie nodded, subtly glancing at Annabel to see what her reaction would be. "OK." She relaxed into the embrace for one second longer and then pulled away. As she and Annabel walked toward York Avenue, away from the school, Stefanie turned around and smiled. Over her shoulder, she called back, "See you tomorrow, Ms. Olson."

At that point, she didn't know that she wouldn't.

When she got home that day, she found an envelope at her front door.

Her mother sat with Stefanie while she opened it, waiting to put her arms around her fragile daughter. She already knew what was in the envelope. She had taken the phone call earlier that morning.

Stefanie didn't go to school the next day, and she didn't return again that week.

– 48 –

The altar was laden with flowers reeking with the happy scent of almost-summer. Lights illuminated the painting of Baby Jesus, just above the tabernacle, and the baby seemed to sparkle. Sun was shining gently through the stained-glass windows, and the organ situated on a balcony above them played slow, quiet music in the background. Stefanie noticed the group of people clustered together in the back of the church, their heads tilted to the sky, clutching hands, and standing together in a circle, all crying. They looked like they were praying.

Uncomfortable and standing conspicuously at the top of the center aisle, Stefanie's eyes searched the crowd. She didn't know where they would be sitting, but she needed to find them. They had to sit together. Soon her palms were clammy, and she wiped them off on her clothing. She was wearing a long skirt, meant to hide the shape of her legs, but people could probably see through her cover anyway. Were they staring at the ice-cream cone shape of her thighs? OK, breathe.

She tried to slow her breath down and think clearly. Where had they said that they would meet her? They'd had this conversation the day before, but Stefanie couldn't really remember anything that had happened since leaving school on Monday afternoon. And it was now Thursday morning. She wondered if perhaps she had been sleepwalking through the past couple of days.

"Stef." A voice surfaced next to her left ear, and she turned quickly.

"Oh, thank God, Naomi." She threw her arms around her friend's neck. "I couldn't find anyone. I've been standing here for, like, ten minutes."

"We're over here." Naomi led her through the growing crowd to the front of the church.

Finally, after tripping over an elderly woman fully clothed in black who was carrying a cane but not actually using it, Stefanie and Naomi slid into the pew beside the others. They hadn't seen each other in a long time, and it was shocking to look at her friends dressed normally, not in the pajamas, slippers, and oversized t-shirts that had comprised their uniforms at Barrett. Her palms were cool and dry now; she gave Abby a hug and blew Lizzie an air kiss.

"Where's Lily?" Stefanie whispered, a slight note of urgency in her voice. Had something happened?

"Not here yet. She called a few minutes ago," Abby held up her cell phone. "She left a message. Jules was supposed to bring her, but she was late to work today. They had to find someone new at the last minute."

Deep sigh. Lily would make it after all. Stefanie knew how much it meant for her to be here. The Barrett Institute didn't grant day passes too frequently, but they had made an exception for Lily. Her second hospitalization had lasted longer than expected. She had resisted and restricted more, and the therapists had been surprised that she wasn't the same docile creature that they had first met back in March. But when Stefanie called to tell her the news, amid broken sobs and many tearful, "I'm sorrys," Dr. Katz had been willing to let Lily go. It was just for the day, just long enough to spend a few hours away, but it was enough for Lily to do what she needed to do, which was to be there with them that morning.

The organ continued to play low, soft, sad music. Mournful and heavy, they didn't talk. Most of the church was silent, except for the few people still huddled at the back. Stefanie watched for Lily from her seat at the end of their pew. She should be here any minute.

"Are you sure she's coming?" Stefanie looked at Abby again. The service was about to start.

"Here," Abby passed the cell phone down the row. "Listen to her message if you don't believe me. It's the third one on there. The first two are from Coach Klay."

"Wait, no, don't call. There she is." Lizzie lifted one hand in the air and waved cautiously. It was nearly the same wave she had given Stefanie four months before.

A slight girl had just entered the church through the double doors and was staying toward the back, as if lost. She too, was dressed all in black, but her skin practically gleamed, too white and pale to look healthy. When she spotted Lizzie's waving hand—a beacon in a sea of dark colors—she moved slowly toward them, as if afraid to move more quickly; as if, perhaps, she wasn't quite steady on her feet.

Their arms wrapped around each other, and Stefanie cringed to feel the ribs beneath Lily's clothing. "You made it."

"Yeah." Lily squeezed back with more strength than she seemed capable of, but her voice shook and her face was wet with tears. "I was so afraid I wouldn't. I was so afraid it'd start without me. I hate it there, Stef. They can't even get someone to take you to a goddamn funeral."

"I know." Stefanie wiped a tear off Lily's cheek. "Shh … it'll be OK." All down the row, they sat with hands clasped together, not saying anything, just holding on as if their lives depended on it.

It was strange. As she stared down the line of teenage girls, Stefanie forgot momentarily that Sarah would not be coming. She looked around, waiting to see the cheerful smile pop up from behind a potted plant or in front of their pew, but it didn't. Sarah wasn't coming; rather, she was already there—on the altar, in the closed mahogany box adorned with flowers. As they waited for the service to start, Abby passed out tissues. They had to fight to hold back the unshed tears that pooled in their eyes.

Sarah Amelia Johnson. It was written on the mass card that they all held in their hands. Perfect, curvy, delicate script. Sarah would have liked it. There was a picture of the Virgin Mary on the front holding Baby Jesus tenderly in her arms. Her name was on the card, but she was gone. No one would see her again, not in this life.

It was hard to believe that only four months before they had stood in a nervous cluster outside the weigh-in room every morning, shivering in the thin hospital gowns. It was during those times that their frailties were most apparent. Each would pinch at her stomach, thighs, or arms, exclaiming over nonexistent fat. Together they had struggled, and together they had contemplated their futures. The possibility of death had occurred to them, even then, but they'd never really believed that it could happen. They had ended their time together with their pact. But Sarah was gone; she'd already changed the agreement.

They used incense during the ceremony. There was a picture of Sarah next to the coffin. She was younger—when her face had been fuller and healthy—but the smile was the same, though it seemed to have a touch of sadness in it too. Stefanie wondered if she had known what was going to happen, even back then. As she sat to have her picture taken on a clear, crisp fall day, had she known that she wouldn't see her twentieth birthday?

The five remaining musketeers sat together in the fourth pew to the side of the altar. No seats had been reserved for them near the center because Sarah's parents wouldn't allow it. "Isn't it enough that we're letting you come?" Their bereft eyes had accused them. Naomi had been offended, but, as Lily had pointed out, their group of five skinny teenage friends came from a time that the Johnsons hoped to forget, wanting to remember only the good in Sarah's life, not the sickness that had claimed her.

The service ended, and they swiped at their eyes, bidding au revoir—until we see you again—to one of their number.

For each, that day had been memorable. Not only because of Sarah's passing, but because, as the other families dried their eyes and went home, the musketeers of the Barrett Institute walked slowly together down the block and seated themselves at a café.

To the Johnsons, their act wouldn't have mattered. The people at the funeral and the priest wouldn't even have noticed. But Sarah would have understood. While the tables around them laughed, enjoying early summer brunches, they ordered and ate in silence, grasping onto each other for support.

Sarah had died over a toilet seat, alone, late at night, when her heart had given out from purging one too many times. And she fell forward, hitting her head on the porcelain rim, bleeding across the white-tiled bathroom floor. Her parents had found her the next morning, blood on the floor and vomit in the toilet. They hadn't needed an autopsy; they could see how she had died. Her death hadn't been in control, and it hadn't been graceful. Sarah wouldn't have wanted her end for any of them.

Stefanie looked at the others, wondering if this time they could change things. Sarah wouldn't want them to join her, but what did they want? It was the same question that had reverberated in their thoughts since discharge: should they get better or not? Was it even possible? The statistics said only nine in one hundred would die from it, but, as she sat there watching the pained expression on their faces, she wasn't so sure.

One had gone down; there were five left to go.

Slowly, each bite of food on their plates disappeared. Toast, egg, salads, a turkey sandwich, cups of soup, grilled chicken. They chewed and swallowed and took the next bite. Tables around them emptied and then refilled, but they didn't rush. They tasted every bite, smelled it, felt it go down, obsessed about it, and then panicked. But they ate it.

Abby was the last to finish, and, as soon as she swallowed the last few pieces of her sandwich and put her napkin down in her plate, the waiter appeared. He was a cute young man in his midtwenties, and he spoke with a slightly Greek accent and a lopsided grin. "Can I get you ladies anything for dessert? Coffee? Tea? Anything else? Or will that be all for today?"

Naomi's pupils dilated, and she looked around the table. "Well, girlies, should we?" Her voice came out distorted and kind of squeaky.

Dessert? She couldn't possibly be serious. Stefanie had a sudden urge to reach across the table to feel Naomi's forehead and check for a fever, or else to smack her. Dessert! Four months ago, Naomi couldn't keep anything in her stomach, now she wanted dessert?

The first mischievous grin that Stefanie had ever seen on Lily's face appeared. "OK, let's challenge ourselves. I only have an hour left before Jules picks me up and brings me back to hell on Earth. Sarah would have wanted to us to."

Lizzie stuck out her tongue and cocked her head as if she was thinking. "Sounds good to me. Hmmm, I'll get—let me see—a vanilla sundae with chocolate sauce, whipped cream, and a cherry. No nuts." Stefanie remembered talking to Lizzie about their favorite desserts. What she had ordered was what she had dreamed about.

Lily scanned the menu over Naomi's shoulder. "I think I'll have some hazelnut Ciao Bella gelato. You, Naomi?"

"Hazelnut gelato, all the way."

Abby was next. Then Stefanie. It would be her turn, and she had no idea what she was going to do. She couldn't concentrate.

"I'd like a vanilla milkshake, please. Wait, no—chocolate or vanilla? Oh, I'll go with chocolate." Abby didn't look entirely convinced, but the waiter moved on down the line.

They had all made their selections. It was her turn next. Stefanie froze. They couldn't be serious. She couldn't have dessert. She'd be breaking the rules. Instinctively, her fingers moved for her hips. The salad that she had gotten for lunch hadn't done too much damage, at least not yet, but she'd better not do any more. She couldn't be too indulgent—and that meant no dessert. The waiter was poised, ready to take her order, but Stefanie just shook her head. "No, thank you. I'm not that hungry."

"All right then. One sundae, one chocolate milkshake, and two hazelnut Ciao Bellas on the way." The waiter returned to the back of the restaurant, tucking his little notepad into the pocket of his gray slacks.

Neither Lily nor Lizzie nor Abby nor Naomi said anything. And Stefanie wondered what they were thinking. She wondered if she had let them down. But she just couldn't have done it. Maybe next time God would finally give the non-anorexic Stefanie the new strength that she needed to resist her sickly counterpart.

- 49 -

Afterward, that day wasn't mentioned again in any of their e-mails or letters or phone calls, but Stefanie knew that the Virgin Mary and Baby Jesus hung in five different rooms, each card in a place of honor. But still, they all struggled. They all struggled, but somehow each of them was moving forward, however tentatively.

Sarah had had enormous faith. Faith was strong. It could change things; it could help you. Then again, it all depended on where your faith was placed. Sarah had placed her faith in the disorder—it was the thing that was going to make everything all better. The disorder had killed her.

Stefanie wrote those thoughts in her journal and recorded the events of the funeral. She wrote it down, not because she was afraid she would forget, but because she felt that she had to. She didn't need it to remember; she would never forget.

She thought about her friends from the Barrett Institute and from school, and she thought about what it meant that she would never see one of them again. She'd had friends move before, but that was only across a state line—it was an easily retraceable path and they were only a phone call away. Wherever Sarah was, Stefanie couldn't just dial a number and wait for her hello. Sarah wasn't going to dance around any more IV poles. She wasn't going to play cards or Life. Stefanie thought about the silver picture frame that had held Ed's picture and wondered what Sarah's parents had done with it. She didn't have any pictures of Sarah—cameras had been forbidden at Barrett—and she wondered if she would forget her friend's face. The harder she tried to focus on it, the blurrier the vision became, and eventually she just stopped trying. Sarah would never again be there to exchange instant messages. And she would never be there to receive another birthday card or a small present in the mail. She would never again see the sun shining, and she wouldn't ever feel drops of rain falling on her head on a spring day.

Her mother had told her that Sarah was better off now, out of the pain that the eating disorder had caused her, but Stefanie was skeptical. Out of the pain? Yes, but also out of the world. Maybe there were more positives than negatives to being alive. She didn't say it out loud, but the thought occurred to her. It wasn't enough to say that Sarah was out of pain. Sarah's life had been overtaken by the negatives, and she'd never again feel the positives. And Sarah had been selfish. What about the pain that she had caused the others? Stefanie oscillated between grief and rage. She lost one of her best friends because her own friend hadn't valued her life enough. Sometimes she wished Sarah were alive just so she could yell at her. How could this have happened? It was obvious that Sarah hadn't thought about the people she was leaving behind. If she had, she just hadn't cared enough. Stefanie felt betrayed somehow, and confused. Was there anything that she could have done to stop it? Was there anything she could have said? In her dreams, she often met up with Sarah. She guessed that the aggression came out at night, and sometimes she woke up sweating and scared—she'd been smacking Sarah and pulling her hair. Or sometimes she woke up crying—she'd seen Sarah in Central Park but hadn't been able to catch up; Sarah had turned her back and just walked away.

Death was final. It had claimed one of her best friends, and she was gone forever. Stefanie didn't want to die. She knew that now, as she remembered Sarah's coffin, but recovery seemed risky and hard. Maybe impossible. She had been sick, maybe still was. And sickness meant a similar coffin could be in her future. But getting better would mean sacrificing Sarah, disregarding her place in the agreement, and potentially leaving the others behind. She'd never believed that it could happen—not to any of her friends, not to her. They were immortal. Until Sarah's funeral, that had always been her firm belief. But what if it wasn't possible for them all to recover together? She was beginning to see a new impracticality to upholding their promise. Was it even possible that the dwindling number of muske-teers could all recover? What if they couldn't? She had a vague sense of what would happen then but didn't want to think about it.

Alone in bed at night or in the morning when she was jolted awake by the bones song, Stefanie wondered about it all. While four of them still clung to life, was Lily the only one who was really keeping her promise? Was going back to Barrett the only way to uphold the pact? And were they obligated to follow? Was dying the only way? Those were questions that Stefanie couldn't answer. Could she get better without betraying her friends?

The night after the funeral, Stefanie closed her journal firmly. Her pages were speckled with tears and had begun to crinkle. She knew that she wouldn't write for a long time. She was full of ques-tions, but the rest of the pages remained empty. She didn't even look in the drawer where the journal was kept. Hoping the memories of that day would fade within a couple of weeks, she didn't want to risk remembering.

One of their number was gone. Could more follow?

– 50 –

Over the course of time, Stefanie watched the others struggle. Lily was back at Barrett—this latest time for a much-prolonged stay. Lizzie had been readmitted temporarily for observation after Sarah died, because the doctors were concerned that Lizzie might take her sadness and anger out on herself. Naomi had hated her father for the longest time, and they hadn't made any progress in the virtually nonexistent family therapy. Abby was still swimming long hours every day and losing strength consistently. Her times were getting slower, and Coach Klay was threatening to drop her from the team. And Sarah, well, she had obviously lost the fight.

It had occurred to Stefanie that she was the only one doing all right. She was the only one who still managed to eat three meals a day, even if she did purge away some of those calories. She was the only one who didn't have to water-load to keep herself out of the hospital. Her weight had been falling, but not too quickly, she wasn't in serious trouble, even Dr. Adler admitted that. She'd gone through the stages of grief, mourning over her lost friend, the anorexia. She'd been angry and jealous and resentful as the others restricted and purged and exercised. She'd had her down days, but also her up moments. Things had been getting better. Even Dr. Grant had said that she was making progress.

But now, one month after Sarah's death, after five months of seeing her friends through tough times, Stefanie wasn't the one watching from the sidelines. She was the one in trouble. Her school friends were long gone on their fabulous summer vacations. New York City had gotten hot and sticky—the garbage smell and low smog never quite lifting. The doctor's appointments seemed to be multiplying as they watched her more vigilantly. And her best friend had become the toilet—or the bathroom mirror. Though she still talked to the Barret girls online, and Lily over the phone once a week, she didn't think about them as often anymore. She only missed them sometimes. Food became her preoccupation again, and she didn't care as much about connection. She forgot what it felt like to really talk to friends, and as each day passed, she became more isolated.

"The shinbone's connected to the knee bone, the knee bone's connected to the thighbone, the thighbone's connected to the hip bone ..."

The CD skipped a beat and began again, the way it had the day before, and the day before that, and the day before that. She was still listening to it. The word *Motivation* still spun, a black blur through the clear front of her stereo. She was still doing her exercises, still pushing herself to the brink of exhaustion (occasionally passed) on a daily basis.

Her parents had finally caught on, to a certain extent.

Faced with fights, arguments, screaming matches, and deceit, they had become a mixture of emotions. They hated Stefanie for what she was doing to them—for the time that it took to get through a meal. When she screamed that she hated them and threw tantrums, they just stepped aside and watched. They had tried holding her, comforting her, rocking her, and talking to her, but nothing worked. There wasn't anything that they could do. Stefanie was slowly killing herself, and she didn't even see it. Like Stefanie had wanted to shake her Barrett friends at times, her parents wanted to shake her. For every lie, they grew a little bit more resentful and a little bit more frustrated. Her mother cried in the living room at night after she thought her daughter had gone to bed. Her parents fought about how to deal with her. Her father wanted to punish her. Her mother tried to force her to eat, sitting there with her, cutting the food, not letting her get up from the table. Both wanted the same thing, but, in the end, they couldn't agree on how to get there. There only came more fights, arguments, and screaming matches.

Finally, exhausted and angry at each other, their daughter, and the doctors who couldn't seem to help her, they gave up. As they had before the hospital, they stopped pleading with her to eat. Her mother made the point that if she wanted to die, so be it. Everything was in her hands. Her eyes were empty when she spoke these words, and Stefanie longed to throw herself at her mother and hit her, beat her, for giving up. If her own parents gave up, how could anyone expect her to succeed? But when she tried to hold onto her mother, not let her leave the room, Madeline Webber walked away. She had to protect herself emotionally; it was time to think of herself. The day came when they gave in to their numbed, willful desire to believe that she had the situation under control—or they had just had enough, and so they stopped fighting.

They knew that she listened to the bones song more than any other. They knew that its presence in her stereo or Discman was a given at any point during any day. But they didn't understand it all, or, as she had thought many times, they just didn't care.

When the CD paused after the words *hip bone*, Stefanie stopped. The muscles of her stomach relaxed, thankful for the slight rest. Her hands flew to her hips. There they were, those hip bones, supposedly instrumental to the body's frame. She pressed down on them hard, testing, always testing. She yawned and closed her eyes, and she lay there on the floor. The last time she had experienced good sleep was after Sarah's funeral. It had been the sleep of exhaustion, both emotional and physical.

Now she laughed at herself. She remembered that night. It was the night that she had decided to get better—really this time, not just in appearance, she really and truly had meant it. She wasn't going to be part of the percent for whom this disease is fatal.

But despite the promises, wishes, and dreams, nothing had materially changed since she'd left the Barrett Institute five months before, or in the month since Sarah had died. The tendencies were all still there, and it was amazing how life had returned to the way it had been so quickly. Initially, she had tried to eat more. The day she came home after the funeral, she had worried when she found her mother at the kitchen table, crying because she could imagine what Sarah's mother must have been feeling. For a while, Stefanie had lost her sense of being indestructible and became mortal. And, for a while, Stefanie cried herself to sleep at night, promising herself that she wouldn't let go of any of her other friends. Sometimes, along with her prayers for thinness, she prayed for the strength to recover. Then the determination wore off, and slowly everything went back to normal. Stefanie would never forget the altar or the words of the priest or the mahogany coffin. But life continued now as if it had never changed—as if it didn't know what change was.

The chorus resumed in the background and with it her drills. Her muscles contracted and relaxed, forced into submission by the strength of her will. The music faded out in response to the end of the song, and, this time, she hit the stop button.

Stefanie rolled over. Standing in front of the floor-length mirror, she swung her hips from side to side in a motion that she'd done a hundred times over or more. She watched as the bones shifted and pinched at the skin on her stomach.

She flicked the music back on and looked into the eyes of her reflection. "Tonight: 421 sit-ups. It took me an hour and forty-five minutes. Tomorrow, I'll push harder and reach 450." The eyes of the skeleton in the mirror were full of determination.

Like always, it was late by the time she had finished, and the rest of the house was asleep as she slipped into the bathroom. This was just another part of the daily routine that she had so quickly fallen back into: workout, school, workout, homework, dinner, purge, workout, weigh-in. *Weigh-in*. Time to see the payoff.

Tentatively, she approached the white demon, as the six musketeers had learned to call it. Obsessively feeling for those places where the bones protruded once again, Stefanie stepped onto the scale. She wasn't sure if her parents even knew that there was a scale in her bathroom. She'd bought it one day after school and hadn't chosen to share the information.

Disappointment. Frustration. Anger. Another day was over, and she hadn't changed. All that work was for nothing. It was never good enough; she'd never see the difference that she was looking for. She'd never be happy. She'd never get people's respect and attention. There wasn't much hope for the future.

And it was now two am, just enough time for a few hours of sleep before it would all begin again. She climbed into bed and took out her temporary journal, a sheet of white, loose-leaf paper, where she wrote down only how many repetitions she had done and her goals.

July 18, 2001.

Under the date, she wrote a number, circled it, and wrote a second: her goal for the next day. The numbers mixed, and Stefanie squinted to see them properly. Everything except for that piece of shining white paper had gone dark around her. It was all black. Her eyes darted around the room, trying to steady themselves and finally rested on the small laminated card taped to her mirror. The Virgin Mary smiled, holding Baby Jesus with a tenderness unreachable in the mortal world. Stefanie knew what the back said; she could even picture the golden letters that spelled out Sarah Amelia Johnson. Underneath the name were the dates 1983–2001.

Sarah. The fact of that death still shocked her, no matter how many times she stared at the back of that card and reminded herself that it was a reality. It had scared her. Sarah had only been eighteen. And then she was gone.

Just a few more sit-ups. She could do it. She'd had an extra handful of grapes today, so she should do it. In the moment, 421 no longer seemed like a satisfactory accomplishment. She set her alarm clock for the next morning and hit play on her stereo.

"The shinbone's connected to the knee bone, the knee bone's connected to the thighbone, the thighbone's connected to the hip bone …" rang out from the speakers.

The music skipped a beat in the same place it always did, and Stefanie willed her stomach muscles to contract, pushing toward her new goal of 450. She was exercising again. And still listening to the bones song. Still striving toward the end that she was beginning to suspect wouldn't really bring happiness. Still trying to lose weight that just didn't want to come off. Had Sarah been happy when she died? She didn't think so. As her chest rose to meet her bent knees again and again, Stefanie wondered if maybe she'd found the answer to that all-important question: Was it even possible to recover? She felt defeated and hopeless.

Stefanie's hands returned to her hips, assessing the day's damage. The song was insignificant. As her parents said and wanted to believe, it was just a thing from the past, a thing from her childhood. But they didn't see the truth. For the remaining musketeers, the past was the present, and the present might well be the future. In the dark by herself, as she resumed the hated sit-ups, Stefanie knew that her lip was bleeding. She was scared of dying.

Her eye caught the mass card again, stuck in the right-hand corner of her mirror. Faith and trust could have saved them, should have saved them. Sarah believed in the power of the disorder to bring happiness. Doctors, therapists, God, anyone. She could have trusted anyone, believed that they would tell her the truth, that they would help her. Sarah could have placed her faith anywhere, except in the disorder and its inherent illusions. Faith should have been a savior; instead, it had been a murderer. She had believed too strongly in the power of thinness.

Stefanie's stomach muscles were aching, but determination was winning out. She licked the blood from her lip and cursed, squinting up at the mass card. She didn't want to keep going. She wanted to stop. But she couldn't. She'd been working at it for so long, strengthening her determination. Stopping would take a new kind of power.

Before bed that night, Stefanie prayed. She didn't ask to lose weight, and she didn't ask for a new trick to avoid eating. Instead, she wrapped her arms tight around Mr. Whiskers and, in the darkness of her room, spoke aloud to no one in particular, hoping that God might be listening, "God, help me know what to do. Help me make decisions. Help me get better. Help my friends. Don't let them die."

– 51 –

The summer continued in a haze of eating, starving, and purging. Annabel and Laura and Julia returned from their trips. They'd invited Stefanie to the movies once, but she'd declined. She wasn't going anywhere near that fattening popcorn and candy. School shopping began in a whirlwind of junior year anxieties, and Stefanie spent most of an afternoon at Staples buying school supplies. Then school began, and within weeks it felt like nothing had changed. As the weather changed and the leaves fell from the trees, dead and shriveled, something else was passing on as well—someone else. There was another funeral.

Stefanie attended, this time fully aware that when the three other musketeers hugged her, they could feel her ribs beneath her clothes. They ate another lunch at their café. And they had another round of desserts, which again Stefanie refused. Months passed. Stefanie hid in her room, exercising on Halloween, even though Laura and Annabel asked them to join her. Things had changed; the weather was warm for November, and a different kind of breeze blew through the city. There were a few days when it was even balmy.

As Thanksgiving approached, the remaining Barrett girls mourned the loss of two from their number, but they also gave thanks. They talked, all of them together on the phone, three days before Thanksgiving and exchanged the usual "I am thankful for's." As Stefanie listened to the other girls tell stories and say what they were most grateful for, she knew they were being honest. She was jealous that she couldn't join them in that.

Surrounded by a chorus of "I am thankful for my body and my health," Stefanie had to admit that she hadn't expected them to acknowledge doing better. But they were. And they were proud of that. They were ready to confess that the disorder was slowly leaving them. They talked of days without thinking incessantly about food. They talked of trusting their therapists, and the insights that they were gaining into their own lives, but also into the lives of others. Sometimes they couldn't quite remember how it felt to be so out of control, so dominated by something so small but so essential. They had become removed from the disorder. The anorexic thoughts were still with them, but there were healthy ones mixed in as well. And sometimes, when the two sides fought, the healthy side was strong enough to win. Somehow they'd leapfrogged over Stefanie's head and progressed, leaving her behind. They'd started over after the second death; she'd fallen back. Half of her prayers had been answered: God had helped them, but he was still ignoring her. She still didn't know what she wanted, and she still wasn't strong enough to resist the music of the bones song. She had put her faith in the disorder again. God wasn't listening, so maybe she just wasn't worth his effort.

Another month passed, and the calendar read December 14: her seventeenth birthday. Stefanie hadn't planned on celebrating. She certainly wasn't having a party for her school friends, but the week before Naomi had called. They were planning another get-together, and her birthday was the proposed occasion. The plan was to come together under happy circumstances.

Stefanie dropped her coat in the kitchen and sat down.

It had been almost five and a half months since Sarah's funeral. Naomi and Lizzie had sent e-cards that sang happy birthday and real mail that had arrived at her doorstep that morning. They were still doing fine. Her? Well, she wouldn't call herself recovered. Not really. Not yet. There was a fear that gripped her around the stomach when she felt the preoccupation with weight and calories trying to slip away, and she couldn't just open her hands to set it free. Sometimes Stefanie didn't want it to go. She looked at her thighs: they were still bubbles blown by her kneecaps, and they still wiggled like Jell-O. And she still yearned to lose weight and get back to her hundred-pound self. She still restricted. Sometimes the tenacity of the disorder lessened, and the claws didn't dig quite so deeply into her skin. Sometimes she could feel it leaving her behind, moving on to torment some other poor teenager. She would look at the mass cards on her mirror and get scared. Her friends had had such faith in the disorder—would she? Stefanie didn't want to join her friends wherever they had landed after life. She knew that that wasn't what the pact had meant. She knew that hadn't been the point. And yet, despite it all, Stefanie was still restricting. She had watched two friends die from this disorder, but she still couldn't give it up. Maybe she hadn't hit rock bottom yet.

Her mother walked into the kitchen and freed her from her own thoughts. "Stef, I didn't tell you this earlier, but Julia and Annabel and Laura will be here in fifteen minutes. They wanted to do a little something for your birthday."

"Oh. OK. Thanks Mom. They're coming here?" She didn't wait for the answer.

She thought of her two sets of friends: very separate, yet both somehow involved in this day. Her Barrett friends were taking her to dinner. Her school friends had arranged to surprise her; maybe she would invite them to join their group for dinner. Stefanie smiled at the idea, but the happiness faded quickly. She'd almost forgotten. Two of her friends wouldn't be there tonight.

She rested her head in her hands and murmured these questions to herself: *Two of the original six are gone; will the next four go too? Can I recover? Can I ever be completely and utterly happy with myself?* Once again, she didn't have the answer.

The doorbell rang, and Stefanie heard her mother close the door behind her school friends.

The four of them went to her room, where she exchanged the bones CD for the Matchbox Twenty album and skipped to the song "Unwell." They sat on the floor, and her three friends unloaded their canvas bags. They had brought gifts and cupcakes.

They told her how they had planned the day in advance. Stefanie thought about but didn't say how much they had surprised her with their kindness. She had wondered if they would forget. But they hadn't. They had come to celebrate with her.

"Open your presents already." Laura shoved a wrapped square at Stefanie. "Open it."

The presents that they had brought were three photo albums of their friendships: one from Annabel, one from Laura, and one from Julia. Stefanie leafed through each and hugged her friends. They had brought her a cupcake with creamy, delicious, melty icing and a cake part that she knew was French vanilla, her favorite. They remembered. She should have known—maybe even did know, deep down—that they were still friends. Maybe they'd grown apart a little bit, but that was fixable. People changed. They had changed, and she had changed. But none of them had lost contact forever. It just might take a little extra work, a little more TLC, a little more quality time, and a little bit more forgiveness to keep the closeness going.

"Stef." Her mother's head appeared in the doorway. "It's nearly six thirty. It's almost time for you to meet the girls at Serafina."

"Thanks, Mom. Be ready in one minute." Stefanie turned to her friends and smiled. "Will you guys join us for dinner? I'm sure they wouldn't mind. And I want you to meet them."

The three girls nodded. They would be happy to. Their calendars had been cleared for Stefanie for the entire night. Laura giggled. "Of course we'll come, we're your best friends, aren't we?"

Stefanie stuck out her tongue but stood to get her coat. The four of them walked across Eighty-third Street to Madison. The weather had turned cold again, and by the time they arrived their teeth were chattering and their legs were shaking. The warmth of the restaurant defrosted their bones, and Stefanie relaxd. She wasn't sure what she would find upstairs—would they still be thinner?—and she didn't know what they would think of her—how'd she put on so much weight?—but she was a little bit excited at the same time.

"This way, please. The others are already here." The maitre d' led them toward the next flight of stairs. They were sitting on the outside patio upstairs. It had always been her favorite place to sit. Airy and open. Comfortable. Homey.

She saw Naomi first. Then the others. They were sitting at a table in the corner and didn't see her come in. The maitre d' pointed to the table, as if she didn't recognize them, and walked away. But Stefanie paused. There they were. Sitting there, talking. They looked happy; they were smiling, and Lizzie giggled. Their faces glowed with the radiance of health. Rosy patches underlined their eyes, making Lizzie's blue ones shine brighter. Their gazes weren't hollow anymore, and the cheekbones didn't protrude from behind grayish skin.

She smiled just watching them. A fourteen-year-old—barely a freshman—with a senior and a college girl. Anyone else would have thought that they were an odd threesome, but Stefanie didn't think that anything was out of place. The smiles were all genuine, and it was the most natural thing in the world.

"Steffie!" Lizzie's cry echoed through the dining room; she had been sighted.

"Hey guys." Stefanie weaved her way across the room, avoiding tables that were already filled with people. She was sure everyone was staring. "These are my friends, Julia, Annabel. And Laura." As they made room for the added dinner guests, Stefanie worried. Did she really want to be there? They'd see her pale cheeks and know that she had been restricting. She didn't want to trigger anyone. She didn't want them to think that she condoned their restrictions. It was just different for her. And more importantly, they'd see that. Although she was obviously malnourished, she wasn't emaciated, and they'd have to wonder why. They'd have to realize that she just wasn't as good at playing the game as she had been before. And she didn't want them to see that.

Embraces passed around the circle. Lizzie's ribs were still noticeable when she squeezed hard. Stefanie cringed. She'd known that they'd still be thinner. And Lily hugged her longer than the others. They'd missed each other; it had been too long.

Stefanie held onto Lily and began to cry. Too many people were missing from the table. Sarah was gone. And so was Abby. She hadn't realized until just now that, after Abby's funeral, Abby would really be gone. She had joined Sarah. Maybe she was the only one who had really upheld the pact. Stefanie missed her; she'd simply slipped away unnoticed, slipped away into a blue abyss that she'd never rise from. No one had realized how seriously she needed help, especially not Coach Klay.

"Don't let go, Lily. Wait another moment. I don't want them to see me cry." After Sarah, Stefanie had thought that if anyone else died, it would have been Lily. She had been doing so poorly for so long, but now she seemed healthy—still thin, but not painfully so. The thought of losing Lily had terrified Stefanie, and there was some relief in being able to hold her tight. But at the same time, the fact that Lily was still there meant that someone else wasn't. And that didn't seem fair either.

"Can I help you, ladies?" The waiter appeared at their table only moments after they'd parted and taken their seats.

What would she get? The others had been there longer and had had time to think. She knew Serafina's menu by heart; unless they'd changed it, she would have been able to recite it. In the past, she'd always gotten the pizza. It had been her favorite, but could she have that now? Bread, starch, cheese—it was too much to handle. She'd have to pick something else. Her runner-up had been penne à la Vodka, but that was starchy too. What else? A full entrée with fish or chicken? No, that was too much food, even though she knew the amounts weren't really overwhelming. An appetizer? No, that would look too suspect, too much like she was still sick. Did she want to look like she was still sick?

Annabel started, and Julia and Laura followed. Ordering food meant nothing to them, and Stefanie wished that they could understand, just once, how it felt to be paralyzed by the very thought of putting something in your mouth.

If she remembered correctly, the Caesar salad had always been good. If she didn't eat the thin slice of Parmesan on top, she'd be okay with that—maybe.

Lily and Lizzie were ready, and Stefanie nodded her head. She could be ready if she had to be. She'd get the Caesar salad and worry about the effects later. She just hoped that the others were getting items equally caloric.

To them, ordering mattered. Stefanie knew it did. But to an outsider, it might not have looked that way. They might have looked like a completely normal group of teenagers.

One pizza: Naomi's; one Caesar salad with grilled chicken: Lizzie's; one order penne pomodoro with mozzarella cheese: Lily's. The other items smelled so good that Stefanie could feel her mouth watering as the food was laid down on the table. She wished she could have gotten pizza, or pasta, or even the grilled chicken that added that little bit of substance to a meal that otherwise consisted of only water and fiber and a little cheese. She felt empty again, and disappointed. Why could they eat those things, and she couldn't? But still, she felt a certain satisfaction from knowing that hers had the least calories in the bunch, though she knew, too, that that was just the eating disorder talking. If the real Stefanie was allowed to be heard, that voice would be crying in frustration. Life just wasn't fair.

"You know what movie I loved?" Lily paused after a large mouthful of penne. "I saw *Real Women Have Curves*, and it was amazing. I highly recommend it."

Lizzie laughed. "L and L give it two thumbs up. I loved it too. My foster mother rented it for us to watch together. I didn't think I would like it, but it was really good."

Lily and Julia started talking about books.

Exchanging recent hits and commenting on mutually experienced flops, Annabel and Naomi and Laura were talking about vacations. Naomi had announced that she was going to Disney World with her dad for some quality bonding time and the Disney World aficionados were filling her in on the hottest attractions, rides, and restaurants.

Lizzie looked at Stefanie, who was sitting back, just listening to her friends talk. "Oh yeah. Stef, I don't cut anymore." She held up a perfectly healed wrist with no new scars.

The table went silent, and Stefanie wondered what Julia and Annabel and Laura were thinking. She'd never told them that Lizzie was the cutter. Even the other musketeers were obviously surprised, taken aback by Lizzie's matter-of-fact statement about a suspicion that they'd probably all had but had never heard confirmed. Stefanie smiled and squeezed Lizzie's hand under the table—it was a relief to hear that—and the others chose not to push it. Within moments, the confession seemed forgotten, and the conversation returned to pop culture and other equally light topics.

It was all so good. They were sitting at a table at her favorite restaurant, talking not about food and calories and horror stories but about normal things. They were teenagers, and for once they were acting on it. The only stories that were exchanged about eating, or anything related, were success stories. They were obviously proud. Stefanie wished she had one to share, but she didn't think they'd want to hear about how the day before she had successfully evaded her mother's probing questions about her lunch at school. She'd felt good about it at the time, but now, listening to them talk, she knew that it wasn't of the same caliber.

As she sat there at the table, surrounded by the familiar cadences of her closest friends in the world, she realized that she was still different. She could just feel it.

She couldn't explain how badly she had wanted to get pizza and dessert. She couldn't explain how badly she wanted to realize that life was a privilege rather than a chore. She wanted to go out with her friends—Lily, Lizzie, Naomi, Laura, Annabel, Julia. She wanted to go out and have fun, like they used to. But so much time had passed. She had missed so much. Birthday parties—Laura had had one, but she'd turned down the invitation. Sleepovers—after her parents found out that she was sick, they'd banned her from all of the weekend slumber parties. That wasn't to mention the countless classes and school activities—the end-of-the-year bashes and the midsummer galas—she'd missed and the memories of her sophomore year that she could never get back. She'd missed the yearly trip to Vail with Laura's family, and she'd spent her summer in doctors' offices and at therapy instead of relaxing and having fun. She had also lost friends—Sarah, Abby, and maybe, in her own way, Julia, who for a time hadn't wanted to put up with the eating disorder.

She'd missed too much. But explaining all of this to her friends wouldn't help them understand why it was so hard for her to do something as simple as eat, especially if they knew she wanted to recover. There were things that people just didn't understand, and, as much as Stefanie wanted to, she couldn't explain.

She took another bite of her Caesar salad and tried to smile, but she knew that it didn't compare to the pizza that sat across from her. She'd thought it earlier that day, earlier that week, and earlier that month; she'd thought it so many times, but now she thought it again: life wasn't fair. This wasn't fair. They were happy. They were experiencing excitement and joy and sadness and pain again. She was shut off from the world, shut off from the emotions that make everything colorful and interesting. Her life was monotonous, in dull shades of black, gray, and white. She didn't know how to change that, even if she had been sure that she wanted to.

Dinner ended. She finished her salad amid the chatter of her friends. Then she excused herself and went down the stairs to the ladies' room. As she opened the door, her hands shook and her front teeth bit hard into her bottom lip.

She closed the door, slid the lock into place, and looked at the toilet.

Tears rolled down her cheeks. She couldn't even grasp why she was crying. There was something that she'd been chasing for so long—happiness. She'd tried one way, and it hadn't gotten her anywhere. Now she couldn't bring herself to try the other way. She couldn't bring herself to try and get healthy.

Standing there, lost and confused, Stefanie heard a knock on the bathroom door. "Shit." She tried to wipe her eyes and knew that she was out of time. She couldn't throw up with someone right outside the door. She slid the bolt away and pulled the door open. When she took a step forward, she walked right into Lily's outstretched arms.

"I thought maybe you could use a hug." Lily had stepped into the bathroom and closed the door behind them both. She slid the lock back into place and, for a few minutes, the two girls just stood.

"You don't understand. I'll lose everything if I give this up. Everything. You'll stop caring. They'll stop caring. Dr. Adler, Dr. Grant, they'll all stop caring. I'll fade into the background. I'll disappear just like that—and all because I've given it up." Her words were coming out slurred and loud. As she spoke, she wondered if the people in the restaurant, just feet away, could hear her. "I want to get better. I want to get past this. I do. I swear. I want to recover. I want to go out with you guys and have fun. I want to have ice cream again. Damnit! I want to enjoy myself without worrying about the calorie count of the food. I hate that I can't even eat a simple meal without coming back to this." She pointed at the toilet. "I want to get back to the place where I can just eat what I want, when I want it. But I can't get there. It's too far away. I can't do it. Nothing will ever get better." The words tumbled out, and she was surprised to hear herself say them.

Exhausted and crying hard, she collapsed into Lily's arms. Lily held her, rubbing her back, until the tears slowed and she could stand again. "Sweetheart, stop. You'll get there. Jump in with two feet, and you'll get there. Swear to God. Look at me."

"But you're stronger than I am. You're so much stronger. I'm just a little nobody who deserves to be left on the bathroom floor."

Lily's voice became suddenly harsh, and she pushed Stefanie away so they could look each other in the eyes. "Bullshit. You're every bit as strong as any one of us, and you're not going to use that excuse with me. Not with me." She let Stefanie fall back into her arms in a new wave of tears.

Stefanie tightened her grip for one last second and then let Lily go. She took a minute to regain her composure. "You're right. I can do this. We better get back upstairs—the others must think we got lost." Her voice shook and she didn't seem all too confident in her assertion, but in a moment of weakness, or perhaps kindness to herself, she had said it. Like the words in her journal, it couldn't be taken back now.

They washed her face with cool water and returned to the table, Lily gently guiding Stefanie with one hand against her back.

"Dessert, anyone?" Naomi unfolded the menu that the waiter had just handed her but didn't read from it. "I believe we have something special for the young woman, correct?" She pointed to Stefanie, and the waiter nodded, then scuttled off to the kitchen.

Lily grabbed Stefanie's hand under the table and squeezed it, just as Stefanie had squeezed Lizzie's. "It's OK. You don't have to if you can't."

Stefanie brought her napkin up to her tear-stained face and rubbed her eyes. "I know." She wondered if the others could see that she had been crying.

When the waiter returned, amid a flurry of action from the kitchen, he produced a cookies 'n' cream ice cream cake with Oreos on the side. There were eighteen candles spread across the top—one for good luck. And slowly they were all lit. As they began to sing "Happy Birthday," Stefanie disappeared into her own thoughts.

They weren't going to abandon her just because she got healthy again. That wasn't the way friendship or parenting worked. Maybe they'd never meant to make her feel neglected. They all loved her. She knew that with the same surety that she knew her name. Sure, sometimes she forgot, but in the end she knew. She thought about those phone calls with Laura—back when she had played Dear Abby. Someone with problems all the time gets tiresome, boring. It was far better to talk to someone vivacious and enthusiastic. That was what really kept people interested. She wasn't going to lose anybody.

She heard the right words ring through her head. They were the words that she had needed to hear. *People didn't want to be around other people who were sick all the time.*

"Stef, blow out the candles." Laura's words brought Stefanie out of her thoughts, and she blew hard. "Don't forget—make a wish!"

Stefanie smiled. She thought of the birthday card her dad had left at her placemat that morning. Inside it said: *"I love you, honey. And we're very, very proud of you."* Still right out of a book, but it wasn't so bad. Not really. Not that night.

Naomi had begun to pass out pieces of cake. "Stef, would you like some?"

She looked at Lily. She'd confirmed that she wanted to get better ten minutes ago; maybe it was finally time to make the exceptional effort that it would take. Before tonight she had just been following along, restricting as the days progressed, waiting for a reason to challenge herself.

And here it was.

Oreos. Her favorite. It was the one dessert that she had fantasized about since the beginning of it all. The one that had filled her dreams on her hungriest nights. And ice cream came in a close second behind the Oreos. But she hadn't had either of them in a long time. And now was her chance.

"Yes, please. A small piece and three Oreos."

Lily smiled, Lizzie laughed, and Naomi passed the cake and Oreos. Laura, Annabel, and Julia didn't know quite what they were seeing, but they watched in silence nonetheless, somehow sensing that for Stefanie, and even for the others, this was an important moment.

She stared at the piece of cake in front of her. This was more than her monthly quota of dessert; it had more calories than a thousand of her meals put together. The china was soft, off-white, with a small Tuscan scene along the edges. The soft cream on her tongue, the contrast of the Oreo cookies mixed in, the combination sliding down her throat and landing in her stomach felt so good. The decadence of this dessert both tortured and thrilled her. But this was what normal people did, especially on their birthdays. And she wanted to be normal.

The ice cream melted slowly on her tongue. She took a bite of Oreo. Crunchy. Sweet. Creamy inside. She licked a crumb off her lip and looked at her friends. She could imagine her parents sitting at the table, watching her closely yet trying hard not to grin too enthusiastically. She took another spoonful of ice cream and another bite of Oreo, eating slowly, trying to make it last. It was worth it.

Later that night, in her room, behind the closed door, Stefanie hummed to herself.

"The shinbone's connected to the knee bone, the knee bone's connected to the thighbone, the thighbone's connected to the hip bone ..."

And suddenly she hated the song. It hadn't given her anything, ever.

Fighting the old urges, she left the Matchbox Twenty CD from earlier that afternoon in the player. When she wanted to listen to music, she played "Unwell" and sang along with the words.

Her tattered journal was lying open on the bed, and Stefanie flopped down next to it with a pen. She wrote the date again, and under it scribbled a circled number: she'd done her sit-ups and leg lifts earlier in anticipation of the party.

It was dark, but Stefanie could still see the two mass cards on her mirror: the second from Abby's funeral. *Sarah and Abby were gone; she didn't have to be.* Gathering her courage, she wrote the second number, her leg-lift goal for the next day, just as she had done the past year. But tonight, the second number was lower than the first. She was going to try. It was down on paper now, and, just like her daily allowances, it couldn't be taken back.

Before Stefanie turned out the lights, she wrote the questions that had plagued her.

We've lost two. Will the other four go next? Can I ever be completely and utterly happy with myself? Is recovery really possible?

Then she crossed the words out. It would still be a daily struggle, but the question was gone. She had found her answer.

978-0-595-41412-3
0-595-41412-5

Printed in the United States
80284LV00009B/28-30